Our Fate

Laura Cole

Published by Laura Cole, 2024.

This is a work of fiction. Similarities to real people, places, or events are entirely coincidental.

OUR FATE

First edition. November 17, 2024.

Copyright © 2024 Laura Cole.

ISBN: 979-8230681342

Written by Laura Cole.

Chapter 1: A Duel in the Shadows

The air around me thrummed with tension, thick with the promise of destruction. In the depths of the ancient amphitheater, the shadows twisted and danced, eager to witness the clash between two rivals who had long since lost any pretense of civility. I could feel the weight of their eyes, the quiet murmur of my name, as if they were waiting for something monumental to break in the air. The crowd was always hungry, always demanding more. But none of their eager whispers could compare to the voice that had haunted my every thought for years—Kael.

His figure loomed just beyond the reach of my flickering light, his dark cloak rippling like a shadow in the moonlit silence. That smirk—the one that always seemed to say he knew something I didn't—stretched across his lips, making my teeth grind. His eyes, as cold and calculating as the city streets we'd grown up on, locked onto mine, daring me to make the first move.

"I see you've been practicing," he said, his voice a low purr of amusement. The tone of his words made me want to strike him more than I cared to admit. His arrogance was a constant, like an itch I could never scratch.

But I wouldn't let him see that. Not now. Not here.

"Don't flatter yourself," I shot back, my voice dripping with venom, even as my fingers twitched, gathering the power that was bubbling just beneath the surface. I had been training for this moment. Years of preparation, each spell learned and perfected, every arcane secret I had uncovered, all brought me to this singular point where the two of us would finally settle the score.

The stones beneath my feet felt alive, breathing in sync with my pulse as the magic in the air thickened. I let the power surge through me, drawing on the energy that the ancient amphitheater seemed to store in its very bones. It was a place of power, built centuries ago, where mages like Kael and I had come to sharpen our skills, our grudges, our very identities. Tonight, the stage was set, and I would not let him walk away with that smug look on his face.

With a flick of my wrist, the air between us shimmered, crackling with the magic I unleashed. It was fast, precise—an elemental bolt of lightning that shot from my hand with the force of a storm. Kael's eyes flared with recognition.

He didn't even flinch. Instead, his fingers twirled lazily in the air, a gesture so casual, it made me want to scream. The lightning bolt arced toward him, only to be swallowed up by the swirling darkness that erupted around him. It was as if the air itself bent to his will, forming an impenetrable shield that sucked the life out of my attack.

"Cute," Kael muttered under his breath, his voice mocking. His hand shot out, and a rush of force sent me stumbling back, the ground beneath me crumbling into jagged edges as I struggled to keep my balance.

I gritted my teeth, eyes narrowing. This wasn't a game. He thought it was.

"You think you can just waltz in here, Kael, and take what's mine?" My voice cut through the air, sharp and biting. Every word felt like a promise—a warning. He didn't know what was coming. He didn't know how far I would go to end this.

Kael laughed. "You really think you have anything to lose?" His words were sharp, like shards of broken glass. "You think you can fight your way out of this, Evanna? You've always been too rash, too eager to prove yourself." His smirk deepened, taunting me, daring me to make a mistake.

I was done with his games. Done with the way he always toyed with me, like I was some puzzle he had yet to solve. Tonight, I wasn't going to give him the satisfaction of being right.

I steadied myself, pushing away the heat of frustration that threatened to cloud my focus. If I let myself get angry, I would lose. And this was the one battle I couldn't afford to lose.

A flicker of motion caught my eye. His spell. He was ready to strike. I could feel the magic crackling at the edges of my senses, the way it bled into the air, promising pain and destruction. But I was prepared.

As his hands moved to cast, I was already one step ahead, weaving a counter-spell into the fabric of the arena. The magic within the stones responded to me, thrumming with recognition. I had spent years learning their secrets, speaking to them as one would to a lover. I called upon them now, pulling the earth itself into my control. The ground rumbled beneath us, and before Kael could fully release his spell, the earth rose up, jagged stone pillars shooting toward the sky like the fingers of some long-forgotten god.

Kael's eyes widened, just a flicker of surprise before the smirk returned. He was fast, too fast, his body twisting out of the way of the rising stone, but he wasn't quite quick enough. One of the pillars grazed his shoulder, and for a split second, he hesitated.

That was all I needed.

In the blink of an eye, I was on him, the power surging through my veins, more intense than anything I had ever felt before. I reached out with one hand, fingers brushing the edge of his cloak, and for the briefest moment, our magic mingled—my pulse, his power—and I knew. This was it. The breaking point.

"You've lost," I whispered, my voice a hiss in the dark.

Kael's eyes locked with mine. He didn't speak. He didn't need to. The tension between us was enough, thick with the weight of everything we had fought for, everything we had lost.

The stone walls of the amphitheater felt like they were closing in around me, the weight of the moment pressing down with an intensity that almost made my knees buckle. The air was thick with magic, heavy with the promise of something—something I wasn't quite ready for. But it was coming, whether I liked it or not, and Kael was still standing there, impossibly calm, with that infernal smirk plastered across his face. It was the smirk that had haunted me since we first crossed paths, the one that made me want to scream and kiss him in equal measure.

"Really?" I said, forcing a laugh. "You think you can just play with me like this?"

Kael didn't flinch. He simply watched me, those eyes never leaving mine, like he was studying me for some secret I wasn't aware I was giving away. That wasn't a good sign. Kael had this way of making you feel like you were the subject of some grand experiment, and I hated it.

His voice was low, almost too quiet, but I heard every word as if it were shouted across the ruins. "You're better than this, Evanna. I thought you'd at least put up a real fight."

Oh, I had been fighting. The problem was, I hadn't been fighting him. Not really. He was right, though. I was better than this. I could be better than this. And for a fleeting moment, I allowed myself to focus—not on Kael, not on the watchers who waited in the shadows, but on the magic. The raw energy of the earth beneath me, the pulse of the air around me, the fire that simmered beneath my skin.

I closed my eyes, just for a second, and let it flow.

When I opened them again, everything had changed.

There was no hesitation now. No second-guessing. The magic was mine to command. I reached out with my senses, pulling threads of power like silk from the depths of the earth. This time, Kael didn't get the chance to mock me. The ground shook, a low rumble that seemed to come from deep within the world itself.

And then, without warning, I unleashed a torrent of energy so intense that the sky above us seemed to darken in response.

Kael's eyes widened for a split second, but his instinct kicked in before I could even blink. His hands moved, and the air around him swirled like a vortex, pulling the magic into himself, redirecting the force I had thrown at him with a practiced ease.

"Impressive," he murmured, and there was something like admiration in his voice that made my blood run cold. "But not enough."

With a flick of his wrist, the air exploded—literally. It was as if the world itself had cracked open. Magic, raw and unrefined, shot outward, and I barely had time to raise a protective shield before the force of his attack slammed into me, throwing me back like a ragdoll. My body hit the stone floor with a sickening thud, and the breath whooshed out of my lungs.

I fought to stay conscious, my vision blurred, but my mind was still sharp. He had the upper hand—again.

"Well, that's one way to do it," I muttered through gritted teeth, rolling onto my side and pushing myself up. The movement was slow, deliberate. I wasn't done yet. Not by a long shot.

Kael, standing with that smug confidence, wasn't even out of breath. He had this way of being completely unbothered by everything around him, as if the world could fall apart and he'd just be there, cool as a cucumber, waiting for the pieces to fall into place.

"You're bleeding," he said, his voice lilting, as if we were discussing the weather. His eyes flicked to the slight cut on my cheek, where blood had started to trickle down. "It doesn't have to be this way, you know."

I took a step forward, ignoring the ache in my side, focusing instead on the power swirling inside me, winding through my veins like wildfire. I wasn't about to let him get away with that.

"Funny," I said, my voice flat, "I was thinking the exact same thing."

Kael tilted his head, his smile faltering for just a fraction of a second. It was almost imperceptible, but I saw it. He was testing me, waiting for me to crack. And maybe, just maybe, I was finally beginning to figure out the game.

I drew a breath, feeling the magic surge again, but this time, I controlled it. This wasn't a fight anymore. It was a dance, a game of wills. His power might have been formidable, but mine had the depth of the earth behind it. I wasn't just going to strike him. I was going to outlast him.

"You think you're the only one who can learn, Kael?" I said, my voice a whisper that cut through the tension between us. "You think I haven't been watching you? Studying you? I've learned your tricks. I've learned your weaknesses."

His eyebrows arched slightly, and I could see the flicker of doubt in his eyes, the first crack in his armor. "You think you know me that well?"

"You're an open book, Kael," I said, a smile tugging at the corner of my lips. "And I've read every page."

Before he could respond, I struck again. This time, I didn't just rely on the magic of the earth beneath me. I wove my spell with intent, pulling threads from the air, from the sky, and from the very essence of the world around us. It was a complex weave—one that took everything I had, but it was perfect.

Kael's smirk faded, replaced by a look of focused calculation, but it was too late. The spell I'd unleashed was one of balance, of harmony, and it was going to bring everything to the edge of chaos. It wrapped around him, binding him as much as it would him—and that's when I realized. This wasn't just a duel anymore. This was the beginning of something far more dangerous.

The air hung thick with the scent of earth and stone, an ancient scent that seemed to pull at my very bones, reminding me of just how deep the roots of this place ran. Beneath the wild sparks of magic that danced around us like fireflies, I could feel the pulse of the city in the distance. New York City—where every moment was a rush of possibilities, yet here, in this forgotten corner, time had slipped its grip entirely. The amphitheater, with its cracked stone and weathered arches, seemed a world apart, an untouched relic of something older, darker.

It was in these shadows that Kael thrived, a predator in his element. His eyes glittered in the half-light as he watched me carefully, too carefully. His every movement was deliberate, measured. As if he were waiting for me to falter. As if he were waiting for me to break.

"You really think you can bind me, Evanna?" His voice was smooth, like butter slipping over hot metal. I hated the way he said my name. The familiarity in it, the challenge. "You're more naive than I thought."

I felt a flare of heat surge through my veins, my magic pressing against the barrier I had placed around my heart. I wasn't naive. I knew exactly who Kael was—and what he was capable of.

"Maybe you're the one who's naive, Kael," I replied, voice cold, even as the warmth of power spiraled through my chest. "You still think this is about one-upmanship, don't you?"

His lips quirked upward, an arrogant smile that only deepened my resolve. "Everything's about winning, Evanna. You know that."

The words burned through me, sharp and bitter. I knew how he thought—always about the win, always about the power. It was how he had risen to prominence. But the problem was, power alone wasn't enough to defeat me. Not anymore.

I raised my hand, the air around us shimmering like heat waves rising from pavement, and Kael's eyes narrowed. He wasn't expecting this. Neither of us had expected it.

"You've forgotten something, haven't you?" I said, just as the ground beneath us rumbled.

Kael's gaze flickered down, just a split second before the ground tore open beneath him. His shield snapped into place, a swirling mass of energy that absorbed the brunt of the attack, but the force still sent him stumbling back.

I wasn't finished yet.

The walls of the arena groaned, ancient stones shifting as I pulled on the earth beneath us. I'd always been attuned to the rhythms of this place, to the pulse of the land—more so than Kael, who relied on his own arrogance, his own wits. The spell wasn't just a barrage; it was a reminder that this battle wasn't his to win.

Kael hissed as jagged rocks shot up, attempting to pin him down. But he wasn't as quick as he thought. The rocks missed him by mere inches, scraping against his cloak, the edges of his magical shield flickering as if unsure whether to collapse or expand. He sneered, his eyes blazing with that infernal light.

"You're good," he said, a grudging respect in his tone. "But you're not invincible, Evanna."

I smiled, but it wasn't a smile of confidence. It was a smile of quiet understanding.

"I don't need to be invincible, Kael," I said softly. "I just need to outlast you."

His face twisted into a scowl, the smirk evaporating like mist in the morning sun. He took a step forward, hands outstretched, and I could feel the pressure building around us. Magic crackled, the air thick with the weight of the two of us facing off. He was preparing his final move, the one that would bring everything to an end.

But something flickered in my peripheral vision—something I hadn't seen before.

The shadows—those silent, watchful figures hidden beneath cloaks—were moving.

No.

I wasn't just fighting Kael.

I turned, instinct pulling me just in time to avoid the blow that came from the left. The world seemed to slow as I twisted, my heart pounding in my chest, and there, in the depths of the shadows, I saw them.

The cloaked figures.

They weren't spectators, not really. They were waiting for something. Waiting for the right moment.

And I had just given it to them.

A cold shock spread through me as the first figure moved forward, hands raised, chanting something in a language I couldn't recognize. My magic recoiled instinctively, but Kael's laugh cut through the rising panic.

"Well, well, Evanna," he said, voice thick with amusement and something else, something darker. "Looks like you've been too busy fighting me to notice the real threat."

I didn't look at him. I didn't dare. My attention was fixed on the encroaching figures, their movements unnaturally fluid, like shadows slipping from the cracks of the world. The ground beneath my feet trembled again, this time not from the force of our magic, but from something far more ominous. The amphitheater, once a place of power and pride, was becoming something else. A trap.

One of the figures raised a hand, and suddenly, I felt it—a draining sensation, like someone was sucking the very energy out of me, the life force being drawn from my limbs.

I stumbled, trying to catch my breath, but the weight of their power pressed down on me, suffocating me. And then, I heard it.

A low, whispered chant, almost too quiet to hear, but unmistakable in its intent.

"No," I whispered, my voice breaking.

Too late.

Before I could react, the world around me splintered. Magic, not my own, twisted and surged through the arena, and everything—everything—went dark.

Chapter 2: The Mark of the Raven

The morning light filtered weakly through the half-drawn curtains, casting long shadows on the floor like something out of a dream I couldn't quite remember. I stretched, letting the silence of the room settle around me, but the moment my arm moved, I felt it—a sudden, sharp pain, like something was burrowing into my skin. I gasped, jerking my arm back to my chest, staring at the darkening mark that now lay across my wrist.

It was as though a shadow had decided to take root, its edges crisp and clean, but the center was a swirling mess of ink-black feathers, as though the very essence of a raven had been burned into my flesh. The design was elegant—too elegant, like something drawn by the hand of a master artisan. It was perfect in its imperfection, a scar that would never fade.

I rubbed my thumb over it, the skin hot to the touch, as though the mark itself was alive, writhing beneath my palm. The realization hit me like a bucket of cold water. It wasn't just a symbol—it was a prophecy. The Ravenmark. The one they'd spoken of in hushed tones, the one that haunted the stories I'd heard as a child. The one that told of a person who would be either the salvation or the damnation of us all.

Fate had never been a friend of mine. I'd seen it twist and turn like a cruel game of chance, but now, it had chosen me. I wasn't sure whether to laugh or scream. Maybe both. A curse and a gift wrapped up in the same dark feathered mystery.

I was still trying to figure out whether I was supposed to be terrified or elated when the door creaked open, and Kael stepped into the room, his dark eyes immediately locking onto the mark on my wrist. He didn't look surprised. No, Kael never looked surprised by anything. He was too damn smug for that.

"Well, well," he said, his voice smooth, the teasing lilt in his words like a dagger wrapped in velvet. "Looks like fate has a cruel sense of humor."

I swallowed hard, trying not to let my frustration show. "What are you doing here?"

He leaned against the doorframe, arms crossed, eyes narrowing slightly as he studied the mark. "I should ask you the same thing. I didn't expect to find you... gifted this morning."

His sarcasm was thick, but I could hear something else beneath it. Curiosity. The kind of curiosity that could be dangerous if given the right spark.

I shifted uncomfortably, pulling my sleeve down over the mark, as though hiding it from him would somehow make the situation less real. But I knew it wouldn't. It was there, carved into my skin for a reason. Kael was smart enough to know that. Too smart.

"Don't act like you knew this was coming," I muttered, avoiding his gaze. "You were just as clueless as I was."

"Oh, I knew," he replied, his voice low, almost too confident. "I didn't know when it would happen, but the Ravenmark? I've seen it before." He stepped closer, his boots thudding lightly on the wooden floor. "I didn't think it would be you, though."

I glanced up at him, his face so close now I could see the faintest scar along his jaw, like a remnant of a battle long forgotten. His scent—the sharpness of pine and something else, something familiar—washed over me, and I had to force myself to focus. This wasn't about him. Not anymore.

"Why would it be me?" I demanded, narrowing my eyes. "You think I'm the one this prophecy was meant for? That I'm some kind of hero?"

Kael smirked, a flash of something almost like amusement crossing his features. "Hardly. But you are the one with the mark. And that's a little hard to ignore."

"Great," I muttered. "So what now? I'm supposed to figure out how to save the world or destroy it with this thing?" I motioned to my wrist, though I had no idea what to do with it.

"You could," Kael said, taking a step back. "Or you could leave it up to fate and see where it takes you." He hesitated, just for a moment, before continuing. "But I wouldn't recommend it. Not unless you're prepared for what comes next."

I didn't ask what that was. I didn't need to. His eyes told me more than enough. He knew things. Things I didn't. Things I needed to know if I was going to make it out of this alive.

"Fine," I snapped, tugging my sleeve down further. "If you're so knowledgeable, why don't you enlighten me, then?"

Kael raised an eyebrow, clearly enjoying my irritation. "It's not so simple as telling you what you want to hear. The Ravenmark chooses. It doesn't care about your desires, your plans, or your comfort. It marks you, and you either rise to the challenge or fall. No in-between."

I clenched my jaw, feeling the heat of the mark pulse beneath my skin, and took a deep breath, trying to ignore the knot that was forming in my stomach. "I didn't ask for this."

"No one does," Kael said softly, his gaze flickering to the mark again, then back to my face. "But it's yours now. And I can help you understand it. If you let me."

I hesitated. The last thing I wanted was to rely on him, but the alternative was standing in the dark, fumbling my way through a prophecy that felt like it had already decided my fate.

"You can't just help me," I said, narrowing my eyes. "You have an agenda. You always do."

Kael smiled, but there was no warmth in it. "Maybe. But sometimes, our agendas line up, whether we like it or not."

And just like that, I knew I was trapped.

Kael's words lingered in the air like a bad smell, and I had to resist the urge to swipe at my wrist, as though I could erase the Ravenmark with a simple motion. It burned hot against my skin, a reminder of the world I hadn't asked for, the one I'd been thrust into without warning or consent.

I wasn't sure how much more of his smug, infuriating grin I could take before I'd scream, but he was already turning on his heel, as though he knew what I needed before I even realized it myself. I clenched my fist, half-expecting to feel the mark flare up again, but it remained still, the ink sinking deeper into my skin, as though it were now a part of me.

"We should go," Kael said, glancing back at me with the same half-amused, half-concerned expression. "You'll want answers, right?"

"Not from you," I snapped, my voice sharp. "I can figure this out on my own."

Kael chuckled under his breath, not even trying to hide the amusement dancing in his eyes. "You can try. But the Ravenmark isn't something you can just 'figure out.' It's not like picking the right kind of coffee beans at the local café, you know."

I resisted the urge to throw something at him. "Coffee, huh? What's next? A recommendation for a pastry to go with my impending doom?"

"Funny you should ask," he said with a mock seriousness that made my blood boil. "I've heard there's a little bakery downtown that makes killer croissants. But I wouldn't go there if I were you. Those things are dangerously good."

I wasn't sure whether to laugh or scream. The man had the audacity to mock fate, but somehow it didn't seem entirely wrong. He knew something. He had to. But the last thing I needed was his smug confidence throwing off the fragile sense of control I'd managed to hold onto. I shook my head, muttering something under my breath about his inability to take anything seriously.

"Where are we going?" I finally asked, needing to steer the conversation toward something I could actually control.

"I know someone who might be able to help," Kael said, his tone suddenly more businesslike. "We don't have time for coffee or croissants, but I think you'll appreciate the distraction. If you want answers, you'll have to trust me on this."

Trust him. It was a laughable notion, but there I was, contemplating the idea of following him into some dark corner of the city to seek out whatever godforsaken information lay waiting for me. Because as much as I hated to admit it, Kael was right: I needed answers. The Ravenmark wasn't something I could ignore.

The ride downtown was a quiet one, save for the sound of the tires humming along the rain-slicked streets. It was a typical morning in Chicago—gray skies, a drizzle that seemed to fall just enough to make everything feel damp without actually washing anything clean. The city felt like it was holding its breath, as though waiting for something big to happen. I wondered if the universe was just as impatient with me as I was with it.

Kael drove with his usual calm, one hand on the wheel, the other resting casually at his side. His eyes were focused on the road, but every now and then, his gaze flicked to me, as though measuring my reactions. I could feel the weight of his scrutiny, but I refused to let it bother me. After all, it wasn't like he'd be around for long once I figured this out. Or so I hoped.

We reached a nondescript building tucked between two high-rise apartments. From the outside, it looked like any other old warehouse, with rusting metal doors and graffiti tags that shouted in neon colors. But Kael didn't seem bothered by its dismal exterior. He parked the car and led me up a narrow staircase, the kind you'd miss if you weren't looking closely.

The door creaked open to reveal a dimly lit room, shelves filled with strange artifacts, and the smell of incense thick in the air. I could hear a low hum, almost like chanting, but when I looked around, there was no one to be seen.

"Who are we meeting?" I asked, suddenly feeling very out of my depth.

Kael didn't answer right away. Instead, he moved to the back of the room, tapping a hidden panel in the wall that slid open to reveal a narrow hallway. He motioned for me to follow.

"Someone who knows more than I do," he said, his voice low. "Someone who can help you understand what you're dealing with."

The hallway felt like it was closing in on me with each step, and the silence between us became heavy, thick with expectation. I had no idea what I was getting myself into, but with every step I took, the mark on my wrist seemed to pulse, as though urging me forward.

We stopped at a door at the end of the hall, and Kael knocked twice before opening it. Inside, the room was even darker, but I could make out a figure sitting at a desk, their face hidden beneath a hood. The person didn't move when we entered, but I could feel their presence like a tangible weight in the room.

"Well," the figure said, their voice smooth but cold, like the edge of a blade, "it's about time you showed up."

Kael stepped forward, his posture stiffening as if he'd been expecting this encounter. "We need answers. You're the only one who can help."

The figure didn't respond right away. Instead, they reached for a set of old scrolls on the desk and unrolled one, revealing symbols I didn't recognize. My heart skipped a beat as I realized they were the same symbols as the ones etched into my skin.

"I know why you're here," the figure continued, their voice steady, almost comforting. "And I know exactly what you've become."

I swallowed hard, feeling a chill run down my spine. I had no idea what they meant by that, but I was about to find out.

The figure's voice rippled through the room like a shiver of ice. There was something too calm about it, like someone who had seen it all before—and I didn't know if that comforted me or made my skin crawl.

"I know exactly what you've become," they repeated, their head still bent low beneath the hood, an indistinct shadow looming in place of a face. I swallowed hard, the words sinking in with a weight I couldn't shake. They sounded like they were speaking of something far beyond the mark, something far older and far more dangerous.

I took a step back, instinct kicking in, but Kael's presence behind me was a wall I couldn't pass through. He was uncomfortably still, waiting for whatever revelation was about to be unveiled. I, on the other hand, was just trying to steady my breathing as the air in the room seemed to tighten, thickening around us like fog.

"What do you mean by that?" I asked, forcing the words out. My voice came out harsher than I intended, laced with a tremor of unease. "I haven't... I haven't become anything. I'm just me."

The hooded figure chuckled, low and almost imperceptible, as though they were reading a joke only they understood. "Oh, you're still you, all right," they said, leaning forward just slightly, and for the first time, I noticed the glint of something dark and sharp in their eyes. It wasn't warmth, nor sympathy—just something cold and calculating. "But you're also something else now. Something... more."

I wasn't sure if that was supposed to be comforting or terrifying, but it sure wasn't either. The mark on my wrist seemed to pulse, as though it recognized the conversation, like it was listening, waiting for its moment to reveal whatever secrets it had wrapped up in its ink.

"I didn't ask for this," I muttered, almost to myself, though I knew it wouldn't change anything. My frustration bubbled to the surface. "I didn't want to be a part of some prophecy. This isn't my fight."

The figure didn't respond immediately, instead letting the silence stretch, as though weighing my words. Then, finally, they tilted their head, their voice quieter but sharper than before.

"Ah, but the prophecy doesn't care about what you want," they said. "It only cares about what is."

I felt my pulse quicken, my skin crawling at the inevitability in their words. I wasn't sure if I hated them or if I was scared of them, but I was definitely starting to feel small in their presence, like a fly trapped in a web I hadn't seen spun around me.

"Look," I said, pushing against the growing unease in my chest. "I don't care what some ancient prophecy says. I'm not a weapon, and I'm not a savior. I'm just trying to make sense of this... this thing on my wrist. If you can help me understand it, fine. If not—"

"If not?" The figure interrupted, their voice smooth and cool as ice. "What exactly do you think you'll do? Leave? Go back to your little life and pretend this never happened? That this mark isn't a part of you now?"

Kael shifted behind me, his presence like a pressure against my back. I could feel his gaze, sharp as ever, but he said nothing. I wasn't sure if I was grateful for his silence or annoyed by it.

"I don't know," I said, lifting my chin defiantly, trying to mask the way my pulse raced. "Maybe. I don't have to play by anyone's rules, certainly not some random prophecy."

The figure straightened in their seat, the shadows making their form look almost ghostly. "You think you have a choice?" Their tone shifted—less condescending now, more... ominous. "You do understand that this mark was made for you, don't you? It chose you. You are not going to walk away from it, not anymore."

I clenched my fists, fighting the tightening of my throat. I didn't want to believe them. I couldn't. There had to be another way out of this, a way to reverse whatever twisted fate had me trapped.

"I didn't ask for this mark. I didn't ask for any of this," I spat, the words sharp like shards of glass.

"Ask all you want," the figure responded, leaning closer now, their hands folding on the desk with a soft thud. "But it doesn't change what's coming."

"What's coming?" I demanded, taking a step forward, my voice steady despite the cold gnawing in my gut. "What exactly is coming?"

The figure looked at me then, their eyes flicking from my wrist to my face, their expression unreadable. "The Ravenmark is more than just a symbol of power. It's a marker of balance. You will be forced to choose, whether you want to or not. The forces that seek you out will not be kind."

I froze, my blood running cold. "What forces?"

The figure didn't answer immediately. Instead, they rose from their chair, a fluid movement that sent the air around them stirring like the calm before a storm.

"You'll know soon enough," they said, their voice low and unsettling. "But be warned. The mark has already begun to draw attention. And the ones who come for you next will be much harder to escape than any prophecy."

I turned to Kael, my mind racing, but his face was as unreadable as the figure's. His usual confidence was nowhere to be found, replaced instead by a flicker of something darker, something I couldn't name.

"Kael?" I asked, my voice a little more desperate than I intended. "What does that mean? Who's coming for me?"

He didn't answer at first. He just looked at me, his expression shadowed, his jaw tight as though he, too, was weighing something heavy.

Then the figure's voice cut through the tension, sharp and final. "You'll find out soon enough. You don't have the luxury of time anymore."

I opened my mouth to respond, but the words died in my throat when I heard it—the unmistakable sound of footsteps, fast and hard, coming toward the door. A knock echoed, loud and insistent, and before I could even blink, the door flew open, and a figure stepped inside.

And I knew, in that instant, we were no longer alone.

Chapter 3: Whispers in the Hall of Mirrors

The hallway stretched endlessly, its polished floors reflecting a thousand flickers of light as though the very air vibrated with untold secrets. Every step I took seemed to echo louder than the last, the delicate chime of my boots on marble grating on my nerves. I hated this place, but it was the only place where the truth seemed to hide, nestled among shadows and whispers. I had to know about the Ravenmark. I had to understand what it was—what it meant for me. And yet, the more I sought answers, the more elusive they became, as though the universe was deliberately toying with me.

I didn't expect to find Kael here, not in the labyrinth of this place where the walls were far more than just stone and glass—they were alive with illusions. A thousand mirrors lined the walls, all twisting reality until I couldn't trust the shape of anything, not even my own reflection. It was in the distortion that I first saw him, his figure flickering between angles like a phantom refusing to be fully caught. He was talking to Seraphina, the enigmatic leader of the society who never gave her name lightly. Her presence alone was enough to make the air thicken, to draw your gaze toward her like a moth to flame. Silver hair, cold eyes, and a smile that never reached her lips. She commanded respect, but more than that—fear.

As I stood there, the conversation drifted into focus, piercing the veil of silence that surrounded me.

"The dark sorceress knows," Seraphina murmured, her voice a snake's hiss, too low for anyone outside their circle to fully grasp the weight of it.

Kael's face hardened, his features pulling taut like the strings of a bow ready to snap. I didn't need to hear more to understand that whatever they were discussing, it wasn't meant for my ears. But that didn't stop the icy fingers of doubt from curling around my chest. What was it about the Ravenmark that could incite such an intense reaction? What did they know that I didn't?

Kael turned, and his eyes locked with mine, catching the reflection of my uncertain expression in the mirror. I swear the glass warped, the edges curling like smoke as our gazes met. There was something unsettling about the way his eyes flickered, a quick, sharp recognition. His lips twisted, not quite in a smile, but not quite in a frown either. It was a dangerous thing to read too much into, especially when his silence carried more weight than words ever could.

Before I could react, he was moving toward me, cutting through the hall with the same fluidity as a shadow darting between beams of light. My heart stuttered, but I refused to flinch. It would be far too easy to let him rattle me. The mirrors seemed to mock me with every step I took, my own reflection following me like an uninvited guest.

"You shouldn't be here," Kael said, his voice quiet but commanding, a low warning that still somehow seemed to echo off every surface. There was an edge to his words, something sharp enough to slice through my resolve.

"I don't remember asking for permission," I shot back, my voice smoother than I felt. The last thing I needed was to appear vulnerable, not when everything about this place, and him, already made my pulse race faster than it should.

He stopped in front of me, close enough for me to feel the heat of his presence, close enough for the world around us to feel like it had narrowed to a single, unavoidable moment. The tension between us was thick, the kind that built slowly and unbearably, and even as I steeled myself against it, a small part of me couldn't help but wonder what it would be like if I just let go. What if I stopped pretending to be unaffected by his mere proximity? But then, that would be far too easy. And easy was never the answer when dealing with people like him.

"You're not ready for this," he said, his voice lowering even further, and something in his eyes flickered. Was it concern? Or was it something else? I couldn't tell, not when his expression shifted so quickly, so effortlessly, like a mask slipping over the face of someone trying to hide everything they were.

"I don't need you to decide what I'm ready for," I replied, raising an eyebrow, trying to keep my cool even as my insides churned. I could hear the murmur of the others behind us, the low hum of voices and the shuffle of feet, but in that moment, it felt like we were the only two people in the world.

He took a step closer, his breath warm against my skin. "You don't understand what you're getting into. This... it's not just some game. These people... Seraphina, they don't play by the same rules you do."

The statement hung in the air, its weight settling over me like a shroud. I could feel it—could feel the deep pull of something dark, something dangerous. And yet, I couldn't look away. I couldn't stop myself from asking, "What game are you playing, Kael?"

His eyes flickered to the side, where Seraphina stood, still watching us with that calculating gaze of hers. Then, his focus returned to me, more intense than before, and I swore I could feel the very air around us crackle with an unspoken promise.

"The kind that only leaves room for winners," he said, his voice a whisper, his lips barely moving as he spoke. "And you're already playing."

I wasn't sure if he was warning me, challenging me, or something far more complicated than either. But as he turned away, leaving me standing there, alone and surrounded by shifting reflections, I knew one thing: whatever game Kael was playing, I was already caught in its web.

The glass around me shifted again, distorting my own image as though it couldn't quite figure out what I was supposed to be. Maybe it was right. Maybe I didn't know either. Kael's words hovered like smoke in my mind, each one thick with implications I was reluctant to unpack. I should've walked away, should've turned on my heel and left before I was dragged any deeper into whatever this was. But I couldn't. I couldn't stop myself from following him with my eyes as he slipped past me, his presence like a shadow that refused to be dismissed.

I turned, watching him approach Seraphina once again. They exchanged a few words—brief, clipped—and I could feel the weight of their unspoken communication like an invisible thread tugging at me. There was something in the way Kael stood, half-turned as though he were already preparing to leave, yet tethered to this space by something far more insidious than duty. The flicker of the lights above caught my attention, casting his face into sharp relief for a moment, and I saw it then—the faintest trace of uncertainty. For the briefest second, Kael's usually impenetrable mask cracked, and I was left with an image I wasn't sure I was meant to witness. But before I could make sense of it, he was already moving again, his back to me as he left Seraphina's side without another glance in my direction.

Chapter 4: Magic In the Air

My heart skipped a beat. There was a tension in the air that hadn't been there moments before. Maybe it was him, maybe it was the conversation, but there was a distinct shift. Something had changed, and it wasn't just the mirrors that now reflected the world in jagged, surreal angles. I reached for the nearest mirror, bracing myself against its cool surface, only for the reflection that greeted me to be nothing like the one I was expecting. It was twisted, warped—a version of myself I hardly recognized. My face seemed older, harder. Was that really me? The reflection blinked, and for a split second, I wondered if it had been watching me all along.

I stepped back, shaking my head as though I could erase the image, but the distortion remained, lingering at the edges of my vision.

It wasn't just the mirrors that had changed. Something else was happening—something beneath the surface, something I couldn't quite grasp. I caught a glimpse of Kael again, standing just beyond the shadows, his form half-buried in the shifting reflections. It was as though he wasn't really there, or maybe he was everything I couldn't see—everything I refused to. His jaw clenched, and I could feel his gaze without even looking. It was as though the mirrors were playing tricks, amplifying the tension between us in ways I didn't want to explore.

I had to find out more about the Ravenmark. I had to make sense of it. But now, in the silence that had descended over the room like a heavy fog, I was beginning to realize that the answers I sought might not be what I expected—or even what I wanted.

And maybe, just maybe, it was already too late.

"Stop looking like you've swallowed a lemon," Seraphina's voice cut through the haze, cool as ever. Her presence slid up next to me, almost too quiet for me to detect at first. I hadn't heard her move, but she was there now, her silver hair shining in the dim light, her eyes sharp and unwavering. "You're in far too deep to back out now."

I glanced at her, unsure of what to say. She was, in a strange way, almost like a reflection of everything I hated about this place. She was poised, untouchable, and entirely in control. I hated how easily she read me, how she could assess my every thought before I even had a chance to voice it. And yet, I couldn't look away. "You think I don't know that?" I replied, the words sharper than I intended. "Why else would I still be here?"

Seraphina's lips curved into something between a smile and a sneer. "I didn't expect you to be the type to back down easily," she said, her gaze flicking over to Kael. The flicker of something—something dark and calculating—passed between them before she returned her attention to me. "But you should know, there's no turning back once you enter this game. Once you wear the Ravenmark, it doesn't just mark you. It owns you."

I wasn't sure if she meant to scare me or warn me, but the chill creeping down my spine told me that whatever she was implying, she wasn't lying. Still, I couldn't let her see how much the words affected me. "I'm not afraid of a little ownership."

She chuckled softly, her voice low and melodic, but it held an edge. "No. You're not," she said, her eyes narrowing slightly. "But you should be. Not everyone who wears the Ravenmark survives long enough to understand what it means."

My pulse quickened, and I could feel the ground beneath me shift as though I were standing on the edge of something far deeper than I was ready for. There was no turning back. There was only the relentless forward momentum of everything that had brought me here.

I glanced at Kael once more, his face unreadable. He wasn't watching me now. He was watching the door, the world beyond the Hall of Mirrors. Maybe he was the one who was afraid. Maybe he knew things I didn't, but I wasn't about to let him off the hook so easily. "And what's the price of survival, Seraphina?" I asked, my voice quiet but insistent.

Her gaze flicked to Kael once more, and for the first time, there was something like hesitation in her eyes. "Sometimes," she said, her voice almost a whisper, "the price is far greater than you can imagine."

It wasn't a warning anymore. It was a threat. And in that moment, I realized that whatever game I had thought I was playing, it was far bigger than me—and far more dangerous than I was prepared for.

I don't know what compelled me to follow them, but I found myself drifting deeper into the heart of the Hall, moving past the fractured reflections that played tricks on my mind. The mirrors weren't just surfaces—they were like doors, each one offering a glimpse of something else. A life I didn't recognize. A world I didn't belong to. I could hear their voices now, Kael's clipped tone and Seraphina's measured one, growing more distant as I moved through the maze.

I wasn't sure what I expected, but the deeper I went, the more I felt like I was closing in on something I wasn't supposed to understand. It was like standing in the middle of a storm, with every gust of wind a new piece of information pushing me further into the unknown. I could hear bits of their conversation. Not enough to piece it all together, but enough to feel that unmistakable twinge in my chest.

"She can't keep playing both sides," Kael said, the words low but heavy.

Seraphina's voice followed, soft yet final. "She doesn't have a choice anymore."

I wanted to stop then, to turn around and leave before it was too late, but I couldn't. Something in me needed to hear the rest. Needed to know what they were saying. Needed to know why it had to be me.

I rounded a corner, and there they were, standing by a large, ornate mirror that stretched from floor to ceiling. The reflective surface shimmered in a way that made the edges seem like they were melting, warping with something darker than the glass itself.

Kael was closer to it, his hands folded tightly in front of him, like he was trying to contain something inside him that wanted to break free. Seraphina stood to the side, her arms crossed with that knowing expression she wore like armor. Neither of them noticed me at first, but I could feel the tension between us—thick, undeniable. The kind of tension that pulled at the seams of reality itself.

"You know why she's here, don't you?" Seraphina's voice cut through the thick silence, her gaze never leaving Kael. She wasn't talking to him as though they were equals. She was talking to him like he was a child, a disappointing one at that.

Kael's jaw clenched, his eyes narrowing, but he said nothing at first. His gaze flickered toward the mirror, and I swear the air around us shifted. "I know," he finally muttered, his voice tight. "I know exactly why she's here."

Seraphina smirked, her lips curving in that cold, calculating way. "Then you know what has to happen next."

I froze. The words sliced through the air like a blade. What did that mean? What was supposed to happen next? I barely registered the footsteps behind me, the faintest sound of leather shoes clicking against marble.

"Are you following me now, or is this just a coincidence?" The voice was too familiar, too knowing. Kael.

I didn't turn around right away. I couldn't. Not with the weight of his gaze pressing against my back. "I'm not following you," I said with a sharpness I didn't feel. "I'm just... curious."

"You should be careful," he said, his tone shifting—suddenly lighter, almost teasing. "Curiosity can get you into trouble around here."

I could feel his presence behind me, hear his breath just a little too close to my ear. His words weren't meant to intimidate, but they did anyway. There was something about the way he spoke, about the way he always seemed to be right there—just when I thought I had a moment to breathe—that made everything feel too much, too fast.

"You're telling me that now?" I scoffed, forcing a laugh that didn't quite reach my eyes. "You're just now telling me to be careful?"

His smile, if you could even call it that, was brief and somewhat exasperated. "You didn't listen the first time."

I wanted to say something sharp, something witty, but I couldn't. The truth was, I didn't know what I was doing here. The mirror before me, the one that had drawn me in like a siren's call, now felt like a threat, like it was pulling me in, deeper and deeper. But why? What was in that reflection that I couldn't see, something just out of reach, gnawing at the edges of my understanding?

"I'm not afraid of a mirror," I said finally, the words louder than I intended. But as soon as I spoke them, I felt the weight of the moment shift. Something wasn't right.

Kael's gaze flickered toward Seraphina before he took a step closer. "It's not the mirror you need to be afraid of," he said softly, his voice barely audible. "It's the reflection."

I turned my head slightly, just enough to catch the way his eyes seemed to darken, the way his expression hardened into something unreadable. "What do you mean?" I asked, my voice quiet, though my heart was racing.

Kael didn't answer right away. He only stared at me, his expression inscrutable. "You'll find out soon enough," he said finally, his tone so detached it felt like he was talking about something entirely unrelated. "Just know this—there's no turning back. Not anymore."

I didn't know what to make of his words, or the way they hung in the air like a threat or a warning. It didn't matter. I was already too far gone to stop. The reflection in the mirror shimmered again, and this time, I wasn't sure if I was seeing myself—or something else.

Something that didn't belong.

The surface of the glass rippled, and for a moment, I thought I saw something move within it. My breath caught, my pulse hammering as the reflection seemed to... shift?

Before I could make sense of it, I heard the door behind me creak open. A shadow stepped through it.

I didn't have time to turn around.

The mirror shattered.

The moment the blood touched the ancient scroll, I could feel something shift within me. A strange pulse, like an electric current running beneath my skin, zipped through the air and hummed in my veins. I glanced at Kael, his features still as impassive as ever, but I could see the slight tension in his jaw—the way his hand flexed against the hilt of his sword as if he was trying to steady himself. I wanted to laugh. I wanted to tell him that this whole thing was absurd, that I was no hero and neither was he, but the words caught in my throat. Instead, I stood there, staring at him, waiting for some sign that this was going to be okay.

Seraphina, ever the calm one, was already folding the scroll back into her satchel. "It's done," she said with a quiet certainty that unsettled me. She didn't look back as she walked towards the door of the ancient library. "Meet me at the docks at dawn. We leave for the mountains immediately."

Kael didn't move for a long while, his eyes locked on mine. The silence between us was thick, filled with unsaid words and a strange, unspoken tension. Finally, he broke the quiet, his voice rough. "So, we're really doing this?" The weight of the question hung in the air, and I didn't quite know how to answer.

"I don't know," I admitted, crossing my arms defensively. "I'm still trying to wrap my head around it." I forced a laugh, though it was more nervous than anything else. "One moment, I'm minding my own business, and the next—poof—I'm caught up in some ancient prophecy about an orb that might save the world. Do you feel like this is your life now?" I tilted my head toward him, my eyes searching for something—anything—to make this whole situation make sense.

Kael's lips quirked at the edges, but there was no real amusement there. "No. I'm still waiting for someone to wake me up from this nightmare."

"Right? Because I could really use a nap right about now," I replied with a half-smile, trying to ease the tension. "A long one."

"I'll make a deal with you," he said, stepping closer. The air between us crackled with the strange magic that was now binding us, and I swore I could feel his heartbeat in time with mine. "You keep your distance, and I'll keep mine. We get through this alive, and we don't have to speak to each other again after it's over. Sound good?"

I didn't trust myself to speak, not with this new, unsettling connection buzzing in my chest. Instead, I just nodded, though the idea of cutting ties with him once this was over seemed too permanent. What if this tether that was pulling us together was more than just a blood pact? What if it was something deeper, something that would make me crave his presence more than I cared to admit?

Without another word, Kael turned and walked toward the door, leaving me standing there alone in the quiet room. His footsteps echoed in the stillness, and I felt the weight of the coming journey settle over me. We weren't friends, not by any stretch. But in that moment, I knew that we didn't have to be. What we had was something far more complicated.

The next morning, I found myself at the docks before the sun had even begun to rise. The sky was streaked with hues of violet and rose, and the faint smell of saltwater clung to the air. I stood near the edge of the pier, watching as Seraphina made final preparations for our departure. She was as composed as ever, her face unreadable, but I could sense the quiet urgency in her every movement.

Kael arrived shortly after, his heavy cloak trailing behind him, the hood pulled low over his face. He looked like someone who had walked straight out of a shadow, dark and dangerous, and for a moment, I wondered if he had ever seen the light. The tension between us was palpable, but we didn't speak. There was no need to. We both knew this was the start of something we couldn't turn back from.

Seraphina approached us as the first rays of sunlight pierced the horizon. "The journey ahead will test you both," she said softly, her eyes sweeping over us. "What you feel now, this bond between you—it will only grow stronger, or it will destroy you."

I looked at Kael, the knot in my stomach tightening. "And what if we can't make it work?"

Seraphina's lips curled into something like a smile, but there was no humor in it. "You don't have a choice."

With that, she motioned toward the boat that awaited us at the end of the pier, its sails already unfurled, ready for the journey ahead. We were headed to the mountains, a place so far removed from the bustle of city life that I could barely comprehend it. But one thing was certain: the farther we went, the closer we would get to whatever destiny awaited us at the top of that craggy, snow-capped peak. And with it, the Orb of Balefire.

I could feel Kael's presence at my side, as solid and unyielding as a mountain, but I couldn't help the flutter of nerves that gripped my insides. There was no telling what we would face out there, or how we would fare with this newfound connection between us. But one thing was clear—this journey wasn't just about the orb. It was about everything we were about to learn about ourselves and each other.

The boat cut through the water with a rhythmic, gentle lapping against its hull, and the salty tang of the ocean air filled my lungs, grounding me in the moment. The city of New Orleans had already faded from view, a distant silhouette on the horizon, and all that lay before us was the open water and the unknown. My fingers brushed the edge of the boat's railing, the wood cool beneath my touch. For a moment, I imagined that the waves would carry us far away from everything, but the gnawing tension between Kael and me made it impossible to shake the feeling that we were tethered to something far darker than the journey itself.

Seraphina was at the helm, her long, raven-black hair catching the breeze, her back straight as a board. She had an almost regal air about her, as if the rough seas and the weight of our mission meant nothing. There were times when I wanted to believe that I could be like her—calm, controlled, unaffected by the gravity of the task ahead. But all I could feel was the strange, pulsing connection to Kael. The bond we'd forged in blood was far more than I'd expected. Every time I glanced at him, my heart beat a little faster, my breath caught in my throat. He felt like a shadow—present, elusive, but untouchable.

As if sensing my gaze, Kael turned to face me. His expression was unreadable, but his eyes... those damn eyes. They held a quiet storm, a depth that I hadn't fully understood until now. There was something raw about him, something that felt both dangerous and magnetic. I couldn't deny it. He was a puzzle I was afraid to solve.

"You're staring," he said, his voice low and steady, but with a hint of amusement, as though he found some quiet thrill in it.

I rolled my eyes and forced a smile, trying to play it off. "I was just wondering if I've signed up for a nightmare," I said, my tone light but carrying the weight of truth beneath it. "I've never been to the mountains. Can't say it's my first choice for vacation."

Kael raised an eyebrow, the barest hint of a smirk curling at the corner of his lips. "Well, I hope you packed something warmer than that." He nodded toward my leather jacket, which felt more like a fashion statement than actual protection against the cold.

"I'm flexible," I replied, flashing him a grin. "I've learned how to make do. Not my first time battling something bigger than me, after all."

His gaze softened, just for a split second, before the familiar coolness returned. "We'll see how well you handle it when the real fight begins," he said, his voice just low enough that only I could hear it. He turned away before I could respond, his attention shifting to the horizon.

I didn't know what he meant by that—what 'the real fight' entailed—but a strange part of me didn't want to ask. Not yet, anyway. I had too many questions about what was happening between us, about the strange pulse that tied our fates together. The blood pact had sealed something I wasn't ready to face.

As the hours passed, the boat crept closer to the far-off mountains, their peaks jagged and looming in the distance. The wind had picked up, and the air had grown colder, the water now choppier as we neared the shore. I shivered despite myself, tugging my jacket tighter around my shoulders, but I knew the worst was yet to come.

The island we'd docked at was small and isolated, surrounded by dense fog that gave the air a thick, impenetrable quality. There was something eerie about it—the silence, the way the mist curled like fingers around the trees. Even Seraphina seemed uneasy, her sharp eyes scanning the surroundings as we stepped off the boat and onto the rocky shore.

"This place is cursed," she muttered, almost to herself, her voice carrying just above the wind. "Don't let the quiet fool you. It's not peaceful here."

I swallowed hard, my pulse quickening. "Cursed? That's... reassuring."

She didn't respond, but I noticed the slight tension in her posture. There was a wariness to her now, a crack in the mask she always wore. It made my stomach flip, but I didn't voice my concern. I had enough of my own fears to deal with.

We started our trek into the woods, the path barely visible beneath the overgrowth. Every step felt heavier, the air thick with something I couldn't place, as though the land itself was alive with secrets. Kael walked ahead of me, his broad shoulders blocking the path, but I couldn't shake the feeling that something was watching us.

"Are you sure we're headed in the right direction?" I asked, trying to push away the unease that crept up my spine. "This doesn't look like the road to a hidden treasure, if you ask me."

Kael didn't look back as he spoke, but his voice was steady. "Trust Seraphina. She knows what she's doing. We're getting close."

I wasn't so sure about that. The mist was growing denser, curling around the trees like a living thing, and the strange sensation of being watched had only intensified. It wasn't just the mist anymore—it was the feeling that something was breathing right behind us, its presence just on the edge of my awareness.

Suddenly, the silence was broken by a crackling sound from the trees to our left, followed by the unmistakable thud of something large hitting the ground. I froze, my heart slamming against my chest. Kael's hand went instinctively to his sword, and Seraphina muttered something under her breath, her hand glowing faintly as she summoned some form of magic.

Something—someone—was out there, and the forest had just become far more dangerous than I had anticipated.

A rustling in the trees made my stomach drop. Then, a voice, low and gravelly, echoed through the mist.

"You're not welcome here," it growled, the words sending a chill through the air. "Not now, not ever."

Chapter 5: The Forest of Forgotten Songs

The forest was thick with the scent of damp earth and old pine, the air heavy with the kind of stillness that only a place untouched by time could carry. Each step we took seemed to disturb a layer of something ancient, like we were walking over the bones of forgotten legends. The trees were gnarled and twisted, their branches interlocking above us in a tight weave, blocking out the sky. It was as if the world outside had ceased to exist. There was no breeze, no birdsong, just the occasional creak of wood bending under the weight of centuries. Yet, beneath that silence, there was a hum, a quiet vibration that reverberated in my chest, too faint to identify but undeniable all the same.

Kael moved ahead of me, his boots sinking slightly into the moss-laden ground with every step. I caught sight of the sharp line of his jaw, his lips set in a permanent scowl. There was always something so self-assured about him, like he never had a doubt in his mind, and it made my skin prickle. His arrogance was infuriating. "You're quiet," he observed, glancing back with a smirk that didn't quite reach his eyes. "Not even a witty comeback? Am I that intimidating?"

I rolled my eyes, though I wasn't sure he noticed. "You're too confident for your own good. We're walking into a place that's been hiding its secrets for centuries, Kael. Confidence won't save you from that."

He didn't respond at first, his eyes scanning the shadows ahead, the hint of a frown tugging at his lips. But then, with that characteristic bravado of his, he straightened his shoulders and answered, "Fear is the enemy. Not the forest, not the darkness. If you show it a crack, it'll find a way to crawl inside."

It wasn't a sentiment I shared, but I kept that to myself, choosing instead to match his pace, despite the uneasy flutter in my stomach. There was something wrong about this place, and I wasn't sure what. I wasn't usually one to give in to superstitions or idle chatter about cursed places, but there was a palpable sense of something watching us, following us from behind the trees. My breath caught as the wind shifted, carrying with it the faintest echo of a song—soft, haunting, like a lullaby half-remembered from childhood. It tugged at something deep inside me, a whisper that slipped through the cracks of my defenses.

"Did you hear that?" I asked, my voice barely a breath.

Kael didn't break stride. "What, the wind?" he scoffed. "That's nothing."

But it wasn't nothing. The air was growing colder, and I could feel the hairs on my neck standing on end. I could've sworn I heard it again—distant but clear, the lilt of a melody winding its way through the trees, coaxing me forward. Something about it was familiar, like a song I had once known but had forgotten.

The silence between us stretched, thick with the sound of my pulse. I was about to speak again when the ground shifted beneath us. It was barely perceptible at first—a slight tremor that rattled my bones, a quick tremor of warning. Before I could react, there was a growl from the shadows, and then a blur of motion. The forest exploded into chaos.

A shadow hound lunged from the darkness, its eyes glowing a feral gold. Its fur was matted with the damp of the forest floor, and its teeth were long, sharp, gleaming under the faint light that filtered through the canopy. Instinctively, I stumbled back, my breath hitching in my throat. Kael moved in front of me in one fluid motion, his hand going to the sword at his hip, drawing it with a practiced swipe. The blade hummed as it sliced through the air.

The hound was fast, its movements a blur of raw power. But Kael was faster. He danced around it with a predator's grace, his strikes sharp and deliberate. I could hear the sound of steel meeting flesh, the hound's growls mingling with the hiss of Kael's blade cutting through the air. For a moment, all I could do was watch, my heart racing in my chest as the fight unfolded before me.

Then another hound appeared, its form slipping from the shadows like smoke. A third, and a fourth. They circled us, their eyes gleaming with hunger, and I realized with a jolt that there were too many to fight off. We couldn't outrun them either—not with the forest closing in on all sides.

I looked at Kael, my throat dry. "There's too many. We can't—"

"Stay close," he interrupted, his voice low and firm, cutting through the panic that threatened to overtake me. He had his back to me now, his sword flashing in the dim light as he took another step forward. "Don't move unless I tell you to."

Before I could respond, one of the hounds lunged again, and Kael's sword met its throat with a sickening thud. But the victory was short-lived. The pack closed in around us, their growls rising to a crescendo, vibrating through the forest. My heart hammered in my chest, the air thick with tension, the scent of blood, and the overwhelming sense that we were surrounded by something ancient—something far older than the forest itself.

"Evanna," Kael's voice broke through the chaos, sharper now. "Move!"

I didn't need to be told twice. I scrambled to my feet, my legs shaking, but I didn't hesitate. The forest seemed to close in around me, and the sound of those eerie songs—those forgotten melodies—sang louder in my mind, almost drowning out the growls and the clash of swords. I could see the way Kael moved, how he cut through the hounds with ruthless efficiency, but I knew we were running out of time.

The forest was alive, yes, but it wasn't on our side. And I had the sinking feeling that it had plans for us.

The forest was a labyrinth of shifting shadows and twisted trunks, a place where even the air felt as though it carried the weight of forgotten promises. With every step, the ground seemed to groan beneath our feet, like the earth itself was warning us to turn back, but we had come too far to consider retreat. My boots sank into the soft, mossy earth, the scent of wet foliage thick and suffocating, but the steady rhythm of Kael's pace kept me moving forward, even if my thoughts were running in circles.

"Do you ever stop talking?" I muttered under my breath, though it wasn't entirely directed at him. The eerie quiet of the forest—broken only by the occasional whisper of the wind—was enough to unnerve anyone. But Kael? No. His arrogance was impervious to anything as mundane as fear. His presence was a storm that swept across the space between us, and it was hard not to feel like a leaf in its path. Even in the face of the unknown, he kept pushing forward, as though he knew exactly what awaited us.

"Tell me, Evanna," he called over his shoulder with a smirk that seemed to mock the very forest around us, "what's the worst that could happen? You can't seriously believe these trees are out to get us."

"You're right," I replied, rolling my eyes despite myself. "They're not. They just happen to be very good at making us feel like we've stepped into a haunted theme park. So, no. I don't think they're trying to get us. But I'm not sure the place itself has our best interests at heart."

Kael chuckled, the sound rough and low, as though the tension in the air had somehow amused him. "Let me know when you start believing in ghosts, Evanna. Until then, I'll keep my eyes on the prize."

I wasn't sure what prize he was chasing—maybe it was the Orb of Balefire, or maybe it was the idea of proving something to himself. Either way, I wasn't so sure that whatever we found here was going to be worth the trouble we were courting. The Orb was more of a legend than a reality. But still, we walked on, the path narrowing in front of us as the trees seemed to press in tighter, their gnarled limbs twisting into unnatural shapes. Every so often, I caught glimpses of something darting just out of sight—shadows shifting faster than they should have been able to.

"Do you feel that?" I asked, stopping in my tracks. A chill had spread through my bones, a creeping sensation of being watched. Kael paused as well, his body language shifting slightly, a subtle tension threading through the way he held himself.

"Feel what?" He turned to face me, his sharp gaze assessing, as though expecting me to make some grand revelation.

"The air. It's... different," I said, my words hanging uncertainly between us.

"Maybe it's the weather," he said, but his tone lacked its usual confidence. The forest had its way of making even the most self-assured falter. "You're letting your imagination run wild."

I shook my head, not fully convinced. But Kael was already moving again, striding purposefully forward, and I had no choice but to follow. The tension that had been growing between us—bubbling beneath our casual banter—seemed to build with each step. He moved with such confidence, like he had something to prove, and I resented how easy it was for him to appear unshaken. If I hadn't seen the way he fought those shadow hounds with a calm ruthlessness, I might have found his bravado charming. Instead, it made my stomach turn. In his world, everything had a place, a purpose. But not here, not in this place.

The whispers were back, but louder now. They threaded through the branches above us, twining through the leaves with a soft cadence that almost sounded like words. A tune? A memory? I couldn't say. But it was enough to make my heart race.

"You're still hearing that, aren't you?" Kael asked, this time slowing his pace to match mine. His voice was low, and I could feel the shift in him, like the song was affecting him too. He was no longer the invincible force I'd seen earlier. He was human, vulnerable, like the rest of us.

"It's... unsettling," I admitted, though I didn't want to. There was something about his presence that made me want to hold my own, not to admit to any weakness. "I'm not sure what it is, but it's pulling me in. I don't like it."

Kael's gaze flickered to the dark depths of the forest, and for a moment, he was lost in thought. "The Orb," he said, almost to himself. "It's hidden here. It's connected to this place. But it's not just the Orb we need to find. It's the magic. And whatever the forest is hiding from us."

I nodded, though it did little to quell the unease spreading through me. The forest wasn't hiding a trinket, a relic. It was hiding itself, its soul, and I wasn't sure if I was ready to confront that.

Then, a rustle broke the silence. At first, it was subtle—just a faint disturbance, like a breeze through dry leaves. But it came again, this time louder, closer, and I knew we weren't alone.

"Stay behind me," Kael growled, his hand dropping to the hilt of his sword.

Before I could respond, a blur of motion appeared, and suddenly the hounds were back, but this time there were more than I could count—dozens, their eyes glinting with that feral hunger. They were faster than before, and the air was thick with their growls, their claws scraping against the bark of the trees as they circled us, their shadows twisting like smoke.

Kael moved first, drawing his blade with swift, practiced ease, but the forest was closing in on us. Every direction seemed to hold new threats, and my pulse quickened as the hounds began to close in, each of them focused solely on one thing: us.

I glanced up at Kael, our eyes locking for a fraction of a second before the first hound lunged. There was no time for words. There was only the sharp sound of metal meeting flesh, the heavy thud of paws against the ground, and the desperate pulse of survival.

And somewhere, deep in the heart of the forest, I swore I heard that song again. Louder now. Stronger. It wasn't a melody. It was a warning.

The forest had become a living thing—its breath cold and quick, every sound amplified, echoing with a strange intensity. Even the low growls of the hounds, now circling us with more determination than I had ever seen in any creature, seemed to resonate with something deep within the earth itself. It wasn't just the hounds that were closing in; the very woods felt like they were contracting, pulling us deeper into their heart. We were intruders, uninvited, and the trees knew it. Their bark, dark and slick with moisture, seemed to pulse with the rhythm of the forest, the shadows lengthening unnaturally as though they were feeding on the very fear that radiated from us.

"Evanna, move!" Kael's voice was sharp, a jolt of command that cut through the tension. His eyes were fixed on the pack of hounds, his grip on his sword tightening as he prepared for another onslaught. There was no bravado in him now—only focus, the kind of fierce calculation that came with knowing death was close by, and only one of you could walk away from it.

I didn't hesitate, darting to the side as the first hound lunged with a growl that rattled my bones. My breath caught in my throat as I spun, the sharp edge of Kael's sword flashing beside me as he cleaved through the beast's throat in one swift motion. But there was no time to celebrate the victory. The forest was alive with them—more than I could count, their eyes glinting like hot embers in the murky light. They were relentless.

My feet barely touched the ground as I twisted and dodged, trying to keep out of the reach of the hounds, but it was no use. The forest was a blur of darkness, the trees pressing in on all sides as I fought to keep my footing. I could hear Kael behind me, his every strike a promise that he would protect me, but even he couldn't save us from everything. The hounds were too fast, too many, and I had no illusions that we'd survive this unscathed.

"Why is it always dogs?" I grunted, ducking under a snapping jaw. "Why couldn't it be something... less bitey?"

Kael's lips quirked for a split second, his eyes flashing with that wry humor I had come to expect from him, even in the face of danger. "You've got a point there. I'd take a well-placed cactus over these hounds any day."

The banter was a brief respite from the chaos, but it did little to stave off the growing sense of desperation gnawing at my gut. I had no idea how long we could keep this up. My lungs were burning, my legs aching with every dodged blow. And yet the hounds kept coming, an endless tide of fur and teeth, shadows that seemed to multiply the deeper we ventured into the forest.

"We're not going to last," I panted, my voice strained, as another hound's claws skimmed my shoulder, tearing through the fabric of my coat.

"Shut up and keep moving," Kael snapped, his tone harsh but necessary. He was already spinning, his blade cutting through the air with expert precision, dispatching another hound with the same ruthless efficiency as before. But his movements were slowing, his focus narrowing with every blow. I could see it in the way he carried himself—his muscles tensed, his breaths coming faster. Even Kael wasn't invincible.

But the worst part? The worst part was that I could feel it. The song. It was louder now, clearer, calling to me from the heart of the forest. It wasn't just an eerie hum anymore—it was a command, something tugging at the very marrow of my bones, urging me forward, urging me to follow it into the depths of the unknown.

"We have to—" I started, my voice a breathless rasp.

"Not now," Kael growled, his eyes flashing with a warning that stopped me in my tracks. But the pull of the song was stronger now, its whispers clearer, its lyrics forming in my mind like a puzzle begging to be solved. "Evanna, no—"

But I was already moving.

The hounds were forgotten. The forest was forgotten. The only thing that mattered was the song, the way it was weaving its threads through me, making me feel something I couldn't understand, something that made my heart ache with longing. I could hear the words now, faint but distinct, urging me forward, deeper into the forest. Something was waiting for me there.

Kael's voice broke through my haze of thought, a low snarl as he reached for my arm. "Don't! You don't know what you're doing!"

But I pulled away, the pull of the song stronger than his words, stronger than anything else. The trees loomed larger now, their trunks twisting in ways that shouldn't have been possible, bending in unnatural arcs, the branches tangling in strange, impossible shapes. But the path I was walking down, the one the song was guiding me to, remained clear, a shining thread in the web of shadows.

Kael's curses were nothing more than distant murmurs now. The world seemed to narrow, the air growing colder with every step I took, the song swelling in my mind like a tide I couldn't control. It felt like the forest was opening up to me, welcoming me, and I couldn't stop myself from moving forward. The hounds were behind me now, their growls fading into the distance, and yet I wasn't looking back. I couldn't.

And then, before I knew it, the forest opened up before me, and I stepped into a clearing. The moment I crossed the threshold, the song stopped. The silence that followed was deafening, and the air was thick with the weight of... something. The Orb of Balefire, they had said, was hidden here. But I wasn't sure if that was all I was meant to find.

There was something in the clearing—a figure, barely visible, but I could feel its presence like a thunderstorm on the horizon. I froze, my breath caught in my throat. The figure's outline was indistinct, wavering like heat on pavement, but its eyes... those eyes were burning with an intensity that made my heart stutter in my chest.

And then it spoke.

"You're too late."

Chapter 6: The Orb and the Warning

I ran my fingers along the surface of the Orb, its cool stone almost too smooth, as though it had been polished over centuries by unseen hands. The warning, etched into the ancient surface in jagged script, glowed faintly, as if alive. Beware the one who walks beside you. The words gnawed at me, settling like a weight in my chest, dragging my thoughts down into a deep, cold pit. It felt as though the stone itself was humming, vibrating with some dark knowledge, and I couldn't shake the feeling that it had recognized something about me—something I hadn't yet allowed myself to fully understand.

Kael was standing a few paces behind me, his tall figure casting a long shadow across the cracked floor of the crypt. His presence, so often a comforting weight at my back, now felt more like a trap. The way his eyes narrowed, studying me with an intensity that bordered on predatory, sent a ripple of discomfort through my veins. I should've been used to it by now. After all, I'd spent enough time around Kael to know that his sharp mind didn't miss much. But this? This was different. The words on the Orb were a warning. And every instinct screamed that they were meant for him.

"You've gone pale," Kael said, his voice smooth, too smooth, as though he'd already figured out something I hadn't. "What aren't you telling me?"

I tried to swallow, the dry lump in my throat refusing to budge. "Nothing," I muttered, hoping the lie wouldn't sound as shaky to him as it did to me. I could feel his gaze boring into my back, could practically hear the thoughts ticking through his mind, his sharp intellect no doubt already dissecting my every hesitation, my every movement. If anyone could pick apart the tangled mess of fear and unease knotted in my chest, it would be Kael.

He took a step closer, his boots scraping against the rough stone floor with an almost predatory quiet. "Don't lie to me, Lila. I know you. That orb was supposed to be a victory. So why do you look like someone just dug your grave?"

I glanced at the Orb again, my hand trembling slightly as I pulled away from it. His words echoed in my ears, twisting into a tangle of fear and confusion. I wanted to tell him, to spill the truth out like a dam breaking, but how could I? How could I admit that the warning was for me? How could I say that I couldn't shake the feeling that I was walking beside a monster in the guise of a man, and that everything inside me was screaming to run before it was too late?

But instead, I just stared at him, my mouth dry, trying and failing to form the words. The silence stretched between us, thick and heavy, until it felt like it might choke me.

Kael's eyes softened for a moment, as if he was seeing something in me that he didn't understand—something that, for once, I wasn't sure I understood either. He ran a hand through his dark hair, his frustration visible, but there was a flicker of something else in his gaze. Something almost like concern.

It made me angry. How dare he? He had no idea what it was like to live with the kind of power I had. He had no idea what it felt like to know that the very thing that made you special was also the thing that made you a target. He didn't understand the weight of the power he was walking beside, the darkness that lurked behind every step, every breath. And yet, here he was, looking at me like I was the one who had something to hide.

"I didn't sign up for this," I said, the words coming out sharper than I meant. "I didn't ask for any of this." My fingers brushed the Orb again, and for a split second, I felt its pulse, almost like a heartbeat, under my skin. The darkness seemed to whisper, to beckon, and I pulled my hand away as if it had burned me.

Kael's expression shifted again, his lips pressing into a tight line as though he was wrestling with some decision I couldn't fathom. His eyes locked on mine, unwavering, the force of his stare now something I couldn't escape. "You've been walking in the dark for a long time, haven't you, Lila? You've been carrying this burden, whatever it is, and you've been doing it alone."

I wanted to scoff, to tell him that he didn't know me, that he didn't know the first thing about the shadows I carried. But instead, I just stared back, my breath shallow, caught between the need to run and the desire to stay. His words were too close to the truth. It had always been like that for me—one step forward, two steps back, caught between the past I couldn't shake and the future I didn't want to face.

"I'm not asking you to carry it for me," I said, my voice quieter now, more controlled. "But I'm also not going to pretend I'm fine when I'm not. You don't get it, Kael. There's more going on here than just this... orb." My hand hovered over it again, my skin prickling as I watched the glow intensify for a moment, casting strange shadows across the stone walls.

His eyes flicked to the Orb, and then back to me, a flicker of realization dawning behind his gaze. "You're scared."

I nodded, too tired to argue anymore, too tired to deny what was so obvious even to him. The truth was, I didn't know what I was scared of. Not completely. I didn't know if it was the power I held, or the man who stood beside me, or the fate that seemed to be pulling us both into a dark corner. But something told me that the warning on the Orb was only the beginning of something much darker. Something I wasn't sure I was ready to face.

I took a step back, trying to put distance between myself and the Orb. The air in the crypt was heavy, suffocating, filled with a sort of static energy that felt wrong in the pit of my stomach. I could hear the faint drip of water somewhere off in the shadows, the sound echoing off the stone walls, but everything felt distant now, muffled by the buzz in my head.

Kael didn't move. Of course, he wouldn't. He wasn't the type to retreat, to give me space when I needed it most. He was the kind of man who would close in, who would push, until there was nowhere to go but forward. And right now, I didn't want to go anywhere with him. But I couldn't seem to stop myself, either.

His expression was unreadable, though there was a tension in his jaw that I knew all too well. He wanted to push, to drag the truth from me, but he wasn't going to get it easily. There were things I wasn't ready to say, even to him. Especially to him.

"Lila," Kael said again, his voice low and steady, each syllable carrying that same undercurrent of something I couldn't name, "this isn't like you. You're not the type to hide your cards."

I turned to face him, meeting his gaze squarely for the first time in minutes. There was a flicker of something in his eyes, something that made my breath catch, but I refused to let him see that. I wasn't going to be the one to break first.

"I'm not hiding anything," I said, my voice sharp. "You're overthinking it. Maybe you should worry less about me and more about that warning." I gestured to the Orb, hoping it would shift the conversation, give me some breathing room.

He didn't budge. Instead, his lips twitched, almost like he was amused by my feigned indifference. "You think I'm overthinking it?"

I nodded, though my chest was tight with nerves. "You're making something out of nothing, Kael. It's just a warning. Cryptic nonsense meant to scare us." I didn't even believe my own words. I could feel the chill that had settled in my bones deepening, spreading like frost across my skin. But I had to pretend I didn't care, even if I was slowly suffocating under the weight of that warning.

Kael's eyes softened, but not in the way I wanted. It wasn't the comfort I craved, nor the reassurance I needed. No, it was the look of a man who could see through the mask, the one I had so carefully constructed. He took a step forward, his gaze never leaving mine, and suddenly the air between us felt even thicker, as if the walls themselves were closing in.

"What's it say?" he asked quietly, his tone shifting. There was something dangerous in his voice now, something that made my heart stutter. "What does it mean, Lila?"

I didn't want to tell him. Part of me wanted to lie, to cover it up, to walk away and pretend none of this ever happened. But I couldn't. The words were already in the air between us, and there was no taking them back.

"Beware the one who walks beside you," I said, my voice barely a whisper, as if saying it aloud would give it more power than I could control. "It's meant for me, Kael. It's warning me about you."

His face didn't change, but his shoulders tensed, and that was enough. I could see the slight hitch in his breath, the way his brow furrowed, as though he was trying to parse my words into something that made sense. For a long moment, neither of us spoke. I could feel the weight of the silence pressing against my chest, the unsaid things hanging between us like an invisible thread.

Finally, Kael exhaled sharply. "You think I'm a threat?" His voice was tight, more clipped than I'd ever heard it, and I had to fight the urge to step back.

I wanted to explain. I wanted to tell him that I wasn't accusing him, not really, but how could I? The warning on that Orb was more than just words—it was a feeling, an instinct that gnawed at my gut. Every fiber of my being screamed that something was off. Something about him.

"No," I said finally, my voice trembling despite my best effort to remain steady. "But I don't know you, Kael. I don't know what you're hiding."

He laughed then, the sound low and edged with something I couldn't quite place. "I'm hiding nothing, Lila," he said, his voice suddenly harder. "But you? You're full of secrets."

I flinched, but didn't let him see it. "I'm not the one with a glowing Orb in my hand," I snapped, gesturing to the object that had suddenly become the center of our universe. It was pulsing with an unnatural light, and I could feel the pull of it, like a magnetic force I couldn't resist. "I didn't ask for this. I didn't ask for any of this."

Kael's eyes narrowed as he watched me, and I could see the wheels turning behind his gaze. He didn't believe me, of course. Kael never believed anything unless he saw it for himself. But he wasn't an idiot. He knew something was wrong.

"You think that Orb is the problem?" he asked, his voice barely a whisper. "Lila, that Orb is just a piece of the puzzle. The real question is why you think the warning is meant for you. Why does it scare you?"

I opened my mouth to respond, but the words caught in my throat. The truth was, I didn't know. All I knew was that the feeling in my gut—this overwhelming, cold fear—wasn't something I could ignore. Not anymore.

I glanced down at the Orb again, the words still shimmering in my mind. They were meant for me. And deep down, I knew that the worst was yet to come.

The tension between us was thick, the kind that crawls under your skin and leaves you itchy and exposed. Kael was still standing there, eyes fixed on me, his body tense like a coiled spring ready to snap. His silence, as much as his questions, was a weapon. I could feel the weight of every unspoken word pressing in on me, making it impossible to breathe without giving myself away.

"Lila," he said again, his voice softer this time, but there was a dangerous edge to it. "You can't keep running from this. Not anymore."

I took a step back, as if that would give me some space to think, but it was pointless. There was nowhere to run. Not from him. Not from the truth.

He didn't move, but I could see the shift in him. The moment he realized he was losing me. Not physically, not yet, but emotionally. Mentally. I had always been a mystery to him, a puzzle he couldn't solve. But this? This was different. The Orb, the warning, the way it felt like the ground was tilting beneath my feet—Kael wasn't used to being in the dark, and I could tell he hated it.

"I'm not running," I said, trying to steady my voice. "But I'm not going to let you dictate my every move either. This... this is my problem. Not yours."

Kael's eyes flicked to the Orb, still resting innocently on the stone pedestal, its glow growing more erratic with each passing second. He stepped closer, and I could feel the heat radiating off him, a magnetic pull I couldn't escape no matter how hard I tried. "You think you can handle this alone?" he asked, his words laced with disbelief. "You think I don't see you, Lila? I see you. You're scared."

The word hit harder than I expected. Scared. The one thing I didn't want him to know. And yet, he was right. I was scared. Scared of the Orb. Scared of him. Scared of the truth I wasn't ready to face. I opened my mouth to protest, to tell him he was wrong, but the words never came. Because deep down, I knew he was right. The truth had been sitting there, mocking me, since the first moment I touched the Orb.

I took another step back, more out of instinct than anything else, but Kael was closer now, a shadow at my side. The air between us felt like it was crackling, filled with all the things we hadn't said, the things we couldn't say. His hand reached out, almost casually, but there was nothing casual about the way his fingers brushed mine. It was like a live wire had just connected between us, a surge of energy that jolted through me with terrifying intensity.

"Tell me what you're thinking, Lila," he said, his voice low, almost a whisper. "You're not fooling me."

I shook my head, taking another step back, but this time, he followed. He always followed. I couldn't remember the last time I felt like I was in control. Every time I thought I had a hold on the situation, Kael's presence, his proximity, shattered that illusion. There was no getting away from him, not in this place. Not in this moment.

"I can't do this," I said, my voice breaking despite my best effort. "I can't keep pretending that everything's fine when it's not. That warning—it was meant for me. It's about me, Kael. Not you. Not this—us. Just me."

His gaze softened, just a little, but it didn't comfort me like I wanted it to. If anything, it made everything worse. His concern, the way he was looking at me like he could fix it, like he could somehow erase all the chaos swirling inside me, only made the storm inside me grow louder.

"That's not how this works," Kael said, his voice firm, his hand finding mine once more. "It's not just you anymore. Not with this. We're in this together, whether you like it or not."

I pulled my hand away, a small act of defiance, but it felt hollow. It didn't change anything. Kael wasn't just with me. He was in me. His presence, his influence, his power—they were all things I couldn't escape. No matter how much I tried.

"We need to leave," I said abruptly, my mind already working on the next step, the next move. I couldn't stay here, couldn't keep feeling like I was unraveling under the weight of it all. "We need to get out of here. Now."

Kael didn't argue, though I could see the questions in his eyes. He knew better than to push me when I was like this. Instead, he reached for the Orb, lifting it gently from the pedestal, his fingers brushing its surface, the pulse of its light momentarily flickering in response. It was like the thing was alive, responding to him. But I didn't want to think about that now. I didn't want to think about what the Orb was doing to him, to me.

We turned to leave the crypt, the silence between us louder than ever. The cold stone floor seemed to stretch endlessly beneath our feet, the shadows clinging to us like a second skin. I could feel Kael beside me, his presence both a comfort and a warning.

As we reached the door, something shifted. A sound, a whisper almost too soft to hear, like the wind brushing against the walls. My pulse spiked. Something was wrong. The warning. The one carved into the Orb. It wasn't just meant for me—it was meant for both of us.

"Kael," I whispered, my voice barely audible, "we're not alone."

He stopped, his body going rigid beside me. His hand dropped to the hilt of his sword, and I knew in that moment, everything was about to change.

The door behind us slammed shut with a deafening crash. And then the shadows in the crypt began to move.

Chapter 7: The Sorceress Unveiled

The city was thick with the weight of twilight when Selene appeared, slinking out of the shadows as though she were made from the very fabric of the night. I had always wondered if darkness could take shape, but there she was, standing in front of me, the embodiment of every nightmare I had ever buried in the back of my mind. The evening air was sharp, the scent of rain looming just beyond the horizon, but none of it touched her. She was a world unto herself, draped in a gown as black as the spaces between the stars, eyes glowing with a malevolent light that somehow felt warmer than it should.

My breath caught in my throat, and for the briefest moment, I questioned if I had somehow wandered into a dream. But no, this was too real. The hum of distant traffic, the faint rustle of a late-night breeze through the trees lining the park, all of it anchored me. I wanted to scream, to run, to do anything to escape her, but my feet refused to move. Instead, I stood there, frozen, as her gaze swept over me, the barest trace of a smirk curling her lips. She knew the effect she had, and worse, she knew I couldn't look away.

"Evanna," she purred, her voice like velvet and honey, and yet colder than anything I had ever known. "I've been waiting for you."

The words slid over my skin like ice, and despite the rising chill, I couldn't bring myself to shiver. I had heard the legends, of course—whispers in hidden corners, hushed tones from those who thought they knew everything. Selene, the sorceress who had once been part of the ruling council of magic, the one who had disappeared without a trace, leaving only rumors and a thousand unanswered questions in her wake. No one knew exactly what she had done or what had made her vanish, but they all agreed on one thing: whatever power she had, it was not to be trifled with.

"Are you a ghost?" I asked, though I already knew the answer. No, she was not a ghost. She was far too alive, too present, too powerful for that.

Her laughter was soft, dangerous, and somehow the sound of it seemed to twist the world around me, making the streetlights flicker, the shadows stretch and sway unnaturally. "A ghost? How quaint. No, I'm something far more interesting. A woman of many parts, some of them you may never understand. But you, my dear Evanna, you're on the verge of something extraordinary. I can see it in you. The potential. The hunger."

I frowned, instinctively taking a half-step back, though it didn't help. The distance between us remained fixed, as though the very air itself conspired to keep me within her reach. "I don't know what you're talking about," I said, but my voice lacked conviction. I wasn't sure if I was trying to convince her or myself.

She tilted her head, as if considering me. "Oh, I think you do. You've always known. The way your power stirs when you're near danger, the way you can sense when someone lies, the things you can make happen when you're angry. You're not like them, Evanna. Not like those who think they control you."

Her words were a blade, slicing through the veil of my thoughts, uncovering things I hadn't even realized I had buried. My pulse quickened, and I hated the way her presence seemed to seep into my skin, as though she were planting something there. Something dark.

"You've been a pawn in their game," she continued, her voice smooth, almost coaxing. "A piece to move around the board, one they've used to do their bidding. Kael—he knows this. He's not what you think."

The mention of Kael brought a knot to my stomach, tightening, twisting. I could hear his laughter echoing in my mind, see the way his eyes always held something back, something far too dangerous to name. He had never been fully transparent with me, always holding pieces of himself just out of reach. The idea that I might have been nothing more than a pawn, manipulated and controlled by him, gnawed at me like acid eating away at the edges of my certainty. But no, I couldn't—I wouldn't—believe it.

"I don't believe you," I said, my voice a little more forceful than I intended. "Kael isn't like that."

Selene smiled, but it was a smile that didn't reach her eyes. "You don't have to believe me now. You'll see the truth eventually. You always do." She took a step closer, and despite myself, I took one back. "I don't offer these things lightly, Evanna. You're more than you realize. More than they ever let you be."

Her words sank into the air, settling heavily, stirring something in the depths of my mind. My pulse raced, but a part of me resisted the pull of her promises. I couldn't give in—not to her, not to whatever twisted game she was trying to play. I had been raised to believe in a world where loyalty mattered, where trust could be earned and respected. But now, standing before Selene, I couldn't shake the gnawing feeling that everything I had ever believed might be built on sand, ready to slip away at any moment.

"I don't need your help," I said, trying to sound resolute, though there was a flicker of doubt beneath the surface. "I'll find my own way."

She didn't respond immediately. Instead, she simply looked at me, her gaze penetrating, as though she could see through to the very heart of me. "Very well," she murmured. "But remember this, Evanna: the truth is not always what we want it to be. And when you're ready to accept what you are, what you could be… you know where to find me."

With that, she turned and vanished into the night, as swiftly and silently as she had come. The city seemed to exhale around me, the streets once again familiar and comforting, though the strange, unsettling sense that everything had shifted lingered in the air. I didn't know if Selene's words were a warning or an invitation, but I knew one thing for certain: my world was no longer as simple as it had seemed a mere moment ago.

The next few days felt like a fog had settled over my life, thick and suffocating, as though the air itself was dense with all the things I couldn't see or touch. I went through the motions of my daily routine—baking bread at my small café, speaking to regulars who asked for the same thing every day without fail, holding onto the semblance of normality like it was a lifeline. But behind my calm exterior, something churned, relentless and insistent. Selene's words echoed in my head, a constant whisper, a gnawing presence that refused to be ignored.

The mornings were the worst. The city of Charleston always looked the same at sunrise, the golden light spilling over the wrought-iron railings of the French Quarter, the air heavy with the scent of jasmine and the briny tang of the harbor. It was peaceful here, deceptively so, with the hum of the city still far enough away to make it feel as though time itself slowed to a crawl. But in the quiet moments, when the steam from my coffee rose in delicate curls, I could still feel her presence, lurking just beyond the edge of my thoughts, waiting.

And then there was Kael.

He had been distant lately, his usual playful smirk replaced by a more cryptic expression. It didn't help that the moments we shared were laced with tension, small things I couldn't put my finger on. The way he would glance over his shoulder as if expecting someone to emerge from the shadows, the way his eyes would linger on me just a little too long, like he was sizing me up.

One evening, after the last of the patrons had left and the cafe had emptied out, I stayed behind, cleaning up as the dim light from the chandelier above cast long shadows across the brick floors.

I didn't notice Kael standing in the doorway until he cleared his throat, a sound that made the hairs on the back of my neck prickle.

"Working late, I see," he said, his voice smooth, but there was something in it that set me on edge.

I forced a smile, though I didn't feel like smiling. "You know me. Always need to make sure the pastries are just right." I set down the rag I had been using to wipe down the counter, giving him a sidelong glance. "Is there something you wanted?"

He stepped into the room, his movements easy and graceful, as if he owned the place. Which, to be fair, sometimes I wondered if he did. "Maybe I'm just checking in on you," he said with that devilish grin that I knew all too well, the one that made my heart do strange things in my chest.

I crossed my arms, leaning against the counter. "You don't check in. You usually show up when you want something."

His eyes narrowed slightly, but the smile didn't fade. "Ouch. That's cold."

I could feel my resolve slipping, like sand through my fingers. I didn't want to let him in, didn't want to entertain the idea that maybe, just maybe, there was something more to him than the charming, enigmatic figure he portrayed. But Selene's words lingered, and I found myself questioning everything.

"What do you want, Kael?" I asked, my voice quieter than I intended.

He took a step closer, so close that I could feel the heat from his body, could smell the faint trace of his cologne—a scent that always reminded me of cedar and something darker, more intoxicating. "You've been distant," he said softly, "Ever since that night in the park. You're not like you used to be."

His words hit harder than I expected. I hadn't realized I had been distancing myself from him. I hadn't wanted to, not really, but every time he came too close, I felt like I was losing something of myself. Something important.

"I've been busy," I said, shrugging off the vulnerability I felt creeping up on me. "The café's been... demanding."

Kael studied me for a long moment, his gaze unyielding. "That's not the real reason, though, is it?"

I tried to look away, but I couldn't. There was something about him, some magnetic force that kept pulling me back to him. It wasn't just his looks, or the way he carried himself. It was deeper than that. Something about him felt familiar, like a shadow that had always been just behind me, a part of me that I couldn't quite shake off.

I opened my mouth to speak, but no words came out. Instead, I found myself reaching for the safe, easy thing—the lie. "I'm fine," I said, forcing a smile. "Really. Just trying to keep my head above water."

Kael didn't look convinced, but he didn't press further. Instead, he reached into his jacket pocket, pulling out a small silver key and tossing it on the counter between us. It was old, intricately carved, and looked far too ornate to belong to something as mundane as a lock.

"What's this?" I asked, picking it up.

"A key to something you'll need soon," he said cryptically, his eyes never leaving mine. "I think it's time you found out what's really going on. I'll leave you to figure it out. Just don't say I didn't warn you."

Before I could respond, he turned and walked out, leaving me standing there with the key in my hand and a thousand questions swirling in my mind. The silence in the café was deafening, and the weight of his words pressed down on me, heavier than I was ready for.

I stood there for a long time, the key cold in my fingers, wondering if I was already too deep into a game I didn't understand. And if I was, how far I was willing to go to find the truth.

The weight of the key in my hand was the only tangible thing in the world as I walked through the streets of Charleston the next evening. The humid southern air clung to my skin, but it did little to ease the chill that had settled deep within me. I wasn't sure what I was walking toward, or what I expected to find, but I couldn't shake the feeling that I had crossed a threshold—a point of no return.

Kael's cryptic warning had burrowed into my mind, but it wasn't just his words that troubled me. It was the fact that I had started to question everything, to wonder if there was a truth that no one, including me, was ready to face. The idea of betrayal, of being manipulated by those I trusted, sat in my gut like a stone. And the more I tried to push it away, the heavier it became.

I turned onto a side street, passing by the weathered brick buildings that had stood for centuries, the faded charm of Charleston's historic district a far cry from the storm brewing inside me. The world felt oddly muffled, as though the familiar sights and sounds were being filtered through a fog. My footsteps echoed too loudly in the quiet, the rhythmic tapping of my shoes on the pavement the only sound that accompanied me.

When I reached the old church on Church Street, the one with the peeling white paint and iron gates that always looked like they belonged in a forgotten graveyard, I stopped. The key seemed to vibrate in my hand, as if it recognized the place before I did. This was it—the answer, or at least a clue. Kael's cryptic message had led me here, but I couldn't shake the feeling that I was walking right into something I wasn't prepared for.

I stood there for a long moment, staring at the gates. They were tall and foreboding, the kind that made you feel as if you were trespassing even before you'd stepped foot inside. A rusted chain and lock secured them tightly, but I had no doubt that the key in my hand would open it. The only question was whether I was ready to step through.

A sharp breeze cut through the night, and I took a deep breath, steeling myself. With a quick, practiced motion, I unlocked the gate, the metallic click echoing in the quiet night. The gates creaked open slowly, as if protesting the intrusion, but I didn't hesitate. I stepped inside, the weight of the moment settling heavily on my shoulders.

The courtyard was overgrown with ivy, the stone path barely visible under a carpet of moss. It felt as though the world had forgotten this place, leaving it to decay in the shadow of time. The air was thick with the scent of damp earth and something else—something almost electric, like the promise of a storm. I walked deeper into the churchyard, the key still clutched tightly in my hand. My heart raced, but I couldn't tell if it was from excitement or fear. Maybe both.

I reached the door of the church itself, the old wooden panels cracked and weathered by years of neglect. There was no sign of life here, no hint that anyone had set foot inside in years. And yet, there was something about the building that felt... alive. As if it were waiting for me.

I placed the key into the lock, turning it with a slow, deliberate motion. The door creaked open, and I stepped inside.

The interior was shrouded in darkness, the faint outline of stained-glass windows barely visible in the dim light. The smell of dust and incense lingered in the air, the scent thick and heavy. The only sound was the soft thud of my footsteps on the worn floorboards as I made my way down the aisle.

Something was off. The silence felt too complete, too heavy. It was the kind of silence that made the hairs on the back of your neck stand on end. My heart thudded louder in my chest, but I pressed on, drawn deeper into the church as if something invisible was pulling me forward.

At the end of the aisle, the altar stood in stark contrast to the rest of the room—clean, polished, almost unnaturally pristine. And behind it, there was a door, hidden in the shadows. My instincts screamed at me to turn around, to leave before it was too late. But I couldn't. Not now.

I approached the door, the key still warm in my hand, as if urging me to unlock it. I hesitated, my mind racing with a thousand thoughts. What was behind this door? And why had Kael sent me here? Was I really ready to face whatever lay beyond?

The key slid smoothly into the lock, and with a click, the door opened.

Inside was a small room, the walls lined with shelves filled with old, dusty tomes. In the center, on a pedestal, sat a single object: a blackened, weathered box. It was small, no bigger than a shoebox, but there was something about it that felt... wrong. Like it was holding a secret too dangerous to be known.

I reached for it, my fingers trembling, but as soon as I touched the box, the air around me seemed to change. It was as though the room itself shifted, the shadows growing deeper, the temperature dropping by degrees. My breath hitched, and I pulled my hand back, but it was too late.

A voice echoed in the room—low, guttural, and unmistakable.
"You shouldn't have come, Evanna."
My blood ran cold. I knew that voice.
Kael.
But how? How was he here?

Chapter 8: Fractures in the Alliance

The coffee shop was empty but for the low hum of the espresso machine, its warm steam curling into the air, thick with the scent of roasted beans and unspoken words. I stood by the counter, fingers gripping the edge as though I could anchor myself to the worn wood and hold off the dizziness spinning in my head. The walls around me, painted a muted gray, felt suffocating. But it wasn't the shop's narrow confines that had me trapped. It was him. Kael. Standing just behind me, silent and unreadable, his presence like an insistent whisper that wouldn't let go, no matter how hard I tried to shut it out.

"I didn't think you'd still be here," I said, my voice sharp, too sharp. A reminder that I was still angry, still hurt, though something darker lurked underneath, tangled with that anger. He hadn't even had the decency to look ashamed. No, Kael was the type to stand tall, his jaw set, his eyes so dark they could swallow the very light that dared to touch them. The weight of his gaze made my stomach twist into a tight knot, though I told myself it was fury, not the flare of something more complicated. "You could've at least pretended it wasn't all for show."

I didn't look at him. I couldn't. Not right now. The truth he'd dropped into my lap—no, more like shoved down my throat—still felt like a bitter pill. The Ravenmark, that damned thing, had always been a mystery wrapped in the kind of danger you could smell from miles away. And now Kael had known all along what it was, how it connected us. How it was supposed to tether us to each other, even if neither of us wanted it.

"I was trying to protect you," Kael said, his voice low, deliberate, as though carefully testing each word before allowing it to escape.

I scoffed, the sound bitter as it left my throat. "Protect me? Is that what you call it? Lying to me for months? Keeping me in the dark like I'm some helpless child?" I could feel my pulse quicken, my chest tightening with the kind of rage that made my skin hot and prickly. "How is that protecting anyone, Kael?"

He shifted, his boots scuffing softly against the polished floor. I didn't need to turn around to know that his posture had changed, the air around him thickening, his restraint slowly starting to fray. "If I'd told you the truth, would you have believed me?" His question was almost casual, but there was an edge to it that made my stomach drop. "You're not exactly the trusting type, are you?"

The words stung more than they should have, and I hated myself for letting them. "Trust is earned," I said, my voice betraying a hint of vulnerability I didn't want him to hear. "You don't just get to walk in and demand it, Kael. You don't get to keep secrets and expect everything to stay the same."

His silence was deafening. I could feel the tension building, a magnetic force pulling at us, too tight, too raw. It wasn't just the Ravenmark between us now. No, it was something worse. Something that had been brewing for months—ever since that first spark of something neither of us had wanted but both had felt. "What is it you're trying to protect me from, Kael? Is it the truth? Or is it... us?" The question hung in the air like a challenge, daring him to answer.

His hands flexed at his sides, and I could almost hear the internal battle he was fighting. His gaze softened, just enough to make my breath catch in my throat, but I wouldn't let him win that easily. I wasn't some damsel waiting to be rescued. I was angry, and I was damn well going to stay that way, no matter how the weight of his stare pressed against me.

"I never wanted this to happen," he said, his voice softer now, though still threaded with tension. "But it's too late for that, isn't it?"

I finally turned to face him. His expression was a blend of guilt and determination, the lines of his jaw tight with frustration. "You're right," I said, voice barely above a whisper. "It's too late." The words were more for me than for him, a reminder that no matter how much I wanted to walk away, there was something inside me that wouldn't let me. Some thread, some invisible bond between us that refused to break, no matter how much I tugged at it.

I took a step back, away from the counter, away from him, but the space between us didn't feel like enough. It never would be. The tension thrummed in the air, heavy and expectant, like a storm waiting to break. And for a moment, I almost thought we were both caught in the same storm, unable to escape. But that wasn't it. It wasn't a storm at all. It was a trap, a snare woven too tightly around us, and the more I pulled away, the more it tightened.

"I don't know if I can keep doing this," I said, the words tasting like ashes on my tongue. "I don't know if I can trust you anymore." There. It was out. And for a moment, I almost felt lighter, as though the truth of my feelings—however jagged—had finally been set free.

His eyes darkened, a flicker of something I couldn't name passing through them, something that made my pulse stutter in my chest. "Then we'll figure it out together," he said, his voice quiet but resolute. "I'm not giving up on you."

I laughed, a sharp, bitter sound. "Well, aren't you noble," I muttered, but even I could hear the uncertainty in my tone. Because, despite everything, part of me still wanted to believe him.

I stood there for what felt like an eternity, the taste of that bitter laughter still lingering in the air between us, clinging to the dusty sunlight filtering through the blinds. The moment felt suspended in time, neither of us moving, neither of us willing to break the silence. Kael's eyes, dark as the night sky, flickered with something I couldn't quite place. Regret? Hope? Or was it just the stubborn determination I knew too well, the kind that had kept us both in this tangled mess for far too long?

"Do you want me to walk away?" His voice was quieter now, laced with an edge that sounded almost... desperate. It made my stomach churn, in the most infuriating way. Because, yes, part of me wanted to walk away. Wanted to rip the thread between us in half and burn the damn thing, leave it all behind. But the other part—the stupid, foolish part—wanted to stay and hear him out. Wanted to believe that this wasn't all some twisted game he'd been playing behind my back.

I didn't answer immediately. Instead, I let the question hang there, heavy and pointless. Because I knew what he was asking, but I wasn't sure I had the strength to answer. The idea of letting go, of walking away from all this, was terrifying in a way that made my bones ache. The Ravenmark, the damn thing that had drawn us together in the first place, was more than just a piece of cursed magic. It was a force, a pull, like a tether I couldn't cut. A tether that Kael and I both had in common, no matter how much we wanted to pretend it didn't exist.

And that made me angry. Because it wasn't supposed to be like this. None of this was how I imagined it, when I'd first started looking for answers. I'd thought I was in control, that I was the one holding the cards. But now, with Kael standing there, with his calm, infuriating silence, I felt like I was the one getting played.

"No," I said finally, turning to face him fully, crossing my arms over my chest in an attempt to shield myself. "I don't want you to walk away. But I don't know how much longer I can pretend everything's fine when it's not."

I saw his jaw clench. That subtle shift in his expression, that tightening of his lips, told me he understood. He knew exactly what I was saying, even if he didn't like it. And for a moment, I wondered if I was being too harsh, too quick to push him away. But no, the doubt was drowned out by the bitterness in my throat, by the raw ache of betrayal.

"You don't have to pretend for me, Charlotte," Kael said, his voice quieter now, but still holding a certain steadiness. He took a step forward, his boots making a soft thud against the worn hardwood floor. I didn't step back. I was too stubborn for that. "I never asked you to."

There was something there—something in the way he said it that made my heart twitch uncomfortably. A vulnerability that I hadn't seen before, hidden beneath all the layers of self-assurance he liked to wear like armor. Maybe that was why I couldn't stay angry for long. Kael had a way of disarming me, making me feel like I was the one being unreasonable. The problem was, I wasn't sure if that was something I should resent or something I should be grateful for.

"So what's your plan then?" I asked, the words coming out sharper than I intended. "You want me to forgive you? Just like that?"

Kael's eyes darkened at my tone, but there was no defensiveness in his reply. If anything, he seemed to be studying me, as if trying to decipher the puzzle I had become in his mind. "I don't want you to forgive me," he said, his voice unwavering. "I want you to understand why I did what I did. And I want us to move forward, together."

Together. The word hit me harder than I expected. We were standing in a small coffee shop in a corner of Seattle, the kind of place people came to forget the world outside, and yet, the world between Kael and me felt like it had just grown ten times bigger.

The Ravenmark, Selene, all of it. It was pulling us apart in ways I couldn't even begin to understand.

"You're asking a lot of me," I said, exhaling slowly as I leaned against the counter, my fingers still gripping the edge. I couldn't seem to shake the feeling that I was holding on to something more fragile than I could afford to lose.

"I'm asking for you to trust me again," he said, each word weighted with the kind of earnestness that made my pulse quicken. "I don't expect things to go back to normal overnight. Hell, I don't even know what normal is anymore. But I'm here. And I'm not going anywhere, Charlotte. Not unless you tell me to."

I wanted to laugh. The absurdity of it all. The way he thought everything could be fixed with a few words. But there was something in his eyes—something genuine—that made it hard to ignore. And it irritated me. The fact that, no matter how much I wanted to push him away, no matter how much I wanted to hate him for what he'd kept from me, I couldn't bring myself to do it.

"I don't know what you want from me," I said, the words feeling like they were being wrenched out of me. "You've already done the one thing I asked you not to do. How am I supposed to trust you after that?"

Kael reached for me then, just a slight movement, but it felt like a declaration. His hand, warm and steady, rested lightly on my shoulder. It was a simple gesture, but it sent a jolt through me, reminding me that no matter how much I tried to deny it, we were both tangled in this mess, and there was no way out without facing it head-on.

"I want you to trust me enough to see this through," he said quietly, almost as if he was speaking more to himself than to me. "Even if it scares you."

I stood there, staring at Kael, the words he'd said still buzzing in my head. "I'm not going anywhere, Charlotte. Not unless you tell me to." The air felt thick around us, charged with something electric that made it impossible to breathe, much less think clearly. His hand still rested lightly on my shoulder, a touch that was too intimate for this moment, but somehow exactly what I needed, even if I hated it.

I wanted to say something, anything, to cut through the tension. But the truth was, I couldn't find the words. What did you say to someone who had done the one thing you'd begged them not to do? The one thing that had shattered whatever fragile semblance of trust we'd managed to scrape together? I couldn't forgive him for keeping secrets about the Ravenmark, but the part of me that still cared—still wanted him, damn it—refused to let go.

Instead of answering, I stepped back, away from him, putting distance between us. It was a knee-jerk reaction, an instinct, but I felt the invisible thread between us tugging at my chest as I did it. His eyes followed me, those dark, unreadable eyes, and for a moment, I thought I saw a flicker of something—was it regret?—before it disappeared into the depths of his guarded expression.

"I didn't ask you to forgive me," Kael said, his voice quieter now, softer. "I just want you to understand that I never wanted to hurt you."

The words hung there in the silence, heavy and loaded. "And yet, you did," I said, unable to stop myself. "Every day that you kept this from me, you hurt me. You hurt us."

His jaw tightened, but he didn't argue. Instead, he dropped his hand from my shoulder, letting the space between us grow, the air thickening as I tried to gather my thoughts.

"I don't know how we move forward from here, Kael," I said, shaking my head. "I can't just pretend it didn't happen."

His eyes softened, just a fraction, and in that moment, I realized that he wasn't trying to excuse his actions. He was waiting.

Waiting for me to make the next move, to decide if this—whatever this was between us—was worth salvaging. But how could I? How could I trust someone who had been keeping secrets about something that could very well kill us both?

"I know it's a lot to ask," he said, stepping closer again, slowly, cautiously, as if he were approaching a skittish animal. "But I'm asking for a chance to prove that I can make this right. Not just for you, but for us."

The words wrapped around me like a warm blanket, and for a moment, I almost let myself believe him. I could feel the weight of the Ravenmark between us, a constant, pressing reminder of the bond we shared, and the danger that bond could bring. And even though I resented it, even though I hated it, I couldn't deny that part of me still wanted him. Still needed him.

"I don't know if I can," I said, my voice barely above a whisper. "I don't know if I can trust you again."

Kael didn't respond immediately. Instead, he took another step closer, closing the gap between us, his presence a force I couldn't escape. He reached up, his fingers brushing against my cheek, sending a shiver down my spine.

"I'm not asking you to trust me right away," he said, his voice low, almost tender. "I just need you to take a chance. For both of us."

I wanted to pull away, wanted to tell him that it wasn't that simple, that trust wasn't something you could just rebuild with a few sweet words and a touch here and there. But I couldn't. I couldn't because something in his eyes, something deep and unspoken, made me believe him. And that terrified me more than anything Selene could ever throw at us.

Before I could say anything else, the door to the coffee shop swung open with a sharp crack, the sudden gust of cold air stealing all the warmth from the room. A figure stepped inside, silhouetted against the bright light of the street. I couldn't see their face, but I could feel their presence like a cold shadow creeping into the room. The tension in the air thickened, and I instinctively took a step back, my heart racing.

The figure moved forward, and as they did, I caught the faintest glint of metal at their side. A knife, glinting in the dim light.

"Kael," I whispered, my voice shaking. "What the hell is going on?"

Kael's eyes darted to the door, his posture shifting, alert. The smile that had been on his lips disappeared, replaced by something colder, something that sent a chill racing up my spine.

"Stay back," he muttered, his voice tight with warning. "This isn't over."

The figure didn't speak, but they didn't need to. The way they moved, the way they held themselves—it was all too familiar. I had seen this before. In the alleyways of Seattle, in the shadows of my past, I had seen people like this. People who didn't leave until they had what they came for. People who had no qualms about spilling blood.

Kael's hand went to his side, and I saw the flash of a weapon beneath his jacket. The Ravenmark pulsed in my chest, the magic thrumming in the air, and I realized in that moment that the battle we were fighting wasn't just against the past. It was against something far darker and it was about to catch up with us.

The figure moved closer, their eyes locking onto mine, and in that instant, I knew. We weren't alone anymore. The war Kael had been trying to protect me from was already here, and the only way out was through the storm that had just begun.

"Kael," I said, my voice barely a whisper, "what are we dealing with?"

But before he could answer, the door slammed shut behind the figure, and everything went black.

Chapter 9: The Festival of Embers

The streets of New Orleans had always thrummed with life, but tonight, they hummed with something more—a wild, electric buzz that wrapped around the entire city like a fever dream. The Festival of Embers was here, and the streets blazed under a thousand lanterns, their flickering flames casting erratic shadows that made the city feel alive, like it had a heartbeat all its own. The scent of sizzling shrimp po'boys and crawfish etouffee hung thick in the air, mixing with the tangy sweetness of sugar-dusted beignets from the French Market. The intoxicating blend of food, music, and the occasional whiff of smoke from the bonfires scattered along the riverfront did nothing to soothe the restlessness in my chest.

Still, for a brief moment, I let myself believe—let myself pretend—that I wasn't standing on the precipice of something darker. The prophecy—whatever it was—had already sunk its claws deep into me, but tonight, I wasn't going to let it ruin everything. The festival was a celebration of fire, of life, of light pushing back the dark. If there was ever a night to lose myself in the warmth of a crowd, this was it.

I should've known better. The second Kael appeared beside me, his black leather jacket catching the light from the lanterns, I knew I was in trouble. The man was trouble wrapped in a mystery I didn't quite understand. His dark eyes scanned the crowd, sharp and focused, but when they landed on me, something flickered—just a momentary, dangerous spark that made my stomach twist.

"You look like you're thinking too hard," he said, his voice low, teasing, and oddly comforting amidst the chaos.

I rolled my eyes, trying to hide the warmth crawling up my neck. "It's the festival. You're supposed to let go, not think."

He smiled—half amused, half knowing—and before I could say anything else, he was pulling me into the dance.

At first, it was nothing more than the sway of the crowd, the pulse of the music tugging us both in time. But then Kael's hand settled on my waist, his fingers warm and firm, and the rhythm of the world seemed to still. It was as if everything else had blurred out of focus, leaving only the two of us, locked in this slow, mesmerizing dance beneath the fire-lit sky.

The sound of trumpets and saxophones wrapped around us, but I could hear nothing but the beat of my own heart, the thrum of it running faster each time he shifted closer. The strange chemistry between us was undeniable, like a spark teetering on the edge of combustion. Kael didn't speak, but I could feel the weight of the unspoken words between us—words I wasn't sure I was ready to hear. He was like the firelight, dangerous and beautiful, and I could feel myself drawn into it, despite the warnings I kept whispering to myself.

"Let's not make this complicated," I said, forcing the words out even though I could feel the heat of his breath against my skin.

He smirked. "I don't do complicated."

I almost laughed—almost. Instead, I leaned in a little closer, letting myself get lost in the rhythm of the music, the flicker of lanterns dancing around us, and for just a moment, I forgot about everything else. The night was ours.

But then the ground beneath us seemed to shift.

The sound of footsteps, harsh and jarring against the music, sliced through the night. People around us started scattering, their laughter turning to frightened murmurs. My heart skipped. The pulse of the city had faltered, and something heavy, something wrong, pressed down on the air like a storm cloud ready to break. Kael's hand tightened around mine, his eyes darkened, a quick flash of something unreadable passing over his face.

Without a word, he pulled me into a nearby alley, the shadows swallowing us whole. The sounds of the festival seemed distant now, muffled as though the world had closed itself off from us.

"Kael?" I asked, my voice steady despite the fear gnawing at my insides.

"It's happening," he said, his tone clipped, low, almost urgent. His grip on my arm was firm, guiding me through the darkness. "Stay close."

Before I could ask what he meant, I heard it—a distant, bone-chilling screech that seemed to come from nowhere and everywhere at once. It wasn't the kind of sound that belonged in a celebration. It was the sound of something ancient, something not quite human. My breath caught in my throat.

"They've come for us," Kael murmured. His eyes flicked to the end of the alley, where figures emerged from the shadows like specters.

I froze. The minions of Selene.

They were here.

The firelight from the festival illuminated their forms, but it did nothing to ease the terror twisting in my gut. Their faces were a patchwork of human and something far darker, far older. Their eyes burned with an unnatural light, predatory and sharp. I could feel the weight of their gaze, each one of them narrowing in on me like a hunter locking onto its prey.

Kael moved before I could say anything else, his body shifting into a stance that was all too familiar, like he'd been preparing for this moment all along. He stood between me and the oncoming threat, his expression hardening.

"You need to run," he said, his voice rough, as though he were gritting his teeth to keep his own panic in check.

"No," I snapped, reaching for the energy inside of me, trying to tap into something—anything—that could help. "I'm not leaving you."

"You don't have a choice," he said, his voice strained as he pushed me backward. "I won't let them take you."

And just like that, everything I thought I knew about the world, about Kael, about myself, shattered into pieces, leaving only the raw, terrifying truth of the moment.

The city's pulse wasn't just thumping beneath my feet—it was a countdown to something far worse than I had ever imagined.

The shadows closed in on us like a thick fog, and the air grew heavier with every passing second. The city's music, once so vibrant and carefree, now felt like a distant echo, muffled by the rising tension that wrapped itself around my chest like a vice. Kael's presence beside me was the only solid thing in the chaos that was rapidly unfurling before us. He stood with his back straight, shoulders squared, eyes narrowed in that familiar, unreadable way that told me nothing, but everything, about what he was preparing to do.

"Kael," I said again, quieter this time, my voice betraying the uncertainty that was creeping into me like the cool night air. "What do we do?"

His gaze flicked over his shoulder, sharp as a blade. "We survive."

Survive. That was the plan? My heart raced, but there was no time to question it. No time to argue. The minions of Selene were closing in, their twisted forms slinking through the alleyway like predators stalking their prey. I could feel their eyes on me, the weight of them burning through the dark. The air around us thickened, the once-familiar sounds of the festival now completely silenced by the heavy presence of the unknown.

I was acutely aware of the fact that, until this moment, I'd never really been afraid. Sure, I'd felt the tremors of unease, the creeping sense of danger, but it had always been an abstract thing—like a shadow at the edge of my vision that could never quite be grasped. But now, standing in the alley, surrounded by creatures who weren't quite human, I understood the true meaning of fear.

A low growl rumbled from one of the figures as it stepped forward, its elongated limbs dragging across the ground with a sickening scrape. A flash of pale skin, translucent and stretched thin over a skeletal frame, caught the dim light of the lanterns. The creature's face was a grotesque blend of sharp angles and hollow cheeks, its lips curled into a silent snarl, revealing jagged, needle-like teeth that gleamed unnaturally in the dark.

I shuddered. "Kael..."

"Stay behind me," he ordered, his voice calm, almost detached, but there was something in his eyes that I hadn't seen before. Fear? No. Something worse. A kind of resignation.

I nodded, although it felt like my limbs had turned to stone, and there was no going back. The weight of everything—the prophecy, the darkness that loomed over us—pressed down harder, pushing all the air from my lungs. I had no choice but to move with him, to trust him, as he led me deeper into the alley, further away from the horror inching toward us.

For all the danger in the air, there was an almost sickening stillness that clung to the moment, like the world was holding its breath, waiting for something to give. And then, it did. A sharp crack sliced through the silence, followed by the sound of rapid footsteps. One of Selene's minions lunged, its body moving faster than anything human should be capable of.

Kael didn't flinch. He was already moving, pulling something from his coat—a thin, glimmering dagger that caught the light like a flash of lightning. Before the creature could even land, Kael's blade was buried deep in its chest. The thing let out a strangled screech, its mouth opening wide, as if trying to let out a scream that was stuck in its throat. But it didn't get the chance. With a swift motion, Kael twisted the blade, and the creature crumpled to the ground, its body going still, its eyes glassy and lifeless.

I stood frozen, my hands pressed tightly against my chest as I watched the scene unfold before me. The realization hit hard and fast: this wasn't just some skirmish. This was a war, one I hadn't been prepared for, one I had barely even known existed.

But then I remembered Kael. The way he moved, so fluid and confident, like he'd done this a thousand times before.

I swallowed hard. "How many more?"

He didn't answer. His gaze flicked to the shadows again, narrowing as more figures emerged, their glowing eyes locking onto us with predatory intent. They were coming from every direction now, like a flood—too many to count, too many to fight off alone.

"We need to get to the docks," Kael said, his voice a quiet command, as though he'd already made the decision for both of us. "Now."

I didn't need to be told twice. My heart pounded in my ears as Kael grabbed my arm, pulling me along behind him with a force that was just shy of desperate. The city's lights, once so warm and welcoming, felt cold now, the glow of the lanterns offering little comfort against the rising storm. As we sprinted through the alleyways, the sounds of the festival, the music, the laughter, were swallowed whole by the sound of our footsteps and the ominous hiss of the creatures stalking us.

I tried to keep up, but the weight of the prophecy—the weight of everything—felt like it was dragging me down, pulling at my feet like gravity had doubled its force. Kael, however, moved with the ease of someone who had run this race before. He didn't break a sweat.

My breath hitched as we turned a corner, the docks coming into view just ahead. The river stretched out before us, vast and dark, with nothing but the distant glint of the Crescent City Connection Bridge looming in the distance. We were close.

But just as hope started to swell in my chest, a figure stepped into the alley before us.

Selene herself.

She was taller than I had imagined, cloaked in shadows and regal in a way that made everything around her seem to fade into the background. Her eyes, cold and calculating, locked onto mine, and the chill that ran through me wasn't just from fear—it was from something ancient, something that made the very air seem to freeze.

"I've been waiting for this moment," she said, her voice smooth, like honey but laced with something venomous.

And then, as if the night hadn't already reached its breaking point, everything changed.

The air around us seemed to crackle with electricity as Selene's presence filled the alleyway, her silhouette stretching impossibly tall in the dim glow of the lanterns. The city, which had been so alive just moments ago, now felt eerily silent. Even the distant hum of the river, usually steady and calming, had taken on a weight of foreboding, as if it too could feel the shift in the air. I couldn't breathe—couldn't seem to think—because the woman before us wasn't just a threat, she was an embodiment of the very darkness I'd been trying to outrun.

Selene stepped closer, the shadows following her like a cloak. Her eyes, pale and cold as winter ice, met mine, and in them was a vast emptiness that made my blood run cold. There was no warmth, no hint of humanity left in her gaze. It was a look that could strip away everything you thought you knew about the world.

"You're a stubborn one," she said, her voice melodic but edged with an unholy precision, like a blade poised to strike. "It's no matter, though. You'll learn soon enough. You're not as untouchable as you think."

I wanted to say something, anything, but the words caught in my throat. My heart raced with the frantic thudding of a panic I couldn't shake, and yet, somehow, I stood my ground. Kael, beside me, was tense, his eyes flickering between me and the woman who had finally come to collect her prize.

"You're not taking her," Kael growled, his voice low and dangerous, the words barely more than a breath, yet they carried the weight of something ancient and deep.

Selene's lips curved upward in a slow, predatory smile. "You don't get to decide that, Kael."

Her name on his lips, like that, twisted something inside of me. The tension between them—sharp as glass—was unmistakable, and I realized, too late, that I had walked into a trap far more complex than I'd understood. This wasn't just about me. This wasn't just about some vague prophecy I had never fully understood. No, this was personal.

The breeze that rustled through the trees suddenly felt colder, as if it carried with it something darker than just the night's coolness. The shadows around Selene began to stir, coiling like smoke around her feet, moving with a will of their own. They twitched and curled, creeping toward us like serpents, and my breath hitched in my throat. The night had turned against us, and I could feel the grip of fear tightening around my chest.

"Why don't we make this easier?" Selene purred, raising a hand as if commanding the very elements. The shadows at her feet thickened, taking form, and with a terrible, unholy shriek, the minions that had followed her sprang forward, their grotesque, misshapen bodies moving with lightning speed. My pulse pounded in my ears as Kael immediately moved in front of me, drawing his blade with a fluidity that belied the urgency of the moment.

I had never been in a battle before—not one like this, anyway. I had never seen creatures like these, creatures that seemed to exist on the cusp of nightmare, their grotesque forms contorting with unnatural, jerky movements. But their eyes—they were human. And that was what made them terrifying. What made them real.

Kael's blade met the first of them with a sickening crack. The creature howled, its sharp, clawed hands swiping toward him, but he was faster. I didn't want to watch, but I couldn't look away as he dispatched the thing with a cold efficiency that left me breathless. Another creature came at him from the side, but Kael was already there, his movements so quick, so precise, it was as if he were part of the very night itself.

But it was not enough.

I barely had time to register what was happening before one of the creatures broke through Kael's defense, lunging for me with a speed that had me stumbling backward, a scream bubbling in my throat.

"NO!" Kael's voice shattered the moment, his hand shooting out to grab my arm, pulling me backward just in time as the creature's claws raked across the air where I had been standing. My heart thudded in my chest as I stumbled, gasping for air, the world spinning around me.

"We need to get out of here," Kael snapped, his eyes wild with a desperation that I had never seen in him before. But how? How could we run with Selene so close, with her army of shadow creatures closing in like a tide?

I turned to him, wide-eyed, "I can't—Kael, we can't fight them all."

"We're not fighting them all. We're running," he said, voice laced with urgency. "To the docks. It's our only chance."

Before I could reply, Selene's laughter rang out, high and hollow, echoing through the alley like a death knell. "You think you can escape me, Kael?" she sneered, her words cutting through the chaos. "You are nothing but a boy playing in the dark. The shadows know you. And they will always be one step ahead."

I glanced at Kael, his jaw clenched tight, his eyes full of something—defeat? No, it was more than that. There was something raw in him, something that told me he'd fought this battle before. He knew what it meant to lose.

But he wasn't going to lose me.

The shadow creatures were closing in again, their eerie wails filling the air as they advanced. I could feel their eyes on me, like they were drawn to me with an intensity that felt like a pull at my very soul. And then, there was Selene, her eyes glinting with malice, her smile full of dark promise.

"Run," Kael said again, his grip on my hand tightening. "Now."

I barely had time to nod before we were running, my heart in my throat, the sound of our footsteps drowned out by the distant growls and shrieks of the minions.

But as we neared the docks, something changed. The air became heavier, thick with magic, like the world itself was bending under the weight of Selene's power.

And then, from the shadows ahead, a figure stepped into the light.

"Not so fast."

I froze.

Chapter 10: The Betrayal

I had never been the type to eavesdrop, but that night, something gnawed at me. Maybe it was the way Kael's phone had vibrated incessantly while we sat in silence, the screen lighting up with notifications he quickly swiped away, a bit too quickly for comfort. Maybe it was the way he kept glancing over his shoulder, as though the walls themselves might betray us. Whatever it was, it set my pulse racing, a gnawing suspicion gnawing at the edges of my mind.

It had started as an ordinary evening. We were curled up in his tiny apartment, the windows cracked open to let in the soft hum of the city below, the clink of ice in our glasses the only sound besides the low murmur of his voice. He had ordered in from that little taco place across the street, the one that sold avocado fries with a side of sarcasm. We had laughed about the ridiculousness of it—avocado fries, of all things. And for a moment, everything felt normal.

But that sense of normalcy slipped away as soon as the doorbell rang.

I knew it wasn't his usual delivery guy. That man always gave us a thumbs up and muttered some variation of "you guys are the best." This one was different, his knock almost too loud, too urgent. When I opened the door, I found a man in a nondescript black hoodie standing there, his hands tucked into his pockets, his face hidden beneath the hood's shadow.

"Is Kael home?" he asked, his voice flat and impersonal.

I stepped back, feeling a slight chill creep up my spine. "Kael?" I called over my shoulder.

He appeared a moment later, moving past me without a word. He gave the man a curt nod, but there was something in the way his jaw clenched that made the hairs on my neck stand on end.

"What's going on?" I asked, trying to read the room, to figure out what this was. But Kael didn't look at me, his eyes fixed on the man in the hoodie as they exchanged something between them—something unspoken.

And then the man left, just as silently as he had arrived, leaving the door ajar behind him. Kael didn't move. He stood there, watching the street, his back to me. I could hear the sharp rhythm of his breath, his body tense with something I couldn't name.

"I need to go out," he said finally, his voice low, but the words scraped against me, as if the sharpness of them cut through the tension in the room.

"Now?" I asked, trying to keep my tone light, as though this were just a casual request, an ordinary part of our evening. But my hands betrayed me, shaking ever so slightly, a reflection of the unease settling in my chest.

His eyes flicked to me, a flicker of hesitation crossing his face before he masked it. "It won't be long."

But something in his tone, the subtle shift of his gaze, told me otherwise. I knew better than to press him for answers. That had never worked. But I couldn't just let him leave, not when the city felt suddenly too quiet, as if it were holding its breath.

"Kael—"

"I'll be fine," he cut in, brushing past me with such finality I couldn't help but feel the door slam between us, metaphorically. The soft click of the door behind him felt like a betrayal, even though it was nothing more than the natural sound of him stepping into the night.

I don't know what made me do it—maybe it was my own restless curiosity, or perhaps I was already picking up on the undercurrents of danger that had begun to surge between us. But I found myself at the window, watching as Kael walked down the street. He wasn't alone.

Another man appeared from the shadows, and I felt a chill settle deep in my bones. I didn't recognize him, but the way Kael greeted him, with the kind of familiarity that only comes from shared secrets, made my stomach turn. And then they talked. Briefly, urgently. Whatever they were discussing, it wasn't casual. It was serious. It was the kind of conversation that pulled people to the edge of something dangerous, something risky.

I couldn't see their faces clearly, but the way Kael's body language shifted when the man leaned in close—too close for comfort—made me feel like I was intruding on something private. Something that wasn't meant for me.

I told myself I was imagining things, that it was none of my business, but my instincts weren't so easily silenced. I needed to know what they were talking about. I needed to understand why Kael had become a man I couldn't trust.

Without thinking, I grabbed my jacket and stepped into the cool night. The streets of the city stretched before me, familiar yet foreign in the dim light. I knew I was taking a risk—Kael would never forgive me if he found out. But at that moment, there was no room for hesitation. Something was wrong, and I had to figure out what it was.

I followed them, my heart pounding in my chest. They moved through the darkened streets with a purpose, turning into an alleyway that smelled of stale beer and the remnants of street food. My feet were silent on the cracked pavement, my eyes fixed on their silhouettes as they came to a stop in front of an old warehouse.

I knew this place. Everyone knew it. It was one of those spots you passed by in the daylight without a second thought but avoided at night. It was the kind of place that carried whispers on the wind—whispers of things better left unsaid.

My breath caught in my throat as Kael and the man disappeared inside. The door creaked open, closing behind them with an almost imperceptible sound.

I should have turned back then. I should have walked away. But I didn't. My legs carried me forward, and as I reached for the handle, I felt something cold and hard brush against the back of my neck.

"Not so fast."

The voice behind me was low, far too familiar for comfort, and yet I didn't need to turn around to know who it was. The warning in his tone was unmistakable, a crackling edge that sent an involuntary shiver down my spine.

"Kael," I said, the name leaving my lips like a confession. I didn't dare to look up at him, not yet. There was too much I needed to process, too much anger tangled up in the pit of my stomach. My fingers tightened around the handle of the door, the cold metal biting into my palms as I steadied myself.

"Don't," he said, stepping closer. His breath, sharp with tension, was warm against my neck as he leaned in. The space between us seemed impossibly small now, his presence suffocating, pressing against every breath I tried to take. "You don't know what you're walking into."

I bristled, a rush of indignation and hurt flooding my chest. I couldn't decide if I was angry at him or at myself for having let him slip so far under my skin. For letting my guard down at all.

"I know exactly what I'm walking into," I snapped, my voice shaking, though I couldn't decide if it was with fear or fury. "I'm walking into the truth. And for once, Kael, I want to hear it from you. Not some half-truths or lies disguised as protection. I want the truth."

He didn't move. I could almost feel the weight of his gaze on the back of my neck, but I refused to meet it. Instead, I stared at the door in front of me, as though the chipped wood could offer the answers I so desperately needed.

"You think it's that simple?" he asked, his voice tight, his words unraveling slowly like he was trying to find the right way to explain something too messy to be untangled. "It's not. It's never been simple."

I felt my pulse quicken, the frustration bubbling up into something darker. "So what, I'm just supposed to keep trusting you? Watching you disappear into the night every time someone calls you?" I spun around to face him, my words coming out in a rush now. "You're meeting with people who are connected to her. Selene. Tell me I'm wrong."

His eyes flickered briefly, a flash of something—regret, guilt, anger? I couldn't tell. But I saw it, and that was enough.

"You don't get it," he said, his voice barely above a whisper, and there was something raw in the way he said it, like he wasn't just trying to explain himself to me but to some part of himself, too. "If I told you everything, you wouldn't understand. You'd run. You'd want nothing to do with me."

His words hung in the air between us, thick with a truth I wasn't sure I was ready to face. But it didn't matter. I was already too deep. I had already seen enough. I couldn't just walk away now, not when everything was beginning to shatter in front of me.

"I already don't understand, Kael," I said, my voice barely above a whisper now, the hurt leaking through. "But I need you to trust me, too. I need you to stop treating me like I'm some fragile thing you can protect by keeping me in the dark."

There was a long silence, a stretch of air where the world seemed to pause, waiting. Finally, he took a step toward me, his boots scraping softly against the concrete. I could smell the faint trace of cologne mixed with something darker, something more dangerous. "It's not about protecting you," he said, his voice hushed. "It's about keeping you safe. You don't understand what's at stake here. You don't understand what I'm involved in."

"Then make me understand!" I cried, taking a step back, my hands shaking. "Make me understand why I should believe in anything you say when you've already shown me who you really are!"

The words came out harsher than I intended, but they were true. This wasn't the Kael I thought I knew. The man who had promised to stand by me, to fight by my side, was nowhere to be found. Instead, I was staring at someone I barely recognized, someone whose secrets seemed to stretch across shadows I was too afraid to venture into.

He opened his mouth, as though to say something—anything—but before he could, a voice rang out behind him, cutting through the tension like a knife.

"Kael, we need to go."

The voice was sharp, authoritative, unmistakably cold. It belonged to the man who had been with him earlier. The one who had disappeared with him into that warehouse. I felt my stomach twist as the realization sank in. It wasn't just a casual meeting. It wasn't just a business deal or an accidental brush with danger. No, this was something planned, something that went far deeper than I had ever imagined.

Kael's jaw tightened, his entire posture stiffening as he turned toward the man. "I'll be there in a minute," he said, his tone so calm, so measured, it made my skin crawl. "Give me a moment."

But the man didn't budge, his gaze flickering between me and Kael, something unreadable in his eyes. "We don't have time, Kael," he said, his voice clipped, almost impatient. "Selene is expecting you."

Selene. The name struck me like a slap to the face. It was the one name I had never wanted to hear. Not like this. Not now.

And in that moment, I realized just how far I had fallen into this world of shadows, of lies and betrayals, without even knowing how to climb out.

Kael didn't look at me as he nodded curtly and started toward the man, his back to me now.

But I couldn't let him go. Not like this. Not with the silence between us so loud it might as well have been a scream.

"Kael," I called out, my voice shaking despite my best efforts to control it. He froze, his shoulders stiffening. "Don't—don't you dare walk away from me again."

For a long moment, he didn't move, and I thought maybe, just maybe, he would turn back. Maybe he would come to his senses. But then, as if the decision had already been made, he turned his back to me and walked into the night, leaving me with nothing but the echo of his footsteps and the crushing weight of a betrayal I was still too terrified to fully understand.

The night stretched on, thick with the weight of unspoken things, each minute heavier than the last. I stood there, on the fringes of the streetlight's glow, my mind unraveling with the understanding that I had been nothing but a fool. I had let my emotions tie me to Kael, a man whose truths I had never truly known, whose loyalty seemed as fluid as the shadows stretching around us. As I watched him disappear into the darkness with that stranger, I realized I hadn't just lost my trust in him—I'd lost myself. The city felt suddenly vast, endless, like a maze I had been trying to navigate, only to find out I had been walking in circles the whole time.

I didn't know how long I stood there, paralyzed by the overwhelming confusion swirling in my head. It wasn't until the biting wind cut through the thin fabric of my jacket that I snapped back to reality, the chill finally pushing me into motion. I couldn't just stand here. I couldn't just let this be how it ended.

"Stupid," I muttered under my breath, my voice raw, as I turned back toward the apartment. But the walk felt different now. The familiar streets of our neighborhood—the hum of life spilling out from the 24-hour coffee shop, the neon sign from the all-night taco truck buzzing in the distance—were no longer comforting. Instead, they were suffocating.

As I reached the building's entrance, I nearly collided with a man coming out, his large frame blocking the way. I looked up, and for a second, my brain took its sweet time processing the man standing in front of me. He wasn't familiar—his face was all sharp angles and cold indifference, like someone who had spent too many years in the city's underbelly.

"Excuse me," I muttered, stepping around him to go inside, but he stopped me with a hand on my arm, far too firm, far too calculated.

"You're not supposed to be here," he said, his voice low and smooth, like he had been rehearsing the line for hours.

I blinked at him, disoriented. "What?"

He didn't repeat himself, just leaned closer, his breath laced with something sharp. "Kael's not someone you want to mess with. Trust me on that."

For a split second, all I could think about was how easy it would be to slap his hand away and tell him where he could stick his unsolicited advice. But something about the way he said it, with such casual certainty, sent a wave of cold dread rolling down my spine.

"Why?" The word left my lips before I could stop it, my voice breaking through the icy walls I had been trying to build. "What do you know about him?"

He didn't answer immediately, just watched me like I was a puzzle he was trying to figure out. Then, with a sharp exhale, he pulled his hand away and shrugged, like he had just made some decision to throw a grenade in my direction. "You'll find out soon enough. But just know, when you do, it won't be pretty."

I stood there, staring at the space he'd left behind as he disappeared down the hallway. The words he left hanging in the air felt like a warning I couldn't ignore, even if I wanted to. The weight of them crushed down on me like a physical force, each syllable a leaden weight dragging me into an even darker place than I had been before.

I forced myself to move, my legs feeling too heavy to lift, but I couldn't stop. Couldn't go back. The world outside had already shifted, already warped, and there was no unseeing what I had just witnessed.

I reached Kael's door, my hand trembling as I slid the key into the lock. The door clicked open, and the silence inside hit me like a tidal wave. His scent lingered in the air, a mixture of musk and the faintest trace of whatever cologne he wore, but that comfort was gone now. The apartment, once a sanctuary, now felt like a crime scene.

I didn't know what I was looking for, but I knew I had to find something. Anything. Something that could explain why Kael had kept so many secrets from me, why his eyes had looked at me with something close to guilt before he walked away.

I moved through the apartment with a quiet urgency, my eyes scanning the room with an intensity I didn't know I had in me. The kitchen was as clean as always—he was obsessively neat, a trait that felt both reassuring and suffocating now. No clues there. I moved toward the small desk in the corner, a place Kael kept organized with precision. Papers, some receipts, a couple of old bills, nothing that seemed out of the ordinary. But then, underneath a stack of notebooks, I saw it: a small black envelope.

It was unmarked. No return address. Just a symbol etched on the front, a symbol I recognized too well.

The same symbol I had seen in the warehouse.

I didn't have to open it to know what it meant. I could feel the blood drain from my face as I stared at it. Selene. It was her mark, unmistakable, the one she had branded her followers with.

A sense of dread coiled in my stomach, gnawing at the edges of my thoughts. I had been right all along—Kael had been hiding things, dangerous things, things that had pulled him deeper into a world I didn't want to be a part of. But it wasn't just him anymore. It was me. I was already in it. And if I didn't move now, if I didn't find a way to untangle myself, I would be swallowed whole by whatever this was.

I turned to leave, the envelope clutched tightly in my hand. But before I could take a single step, the front door slammed open, and I froze.

"Looking for something?"

The voice was low, smooth, too familiar for comfort. I didn't need to look up to know who it was.

Kael.

And behind him, standing in the doorway, was the last person I expected to see.

Selene herself.

Chapter 11: Secrets Beneath the Citadel

The air in the hidden chamber beneath the citadel was thick, a strange heaviness that made my chest feel tight, as though the very walls themselves were holding their breath, waiting for something. The faint light of flickering candles cast long shadows over the rows of ancient books, their leather bindings cracked and faded with age. Every corner seemed to hold a secret, every dust mote suspended in the air a whisper from a time long past. I could almost hear the faint murmurs of the forgotten souls who had once tread these very stones, their voices entangled with the magic that still hummed in the corners of the room.

My fingers brushed against the edge of a nearby bookcase, the wood smooth but cool beneath my skin. The scent of aged paper and ink filled my nostrils, grounding me in the present, reminding me of the path I had chosen, one that was tangled in uncertainty and the undeniable weight of destiny. I glanced over at Kael, his tall frame standing in the doorway, his eyes shadowed in the dim light. His presence was both a balm and a burden. The kind of comfort you sought when the world was too much, but also a reminder of the responsibility I carried—of the truths I had yet to face.

"I told you to stay back," I muttered, though my voice was softer than I intended. He didn't move, just leaned against the doorframe with that quiet intensity of his, the one that made it impossible for me to pretend I didn't know he was there.

Kael wasn't the kind of man who could be ignored. Not when his gaze had the unnerving habit of finding its way beneath your skin, unraveling the parts of you that you'd prefer to keep hidden. I had never let him close enough to see the real me, the one that trembled at the thought of making the wrong choice, the one that feared the consequences of uncovering too much. But here, in this chamber, surrounded by forgotten knowledge, there was no room for secrets. Not anymore.

"Whatever you're planning, don't shut me out," Kael said, his voice low, like a promise—or perhaps a warning. It didn't matter. I wasn't sure I could trust him, not yet, not with this. The Ravenmark—an ancient and dangerous magic—was something I had never wanted to get involved in. But now, standing in front of a collection of cursed books and artifacts, I realized that my involvement was no longer a matter of choice. It was fate. The same fate that had led me here, to this very moment, where everything could change.

The Ravenmark wasn't just a name or a legend. It was a burden, a devastating gift passed down through generations, and I had just uncovered its true purpose. The choice it demanded was one I couldn't ignore. It wasn't just about power—it was about sacrifice. And when the time came, there would be no going back.

I exhaled slowly, feeling the weight of my discovery settle in my chest, tight and suffocating. Kael pushed off the doorframe and took a step toward me, his boots clicking softly against the stone floor. He was still too far to reach, but the space between us felt smaller now, somehow. I wanted to step back, to distance myself from the force of his presence, but I stood still, rooted to the ground as if the very chamber had claimed me.

"Talk to me, Elys," he said, and there was something in his voice—a note of quiet desperation, the kind of desperation that only came when someone had something to lose. And maybe, for the first time, I understood that Kael wasn't just chasing shadows. He was chasing me. And maybe, just maybe, I wanted him to.

But the truth... the truth was something I wasn't ready to share. Not with him. Not with anyone.

"There are things here, things I'm not sure I understand yet," I replied, my voice sharper than I intended, the words tumbling out in a rush. "Things that could change everything. And I don't think you should be a part of it, Kael." My fingers curled around the edge of an ancient tome, its pages delicate and brittle, as though it might disintegrate the moment I dared to open it.

Kael's gaze flickered to the book in my hand, then back to me. He was silent for a moment, studying me as if I were a puzzle he hadn't quite figured out. "You don't get to decide that alone," he said, his tone surprisingly gentle.

I clenched my jaw, willing myself not to react. "You don't understand," I whispered, my voice faltering in spite of myself. "You have no idea what's at stake."

"No," he said, his gaze unwavering, "but I know you."

The room seemed to contract, the air thick with unsaid things, with unspoken fears and desires that neither of us wanted to acknowledge. I could feel him edging closer, not physically, but emotionally, and it made my heart race, that stupid traitorous thing that had no place in this madness.

I had thought I could keep him at arm's length, protect him from the mess I was about to make of everything. But as I glanced up at him, I realized it wasn't that simple. He wasn't going to let me. Not now, not when I needed him most.

"Maybe," I said slowly, my voice quieter now, "you should stay out of this, Kael. You deserve better than whatever this is going to become."

His lips quirked into a faint smile, the kind that made my stomach twist in ways I didn't want to acknowledge. "And yet, here I am. Because you don't get to push me away."

The truth hung between us, suspended in the space of a heartbeat. I wasn't sure if it was the Ravenmark that had brought us together or something else entirely. But what I did know was that no matter how hard I tried to push him away, Kael wasn't going anywhere. Not this time.

And that scared me more than anything.

I tried to ignore the way Kael's presence seemed to fill the room, the air buzzing with an energy that both comforted and unsettled me in equal measure. He was too close, too solid, standing just a few feet away with those dark eyes trained on me, watching me like I was the only thing that mattered in this dusty, forgotten corner of the world.

I didn't want him to matter, not in the way he did. But the way he leaned against the stone wall, casually relaxed as though this whole situation wasn't about to spiral into something I couldn't control, left me struggling to keep my focus on the books.

I could feel the pulse of magic in the air, drawing me toward the artifacts like an invisible thread pulling at my chest. And I hated it, the way this place seemed to draw me in, like I was meant to be here, as though the decisions I was about to make had already been written. The Ravenmark. A relic of something old, something dangerous, something that had the potential to ruin everything I had ever known—or worse, make me a part of something far darker than I was ready to confront.

But there was no turning back now. I had already uncovered too much.

"I told you to stay back," I said, the words coming out too softly, like a futile attempt to push him away, to keep him from seeing the fear creeping in from the edges of my mind. I couldn't afford to let anyone in, least of all him. Not now. Not when everything I thought I knew was starting to crumble.

Kael didn't move, just stood there, that infuriating smirk playing on his lips. "You really think I'm going to let you walk into this alone?" he asked, and there was a humor in his voice, but it didn't mask the concern underlying his words.

I spun around to face him, irritation flaring. "You don't understand," I snapped. "This isn't some game, Kael. It's not something I can just walk away from."

"Never said it was a game," he said, his tone turning serious, the hint of a smile slipping away like a shadow retreating at dawn. "But I do know you, Elys. And I'm not going anywhere."

I could feel my heart rate quicken. I didn't want him to be right, didn't want to acknowledge that, maybe, I wasn't as capable of handling this on my own as I liked to believe. The Ravenmark had its claws in me, and the deeper I looked into the ancient texts scattered across the chamber, the more I realized how little I understood about its true nature. The power it promised wasn't something I could control—not if I didn't take the right steps, not if I wasn't willing to make sacrifices I wasn't prepared to face.

Kael took a slow step forward, as though testing my resolve. "You're not alone in this," he repeated, a quiet determination in his voice.

I laughed—a sharp, bitter sound that echoed too loud in the cramped space. "What do you think I'm going to do, Kael? Let you waltz in and be the hero? This is beyond your control. This isn't about saving anyone." I gestured toward the bookshelves, the relics that seemed to hum with unspoken power. "It's about survival. And right now, I'm the only one who's got a chance at that."

Kael's gaze softened, just a little, like he wasn't quite buying the bravado I was selling. "Elys," he said gently, taking another step closer, "you don't have to do this by yourself. Whatever it is that you're afraid of, whatever choice you think you have to make, you don't have to bear it alone."

His words sent a tremor through me, and for a moment, I couldn't breathe. The walls felt like they were closing in on me, and I realized with a start that it wasn't the chamber that was trapping me—it was the weight of my own fears, of all the decisions I had yet to make.

I should have pushed him away. I should have said something harsh, something that would drive him back to the door and out of my life. But instead, I just stood there, my fingers trembling as they skimmed the edge of the book I had been studying. The Ravenmark was more than just a relic. It was a force that could bend the world to its will—and if I wasn't careful, it would bend me with it.

I sucked in a breath, forcing myself to steady my hands. "There's no easy way out, Kael," I said, the words coming out more like a confession than a warning.

He didn't respond immediately, just watched me, his expression unreadable. Then, to my surprise, he reached out and touched my arm—lightly, as though testing the waters. It wasn't a gesture I had expected from him, but it was enough to make me feel something stir beneath my ribs, a flutter of awareness that made me want to step back.

But I didn't.

"Tell me what it is you're afraid of," Kael said, his voice low, the usual flippant tone replaced by something softer, more vulnerable. "Let me help."

I laughed again, but this time it was hollow. "You really want to know, Kael?" I asked, meeting his gaze head-on. "I'm afraid of losing everything. I'm afraid of making the wrong choice. And worse... I'm afraid of choosing the wrong person."

He didn't flinch, didn't pull back from the weight of my words. Instead, his hand slid down to my wrist, his fingers warm against my skin. "Then let me be the one to walk this path with you," he said, his voice so earnest it almost hurt. "I don't need to be the hero. I just need to be with you."

I should have said something then—anything. I should have pulled away and refused him. But instead, I stood there, feeling the full force of his words hit me like a wave, knocking the breath out of me.

The silence between us stretched, taut as a wire, and my heart stammered in my chest. Kael's touch lingered, his fingers still lightly grazing my wrist, and I could feel the warmth of his skin seeping through the thin fabric of my sleeve. It was almost too much—his presence, the pressure, the hum of the Ravenmark's power curling in the air like a living thing. Everything felt like it was spiraling, and yet, I couldn't bring myself to pull away from him.

I knew I should. I knew I should push him out of this mess, tell him to go back to whatever life he thought he had before he stumbled into my orbit. He deserved better than to be tangled in the mess I was about to make. But every time I thought I could sever that tie, every time I tried to tell myself I was doing him a favor by keeping him at arm's length, his eyes—those damn eyes—held me captive.

I tore my gaze from him, letting it fall to the old tome resting on the table before me. My fingers hovered over the pages, but I couldn't bring myself to open it. It felt like an invitation to disaster, like every word on the page would bind me even tighter to the fate I was trying so desperately to escape. But there was no avoiding it. The Ravenmark wasn't something you could ignore—it carved its mark on your soul, whether you wanted it to or not.

"You don't have to carry this alone," Kael said again, his voice quieter now, a subtle plea buried beneath the layers of his usual bravado.

I pressed my lips together, fighting back the instinct to pull away. "I can't," I whispered, more to myself than to him. "I can't ask you to help with this. I can't ask anyone to help. The choice I have to make—it's... it's not something anyone should have to face."

Kael moved closer, his footsteps barely a sound on the stone floor. He stopped beside me, and for a moment, I thought he might pull me into some kind of comforting embrace. But he didn't. Instead, he simply stood there, close enough that I could feel the heat radiating off him, but not so close that it overwhelmed me. It was a strange, calculated distance—a space that left room for something unspoken, something unacknowledged.

"Maybe you don't have to make it alone," he said softly, the words landing between us like a quiet challenge. "Maybe that's the whole point, Elys. Maybe it's not about facing it by yourself. Maybe it's about facing it together."

I blinked, the weight of his words pressing down on me. For a heartbeat, I considered the possibility. The sheer relief that such a thing could bring. But then the reality of what I was dealing with—what I was becoming—came crashing back in. I couldn't drag anyone else into this.

The Ravenmark was more than just magic—it was a curse. And curses had a way of pulling others down with you, no matter how hard you tried to keep them at bay. Kael didn't know that. No one could.

"Kael," I started, my voice raw, a bit too shaky. "This—this isn't something you can fix. You think you can just... show up, say the right words, and everything will magically get better? It doesn't work like that."

His expression didn't falter. "Then let me try," he said, his eyes searching mine. "Let me help you with whatever it is you're facing. You don't have to do this alone."

I wanted to scream, to push him away, to tell him that the best thing he could do was walk out and never look back. But I didn't.

I swallowed the lump in my throat, eyes darting back to the book on the table, feeling the pull of its dark promise. It was ridiculous, this fight. We both knew it. Kael was right, and I was just too scared to admit it. The more I resisted, the more the truth became undeniable: I needed him. I needed someone, anyone, who wasn't as afraid as I was of facing what lay ahead. But admitting that felt like a betrayal of everything I had tried to protect. It felt like signing my own death sentence.

"What if I told you that the choice I have to make..." I trailed off, my voice breaking at the words I hadn't wanted to say out loud. The weight of it all—the knowledge, the consequences, the inevitable—seemed too much for one person to bear. How could I ask anyone else to carry it with me?

I didn't have to finish my sentence. Kael already understood. I could see it in the shift of his expression, the way his jaw clenched just slightly, as though he was realizing something he hadn't known before.

"You're trying to protect me," he said quietly, almost like a realization, and for a moment, it made my heart ache.

I said nothing. What was there to say? Of course, I was trying to protect him. I was trying to protect everyone I cared about from the fallout of what was coming.

A long silence stretched between us. Then, as if to break the tension, Kael took a deep breath and said, "If this thing you're facing—this choice—has already been made for you, then maybe it's not about controlling the outcome. Maybe it's about who you choose to be when it's all said and done."

My heart gave a strange lurch at his words. They were too true, too raw. It wasn't about the magic, or the relics, or the Ravenmark itself. It was about the choices I made. And the people I let in.

But before I could process it further, a loud crash rang out from somewhere deep within the citadel—louder than any sound I'd heard since entering this forsaken place.

Kael's head snapped toward the sound, his expression darkening. "What the hell was that?"

I didn't wait for an answer. I turned, instinctively reaching for the hilt of the dagger strapped to my waist. Whatever it was, it wasn't good. And I could feel it—whatever force had been lying dormant beneath the citadel had just awoken.

A voice, distant but clear, echoed through the chamber.

"Elys..." It was low, guttural. "You can't run forever."

My blood ran cold.

Chapter 12: A Test of Loyalty

I never expected loyalty to feel like a knife twisting in my gut. It's the kind of thing they don't warn you about—how devotion can become a weight, a responsibility, that follows you like a shadow, always just behind your back, pressing on your shoulders when you least expect it.

The test was designed to break us down, to see who we really were beneath the polished surfaces we all showed to the world. There had been whispers before, casual comments in the corners of rooms, about Seraphina's methods. People talked about her as though she were some kind of mythic figure, a woman who could peer inside your very soul and expose the things you'd rather keep buried. But I didn't understand the weight of it all until I stood in front of her, under her gaze.

Kael had been unwavering from the start, his every move calculated and steady. I watched him with a mixture of awe and envy, as though he could read the test like an open book, while my insides twisted in knots, unsure of what the next moment would bring.

We'd been in the room for hours. The walls of the small building were lined with shelves of old books—ones that I suspected Seraphina had never read, ones that were there just to make people feel small. But it wasn't the setting that unnerved me. It was the silence. The waiting. And Kael, of course.

Seraphina hadn't given me a direct challenge like she had with Kael. Instead, she'd given me a look, a kind of half-smile that spoke volumes, and I had found myself fighting against something I couldn't quite define. Was it guilt? Doubt? Or was it something far worse—a strange sort of affection for the man standing beside me, the one who was seemingly impervious to everything?

"Look at me," she had said, her voice as calm as still water. But the words carried more weight than they should have. "You're loyal to something. Or someone."

The way she said it made the room tilt. It made me question my own heart, the tiny flutter it had every time Kael looked at me in that way, like he saw everything. Too much, sometimes. And I hated that about myself. That I couldn't seem to trust my own instincts anymore.

Kael had taken the test in stride, his confidence something I'd always admired from a distance. But when it was my turn, it felt like the floor dropped out beneath me. She'd asked me simple questions at first. Questions about what I valued most, what I'd die for. And I answered quickly, almost automatically. Family. Freedom. But then the questions became personal, prying into places I didn't want to go.

"Who would you betray?" Seraphina had asked. Her eyes were sharp, like a hawk's. She wasn't just looking at me. She was studying me, dissecting me piece by piece.

I'd hesitated. What was the right answer? Could I betray Kael? Could I betray anyone I loved, for something more important? My heart pounded in my chest, and I could hear the ringing in my ears as though I were underwater, drowning in my own uncertainty. I could feel the heat of Kael's gaze on me, but it only made the pressure more unbearable.

"I don't know," I had finally admitted, the words coming out weaker than I wanted them to.

Seraphina smiled. "You don't know," she repeated, almost amused. "That's the problem, isn't it?"

She didn't need to elaborate. I could see it in her face—the way she had been watching me like a hawk, waiting for the moment when I would falter.

The silence was crushing. I felt as though the weight of everything—the uncertainty, the fear, and yes, the growing feelings I had for Kael—were all pressing in on me at once. And that was the moment, the turning point, when I knew I was in trouble. Because loyalty—true loyalty—had never felt so heavy before.

When it was over, when the test was completed and I was left standing there with my own failures like a scar on my soul, Seraphina had pulled me aside. Her eyes were still assessing, though softer now, as if she saw something in me that I hadn't been able to see myself.

"You're stronger than you know," she said, her voice low and full of meaning. But I didn't feel strong. I felt shattered, like a fine china plate dropped on a stone floor.

"Strength isn't the problem," I had replied, barely able to meet her gaze. "It's the rest of it. The fear. The... connection."

Seraphina's lips quirked into a half-smile, the kind that made me wonder if she knew more than she let on. She probably did. "Ah," she said, as though she'd been expecting that answer all along. "That's what makes you human."

I wanted to argue with her. I wanted to say that it wasn't the connection with Kael that made me human, it was the part of me that was still capable of seeing the bigger picture. But I couldn't. The truth was too raw. Kael, with his quiet intensity, had become a force in my life, pulling at my every thought, my every action. And it terrified me. The way he made me feel—like I could lose myself in him, like I could forget everything else that mattered.

And I wasn't sure if I could ever forgive myself for that.

I stood there, on the edge of everything, my heart a tangled mess of emotions I couldn't quite unravel. The city hum of downtown Seattle felt like a distant hum now, like a different world entirely. The air was thick with tension, and not just from the remnants of the test. No, it was the knot inside me, the one that had been growing tighter and tighter since the moment Seraphina's gaze had bored into me, daring me to show my true colors. And I'd failed.

Kael, on the other hand, had navigated the whole ordeal with a kind of grace that made my skin burn with inadequacy. He was stoic, unwavering, as though the thought of betraying anyone—let alone the woman who could probably read the deepest corners of his soul—had never crossed his mind. Watching him in that moment had only solidified my fear: the fear that I was getting in too deep, that the pull between us was no longer just the product of a shared mission but something else entirely. And if that was true, if I really was that close to him—close enough to risk my own integrity for him—then everything I had worked for, everything Seraphina had drilled into us, was slipping away, piece by piece.

When Seraphina had pulled me aside, her words hadn't offered comfort, not really. "You're stronger than you know," she'd said, and I'd wanted to argue. I wanted to scream, No, I'm not. But what would be the point? I had no more fight left. Not now. Not after everything that had unfolded.

"You can say that all you want, but it doesn't change what's happening." I said the words before I could stop them. They hung between us, raw and unpolished, but they were the truth. The truth I was unwilling to face.

Seraphina didn't respond right away. Instead, she just stared at me, her eyes the sharp, analytical kind that could cut you open and find things you didn't even know were there. And maybe I had been foolish, maybe I had believed—just for a moment—that I could pull off this mission without any personal stakes. But I wasn't naïve anymore. Not after the test. Not after Kael had been standing there, watching me with those eyes, his quiet strength pulling me in like gravity itself.

"I'm not the one you need to be afraid of," she said finally, her voice taking on an almost sinister edge.

I blinked, caught off guard. "What does that mean?"

Seraphina smiled, but there was no humor in it. "You think the test was about loyalty, but it wasn't. It was about something much more dangerous. It's about trust. And trust is a fragile thing. Once it's broken, it can never be fully repaired."

I swallowed hard. The words hung in the air, too heavy to ignore.

"Why are you telling me this?" I didn't recognize the desperation in my own voice. It was a small crack, one I couldn't stop from forming.

She didn't answer. Instead, she simply turned on her heel, her long coat swishing behind her as she made her way toward the door. I stood there, caught between wanting to follow and needing to collapse onto the nearest chair and bury my head in my hands. But Kael's presence was a constant, pressing weight in the back of my mind. He had passed the test. He had done what I couldn't, what I had failed to do. And what was I left with?

As if reading my mind—or perhaps sensing the heavy atmosphere in the room—Kael stepped forward, his figure blocking the doorway, his gaze unwavering.

"What did she say to you?" he asked, his voice smooth but laced with an intensity I couldn't ignore.

I felt my pulse quicken, my thoughts racing to put up a wall, something to hide the confusion swirling inside me.

"Nothing that matters," I muttered, too quickly. "Just... words. She's always got something to say, doesn't she?"

Kael didn't move, didn't look away. His eyes searched mine, the silence between us heavy and pregnant with things left unsaid. "I know you're struggling," he said quietly. "But you don't have to do this alone."

His words hit me harder than I anticipated. Alone. The one word that had always echoed through my life, despite the people who had surrounded me, despite all the years of pretending to be something I wasn't. And now, here he was, offering something I hadn't known I wanted—or maybe something I had always been too afraid to accept.

"I'm not struggling," I said, but the lie tasted bitter on my tongue.

Kael's lips pressed into a thin line, his jaw tight. "I think you are. You don't have to lie to me, not after everything we've been through."

I opened my mouth to respond, but the words wouldn't come. Instead, I just stood there, caught in a storm of emotions I wasn't ready to face. The walls I had spent years building around myself were crumbling, piece by piece, under the weight of his gaze.

"I don't need your help," I whispered, but even I didn't believe it.

Kael took a step closer, the distance between us now barely enough to breathe. "You're wrong," he said, his voice so low that it sent a chill down my spine. "I'm not offering you help, Sera." He paused, his eyes holding mine. "I'm offering you trust."

Trust.

The word lingered, and for a moment, everything else seemed to disappear. The weight of the test, the guilt of my failures, the fear of what might happen next. Everything except for him and the way his presence seemed to fill the room, wrapping around me like a fog I couldn't escape.

I had been terrified of losing myself to this connection, terrified of giving in to the pull between us, but in that moment, I realized something. Maybe it wasn't about losing myself at all. Maybe it was about letting go—of the fear, the doubts, the walls—and finding something else. Something real. Something that felt like home.

But the question remained: could I trust him? Or had I already made my choice?

It was late, the kind of Seattle night where the fog rolled in thick, settling like a damp cloak over the city. The neon lights of Pike Place Market flickered in the distance, casting a soft, eerie glow across the streets. The usual bustle of late-night wanderers had quieted, leaving the alleys and sidewalks drenched in stillness. And yet, in that stillness, everything felt alive—alive with things unsaid, with secrets that hovered in the air, waiting to be discovered.

I found myself standing near a window, the glass fogged by the chill of the night. Kael's presence lingered, though he'd gone. The weight of his words, that quiet promise of trust, weighed on me. But what did trust even mean anymore? After everything we'd been through, after the test, after the way I'd let my own fears and doubts twist around me like a noose, how could I be sure that trusting him wouldn't lead to my own destruction?

But what if it was the only thing that would save me?

A soft knock broke the silence, a rhythm almost too familiar. I didn't have to turn around to know who it was.

Kael's voice was quiet but firm. "You're still up."

I didn't answer right away. My eyes lingered on the dark shapes of the city beyond, the distant hum of traffic a comforting background noise. What could I say to him? What words could possibly express the war I felt inside?

"You should be sleeping," I said finally, my voice hoarse, betraying the unease I had tried so hard to hide.

"I've never been good at sleeping," he replied, his tone as dry as the air outside. "Not when I'm thinking about things that matter."

I swallowed, his words hitting too close to home. He had no idea how right he was. But what could I say? What could I tell him without unraveling every piece of me that I had so carefully hidden?

"About what?" I asked, my back still to him.

Kael didn't answer immediately. I could hear the faint rustle of fabric as he shifted, and then, the floor creaked under his weight as he moved toward me. There was a heat to his presence now, something palpable that I couldn't shake. It was as though he had become an extension of the room itself, pulling me into his orbit with every quiet step he took.

"You," he said simply, the word hanging in the air like an unspoken confession.

My breath caught in my throat.

"Me?" I asked, unable to keep the incredulity from my voice. "What about me?"

"Everything," he said, his voice softer now, as though the words were meant for me alone. "You're not as hidden as you think. And I'm not blind, Sera. I see you—everything you are, everything you're afraid of."

I wanted to laugh. A sharp, bitter sound. But it died on my lips. Instead, I turned to face him, my hands fisted at my sides as I forced myself to meet his gaze.

"You think you know me?" I said, though it came out more as a question than a challenge. "You think you see me, but you have no idea what's really inside."

He didn't flinch. Instead, he took another step toward me, the distance between us shrinking in a way that felt inevitable. "I don't need to know everything. I just need to know what matters."

I opened my mouth to argue, to push him away, but the words caught in my throat. Because, deep down, I knew he was right. He didn't need to know every part of me, didn't need to understand the cracks in my heart or the secrets I had buried. He just needed to know that I wasn't going anywhere. That when it all came down to it, I'd stand beside him. But could I? Could I trust myself enough to trust him?

"I'm not what you think I am," I said, the words coming out before I could stop them. "I'm... I'm not the person you think you can rely on."

Kael's eyes softened. He took another step forward, his hand reaching out, hovering just in front of me as though waiting for permission. I could feel the warmth radiating from his palm, tempting me to close the gap between us, to feel what it would be like to give in.

"I don't need you to be perfect," he said, his voice barely above a whisper. "I need you to be real."

It wasn't a promise. Not in the way I needed it to be. But it was enough.

For the first time in what felt like forever, I felt something shift inside me. It wasn't the surge of confidence I had been waiting for, the clarity that would tell me everything would be okay. It was more like a crack, a fracture in the wall I'd spent so long building around myself. And in that crack, something dangerous had begun to bloom.

I didn't pull away when Kael's hand brushed mine. I didn't pull away when his fingers curled around my wrist, gentle but firm. I let him lead me to the couch, where we sat in the quiet, the only sound between us the rhythmic ticking of the clock on the wall.

I wanted to ask him why he was doing this. Why he was still here when I had nothing to offer him but uncertainty and fear. But the words never came. Instead, I let the silence stretch, the weight of it heavy and familiar. It was almost as if we were two pieces of a puzzle, fitting together in a way neither of us had planned.

And then, just as the tension between us seemed to reach its peak, the phone rang, slicing through the stillness like a knife. The sharp, shrill sound cut into the moment, pulling us both back to reality. I didn't need to look at the screen to know who it was. The name lit up in red, flashing like an alarm.

Seraphina.

I glanced at Kael, his face unreadable, and then back at the phone, wondering if this would be the moment everything changed.

Chapter 13: The Siege of Veylian

The first crack of thunder felt like a harbinger of doom, an omen too real to ignore. I stood at the edge of the battlefield, the storm clouds swirling overhead, a reflection of the tempest brewing in my heart. The city of Veylian sprawled before me, an ancient, proud fortress that had withstood the tides of time, yet today, it would be caught in the vice grip of war. The air was thick with the metallic scent of blood, burnt stone, and charred magic, crackling like the breath of a beast too wild to tame.

I could feel the hum of magic running through the very ground beneath my feet, pulling at the strings of my power, coaxing them to the surface like an old friend calling you home. The pull was almost seductive, luring me into its depths, but I resisted—barely. Magic was both a gift and a curse, and tonight it felt more like a curse than anything else. Selene's forces were relentless, their dark powers swirling in unnatural patterns, slashing through the air with vicious intent.

Beside me, Kael was a storm incarnate. His presence was a balm to my frayed nerves, his familiar power grounding me, tethering me to reality when everything else seemed to blur into chaos. His focus was absolute as his magic sliced through the enemy's ranks, each strike leaving a trail of scorched earth and shattered shields. There was something graceful about his violence, something calculated in the way he moved, as if every action was a response to an ancient rhythm that only he could hear.

"Hold the line!" Kael shouted, his voice carrying over the clamor of battle, and I didn't need to ask what he meant. I knew, as surely as I knew the pulse of my own heartbeat, that we were the last bastion. Without us, the city would fall. I raised my hand, summoning the wind, the air heavy with the scent of impending rain. A gust howled around me, tearing through the ranks of Selene's soldiers, forcing them back just enough for a brief reprieve.

But that was all it was—a reprieve. The battle was far from over, and I could feel the shift in the air, the subtle change that told me something darker was approaching. Selene's magic had grown bolder, more desperate, as though she sensed her end was near, but she wouldn't go down without a fight. And it was that fight I feared the most.

Kael glanced at me, his dark eyes flashing with unspoken words. We'd been through this before—battles that raged without mercy, moments when time itself seemed to stand still, and our powers meshed in a way that felt less like strategy and more like fate. But today... today was different. I could feel it deep in my bones, a stirring that suggested something was about to shatter.

"You're unsettled," he said, his voice low but intense, the kind of voice that made you listen whether you wanted to or not.

"I'm fine," I lied, my fingers tightening around the staff in my hands. It wasn't fine, none of it was. The city around us was crumbling, and despite all our efforts, I couldn't shake the nagging thought that we were missing something.

Kael's lips quirked, a smile that was more a challenge than comfort. "I've known you long enough to know when you're lying."

"Good for you," I shot back, though the edge of my voice faltered just a little. I didn't want him to see how rattled I truly was, how every instinct inside me screamed that something wasn't right. And as if to prove me right, the ground beneath us trembled, the distant rumble of thunder now accompanied by something far worse—a roar, guttural and unnerving, that made the hairs on the back of my neck stand on end.

From the depths of the city, a dark shadow rose—a creature too large to be comprehended in a single glance. Its body was a mass of shifting shadows, eyes glowing with a feral hunger that sent chills down my spine. Selene had unleashed her greatest weapon, a beast of nightmare and myth, a creature born of magic too dark to name.

"Well, this should be fun," Kael muttered, his fingers already weaving through the air, ready to engage. I wasn't so sure, but I didn't have time to second-guess. The beast lurched forward, its roars echoing off the city walls as it barreled toward us. It was the very embodiment of destruction, a force that would tear through everything in its path.

We met it head-on.

I called the wind, summoned it into a vortex that whipped around the beast, attempting to disorient it. But it was like trying to stop a storm with a breath. The creature staggered but did not fall. Instead, it shrieked in fury, its dark magic countering mine in a clash of raw, untamed power. The sky above seemed to bend, torn asunder by the sheer magnitude of the creature's magic.

Kael moved like liquid fire, his own magic flaring to life in the form of molten energy, lashing out at the beast's hulking form. But for all its size and rage, the creature was fast, too fast for us to land a killing blow. It swiped at Kael, its claws leaving deep gouges in the earth where they struck. I didn't have to see the damage to know that it was worse than anything we'd faced before.

"Fall back!" I shouted, my heart hammering in my chest. I could feel the weight of the decision settle in my gut. We couldn't beat this thing in direct combat. Not like this.

"Not yet," Kael responded, his voice steady, even as the ground cracked under the force of the creature's next strike. His expression was determined, unyielding. But I saw the shadow in his eyes. He knew, as I did, that this battle had shifted in a way we couldn't control. We were no longer fighting just for victory. We were fighting to survive.

And that, for all our power and resolve, was the one thing that none of us had truly prepared for.

The city of Veylian had become a war zone, and even in the chaos, I couldn't shake the sensation that we were no longer fighting for victory—at least, not in the traditional sense. We were merely buying time, though I wasn't sure for what. The once-pristine stone streets, so revered in their grandeur, had been marred by jagged cracks, as if even the earth itself was attempting to flee from the unnatural storm Selene had summoned. The air was thick, not just with magic but with something darker, something that seemed to pulse and throb in a way that wasn't natural.

Kael's magic flared beside me, a brilliant burst of white-hot energy cutting through the air as we fought side by side. We had always been a force to be reckoned with, our powers complementing each other with a synchronicity that felt almost deliberate, like the world had arranged us in this moment to stand together against the tides of destruction. Still, there was something different about tonight, something that tugged at my instincts, warning me that our unity, however powerful, was not enough to ward off the encroaching darkness.

I glanced over at him, his face set in grim determination, the sweat clinging to the sharp lines of his jaw. His hair was a dark mess, dampened by the heat of the battle and the glow of his magic. There was a fierceness in his eyes that mirrored mine, but there was also a flicker of something else—something I couldn't place, though it unnerved me more than I cared to admit.

"You're staring," he said, voice low but carrying over the clamor of battle. He didn't even look at me, his focus entirely on the shifting mass of enemies charging at us, but I could feel the smirk in his words.

I rolled my eyes, though a part of me couldn't help but appreciate the rare moment of humor amid the madness. "Trying to figure out if you're actually enjoying this," I replied, my voice sharper than I intended. "It wouldn't surprise me."

He flicked a glance at me then, his smile turning wry. "I'd never claim to enjoy chaos, but I'm good at it. And you?" He tilted his head, his lips curling in that way that made it impossible for me to stay angry for long. "You look like you've been handed a plate of bad decisions."

"Very witty," I shot back, stepping forward, my hands raised as I summoned a gust of wind that sent a few of Selene's soldiers tumbling backward, giving us a brief opening. "I'm just trying to figure out if we're winning. Or if we're already dead and don't know it."

"You'll know when we're dead," Kael said dryly. "I'll be the one yelling."

The laughter died in my throat when I saw it—an unsettling shift in the battlefield, a tremor so deep I felt it in my bones. I didn't need to look to know that something was wrong. The magic in the air had changed, twisting, warping, as if it had suddenly been infected by something unnatural. The ground beneath us shifted again, but this time, it wasn't the tremors of a city under siege. This was deliberate, like something massive was pushing its way through the earth itself.

My eyes snapped toward the horizon, and I saw it—Selene's monster, the one we had only heard whispers about. It wasn't just a creature; it was a nightmare made flesh. Its eyes glowed with an eerie, otherworldly light, and its very presence seemed to suck the air from my lungs. We were no longer fighting just for survival. We were fighting to keep this thing from wiping us all off the map.

Kael cursed under his breath, already stepping forward, his power crackling in the air like a live wire. I followed, though every instinct told me that we were facing something beyond our abilities, something designed to obliterate us. The creature's roar was deafening, its form a shifting mass of darkness that seemed to devour the light around it.

"Whatever you do," I muttered, eyes narrowed as I readied myself for what was to come, "don't die on me. I'm not carrying your corpse out of here."

Kael shot me a sidelong glance, a flicker of something—was it affection?—before he focused back on the creature. "You think I'm dying?" he scoffed. "I've got at least a few more tricks left up my sleeve."

"Good. Because I'm fresh out of ideas."

I didn't wait for him to respond. I lunged forward, conjuring a powerful windstorm that swept around the creature, tearing at its form in an attempt to disorient it. The creature staggered, its glowing eyes flashing with rage. But it wasn't enough. For every gust of wind I summoned, the creature's dark magic countered it, sending shockwaves of power that knocked us both back.

"Too strong," Kael grunted, stumbling as the force of the magic sent him to his knees. "We can't hold this."

I looked over at him, the fury and frustration of the situation boiling over inside me. "What do you suggest we do? Wait for it to take the city?"

He gave me a sidelong glance, and for a moment, the determination in his eyes softened. "I was hoping you'd have a better idea."

"Great. No pressure," I muttered, my mind racing. We had no choice. It was either stop the creature now or let it tear everything apart. I could feel the weight of every life in the city pressing down on me. "Kael, I need everything you've got."

He gave a terse nod, standing and gathering his energy in a way I had only seen in the direst of situations. But there was something about his presence, the way his power surged with barely contained force, that made me feel as though we might have one shot at this. His magic, when combined with mine, had always been our greatest strength. But this—this was a different kind of battle. It was a test of more than just magic; it was a test of whether we could push beyond our limits and defeat the thing that threatened to destroy us all.

We were running out of time.

The ground beneath us shifted again, the tremor more violent this time, as though the earth itself were recoiling from the unnatural weight of the creature's presence. I could feel the pulse of its dark magic like a heartbeat, slow but steady, thumping through the ground and into my very bones. My heart thudded in time with it—slow and heavy, and then, suddenly, a rush of adrenaline burst through my chest, speeding up my pulse and tightening my focus. This was no longer just a battle. It was a reckoning. A final test.

Kael's magic crackled beside me, a brilliant pulse of light, but even that felt diminished against the weight of the beast's power. We had always been in sync—his fire and my air, a combination that had torn through countless enemies with ease. But this? This was something else entirely. It was like fighting a storm that didn't just destroy; it consumed.

"Get ready," Kael's voice sliced through my thoughts, low and steady. I caught a glimpse of him, his stance solid and resolute. There was something in his gaze now, something darker than I had ever seen before. Maybe it was the realization that we were on the edge of something we couldn't control. Maybe it was the look of a man who had come to terms with the fact that sometimes, you don't win battles—you survive them.

"You think I'm not?" I shot back, though the doubt clung to my words, thick and uninvited. I raised my hands, calling the wind again, the gusts fighting against the beast's raw power, but it was like trying to hold back the ocean with a bucket. The creature snarled, its massive claws tearing through the earth with every step, sending chunks of stone flying into the air. The force of its approach made the city feel as though it were cracking open, and for the first time, I felt the weight of my own vulnerability.

There was a hiss as the creature's claws scraped the earth, followed by a sound that wasn't quite human, but far too close to it. It roared again, a sound that made the hairs on the back of my neck stand on end. I tried to shake off the rising dread in my gut, but it lingered, heavy and suffocating. "What the hell is that thing?" I muttered, half to myself.

"A nightmare," Kael replied, his lips curling into a smile that didn't reach his eyes. "But you didn't hear it from me."

I shot him a glare, but before I could respond, the creature lunged. There was no warning, no hesitation, just a massive black blur of claws and teeth that swallowed up everything in its path. The force of its attack sent me flying backward, my breath knocked out of me as I hit the ground hard. A sharp pain ricocheted through my spine, but I didn't have the luxury to feel it. Not with the creature bearing down on me.

I pushed myself to my feet, heart racing, my pulse like a drumbeat in my ears. Kael was already back on his feet, too, flames sparking from his fingers, his focus razor-sharp. But I could see it in his eyes—the same realization that had hit me earlier. We weren't fighting a monster; we were trying to stop a force of nature.

"I can't keep this up forever," Kael said, his voice tight, his brow furrowed with concentration as he unleashed another wave of fire at the creature. The flames hit its hide, but it didn't even flinch. If anything, the creature's eyes glowed brighter, its hunger seeming to intensify.

I gritted my teeth, pushing forward, but I wasn't sure if it was the creature or the weight of the situation that was slowing me down. It was like the very air had thickened, thick with dread, thick with something I couldn't name. I pushed that feeling aside as best I could and tried to call the wind again, gathering it into a force that would push back against the monster, but the moment I reached for the power, something shifted.

The creature screeched, a sound that was both physical and mental, the kind of sound that burrowed into your skull and made your teeth ache. I felt the pull of it in my gut, a cold rush of panic clawing at my chest. The wind that I had called on faltered for just a moment, and that moment was all the creature needed.

It lunged, and this time, there was no time to dodge.

I screamed in surprise as something sharp and brutal caught my side, pain ripping through me as I staggered back, barely able to keep my footing. The creature's claws had torn through my armor like it was paper, and I felt the warm trickle of blood against my skin.

"Selene's going to love this," Kael muttered, his voice strained as he cast another flame at the creature, but it didn't seem to do anything to slow it down. His gaze flicked to me, sharp and concerned, but before he could move to help, the beast's claws slashed the air again, aiming directly at him.

"Kael!" I shouted, but it was too late. The creature was faster than either of us had anticipated, and its attack sent Kael reeling back, his magic sputtering out like a candle's flame in a gale.

I took a shaky breath, panic crawling at the edges of my mind, but I forced it back down. Not now. Not yet.

The creature, its eyes glowing like molten amber, advanced again, its hunger apparent, its power unyielding. I couldn't afford to think—couldn't afford to doubt. I raised my hands, calling everything I had left, every last shred of energy, of magic, and of will.

And just as I felt the very last reserves of my power start to flare in my chest, something—something—shifted in the sky above us. A crack of light, brighter than anything I had seen in the chaos of the storm.

OUR FATE

And then, the ground beneath us buckled.
I barely had time to scream before the earth split wide open.

Chapter 14: The Price of Power

I had always known there would be a price, but no one ever told me the cost would be this heavy. It wasn't just the ache that clung to me after each use of the Orb—though that alone could keep me up at night, a cold weight pressing on my chest, the desperate desire to reach for it, just one more time. It was more than that. It was the taste of something I wasn't sure I should want. The kind of craving that starts as a whisper and becomes a shout in the back of your mind, loud enough to drown out everything else. I'd felt its tendrils slip into me the moment I first touched it, but back then, it had seemed like a means to an end, a tool to help me control what was spiraling out of my grasp.

Now, I wasn't so sure.

The world around me felt different. Lush, vibrant, but too sharp. Colors seemed to pulse unnaturally; every sound was amplified, every movement too quick. I caught my reflection in the window as I passed by—a pale ghost of myself with eyes that looked too wide, too knowing. I could see Kael's shadow trailing after me, his gaze never leaving my back, his quiet concern a constant hum.

We were in the heart of Boston, where cobblestone streets still wound their way through neighborhoods that boasted a history as thick as the air. The city, with its salty breeze off the harbor and its blend of modern glass towers and crumbling brick buildings, had always been a little too proud of itself, a little too eager to remind anyone who'd listen that it was the cradle of revolution. And yet, there was something that tethered me here, something both ancient and immediate, as if the city had recognized the power growing inside me before I did.

"You're quiet," Kael said, his voice low and careful, like I might shatter if he spoke too loudly.

I looked at him, at the lines of worry etched into his face, the way his eyes darted toward me when he thought I wasn't paying attention. "I'm fine," I said, a lie I'd become too accustomed to. I kept my steps brisk, forcing myself not to drag my feet. The urge to collapse into the nearest alley and reach for the Orb, just to quiet the chaos inside me, was overwhelming, but I swallowed it down. Not now. Not here.

Kael reached out, touching my arm with a gentleness that seemed to surprise him as much as it did me. His fingers were warm, grounding. It was a sharp contrast to the cold fire curling in my gut. "You don't have to do this alone, you know."

I didn't respond at first. I couldn't. The words tasted like ash in my mouth. What was I supposed to say? Yes, I do. Because I'm the only one who can bear this power. The thought felt less like truth now, and more like a prison sentence I'd signed without realizing the full terms. But there was something in Kael's eyes, an unspoken plea, that made me hesitate, just for a moment.

"I'm fine," I said again, though it was harder this time. My voice faltered, betraying the cracks I was trying to ignore.

He didn't back down, though. "You've been saying that a lot lately," he observed, his tone sharp with concern. "But I'm not blind, and I'm not stupid. I can see it. The way you pull back from me, the way you can't let go of that damned thing—" He stopped himself before he could say more, his mouth tightening as if the words had physically pained him to release.

I had no answer for him. How could I explain that the Orb was no longer just an object? How could I tell him that each time I used it, I felt the threads of who I used to be unraveling, leaving behind something new, something unrecognizable? It felt like I was becoming a stranger to myself, and every time I used the Orb, I was a little less human. I wanted to tell him everything, but the words stuck in my throat, tangled up with the fear that had been gnawing at me since I first started down this path.

The city felt louder now, as if it was closing in on me. The incessant beep of car horns, the muffled conversations of passersby, the scrape of shoes on concrete—it all blurred together in a cacophony that seemed to reverberate in my skull. I was reaching for something—anything—to quiet the noise when Kael's voice broke through again.

"Let me help."

I glanced up at him, and this time, there was no avoiding the truth. Not the one I told myself, anyway. His words were a lifeline, but they were also a temptation. A promise I wasn't sure I could accept. Let me help.

Could I let him? Could I share the weight of the magic, share the burden of the things I'd done to keep us safe? The fear that bloomed inside me wasn't just about Kael's safety—it was about my own. I didn't know how much of me was still intact, how much I could give before there was nothing left but the power, the magic, the hunger.

I stopped walking and turned to face him. The streets of Boston stretched out behind him, full of people who never noticed the two of us standing there. It felt like we were the only ones who mattered, and the world was waiting for me to make a choice.

Kael was close now, his eyes searching mine with a mix of determination and uncertainty. "I can see what it's doing to you. I don't want you to lose yourself." His voice cracked, but he didn't back down.

For a moment, I let the silence hang between us, a fragile space where nothing else existed but the weight of his words and the tug of the Orb in my bag. I should have said something—anything—but I didn't. I wasn't sure I was ready to admit it, but Kael was right. The cost of power was already too high, and I wasn't sure how much longer I could afford it.

I could feel the weight of Kael's gaze, steady, unyielding, like the cool touch of the ocean against the rocks. I hated that he could see through the cracks in my armor, the ones I thought I'd sealed long ago. The worst part? I wasn't entirely sure I wanted him to look away. His concern, as unwanted as it was, was a tether to something real, something human.

But could I trust it?

Boston hummed around us, the rhythm of the city like a pulse beneath my feet. The crisp autumn air tugged at the edges of my coat, sending a chill that had nothing to do with the temperature. It was that same sensation I had each time I stepped out of my apartment—like I was slipping between worlds, where everything looked the same, but nothing felt familiar. The neon lights of South End flickered ahead, and I could smell the tantalizing scent of fresh seafood from the nearby stalls. People passed by, oblivious to the war that had started inside me, like the world had no idea I was unraveling at the seams.

I wasn't even sure I had the strength to keep it together.

Kael's hand brushed mine, a fleeting touch that sent a tremor through me. I could feel the warmth of his skin against mine, grounding me in a way the magic never had. He didn't say anything more, but his silence was louder than his words had been. There was a quiet understanding between us now—something unspoken but present all the same.

"I don't know what I'm doing," I admitted, the words slipping out before I could stop them. "It's too much. I can feel it, Kael. The pull... It's all I can think about. The magic. The hunger." I hesitated, my eyes catching on the distant city lights, anything but him. "It's eating me alive."

There it was. The thing I'd been avoiding, the thing that had been gnawing at the edges of my thoughts for days now. The truth. The power was seductive in a way I hadn't expected. And I was starting to understand why people went mad for it. There was a certain joy in it, an intoxicating sense of control, as if I could reach out and reshape the world with a flick of my wrist. But it wasn't the kind of joy that made you feel alive—it was the kind that made you feel like you were dancing with death and forgetting to care about the final note.

Kael exhaled slowly, the air thick with the tension that had been building between us. "I can see it. You're slipping, and you don't even realize it. But it's not you, not really. It's the power. The Orb. It's changing you."

I let out a short, humorless laugh. "Yeah, well, that's the problem, isn't it? It's changing me, but I don't know who I'll be once I'm on the other side."

Kael was quiet for a beat, his eyes narrowing with a mixture of frustration and something else—something softer that made my chest tighten. "I don't want to see you lose yourself. And I won't stand by and watch it happen. You don't have to carry this burden alone."

I shot him a look, more defensive than I meant it to be. "You think I want to drag anyone into this mess? You think I'm looking for a hero? I'm not. I'm not some damsel in distress waiting for someone to come save me."

His brow furrowed at my words, but he didn't flinch. "I'm not trying to save you. I'm trying to help you. Let me."

For a moment, we stood there, locked in a kind of standoff, both of us too proud, too stubborn to bend. I didn't want his help. I didn't need it. And yet, there was something about the way he stood there—so solid, so unwavering—that made me want to break down, to let him in. But I couldn't. I wouldn't.

The city stretched out before us like a living thing, the crowd flowing past in their own little bubbles of distraction, never knowing the storm brewing on the inside of one of their own. I tried to swallow the lump in my throat, but it stuck there, like a stone I couldn't get rid of. The taste of failure, of fear, of everything slipping through my fingers.

"What happens if I lose control?" I asked, my voice small in the sea of noise. "What happens if I give in? If I let it consume me?"

Kael's eyes softened, and for a second, I saw the man I'd known before all of this had started. Before the magic had come crashing into my life like a tidal wave. "Then I'll be here. I'll be here, no matter what. Because I know who you are underneath all of this. And I believe you can find your way back."

His words made my chest ache in a way that almost hurt. I wasn't used to being seen, not like this. Not with such certainty.

But I wasn't sure if I could be saved, or if I even wanted to be.

"I'm not the person you think I am," I said quietly, turning to face him fully now. My breath hitched in my chest, and I forced myself to meet his gaze. "I'm not some hero. I'm just... trying to survive."

He shook his head slowly, a rueful smile tugging at the corner of his lips. "You're wrong. You're stronger than you think. You're more than just surviving."

It was the kind of thing someone says when they don't understand the kind of weight you're carrying, the kind of pressure you're under. But Kael had never been someone to back down, and I couldn't decide if I hated that about him or loved it.

"I don't know how to stop it," I whispered, more to myself than to him. "I don't know how to make it stop."

The wind picked up, tugging at the strands of hair that had come loose from my ponytail, and I shivered. There were moments when I felt like I was slipping into darkness, moments when the magic felt too big, too powerful, and I wasn't sure if I could keep fighting it. But in that moment, as I stood there with Kael, I also realized something else.

Maybe, just maybe, I didn't have to face it alone.

The city was waking up around us, as if it had a mind of its own. Boston had a pulse, a rhythm that people seemed to follow blindly. But today, the streets felt louder, the world more alive than usual. It was the kind of morning when the sun broke through the gray sky with just enough heat to make you squint. It felt like the beginning of something, though I couldn't tell if it was something good or something terrible. Either way, I wasn't sure I was ready for it.

Kael hadn't moved, still standing close, as if he were waiting for me to make some kind of decision. It was maddening, how patient he was. How much space he gave me to decide what I wanted, as if I even knew anymore. He was a constant in a world that was becoming increasingly unrecognizable, a fixed point in the swirl of chaos that had overtaken my life since the Orb had come into my possession.

"Why do you keep doing this?" I asked, the words slipping out before I could stop them.

He raised an eyebrow, a slight smirk tugging at the corner of his mouth, but there was something in his eyes that told me he wasn't laughing. "Doing what?"

"This. Sticking around. Watching me drown in something I can't control." I gestured vaguely, as if I could encompass the mess of my life in a single movement.

His expression softened, and for a second, I saw the care he tried so hard to hide behind that careful veneer of indifference. "Because I believe in you," he said quietly. "And I think you're worth saving."

I laughed, though it felt bitter, a sound I didn't recognize coming from my own mouth. "Save me? I don't need saving, Kael. I need control."

"And you think that's what the Orb will give you?" His voice was incredulous, but the edge of it made me bristle. "You think you can control something that powerful without losing yourself in the process? You're not invincible, Alina."

His words hit harder than I expected, a sting that rattled around my chest like a rock in a tin can. He was right, of course. The Orb wasn't something I could control. Not completely. Every time I reached for it, I felt it pulling on me, like a siren song I couldn't stop singing along to. Every moment spent using it made the next one more urgent, more frantic. The idea of stopping—of letting go—was like trying to stop a freight train with bare hands. I didn't know how to do it.

"I'm not invincible," I muttered, more to myself than to him. The words tasted like iron, bitter and sharp.

Kael was quiet for a long time. I felt the weight of his stare as if it were pressing into me. He was too close, too close to see the mess I had become. But then he stepped forward, closing the gap between us. His proximity was suffocating, but there was something comforting about it, too, like a rope thrown to a drowning person.

"Then let me help," he repeated, his voice steady, calm.

I shook my head, my thoughts spiraling too quickly for me to process. "I don't know how to let you help," I said softly, the words a confession more than an admission of anything else.

There it was. The real fear I'd been avoiding for so long. The idea that letting Kael in meant letting go of control. It wasn't just the Orb I was holding on to—it was everything. The power, the magic, the way it made me feel like I was on top of the world, even as I felt myself slipping beneath the surface.

Kael reached out again, this time placing his hand on my shoulder. I stiffened under his touch, the instinct to pull away kicking in. But he didn't let go.

"You don't have to do this alone," he repeated, his tone softer now. "I'm here, Alina. Let me help you fight it."

I opened my mouth to respond, but before I could form the words, a sharp pain shot through my chest, a jolt so strong that I gasped. It felt like the world had turned upside down in an instant. The Orb, still tucked safely in my bag, was thrumming with power, as if it had awakened from a deep sleep and was demanding my attention. The magic was no longer a subtle thing. It was a presence, pressing against my skin, curling under my ribs like a living thing, hungry, insistent.

My hand went to my bag instinctively, but Kael caught my wrist before I could reach it. His grip was firm, unyielding, but there was panic in his eyes now.

"No, Alina. Don't."

But it was too late. The Orb had me, its pull too strong to fight. I could feel it coursing through me, its fire licking at the edges of my soul, and I was helpless against it. The city around us seemed to blur, the sounds fading as everything else went quiet, as if the world were holding its breath.

"Kael," I breathed, my voice barely a whisper, though I didn't know if I was calling out to him or to something else entirely. The power surged within me, and I felt it rip through me, my mind splitting in two as I struggled to hold on.

Kael's grip tightened, and for a second, I thought I saw fear flicker across his face. But then, just as quickly, his expression changed, his features hardening. He stepped closer, his face inches from mine, and I could feel his warmth seeping into me, even as the fire from the Orb burned hotter, stronger.

"You need to fight it," Kael urged, his voice low, but there was a kind of desperation in it now, something raw, something I had never heard from him before.

I swallowed, trying to focus, to push back against the magic that wanted to consume me. But the fire was too bright, too powerful. It was suffocating.

And then, just as quickly as it had started, everything stopped.

The world shifted back into place, and I was left standing there, gasping for breath, my head spinning.

But something was wrong.

I looked at Kael—his eyes wide with disbelief—and then at my hand.

And I realized, with a sinking feeling in my stomach, that the Orb was no longer in my bag.

It was in my hand.

And it wasn't just glowing—it was alive.

Chapter 15: The Veil of Deception

The room was alive with whispers, the air thick with the scent of expensive perfume and the delicate hum of violins. Velvet curtains in deep shades of burgundy framed the tall windows of the citadel, where the moonlight spilled in like liquid silver, pooling on the marble floors. It was a world of opulence and mystery, where every corner seemed to hold a secret, and every mask concealed more than just a face. The masked ball had been heralded as the event of the season, and the city's elite were out in full force, gliding across the floor in silk gowns and tailored suits, their steps measured, their eyes sharp.

    I stood at the edge of the grand hall, taking in the scene, my own mask feeling more like a cage than a disguise. It was intricately designed, with thin black lace and glimmering silver threads, but under it, my expression was anything but elegant. Inside, my thoughts were a chaotic swirl of strategy and suspicion, with one name echoing in my mind—Selene. She was here tonight, somewhere in the crowd, her schemes as murky as the gown she wore. The night would be the perfect opportunity to gather information, and I had no intention of letting it slip away.

    I could feel Kael at my side before I saw him, a shadow of danger that seemed to linger in the air around us. His presence was magnetic, like a storm waiting to break, but the mask he wore, a simple black one that hid his sharp features, didn't lessen the tension between us. It only made it sharper. There was something about him tonight, something different in the way he moved, his body language more guarded, like he had something to hide. But then, hadn't we all come to this ball with secrets?

    "You look like you're about to turn this place upside down," Kael's voice was a low murmur, his lips curving into a smile that didn't reach his eyes. He leaned in closer, his breath warm against my ear, sending a shiver down my spine. "Careful, it's not as easy to hide here as you think."

I shot him a sideways glance, our eyes locking for a brief, electric moment before I looked away, pretending to adjust the lace at the edge of my sleeve. "You underestimate me, Kael. I've spent my life hiding in plain sight."

His laughter, soft and dangerous, lingered in the air. "Oh, I don't underestimate you," he said, his voice dropping lower. "But you're not the only one with secrets tonight."

I turned back to face him, my gaze narrowing slightly. "What are you trying to say?"

"Nothing," he replied too quickly, his eyes flickering toward the other guests, his hand subtly brushing against mine, sending a spark through me. "Just... be careful who you trust. Not everyone in this room is here for the same reason you are."

I felt the weight of his words settle in the pit of my stomach. Something was off, but I couldn't put my finger on it. Not yet. The night was still young, and every step I took brought me closer to a truth that might be far more dangerous than I could imagine.

A flicker of movement caught my eye. Selene, her dark hair pinned into a sleek chignon, was making her way toward the grand staircase at the center of the ballroom. She moved with the grace of a dancer, her gown sweeping behind her in a cascade of midnight blue fabric. It was difficult to read her, but I could feel the air shift when she passed, as if everyone knew she held the strings to something far bigger than any of them could understand.

"She's here," I murmured under my breath, almost to myself. But Kael heard me, his body tensing beside me.

"Then we'll get closer," he said, his voice sharp. "You know the plan. I'll stay with you, and we'll find out what we need to."

I nodded, though my pulse was quickening. The thought of being so close to her, to finally having a chance to unmask her—both figuratively and literally—sent a thrill through me. But that same thrill was tempered with the dark, nagging feeling that there was something more to this than just a simple game of cat and mouse.

As I moved through the crowd, my eyes never leaving Selene, Kael's presence beside me was a constant reminder that I wasn't alone in this. His proximity was both comforting and unsettling, and the way he seemed to anticipate every shift in the crowd, every subtle change in the air, left me wondering just how much he knew. The tension between us grew with every passing second, as if we were walking a tightrope, one wrong move away from falling.

And then, just as I was about to reach Selene's side, Kael stopped me with a hand on my arm.

"Wait," he said, his voice low. "Look around. This isn't the only game being played tonight."

I hesitated, then slowly turned my head. A small group of men stood just beyond the edge of the crowd, their faces obscured by elaborate masks. But there was something in the way they held themselves, something in the way they watched the room. It was the same kind of intensity that Kael exuded when he was on edge. And suddenly, the room seemed smaller, the shadows deeper. I swallowed hard.

"What are they doing?" I whispered, my voice barely audible over the music.

Kael's eyes darkened. "They're watching her," he said, his grip tightening around my arm. "And they're waiting for the right moment to make their move."

The realization hit me like a slap. Selene wasn't the only one with plans. This night, this ball, wasn't just a chance to learn her secrets—it was a battleground.

The ballroom was a living thing, alive with the murmurs of the wealthy and the hidden agendas of the powerful. Every masked face around me held a piece of the puzzle I had been trying to solve for months. But even as I tried to focus on the task at hand, I couldn't shake the unsettling sensation of being watched—watched by eyes that weren't as interested in Selene as they were in me. They followed me in subtle shifts, like ghosts lingering just out of sight, their presence far too palpable.

Kael didn't miss the change either. He moved closer, brushing against me in a way that wasn't quite accidental. His scent, faintly cedar and something darker, something earthy, clung to me as if it had always been there. "Stay close," he murmured, his voice a low promise that didn't feel like an instruction but more like an order wrapped in velvet.

I didn't argue. It wasn't that I trusted him completely—no, that would be foolish—but there was something about the way he seemed to anchor me in the madness of the crowd, something that made me feel less like a pawn in a game and more like someone with a purpose.

We moved slowly through the throng of guests, our steps in time with the waltz that echoed through the cavernous hall. The music was an undercurrent to the conversation, a gentle hum that tried to mask the unspoken tension in the room. Each footstep, each glance, felt deliberate. But it was when I caught the eye of one of the men from earlier, standing near the grand staircase with his back to the wall, that I felt the first real pang of danger.

His mask was simple, a matte black with no embellishment. Yet the intensity in his eyes could have burned through steel. A shiver ran down my spine, and I could feel Kael stiffen beside me, his posture straightening as if preparing for a threat.

"Do you know him?" I asked, though I wasn't sure I wanted to know the answer.

"Not exactly," Kael replied. He didn't look at the man, but his gaze had already moved to a different corner of the room. "But that's a face you don't forget. He's been part of Selene's inner circle for a while now. Very loyal, very dangerous."

My mind raced. The pieces were coming together, but not in any way I had imagined. If Selene's men were so close, I was standing on the edge of something far deeper than a mere social gathering. I tried to push the thought aside—this was the moment to act, not to second-guess.

Just as I took a step forward, a sudden voice at my elbow made me freeze. "You seem lost, my lady."

I didn't need to turn to know who it was. His voice was smooth, too smooth, like oil on silk. I'd heard it too many times in my nightmares. Selene's right hand.

"Lost?" I said, turning slowly, maintaining the poise I had perfected over years of navigating such high-society gatherings. My gaze flickered to Kael, who had not moved an inch, but his body was taut as a wire.

The man in front of me, tall and lean with hair that glimmered under the soft chandeliers, wore a mask that was just flamboyant enough to be unmemorable—a simple gold leaf design, meant to blend in yet catch the eye all at once. I had learned long ago that it was the people who wanted attention the least who could be the most dangerous.

"You're far too composed to be here for the social scene," he said, his lips curling into something that resembled a smirk. His eyes, sharp and calculating, never left my face. "What's your true purpose, hmm? I've been trying to figure it out all evening."

"I could ask you the same thing," I replied, my tone playful but not quite convincing. "But I'm afraid the only answer I'll get from you will be a riddle."

His laugh was low, almost imperceptible. "Touché," he said, his gaze flickering to Kael, who was still a shadow at my side. "But I can't help but wonder—what would a charming, clever woman like you be after in a place like this? It's all far too... well, predictable."

There was an edge to his words now, something darker that seemed to crack through his polished veneer. He wasn't just playing a game anymore; he was testing me. And I was starting to feel the heat of it.

"Predictable?" I raised an eyebrow, glancing around the room at the swirl of silk, satin, and whispered secrets. "You must be attending a different party, then."

His smile widened, but it didn't reach his eyes. "You don't know as much as you think you do, my lady."

Before I could respond, a hand—bigger, stronger, more commanding—clamped down on his shoulder, spinning him around to face someone far more intimidating than me. I recognized the other figure instantly—a man with a jaw set like stone and eyes that pierced through the mask.

"Leave her be, Dorian," the newcomer said, his voice cool and cutting. "We don't need to play your games tonight."

Dorian's lips twitched as if holding back a retort, but he straightened and offered a half bow, an exaggerated gesture of submission. "Of course. My apologies."

Without another word, he turned and melted into the crowd, disappearing as quickly as he had appeared. But the sense of unease remained, a knot in my stomach that tightened with every passing second.

The man who had intervened—tall, broad-shouldered, and with a presence that commanded attention even in a room full of powerful people—turned to face me. His eyes, a cool shade of gray, assessed me with the precision of someone who'd seen far too much.

"Are you all right?" he asked, his tone low but sincere.

I blinked, taken aback by his sudden appearance. "Yes, thank you. I suppose I should thank you for your... timely intervention."

His lips curved, just slightly. "It's no trouble. Dorian has a knack for creating trouble. I've been keeping an eye on him for a while."

"Good to know," I muttered, trying not to feel the sting of his piercing gaze. The weight of his attention was unsettling. "And you are?"

"Callum." He extended his hand, his grip firm and steady. There was no pretense about him, no games. Just the raw, unsettling reality of a man who was as much a part of this world as anyone else.

I shook his hand, but something about the way his fingers wrapped around mine sent a shiver down my spine. Callum wasn't here just to play the part of an innocent bystander. No, he was here to stake his claim. And that meant, I was no longer sure where the game began and where it ended.

The conversation with Callum hung in the air, thick with unspoken things. The brief contact of our hands had left a ripple, a tiny fracture in my carefully crafted armor. His eyes, unblinking and steady, weighed me like a book, each page turned with an ease that unnerved me. There was no sense of pretense with him, no elaborate mask or careful flirtation. He was, at the core, entirely unbothered by the games that the rest of the room seemed to thrive on. It was in the way he stood—still, grounded—and the way his presence seemed to swell in the spaces between us. I should have felt safe with Kael close by, but something about Callum made my skin prickle, as if the air itself had grown heavier.

"I've been meaning to introduce myself," Callum said, his lips curling into a subtle, knowing smile. "But I hadn't expected to do it quite like this."

"Seems like the night's full of surprises," I replied, my tone light but my mind on edge. I glanced over my shoulder to where Kael had begun to drift toward the edges of the room, blending seamlessly with the guests. I couldn't help but feel the pull between us, a strange tug-of-war I couldn't explain. "I'd say you've already done more than enough for introductions."

His eyes lingered on me, thoughtful and calculating, as if weighing every word I spoke. "I'm here to watch," he said, the words almost lost beneath the low hum of music and laughter. "To see what you might do next."

I raised an eyebrow, letting the words sink in. "And what exactly do you think I'm going to do?"

A flash of something dangerous flickered in his eyes before he answered. "I don't know. But I'm betting it's something far more interesting than the charades going on around us."

I opened my mouth to respond, but the sharp crackle of tension from across the room made me pause. Dorian had returned, only this time he was not alone. The group of men he'd been with earlier had gathered, their heads bent together in quiet, urgent conversation. Selene's name was barely a whisper between them, but I caught it on the wind, along with the promise of something deeper, something much darker than I had anticipated.

I excused myself, offering Callum a polite smile that didn't reach my eyes. There were far more important things to focus on, and the night was beginning to fracture into something that no longer felt like a simple masquerade.

Moving toward Kael, I noticed a slight shift in his posture as I approached. He didn't look at me, but I could sense his awareness, his intuition honed by years in this world of smoke and mirrors. It was clear he was watching for something—someone. The way his eyes flicked toward the back of the room was enough to make my heart race.

I stopped next to him, close enough to feel the heat of his body but far enough to avoid the intensity of his gaze. "What is it?" I asked, my voice low enough to blend with the music.

Kael didn't speak right away. Instead, he scanned the room, his eyes narrowing as they lingered on a shadowed figure standing just beyond the grand chandelier. It was a woman, dressed in a dark gown that shimmered like liquid night. She was still, her back to the crowd, her posture unnaturally rigid. She had the look of someone who didn't belong in a room filled with glittering masks, her presence too heavy, too deliberate.

"Selene?" I ventured, though I wasn't sure.

"Not yet," Kael muttered, barely more than a breath. His fingers brushed mine, a quick but deliberate touch that sent a tremor through me. "But someone is moving against her."

I turned toward him, startled. "What do you mean?"

He took a half-step away from me, his eyes scanning the people around us like a hawk searching for prey. "There's more at play here than just her. And I think we've just stumbled into the middle of it."

The sudden proximity of the woman—who, as it turned out, was Selene herself—was enough to freeze the blood in my veins. She glided toward the back of the ballroom with a single-mindedness that sent waves of unease through me. As her steps became more confident, more deliberate, I realized what Kael meant. Whatever she had planned for this evening, it was no longer about gathering power. It was something far more dangerous.

I leaned in closer, my voice barely a whisper. "We need to get to her, now."

Kael hesitated, his eyes flickering toward the path I intended to take. "Wait." His hand shot out to stop me, a firm grip on my wrist. "Not yet."

"Not yet?" I repeated, disbelieving. "She's about to disappear into that room, and you want me to wait?"

He gave me a hard look, his expression unreadable. "Do you really think you can take on whatever she's planning by yourself?"

My heart skipped a beat. Kael was right. The night wasn't just about uncovering Selene's plans—it was about surviving them.

Before I could protest, a shout rang through the air, sharp and sudden, cutting through the music and chatter like a knife. The crowd froze, and I spun toward the sound, instinctively grabbing Kael's arm to steady myself. The woman who had been watching us, who had been waiting for this very moment, was now gone, swallowed by the crowd.

And in her place was a figure—a figure whose mask was not the typical silver or gold, but black as midnight, with streaks of crimson running down either side. The man behind it, or whatever he was, was cloaked in shadows so deep that even the chandeliers above couldn't touch him.

The air shifted. The room grew colder.

And then, without warning, he turned toward me. His eyes—deep, bottomless black—locked with mine. My breath hitched.

"Run," Kael whispered, his voice sharp as glass. "Now."

Chapter 16: The Edge of Truth

The pages smelled of aged parchment and forgotten knowledge, a scent that was both comforting and unsettling. I had spent countless hours in this room, reading, learning, unraveling the secrets of the Ravenmark, yet every word seemed to lead to more questions than answers. The runes danced across the pages, their meanings shifting as if mocking my attempts to make sense of them. I had become too familiar with the ancient language, yet not nearly familiar enough. Each time I thought I understood, something new would appear, elusive, like the edge of a dream slipping from my grasp the moment I tried to hold on.

Kael's presence lingered in the doorway, heavy and unmoving, a shadow among shadows. His silence was a weapon in itself. I could feel his gaze on me, sharp as a blade, and I was acutely aware of how it twisted the air between us. His very stillness seemed to vibrate with tension, an energy that hummed beneath my skin, demanding attention. He had never been a man of many words, but tonight his silence spoke volumes. It felt as though he were waiting for something—a moment, a decision, something that would tip the scales between us.

The crackle of the fire in the hearth barely registered in the background, its warmth a faint comfort against the chill of the stone walls. I couldn't seem to focus on anything but the words on the page, the weight of them pressing into my mind. The Ravenmark wasn't just a curse; it was a weapon, an ancient power that could change the course of everything. The prophecy was clear, but its implications... they were far from simple. In order to wield this power, I would have to cross a line, a line I wasn't sure I was ready to cross.

The pages blurred before my eyes as I read the same passage for the third time. The prophecy was written in fragments, pieces scattered across various texts, many of them lost to time. But the fragments I had found spoke of destruction, of rebirth, and of a bloodline marked by the Raven, its power passed down through generations. I was the heir to that power—whether I wanted it or not. The Ravenmark was not just a symbol of my curse; it was a key, a way to unlock the true extent of what I could become. And yet, there was a price.

"You're wasting your time," Kael's voice finally broke the silence, low and edged with something I couldn't place. He pushed off from the doorframe, his boots making soft echoes against the stone floor as he crossed the room to stand beside me. He didn't touch me, but his presence was a tangible force, as though he were magnetized to the very air around me. "You're looking for answers, but you're not ready for the truth."

I glanced up at him, my heart skipping in my chest. I wasn't sure if it was the weight of his words or the way his presence filled the space, demanding my attention, but I couldn't look away. "And what do you know about it, Kael?" I asked, my voice sharper than I intended. "You've never known what it's like to carry this... burden."

His expression didn't change, but there was something in his eyes—an old hurt, a sharpness, a memory—that made me second-guess my words. He didn't react the way I expected. There was no anger, no cutting retort. Just quiet. His gaze flicked to the book in my hands, then back to me.

"You think I don't know what it means to carry a weight?" His voice was low, controlled, but I could hear the underlying tension. "I've seen it, felt it, lived it. I know what happens when you let something like this consume you. And you're walking a dangerous path, Lia."

I could feel the truth of his words pressing down on me, the way his voice had dropped to something barely above a whisper, but I couldn't let go of the book. I had come too far to turn back now. "I don't have a choice," I whispered, more to myself than to him. The words tasted bitter, but they were true. This was bigger than me. Bigger than anything I could have imagined.

Kael's eyes softened for just a moment, his expression unreadable once again. But the brief flicker of something—compassion, maybe?—was enough to make my pulse race. It was the first time I had ever seen that side of him. The mask of the warrior, the hard edge that he had always worn so carefully, cracked just enough to show a glimpse of the man beneath. I wasn't sure if it made him more dangerous or more human, but either way, it unsettled me.

"You always have a choice," he said, his tone gentler now, almost pleading. "And you can choose not to carry this burden. You can choose to put it down."

I shook my head, a harsh laugh escaping me. "And let Selene win? Let her destroy everything we've fought for? No, Kael. I have no choice." My fingers tightened on the edge of the book, as if I could grasp onto the words themselves for strength. "I have to do this."

The room seemed to contract around us, the air thick with unsaid words and unspoken fears. He stood there, still as stone, watching me with that same unreadable expression. I wanted to say something more, to convince him, to make him understand. But something in his gaze stopped me. He knew. He had always known.

"So what's next?" he asked, his voice rough, like it had been dragged through gravel.

I looked back down at the page, at the cryptic runes that seemed to pulse in the dim light. "Next?" I repeated, my voice sounding hollow in my own ears. "Next, I find a way to control the Ravenmark. And then... then I destroy Selene."

I didn't look up as Kael's footsteps came closer, the soft tread of his boots on the worn stone floor punctuating the quiet like the ticking of an unseen clock. It wasn't that I was avoiding him; it was more that the words he'd spoken—those heavy, ominous words—hung between us like a fog I couldn't clear. My eyes remained locked on the text, not because I had any hope of deciphering it, but because it gave me something to focus on, something tangible to grasp as the world seemed to shift around me. I had come here seeking answers, but now, I was starting to wonder if the questions were even worth asking.

Kael's shadow fell over me, blocking the soft glow of candlelight from the ancient pages. He was always so impossibly close, and yet so distant. I could feel his heat at my back, but it wasn't a comfort. It was a reminder that he could slip away just as easily as he had come. His voice was near, but not near enough. "You don't have to do this, Lia."

I let out a soft, dismissive laugh. "You're not the first one to tell me that."

"Then why are you still here?" His words weren't harsh, but they still carried a weight. There was something in his voice that made me pause, a subtle shift in the cadence of his words, a plea buried under the layers of restraint. Kael was used to keeping his emotions under lock and key, a soldier's demeanor honed by years of survival in the unforgiving shadows of war. But tonight, there was an edge to him. One I wasn't sure I understood.

I pushed the book aside with an almost violent motion, the pages ruffling in protest as if they were angry to be abandoned. The silence that followed felt thick, oppressive. A fog in my lungs. I finally turned to face him, my gaze lifting to meet his. He was still as unyielding as a mountain, his expression unreadable. But his eyes—those stormy eyes, always watching me like he could see straight through my skin—were different now. It wasn't just the weight of the situation that made me feel like I was standing at the edge of something I didn't want to understand. No, it was the way Kael was looking at me. The quiet urgency there, the unsaid things hanging between us.

"Because there is no choice," I said, my voice flat but firm. "Not for me, not for any of us. If I don't do this, Selene will win. And we both know what that means."

He didn't respond immediately, which made me realize just how much I hated that silence. We could have filled it with words, or arguments, or the sharp clatter of our usual banter, but instead, it lingered between us, like an invisible thread pulling tighter and tighter.

"I'm not asking you to be a hero, Lia." His voice was softer now, a hint of something else slipping through the cracks—something more vulnerable, more raw. But I wasn't sure if it was meant for me, or just for himself. "I'm asking you to think. To stop rushing into this. We don't have the luxury of making mistakes anymore."

I swallowed, the words feeling like sandpaper against my throat. The truth was, I hadn't stopped to think. Not really. Every move I made, every step I took, was in response to a world on the brink of destruction, a world where I was the only one who could stop it. The weight of that responsibility sat heavily on my chest, pressing down, making it hard to breathe. And yet, Kael's words—those carefully measured words—suddenly felt like an anchor in a storm.

"You think I don't know that?" I said, my voice low, but not without the bite of frustration I felt. "I'm the one who's been living with this mark, this power, this curse. I'm the one who has to figure out how to use it without destroying everything I care about. You think I don't understand the stakes?"

He exhaled, a sharp sound that sliced through the tension in the room. "I know you understand. But that doesn't mean you have to carry it all alone."

I stared at him, unable to say anything for a long moment. His words felt like they should have been comforting, but instead, they only served to remind me of the one thing I couldn't escape: we were running out of time. I could feel it in the marrow of my bones, in the tightening of the air around us. The clock was ticking, and we were inching closer to an end I wasn't sure I could prevent. The weight of that truth pressed on me harder than anything I'd ever known.

"I'm not alone," I said, my voice small now. The bite was gone, replaced with something fragile. "I have you, don't I?"

His silence was enough to make me wish I could take the words back. Kael's gaze hardened, the mask slipping back into place as quickly as it had fallen. He stepped away from me, his posture stiffening. "I'm not here to be your crutch, Lia. I'm here to fight beside you. But if you think you're the only one carrying a burden in this fight..." He trailed off, and I couldn't help but feel the sting of something left unsaid. The weight of something he wasn't ready to share, not yet.

The fire crackled in the background, but the warmth it offered seemed distant, irrelevant against the chill that had settled between us. I wanted to say something, to fill the silence, but my words felt inadequate, lost in the vastness of everything that loomed ahead. Kael didn't turn back to look at me as he moved toward the door, his steps deliberate and resolute. Before he left, though, he paused, just long enough for me to feel the weight of his presence without a word.

"You're not alone, Lia. Not unless you choose it."

And with that, he was gone. Leaving me alone with the echo of his words, and the promise of the storm to come.

The silence in the library was suffocating, wrapping around me like a heavy cloak, so thick I could hardly breathe. The shadows seemed to stretch longer, reaching for the edges of the room, and I wondered, not for the first time, if the walls had always felt this close. The warmth of the fire flickering in the hearth had turned to a distant hum, as if even it recognized the weight of the moment.

I stood there, my fingers still pressed against the ancient parchment, feeling the grooves of the runes beneath my skin, almost as if the text were alive, pulling me in, urging me to trust it. But Kael's words rang in my ears, far too close for comfort. Searching for answers I wasn't ready to find. Was it possible? Could I really be unprepared for the truth that lay buried in these texts? I'd always been the type to demand answers, to chase after every thread until I had unraveled it all. But this—this felt different. It wasn't the type of knowledge you could scrub from your mind once it had taken root.

"Does it ever bother you?" I asked, breaking the tension that had built up between us. My voice felt small, but the question wasn't. "That you can't control what's coming?"

Kael's eyes flickered toward me, but his face remained impassive. "We don't get to control it, Lia. That's the lie we tell ourselves. We can only respond to it."

I frowned, my fingers absently tracing the ink on the page as I absorbed his words. "That's not very comforting."

His lips twitched, just the slightest hint of a smile that I almost didn't catch. "Comfort isn't the point. The point is survival."

I shook my head, the frustration of not having a clear path forward gnawing at me. I turned away from the book and moved to the window, letting the cool air brush against my skin as I gazed out into the city. The skyline of Denver was still lit with the remnants of the day, the bright lights of downtown mingling with the darkness that was falling like a heavy curtain. There was something about this city—the pulse of it, the way it never really slept—that made the uncertainty feel worse. Here, every choice I made carried weight, and every decision felt as though it had the potential to change everything.

The weight of the Ravenmark on my chest seemed to grow heavier with each passing moment, an invisible weight I could neither escape nor embrace. I glanced down at the mark, still hidden beneath the layers of my clothes, and wondered how long I had left before it consumed me, before it overtook my every thought and action. Would I recognize the moment when the transformation would be complete, or would I wake up one morning to find myself someone I didn't recognize?

I pressed my fingers to the glass, my reflection staring back at me, distorted in the fractured light from the streetlamps below. "Do you ever wonder what's going to happen when this is all over?" I asked, barely recognizing my own voice. The words felt too fragile to speak aloud, but I couldn't stop them. "When we win—or lose—what's left for us?"

Kael moved to stand beside me, close but not too close, just far enough to remind me that we were both still standing at the edge of something we couldn't predict. "We'll deal with it when we get there."

"But what if 'getting there' means something we can't come back from?" My voice cracked, and I bit my lip, immediately regretting my words. This wasn't like me. I didn't hesitate. I didn't second-guess myself. But there was something about the Ravenmark, something about the power it promised, that had begun to twist my thoughts into unfamiliar shapes.

"I'm not worried about what we can't change." Kael's voice softened, though the firmness was still there, like a line drawn in the sand. "I'm worried about what we can."

I turned toward him, finally meeting his gaze fully. "What's that supposed to mean?"

His jaw tightened, and I could see the muscle there working under his skin, as though he were fighting to keep something—an emotion, a truth—tucked away. "It means you don't have to carry the weight of the world on your shoulders alone. But if you're determined to do this, if you're going to walk this road, then you'll need to decide right now whether or not you're willing to become the person you're meant to be. Because that person won't just be a savior, Lia. She'll be a weapon. And once you take that step, there's no going back."

His words, sharp and final, hung in the air between us. I felt something stir in my chest, a knot that had been sitting there, tight and cold, for what felt like years. But there was something else there too, something heavier. A sense of inevitability, as though the fates had already chosen their path for me, and all I could do was follow.

I swallowed, my throat dry as I tried to steady my breath. "I don't know if I can be that person," I admitted quietly. "What if I can't control it? What if I become everything I've been trying to avoid?"

Kael's eyes softened, the hardness of the soldier within him giving way to something else—something softer, more human. He didn't touch me, but I felt his presence in the air between us, solid and grounding. "You won't be alone, Lia," he said, the sincerity in his voice making my heart skip. "I'll be right there with you. I swear it."

I wanted to believe him. I wanted to believe that, no matter what happened, we could face it together. But in the pit of my stomach, there was a gnawing doubt I couldn't shake. The Ravenmark wasn't just mine to control. It had a life of its own, and when it rose, it would rise with all the power of a storm.

I opened my mouth to speak, to tell him I was ready to face it, whatever it was. But before the words could leave my lips, a loud crash echoed from somewhere below, followed by the unmistakable sound of footsteps, fast and heavy, moving toward the citadel's entrance.

We both turned toward the door at the same time, our expressions mirrored—alert, wary, ready for whatever was coming next.

But neither of us were ready for the figure that appeared in the doorway, bloodied and breathless, eyes wild with fear.

"They're here," the figure gasped, falling to his knees. "They've found us."

Chapter 17: Flames and Shadows

The air in the training arena was thick, cloying with the acrid tang of smoke and the raw heat of magic being bent and twisted, desperate for control. I could barely hear the crackle of flames over the pounding of my heart, the rhythm of it a steady drum that matched the chaos of our battle. Kael and I were in the middle of it all, two forces of nature locked in a fierce, almost desperate dance, and every step we took felt like an argument. A fight, but not just with magic.

Kael's presence loomed at the edge of my peripheral vision—his shadowy form shifting as he commanded ice and fire in a whirlwind of controlled chaos. He didn't need to say anything to make his opinion known. His actions did all the talking. A sharp flick of his wrist sent an avalanche of glittering frost streaking toward me, and I raised my own hands to counter it with a burst of fire. The two elements clashed in a violent hiss, steam rising in an angry cloud. We were supposed to be allies. Supposed to be learning to fight as one. But every move we made felt like a challenge, a battle to prove who could dominate the arena.

"Stop trying to lead," he barked, his eyes burning with something fierce and untamed. The flames in his hair seemed to flicker brighter with every word, the heat radiating from him intense enough to make the air warp.

I gritted my teeth, my own temper flaring in response. "You think you're the only one who can control magic?" I shot back, launching a surge of power at him. It was sloppy, wild—barely controlled—but it was enough to send him skidding backward, his cloak catching fire for a split second before he doused it with a swift swipe of ice.

For a moment, I stood there, chest heaving, fire flickering in my palms, and I realized that the burn in my veins wasn't just from the magic. It was from him. The way he never asked, only commanded. The way he looked at me like I was just another force to be conquered.

"You're impossible," I muttered under my breath, wiping sweat from my brow.

"You're not exactly easy to work with, either." His voice was edged with frustration, and I could see the muscle in his jaw twitch. But, for a fleeting second, there was something else there too—something almost... apologetic. He didn't say it, but the softening of his expression was enough. Maybe it wasn't all just anger between us. Maybe there was something more.

But then he raised his hands, ready to throw another wave of icy fury, and the moment passed. We were back to the fight.

"I didn't sign up to be your second in command," he added, his eyes flashing as his power coiled around him like an unchained beast. The ice at his feet groaned, the pressure of his emotions pulling at the very air around us.

"I'm not asking you to follow me, Kael," I shot back, my voice barely contained. "I'm asking you to stop trying to control everything."

His lips pressed into a thin line. "You want me to sit back and watch as you make a mess of this?" The words were harsh, but there was a crack in his armor—just a sliver of something real, something unguarded.

My eyes burned, and I felt the heat from my magic flare up in response to his challenge. "I can handle myself just fine. I don't need your help," I hissed, even though part of me knew the words were a lie. I wasn't just mad at him. I was mad at myself. For every time I thought I had control over my magic, only for it to slip through my fingers. For every time I tried to make a plan, and he derailed it with that cold arrogance of his. And yes, maybe a small part of me—just a small one—was mad because he made me feel like I wasn't good enough.

He took a step closer, his eyes locking on mine, and in that moment, the world seemed to narrow until it was just the two of us. The dust around us settled, the flames dimmed, and the magic in the air vibrated with a sharp, electric tension. For a heartbeat, there was silence—just the two of us, standing in the storm of our power, neither of us willing to back down.

"Then what do you want, Lia?" His voice was softer now, no longer laced with anger, but with something more dangerous. "What do you want from me?"

It was a question that hung in the air like smoke. I didn't have an answer, not right away. But there was something in his gaze that made my heart twist. It was vulnerability, thinly veiled beneath layers of ice and flame. The kind of thing that made you want to reach out and shatter it all—tear down the walls that kept him distant, kept us at odds. But I couldn't. Not yet.

"I want you to stop thinking you know everything," I finally said, my voice quieter now, more measured. "I'm trying, Kael. But I can't do this alone."

The words were out before I could stop them, and I instantly regretted them. This wasn't supposed to be a confession. This wasn't supposed to be about vulnerability. But there it was, hanging between us like a fragile thread.

For a long moment, he didn't speak. Then, slowly, he lowered his hands. The fire in his eyes dimmed, replaced with something I couldn't quite place. "We'll never win like this," I muttered, more to myself than to him.

To my surprise, he didn't argue. Instead, he extended his hand toward me, his voice softer than I had ever heard it. "Then let's figure it out together."

And just like that, the tension broke. The storm inside of me—inside both of us—began to subside, leaving behind something I hadn't expected: a sliver of hope, fragile and uncertain, but real.

I hesitated for a moment, unsure if I was imagining the softness in Kael's voice or if it was truly there, buried beneath the usual tension and cold arrogance. His hand hovered in front of me, a lifeline thrown across the chasm of our conflict. The fire in my veins simmered, but it wasn't from anger anymore. It was something else, something too quiet to name.

For a heartbeat, we simply stood there, surrounded by the remnants of our magical battle. The arena was a mess—charred earth, shattered ice, and the faint scent of sulfur hanging in the air like an old memory. My heart still raced from the exertion, but there was a strange calmness that had settled over me. I hadn't expected that.

His eyes met mine, the raw intensity in them still there, but now, under the flickering light of our combined magic, there was something vulnerable—almost tentative. It was the last thing I expected, but it was also the first thing that made sense.

I took a step forward, tentatively reaching out to grasp his hand. For a moment, there was just the quiet of the arena, our breaths the only sound breaking the silence between us. His fingers curled around mine with a gentleness that caught me off guard, as though he was afraid I might shatter if he held on too tightly.

"We need to stop fighting against each other," I said softly, looking up at him. "If we're going to survive whatever's coming, we have to trust each other."

Kael's gaze didn't leave mine, and for the first time in a long while, I saw something flicker in his eyes—something more than the cold distance he wore like armor. Something real.

"Yeah," he said, voice low, the sharp edge gone. "Maybe you're right."

And just like that, the air between us shifted. It was subtle, like the first breeze before a storm, but it was there. We were no longer enemies, no longer competing for control. We were allies. And for the first time in weeks, I felt a flicker of hope that maybe—just maybe—we could make this work.

The arena had grown eerily quiet, the magic in the air crackling with the residue of our power. It felt like the calm before a new battle. But instead of pulling away, Kael moved closer, his hand still gripping mine, not in a possessive way but in a way that suggested he was willing to give as much as I was. I met his gaze, unsure if I should say something, if I even had the right words to match the moment.

He smiled, a small, almost reluctant curve of his lips that softened his usually intense features. "Well, we've made a mess of this place," he muttered, glancing around at the destruction we'd caused. "But it looks like it's worth cleaning up."

The tension that had been building between us for weeks finally broke with that simple observation. I laughed, a quiet chuckle that bubbled up despite myself. "Maybe we should focus on getting through today before we start worrying about the arena," I said, feeling lighter than I had in what felt like forever.

Kael raised an eyebrow. "And how do you propose we do that?"

I met his eyes and shrugged, a sense of mischief creeping into my voice. "We stop throwing fire at each other and start figuring out how to make it work. Together."

His lips twitched into a smile again, this time genuine, and for the first time, I saw something resembling warmth in him. "I think I can manage that," he said, his grip on my hand tightening for just a moment before he released it, stepping back.

But there was a shift. A quiet understanding between us, unspoken but undeniable. We were in this together. Whatever it was. Whatever came next.

As we made our way toward the edge of the arena, the clang of armor and the sound of footsteps interrupted the silence. Seraphina appeared from behind a pillar, her presence like a weight settling over the scene. She took one look at the wreckage—burnt ground, shards of ice scattered across the floor—and raised an eyebrow. "Well, it seems you've made progress."

Kael and I exchanged a look. "It's a start," I said, my voice steady, though there was a hint of uncertainty that I couldn't quite hide.

Seraphina crossed her arms, surveying us with a calculating look. "That's one way of putting it. But if you two are going to survive the war coming our way, you'll need more than just a truce. You need to learn how to think as one."

She wasn't wrong, of course. But somehow, in that moment, I felt more confident about the road ahead than I had in weeks. Kael and I had always been on opposite sides, fighting for control, fighting for our own survival. But there was something different now. Something stronger. We had found common ground, something we could build on.

"One step at a time," I said, glancing at Kael. "We'll figure it out."

Seraphina's gaze softened, just a fraction, before she turned away. "I hope so," she said. "Because the clock is ticking."

The weight of her words hit me then, a sharp reminder that we weren't just training for some petty competition. The war was coming. And whether we liked it or not, Kael and I would have to stand together if we had any hope of surviving.

But, for the first time, I wasn't afraid of what came next. I was ready to face it. With him.

The walk back to the compound was quieter than I expected, the tension between Kael and me having dissolved into something like an uneasy truce. The streets of the city stretched out before us, the fading evening light casting long shadows that seemed to match the quiet in my chest. I should have been worried—Seraphina's warning still echoed in my ears. We weren't prepared for what was coming. But in that moment, walking beside Kael, a strange sort of peace had settled over me. Something I hadn't felt in weeks.

The world outside the compound was bustling as usual, the traffic of the late afternoon moving like a river through the heart of downtown. People were rushing in and out of shops, catching up with friends, grabbing coffee from the corner cafe. It was the kind of city that never slowed down, a mix of grungy streets lined with vintage boutiques and towering office buildings that spoke to its quiet ambition. Denver had a way of taking everything—its thunderstorms, its snow-capped mountains, its neon-lit nights—and making them feel like part of a living, breathing thing. And for the first time since I'd come back, I felt like I might be able to breathe again, too.

But the quiet between Kael and me didn't last for long.

"I never asked for any of this," he muttered, his voice low, rough. We were almost at the gates of the compound, and I could feel his unease creeping back into his tone. "You think I wanted to be dragged into some magical war? Or be stuck with someone who—" He stopped himself, clenching his jaw as if the words had tasted wrong on his tongue.

I raised an eyebrow at him, catching the way his shoulders tensed. "Someone who what? Someone who can't control their magic? Someone who's only here because they didn't have a choice?"

Kael's eyes flickered with something—hurt, anger, frustration—and I realized too late that I'd pushed a button I shouldn't have.

"Maybe I didn't ask for this," he said, his voice quieter now, less defensive. "But I'm here, aren't I? Just like you are. And I don't walk away from things I start."

I could feel the words hanging there, unspoken between us. I had heard those words from him before—only in different contexts, and often spoken in anger. But now there was something else behind them. Something that made me pause.

"You're here because of duty," I said, my voice softening. "But what if it's more than that? What if it's because you know this is where you belong?"

He looked over at me, his expression unreadable. "Belong?" He almost laughed, though it lacked humor. "This isn't some fairy tale, Lia. People don't belong in wars. They survive them. If they're lucky."

The truth of his words hit me harder than I expected. What had I been thinking? That we could just walk through this together, that somehow we'd be better than the sum of our parts? The war wasn't going to be kind. No matter how much we trusted each other, no matter how many walls we tore down between us, the reality was still there, looming in the distance.

"We don't get to choose our battles," I said finally, the words tasting like ash on my tongue. "But we do get to choose how we fight them."

Kael nodded slowly, his lips pressed together in a thin line. "Yeah. That's true."

We walked in silence the rest of the way, the heavy weight of what was coming pressing down on us both. There was no denying it—Seraphina had been right. We were nowhere near ready for what we were about to face. The training, the magic, it was all just the beginning. We had no idea what was waiting for us on the other side.

But maybe that was okay. Maybe it was just a matter of putting one foot in front of the other.

The compound was quiet when we entered, the only sound the hum of the overhead lights and the occasional click of shoes on tile as we made our way toward the main hall. The walls here felt like they were made of something other than stone, like they had witnessed too many battles to remember. Seraphina was waiting for us, her back turned as she gazed out the tall windows that looked out over the city. She didn't move as we entered, didn't acknowledge us right away. But I could feel the tension in her posture. The warning.

"You've made progress," she said after a long moment, her voice clipped. "But not enough. Not nearly enough."

I sighed, rolling my shoulders. "We're getting there."

"We don't have the luxury of time," Seraphina shot back, finally turning to face us. Her eyes were sharp, calculating, the weariness of leadership etched into every line of her face. "You need to be ready. You need to learn to fight as one."

I exchanged a glance with Kael, who gave a subtle nod. We were used to her unyielding expectations, but the weight of her words hung heavy on both of us. If we didn't figure this out soon, we were in trouble.

"We will," I said, more determined than I felt. "We'll get it right."

She eyed me, her lips pressing into a thin line as if she were weighing my words. Finally, she nodded. "I hope so. Because the Council has just made their move."

Kael stiffened beside me. "What does that mean?"

Seraphina's gaze shifted to the windows, her expression hardening. "It means the war has begun."

I felt a chill that had nothing to do with the temperature of the room, a cold realization creeping through me. But before I could speak, the doors to the hall slammed open with a deafening crack, and a figure stepped into the doorway—dark eyes, shadowed features, the faintest smirk playing at the edge of his lips. He was dressed in black, his presence like a storm cloud gathering on the horizon.

And I knew, before he even spoke, that nothing would ever be the same again.

"Seraphina," he said, his voice cold and smooth. "I think it's time we had a little talk."

Chapter 18: The Web of Lies

The weight of Emberfall hung thick in the air as Kael and I stepped over the cracked cobblestones of the village square. The place felt like a forgotten dream, the kind that lingers at the edges of your mind, half-remembered but never fully understood. There were no birds, no children's laughter, only the eerie whisper of the wind brushing against the remnants of what once might have been a thriving community. Once, I imagined it had been a town alive with stories—maybe small-town gossip, maybe love affairs behind drawn curtains. But now? Emberfall had been abandoned to its ghosts, and they weren't the kind you could shake free with a laugh or a prayer.

The buildings were crumbling, their windows like hollow eyes staring out at us, watching our every step. A thick fog had rolled in from the surrounding forest, swirling around our boots as though it had a life of its own. I shivered involuntarily, wishing I could shake the sense that I was being pulled into something I had no business understanding. The mist was too thick, too heavy, like a curtain that kept us from seeing what lay beyond it.

Kael's silhouette beside me was the only anchor to reality. His presence, though steady, didn't bring the comfort I had once relied on. There was a space between us now, an unspoken distance that stretched wider with each passing hour. When we first started this mission, we were like two sides of the same coin—inseparable, a seamless partnership that cut through the chaos around us. But now? Now, it felt like we were just two people walking in parallel, barely touching but always aware of the silent divide.

The coded message that had come through our lines was the spark that set everything in motion. It was a warning. The traitor was here, somewhere in this ghost town, hiding in the ruins like a rat in the walls. And despite the layers of fog and the remnants of past lives, we were supposed to find them. I didn't know who I feared more—the traitor or the truth that would come with uncovering them.

"What do you think happened here?" I asked, my voice barely breaking through the heavy silence.

Kael's gaze swept over the empty street, his jaw clenched, his movements precise as always. "Maybe they ran. Or maybe... they knew too much." His words hung in the air like a dark omen, and I couldn't shake the feeling that the 'too much' might involve us.

I nodded absently, turning my gaze toward the distant outlines of the village's chapel. The doors hung open, abandoned to the elements. I took a step forward, drawn to the place despite myself. There was something about the hollowed-out buildings that invited you to search, as if the answers were buried under the ashes of what once was. Kael followed me, though his steps were slower, measured. His eyes flicked to me, searching my face for something—what, I couldn't tell. Something was off with him too, but I wasn't sure what.

The chapel's interior was dim, the only light filtering through the cracked stained glass windows above the altar, casting ghostly shadows on the dusty pews. The air inside felt thicker, as though it had been waiting for us. The scent of mildew mixed with the faint remnants of incense, a smell that clung to the walls and the bones of the place. I walked down the aisle, the tips of my boots scraping against the wooden floor with a sound far too loud for the stillness.

At the altar, the air shifted. The hairs on the back of my neck prickled, and I knew—something was here. But what? My fingers brushed against the edge of the wooden pulpit, and there, wedged between the cracked floorboards, I found it—a scrap of parchment, folded neatly as though it had been hidden in a hurry. I unfolded it carefully, my heart thudding in my chest.

It was a map.

Not just any map, though. This one was marked with symbols I didn't recognize. It was a blueprint of the village, but it wasn't drawn with ink. The lines were too precise, the edges too clean. I didn't need to be a scholar to know this wasn't some forgotten village map. This was something else entirely.

A whisper of a shadow crossed my peripheral vision, and before I could process what was happening, Kael's hand shot out, gripping my wrist. "We're not alone," he murmured. His voice was low, controlled, but there was a tension in it that spoke volumes.

I felt the hair on my arms rise, and I didn't need to look to know he was right. Every instinct told me that we had just stirred something we weren't ready to face. My grip tightened on the map, my eyes flicking toward the doors. There was a creak, a whisper of movement. Then, from the back of the chapel, a figure stepped out from the shadows.

It was him. The man we had been hunting. But it wasn't the face I expected. This wasn't some mysterious outsider, some foreign agent who had slipped through our fingers. No, this was someone I knew. Someone I trusted.

The realization hit like a punch to the gut. It wasn't just betrayal that we were facing—it was the kind of treachery that came from within.

And suddenly, it all clicked into place. The whispers. The false leads. The strange silence between Kael and me. The traitor wasn't just some anonymous force trying to destroy us. They had been in our midst the entire time.

"Welcome home," the figure said, a smirk playing at the corner of his lips.

And just like that, everything I thought I knew unraveled before me.

The man's voice carried through the chapel, but it wasn't just the words that struck me. It was the cool certainty in his tone, the smugness of someone who knew they held the upper hand. I fought the instinct to react—my first impulse was to scream, to demand explanations, to shove him into the truth I knew he couldn't deny. But I didn't. I didn't move, didn't even breathe. I held onto the map like a lifeline, its edges digging into my palm.

Kael's hand was still wrapped tightly around my wrist, and I could feel the pulse of his heart beating against my skin—fast, too fast. But it wasn't fear. It was something else. Something deeper. Something I didn't want to acknowledge.

"Lucas," I said, my voice steady despite the tremor that was threatening to break free. His name felt foreign in my mouth. "What are you doing here?"

The man—Lucas, a name that now tasted bitter—took a slow step forward, his boots making no sound on the old wood. There was something unnerving about the way he moved, like he was part of the shadows themselves, blending seamlessly into the dark corners of the chapel. His eyes, cold and calculating, never left mine.

"I should be asking you the same question, sweetheart." His lips curled into something too charming to be genuine. "But I suppose you've already figured it out. Haven't you?"

My stomach twisted into a knot, the reality settling over me like a blanket of ice. I had known something was wrong. Something had been off for weeks, since we started this mission. The way he always seemed to know too much. How he was always there when we needed him. His smile had been the same—charming, disarming. But now it felt like a mask, a façade that could shatter in a single breath.

Kael stepped in front of me, his posture tense, his hand still gripping his sword's hilt. He didn't speak, but I could hear the silent warning in his stance. He was ready, prepared for whatever Lucas was about to throw at us. And yet, the air between us had changed.

It wasn't just the presence of the traitor—it was the realization that our small, fragile world of trust had just been shattered.

I swallowed hard. "You're working for Selene." It wasn't a question—it was a statement, the truth crystallizing in my chest.

Lucas's grin only widened. "Oh, don't sound so surprised. I'd like to think I'm a man of ambition. A man who knows how to make the right alliances." He took another step forward, his eyes darting to the map in my hand. "But don't you worry, darling. I'm not here to make enemies. Well, not unless I have to."

The words hung in the air, like an unspoken threat. I could feel the tension tightening around us, knotting my chest with every passing second. Lucas wasn't here to chat about alliances or strategies. He was here to make sure we didn't leave this chapel alive.

Behind me, Kael's hand tightened around the sword hilt. "Get out of the way, Alys," he said quietly, his voice low and dangerous.

I didn't need to ask him what he meant. I'd never seen him so cold. His resolve was absolute—there was no room for hesitation in his tone. He'd do what had to be done, no questions asked. But I wasn't sure if I could let him.

Lucas raised an eyebrow, his eyes flicking between us, amused by the tension. "Alys, Kael. A fine little team you make. Did you ever stop to wonder what would happen if one of you betrayed the other?"

I stiffened. The question hit too close to home. "I don't know what you're talking about," I muttered, but the uncertainty in my voice betrayed me. Because deep down, I did know. The cracks were already there, waiting to widen.

"Don't you? I think you do." Lucas's voice dropped to a low murmur, and for a moment, it felt like he was speaking directly to me. "You've been on the edge of something for a while now, haven't you? Always asking questions, always wondering who's really behind the curtain." He tilted his head, watching me with that unnerving calm. "It's funny. You've spent so much time looking for the traitor that you forgot to look right in front of you."

I felt the ground shift beneath my feet, the weight of his words pressing down on me like a ton of bricks. The irony of it all wasn't lost on me. I had trusted Lucas. I had believed in him. And now, standing here, I realized just how wrong I had been. The betrayal stung deeper than I could have ever anticipated.

"You think this is a game?" Kael's voice snapped, harsh and cutting through the thick silence. "You think we're just pawns on your board?" His words were like a whip, snapping in the air, but Lucas didn't flinch.

"Isn't it all a game, my friend?" Lucas said smoothly, his gaze never leaving mine. "All of this, the scheming, the secrets. It's all part of the same dance, don't you think? The only difference is that some of us are better at playing it than others." He stepped closer, now only a few feet away from us.

Kael's hand twitched at his side, ready to draw his blade, but I reached out and caught his wrist, my grip firm, though my own heart was racing. "Not yet," I said, the words coming out rough.

Kael's gaze met mine, his jaw clenched. "He's not worth the time, Alys."

"I know." The words came out soft, but there was steel beneath them. I couldn't let Kael kill him—not yet. Because there was something bigger here, something more than just Lucas's betrayal. It was the web of lies that had entangled us all, and I wasn't ready to cut it loose. Not until I had answers.

The tension in the room was suffocating, each breath a struggle. I could feel the weight of it pressing down on my chest, the sense of inevitability creeping closer. But for now, I held onto the fragile thread of control, the only thing that kept us from falling completely into chaos.

"Tell me what you're after," I said, my voice steady despite the storm inside me. "And maybe—just maybe—I'll let you walk out of here alive."

Lucas didn't even blink at my challenge, his eyes glinting with something close to amusement. "Alive? Darling, you're already dead." He took a step closer, his voice lower now, dripping with an eerie calm. "The moment you walked into Emberfall, you sealed your fate. You think this is about you or Kael? No, no—it's about the bigger picture. The one you've been too blind to see. But don't worry, you'll understand soon enough."

My chest tightened. My fingers clenched around the map, its edges digging into my palm like a reminder that there was still something tangible in this madness. But the air around me felt impossibly thin, as if we were all suspended in some strange place where time was held hostage, where nothing would ever be the same again.

Kael's posture hadn't shifted, but I could feel the battle waging inside him—his instincts, his loyalty, his desire to protect me, all warping into a slow burn of frustration. "Enough of this cryptic nonsense," he said, his voice edged with steel. "Either you talk or I make you talk. I don't care which."

Lucas's laugh rang out, low and mocking. "You've got guts, I'll give you that. But you've got no idea who you're dealing with, Kael." He flicked a glance at me. "None of us do. But you will." His lips twisted into a smile that didn't reach his eyes. "This place isn't as empty as you think. Not anymore."

The silence between us stretched, thick and heavy, and I felt something shift in the air, a subtle disturbance that didn't belong. It was too quiet. Too controlled. It didn't sit right, not with Lucas's calm arrogance or the fact that I could hear the faintest rustle behind us, like the faintest whisper of footsteps. My pulse quickened, a sudden, unsettling awareness sinking in.

My hand dropped instinctively to the side, my fingers brushing against the hilt of the knife tucked in my belt. But the movement was slow, deliberate, careful—because I knew, deep down, that if this was a trap, one wrong move would put us all at its mercy. My eyes flicked to Kael, and for a brief second, I saw it—his expression, all resolve, but also something else. Fear.

It was the first time I'd ever seen it in him.

Before I could process the thought further, Lucas's voice sliced through the tension again. "There's more than one of us here. You really think we'd let you waltz in, all righteous and unaware? Emberfall was never abandoned. It was a sanctuary. A breeding ground. A place to hide until the time was right."

I shook my head, trying to piece it all together. "Sanctuary for what?" The question hung between us, too heavy to ignore. I could feel the weight of it pressing down on my chest as if the very walls of the chapel were closing in.

Lucas tilted his head, eyes narrowing. "Not what. Who." He smiled, slow and chilling. "You've been walking into the heart of something much darker than your little rebellion. You've been chasing ghosts, Alys—only to realize you've been one yourself." His words dripped like poison, and with every syllable, the world around me seemed to twist tighter, more suffocating.

I swallowed, the truth starting to sting. "What are you saying?" The doubt I'd tried to ignore was creeping in, and I couldn't outrun it any longer. Lucas wasn't just a spy. He wasn't some rogue soldier who'd betrayed his country for money or power. No, he was part of something much bigger. A web of lies and betrayal that ran so deep it reached into places I wasn't sure we could survive.

"You're not ready for the truth," he said, his tone suddenly lighter, almost pitying. He took another step closer, his presence overwhelming. "None of us are. But don't worry, you'll see it all soon enough. And by then, it won't matter."

I was about to say something, anything, to demand answers, when a sudden crash of wood splintering echoed from the back of the chapel, and a gust of cold air swept through the doors, rattling the stained-glass windows like they were made of paper. We all froze, the tension snapping like a taut wire pulled too tight.

"Looks like we have company," Kael murmured, and without a word, he was moving—drawing his sword, his muscles coiled and ready. But his gaze, sharp and intense, flickered to me. "Stay behind me."

I didn't hesitate. My hand tightened around my knife, and I stepped closer, my eyes scanning the darkness at the back of the chapel. The shadows seemed to move on their own, shifting in a way that made my skin crawl. Then, from the darkness, a figure stepped forward, a silhouette against the fog that had begun creeping in through the open doors.

The figure's face remained hidden in the gloom, but there was something about the way they moved—too smooth, too deliberate. My heart skipped a beat. Something wasn't right.

I felt it, the shift in the air, the quiet promise that this wasn't just a confrontation. It was a beginning. And it would end in chaos.

"Kael," I whispered, the words almost catching in my throat, but I couldn't help it. The sudden realization hit like a freight train. The figure in the shadows wasn't just a threat—it was the final piece of the puzzle. The web of lies had finally come together, and we were caught in its center.

Before Kael could respond, a voice, cold and sharp, cut through the thick silence. "You've taken too long to find the truth, Alys. But don't worry... you'll have plenty of time to understand now."

And then the world around us erupted into chaos.

Chapter 19: The Heart of the Storm

The storm cracked open the sky, its roiling mass of gray and violet clouds like some ancient, furious deity awakening from a deep slumber. Thunder rolled over us in waves, too powerful to be anything but alive. The air tasted of salt and ozone, sharp enough to make my teeth ache, and the wind whipped through my hair, tangling it in wild knots that no comb could ever hope to untangle. Every wave felt like a battering ram, each gust of wind like a fist pounding against the hull of our skiff, but we pressed on.

Kael's hands were steady on the rudder, his face set in that familiar mask of calm, as if he wasn't standing on the brink of the end of the world. He turned toward me for a brief moment, his eyes catching the glow of the storm, and I saw the flicker of something in them—something I didn't quite recognize. Something that made my heart give an unexpected lurch, as if it wanted to leap into the void between us.

"We're almost there," he said, his voice steady despite the chaos around us, the wind fighting him at every turn.

I nodded, even though the knots in my stomach twisted tighter. How could we possibly be "almost there" when the entire world seemed to be coming apart at the seams? When every gust felt like the storm itself was trying to tear us from existence?

The Wraithsea was no place for mortals—yet here we were, fighting the impossible. The waves had grown monstrous, towering above us like giant, dark sentinels, their crests foaming and crashing with a terrible power that sent tremors through my bones. I could feel the pull of the sea's magic, ancient and dark, curling around us like a lover with cruel intentions. And through it all, Kael's quiet presence beside me was a tether, grounding me in a world that felt increasingly unreal.

The ritual, I knew, had already begun. Selene's magic had already begun to weave itself into the very heart of the storm. She wasn't just calling upon the power of the Wraithsea anymore. She was the storm now. Every crack of lightning, every gust of wind, every surge of water—it all bore her mark. She was using it, manipulating it, shaping it to her will. She had grown more powerful than I had ever thought possible, her ambitions reaching far beyond anything I'd imagined.

But what I hadn't anticipated was the way it made my blood burn.

I had seen Kael's power before, in flashes—his magic an extension of him, fierce and unyielding. But as we drew closer to the eye of the storm, something inside me began to stir. A recognition that I was not just a bystander in this conflict. That my own power, too, had been growing, deepening, like the roots of an ancient tree. I could feel it, pooling in the pit of my stomach, sending tendrils of heat through my limbs. The air crackled with the electricity of it, almost as if the storm itself was responding to me. Or perhaps it was the other way around.

I glanced at Kael again, wondering if he could feel it too. The way the storm and the magic hummed in our veins, urging us to act. To fight. To take back control before everything slipped away.

"We need to get closer," I said, my voice sharper than I meant it to be. It was hard to keep my thoughts straight, with the storm screaming in my ears, with the chaos pressing down on us.

Kael's brow furrowed, and his jaw tightened, but his hands never wavered from their hold on the skiff. "You're not thinking clearly," he said, his words heavy with concern.

"Like you are?" I shot back, the bitterness in my voice more obvious than I wanted it to be.

The words hung between us for a moment, charged with a weight that neither of us wanted to acknowledge. But the storm, the roaring of the waves, the crackle of magic—none of it waited for us to work out our feelings. It pressed down harder, demanding our attention, forcing us to focus on the task at hand.

The eye of the storm was closer now, a hollow space in the chaos, where the winds and waves gave way to an unnatural calm. It was in that eerie silence that we saw it—the truth I'd been avoiding for too long.

Selene wasn't waiting for us. She was already there, standing at the center of the swirling, glowing waters, her form bathed in the light of the storm. The sea itself bent to her will, the waves rising and falling with her command. I could see the magic coiling around her, a dark, liquid thing that moved with a life of its own, wrapping around her like a lover, an extension of her will. Her hair, long and wild, whipped in the wind like a thousand strands of lightning, and her eyes—gods, her eyes—glowed with an otherworldly light, the depths of them promising a destruction so complete, so devastating, it made my heart freeze in my chest.

But it was her smile that stopped me cold.

It wasn't cruel. It wasn't the smile of a madwoman, bent on destruction. No. It was something else entirely.

"Did you think you could stop me?" she asked, her voice a low purr that echoed in my bones.

I couldn't speak for a moment, my mouth dry. Every instinct screamed to run, to turn the boat around and flee, but something inside me refused. Something else was stirring. The storm had already started, and I wasn't going to let it win.

"We're running out of time," Kael said, his voice tight with urgency. But it was more than just the storm that had him rattled.

It was the truth.

The storm, once merely a threatening hum on the horizon, had grown into a behemoth of wind and water, a monster with a mind of its own, determined to swallow everything in its path. Even as we drew closer, I couldn't shake the feeling that this wasn't just some cosmic anomaly, some freak occurrence of nature. No, this storm was alive. It pulsed with an energy that felt almost sentient, twisting around us like a predator testing the strength of its prey.

My grip on the sides of the skiff tightened as a particularly violent wave sent a shock of cold saltwater spraying across my face. I didn't flinch, though, because to flinch would be to admit that this was too much. I wasn't going to give in to that—especially not when I could feel Kael's presence beside me, solid and constant. There was something oddly reassuring about the way he handled the chaos. He was like the eye of the storm, unfazed, his steady hands pulling the skiff through the tumultuous sea with the kind of calm I could never seem to muster.

"Hold on tight," Kael warned, his voice a low growl above the howling wind.

I nodded, even though my fingers were already white-knuckled from holding onto the side. It was hard to feel like you were doing something useful when the world itself seemed to be on the verge of unraveling. The storm, the magic, Selene's growing power—everything seemed to be falling apart. I could feel it, this overwhelming weight of inevitability, as though fate itself was mocking me. I was only one person. One very human person, with nothing but the odd magic of my own and a tendency to act without thinking. And yet, I couldn't stop myself from moving forward. From reaching for the danger.

"You're tense," Kael said after a long stretch of silence. His voice was too easy, too casual.

"Funny," I said, barely able to hear myself over the cacophony of the storm, "I was going for 'calm and collected.'"

He shot me a sideways glance, the faintest trace of a smile tugging at the corner of his lips. But his eyes were still focused, sharp, calculating. I caught the flicker of something in his gaze—the same realization that had been creeping into my own thoughts for days now. We weren't just playing at this anymore. The stakes had shifted, and this was real. This was the heart of the storm.

The skiff lurched again, sending us both sprawling momentarily, but Kael's reflexes were faster than the rage of the sea. He caught the edge of the boat and hauled me back upright before I even had a chance to swear.

"Thanks," I muttered, wiping water from my face.

"You're welcome," he said with the faintest trace of a smirk. But it was gone as quickly as it came, replaced by something heavier. Something that mirrored the storm itself.

When we finally broke through the last of the waves, the world seemed to freeze. It was as though time had momentarily surrendered to the overwhelming presence of Selene. She stood in the center of the eye, the storm swirling around her, the very sea itself bending to her will. Her hands were raised, palms open, as if she were gathering the very essence of the ocean. And in that moment, I realized something that made the blood freeze in my veins.

She wasn't just wielding the power of the sea. She was the sea. The tempest, the fury, the unrelenting force of nature—Selene had become one with it, and that made her infinitely more dangerous than I had ever realized.

"You're too late," Selene's voice rang out, a soft, almost musical thing that sent shivers down my spine. Her eyes glowed with an unnatural light, and I could feel the pull of her power, curling around me, coiling into my bones like something alive.

I opened my mouth to speak, but no words came. How could I respond to something like this? How could I face the fact that the very thing I had been trying to stop was already here, breathing down my neck, and there was no escaping it?

Kael's voice, low and filled with a quiet anger, cut through my paralysis. "You think you've won?"

Selene's smile stretched across her face, cruel and knowing. "Oh, Kael, you're so predictable. But you've always been predictable, haven't you?"

I shot him a quick look, but his expression was unreadable. Whatever this was, whatever Selene had meant by that, I wasn't sure, but it didn't sit well with me.

"You're playing with fire," I said, my voice louder than I meant it to be, as though challenging her would somehow shift the balance of power.

Her gaze flicked to me then, and the mockery in her eyes was undeniable. "Fire?" she asked with a raised brow. "Is that what you think this is? Fire?"

The air around us began to pulse with a strange heat, and I realized with a jolt that I wasn't mistaken. This wasn't fire. It was something worse.

"Kael," I murmured, my throat dry. "She's... she's not just controlling the sea. She's become it. She is the storm."

Kael's eyes narrowed, his jaw set. There was no fear there, not like I felt in my gut, but I could see the realization dawning in him as well. He hadn't underestimated Selene—but now that we saw what she was truly capable of, it was clear that we were barely scraping the surface of the danger we faced.

The tension between us was palpable, thick with the weight of unsaid things, but there was no time for that now. No time for anything other than survival.

"We need to move," Kael said, voice clipped, already spinning the rudder. His focus shifted away from Selene for the briefest of moments, and that's when I saw it—too late. A jagged bolt of lightning split the sky, casting everything into stark, white relief for an instant, and the force of it hurled us sideways.

I didn't even have time to scream before the boat tipped violently. The sea, in its chaotic fury, had claimed its first victory.

The boat tipped violently, and the world became a blur of saltwater and crashing thunder. My heart slammed against my ribcage, and for a moment, everything went dark—my body fully immersed in the icy grip of the Wraithsea. The chaos was instant, a maelstrom of water and noise, but I fought my way to the surface, gasping for air as I felt my chest tighten. My hands reached for anything, the slick surface of the skiff slipping through my fingers. And then, I heard it—a voice cutting through the roar of the storm.

"Hold on!"

Kael's voice. I wasn't sure where he was, but the urgency in his tone had me clawing my way toward it. Through the disorienting swirl of water, the world felt like it was unraveling at the edges. The boat had capsized completely, and the waves kept rising, swallowing us whole with every passing second.

A splash beside me, followed by the firm grip of Kael's hand around my wrist, yanking me toward him. His eyes, bright and sharp even in the midst of this madness, locked with mine.

"Can you swim?" His voice was fierce, but there was something else buried beneath the surface—a soft undercurrent of something I couldn't quite place.

"I'm not the one who's drowning," I muttered, barely able to keep my head above the water, the shock of the cold settling deep in my bones. But I knew the game was far from over. Selene's power pulsed around us, as tangible as the storm itself, and I had a sinking feeling that her magic wasn't done with us yet.

Kael's grip tightened, pulling me closer. "We're not going to make it if you don't swim."

It was more than just an order. It was a warning. If we didn't get out of the eye of this storm, we wouldn't make it at all.

I pushed aside the panic crawling its way up my throat, kicking my legs in an attempt to follow Kael, whose strokes were strong and purposeful. The water raged around us, but there was something almost comforting in the steadiness of his movements, even as the sky split open with another flash of blinding light.

We were both exhausted, and it was all I could do to keep my head from sinking under again, but I kept my eyes fixed on Kael's back, the sharp curve of his shoulders silhouetted against the madness of the waves. His presence was like a beacon, pulling me forward when everything inside me wanted to collapse.

As we neared what seemed to be a small patch of calmer water, I finally managed to catch my breath enough to speak.

"Do you think... do you think Selene will stop?" I gasped, my words barely audible over the wind.

Kael didn't answer immediately, and I could feel him tensing as we drew closer to a rocky outcropping jutting from the water. His eyes never left the horizon, where the storm still raged, a fury that felt endless, unyielding.

"She won't stop. Not until she has everything," Kael said, his voice sharp with the same frustration and anger I felt in the pit of my stomach. There was something deep in his gaze, something fierce, and I couldn't help but wonder what more there was to him, what more he wasn't saying.

Before I could ask, he turned and, without warning, hauled me toward the rocks. I barely had time to process the movement before the water surged, sending us both crashing against the jagged edges of the outcropping. Pain flared through my side, but it was nothing compared to the shock of cold, the weight of the storm pushing me further down.

"Get a grip!" Kael shouted, his hands grasping me, pulling me up.

We both scrambled, breathless, water flooding my mouth and nose, until finally, I found a ledge to cling to. My fingers burned from the cold and the effort, but there was no time to focus on that. Not with the storm still raging above us, the violent dance of lightning illuminating the chaos in sporadic bursts. The air was thick with the sharp scent of the sea, but beneath that, something else lingered—something metallic, something wrong.

I glanced over at Kael, whose jaw was clenched tight, his gaze flickering to the horizon. "We need to move," he said again, but this time, his voice was edged with something more desperate.

"Where?" I gasped. "Where do we go?" The question was almost laughable in the moment. The whole world felt like it was coming apart at the seams, and the idea of finding safety seemed almost absurd.

Kael's eyes darkened, and he reached down, pulling a dagger from his belt. It gleamed cold and sharp, a weapon built for more than just defense. "We go to the heart of it," he said, his voice low, the weight of the decision hanging between us.

I blinked, my breath coming in short, sharp bursts as I tried to process his words. "You're insane," I muttered, even as I realized he wasn't joking. He meant it.

"We have no choice."

I wanted to argue. I wanted to tell him that it was too dangerous, that we were both on the verge of collapse, but the way he said it, the weight in his voice, told me there was no other option. Not anymore.

He extended his hand to me, and I took it, not even considering the consequences. The storm had already claimed everything else—now it was going to claim us, too, if we didn't act.

As we clambered up onto the rocky ledge, a new sound reached my ears, distant but growing louder with every passing second. A hum, a low, almost rhythmic pulse. It was as though the storm itself had found a new voice, something darker, something more... deliberate.

"We're not alone," Kael murmured, his voice barely above a whisper.

The hum grew louder, and I felt it in my bones, deep and unsettling. And then, just as I looked up, a figure appeared from the mist of the storm—tall, shadowed, with a presence that felt far too familiar.

Kael froze, his grip on my arm tightening. I followed his gaze, my heart in my throat, as the figure stepped closer.

And then, in a voice that chilled me to the bone, the figure spoke.

"You're not going to make it. Not this time."

The words were a warning. But what I didn't understand was whether they were meant for Kael, or for me.

Chapter 20: The Forbidden Tower

The city buzzed with life around me, a stark contrast to the isolation I felt standing on the sidewalk, watching the world move in currents while I was tethered by invisible strings to something heavier. Chicago was always a little wild—its constant hum of activity a comforting reminder of how easy it was to lose yourself among thousands of others. The early morning sunlight filtered through the skyscrapers, casting long shadows and lighting up the details of a city on the move. I could almost feel the heat of the pavement beneath my feet, warm enough to promise the start of another sticky, sun-drenched day. The aroma of coffee and fresh croissants leaked out from the bakery on the corner, mixing with the faint smell of exhaust and early morning rain still clinging to the air. It was all so vibrant, so tangible, and yet... none of it reached me.

I shifted on the spot, my hand wrapped tightly around the handle of my coffee cup, the one thing I was sure would get me through the next few hours. Every morning, this was my routine—crossing the street from my small apartment and stopping at this same bakery, making small talk with the barista, pretending to care about the weather or her latest relationship drama, which was always happening with someone named Dave. I didn't know why I kept doing it—maybe it was the familiarity, or maybe it was the desperate hope that someday, I'd feel normal enough to enjoy this nonsense like everyone else. I hated it, but I kept doing it. A little like everything else in my life.

"Hey," a voice called from behind me, pulling me out of my internal reverie.

I turned, a little too fast. "Jared, don't sneak up on me like that."

He shrugged, his grin wide and charming in that way that made women drop everything to stare. I, of course, had long since stopped being impressed by his ridiculous smile. He was one of those people whose energy could fill a room whether he wanted it to or not. Today, he was wearing a leather jacket, a little too perfect for a morning coffee run. His dark hair fell just over his eyes, making him look like some kind of rogue from a romance novel. I suppose it helped that he was actually a damn good lawyer. They always said the good ones could sell ice to an Eskimo. Jared could sell snow to a polar bear.

"You look... distracted," he said, cocking an eyebrow as he studied me. "What's going on? You're normally all fire and fight before your first sip."

"Nothing's going on. Just thinking," I muttered, lifting the cup to my lips and taking a long sip, hoping the steam would buy me some time. I should have known better. Jared could see right through me, and if I tried to pretend that everything was fine, he'd dig until he found the crack in the armor.

"Well, that's a great way to sound unconvincing." He leaned in a little closer, the faintest hint of mischief in his eyes. "You sure there's nothing to tell? Because I know you, and I'm pretty sure you'd rather not be standing here right now."

I paused. He was right. I'd much rather be anywhere else. The truth of it was, I'd been staring at the empty apartment for hours last night, wondering if I'd ever get back to something that felt like life again. My job was fine. My friends were fine. Everything in my world was fine. And that was exactly the problem. I didn't want fine anymore. I needed something else, something sharp and wild, something that might cut through this stale monotony.

"I'm just... I don't know," I finally said, lowering my gaze to the street. "I guess I'm looking for something. Something I don't know how to find."

Jared's lips curled into a knowing smile. "Well, that's a cryptic way of saying you're bored out of your mind." He reached over and swiped my coffee cup, taking a sip before I could protest. "I've got an idea. Why don't we go do something stupid today? You know, something to shake off that little existential crisis you've got going on. I've got tickets to a show at The Vic tonight, and the after-party's gonna be ridiculous. You in?"

I stared at him, stunned. That was not the kind of suggestion I had expected. Usually, Jared's ideas were more like impromptu bar crawls or last-minute flights to Vegas. But this... this sounded almost... normal. Too normal. My fingers tightened around the edge of the sidewalk as I struggled with the idea.

"Tonight?" I asked, my voice flat.

"Yeah, tonight." He grinned wider. "Come on, let's do something different for once. Break the cycle."

I hesitated, the stillness of my thoughts refusing to break free. I didn't know what I wanted. Maybe that was the problem. But then again, maybe this was the spark I needed—something to kick-start whatever was missing. "Fine. Let's go. But I'm warning you, I'm not going to be your wingwoman."

He scoffed. "Please. Like I need you to swoop in and save me from myself."

"Trust me, you do."

I turned, already knowing that this decision would either be the best or the worst one I'd made in a long time. And either way, I couldn't wait to see what would happen next.

I'd forgotten how much I hated the noise of the city until I was standing in the middle of it, flanked by Jared's endless chatter about the show and the people we'd meet. It wasn't that I disliked him—far from it. It was just that, sometimes, the world felt too big. Too noisy. I could feel the vibration of car engines under my feet as we walked, hear the shriek of the subway beneath the surface, and the calls of street vendors hawking everything from newspapers to phone cases. My mind was swirling with it all, the rush of life moving at a pace I couldn't keep up with.

As we walked past the garish neon signs and the hipster cafes, I realized I was more out of step with everything around me than I had first thought. Chicago's North Side was alive with the kind of frenetic energy that only a city of its size could produce—people on bikes whizzing past, dogs barking, strangers laughing too loud, music spilling out of open windows. But none of it touched me. Jared's voice was a lifeline in the sea of dissonance, but it was also a lifeline I wasn't sure I needed anymore.

"I swear, you've been quieter than usual today," he said, glancing over at me as we passed a row of old brick buildings with graffiti tagging their sides. "This is your brand of entertainment. I mean, the Vic is a hole in the wall, but it's our hole in the wall. You should be excited. Or, I don't know—smile, or something."

"I'm smiling," I replied flatly, my hand fumbling for the strap of my purse as if it were a comfort. "It's just... I don't know. I think I'm realizing I've been stuck in a loop, you know? You get to a point where everything feels the same, and it starts to drag you under."

He stopped in his tracks, peering at me like I had just told him I was considering a career as a trapeze artist.

"Alright, enough of this," he said, placing a hand on my shoulder and pulling me to a halt. "There's obviously something you're not saying. So, say it. Let it out, and let's be done with it. Because right now, you're torturing yourself. And I'm getting really tired of you torturing me by proxy."

The truth was, he wasn't wrong. I had been torturing myself for months. I just didn't know how to make it stop. The life I had was one that many would envy—stable job, good friends, a home with just enough space to make it my own. But none of it felt like it belonged to me anymore. It was as though I was watching myself from the outside, playing the part of someone who had it all together while the real me was somewhere lost in the details, unable to find her way back.

"I don't know who I am anymore," I said before I could stop myself, the words slipping out in a rush of honesty that caught me off guard.

There it was, the heart of it all. The thought I'd been dodging for so long. Jared was right. I didn't feel like myself. And it terrified me.

Jared exhaled slowly, his grip on my shoulder tightening as if he was trying to pull me back from the edge of whatever abyss I'd fallen into. He studied me for a moment, his eyes searching my face, trying to read between the lines of what I wasn't saying.

"Okay, I get it," he said finally, his tone more serious than I'd ever heard it. "You feel like you're losing control, right? Like you're watching everything slip through your fingers and you're just... waiting for something to give. But here's the thing—no one's asking you to have it all figured out. Life isn't a race to be won. It's just... living. It's about finding moments that make you feel alive. And if that means going to a random concert with me, then fine. Let's do that. But you've got to stop running away from whatever's eating at you."

I stared at him, unable to form the words to explain how he had just hit the nail on the head in a way that made my insides ache with the clarity of it. There was a deep, gnawing truth in what he'd said, one that made me feel both relieved and more lost than I had been before.

"I don't want to be stuck, Jared. I don't want to be stuck in this safe little life that doesn't scare me. I just... I don't know what's next. I don't know what I'm supposed to do with all these feelings, or how to make them stop. But it's like..." I trailed off, the words tangled in my throat. "Like if I don't do something, I'll drown in them."

Jared's expression softened, and he reached up to ruffle my hair in that annoying, almost brotherly way he had.

"You're not going to drown, okay? And if you do, you've got me to throw you a life raft. You're not alone in this. You don't have to figure everything out today, but you do have to let it out. Stop bottling it up. It's exhausting just watching you do it."

We walked for a few more blocks, his words still hanging in the air between us like the ghost of something I didn't want to face. But somewhere in that silence, I realized that I wasn't alone. Not entirely. And maybe that was all I needed. A reminder that I wasn't the only one who could save myself.

The show turned out to be everything I expected—loud, chaotic, and slightly ridiculous. But for the first time in what felt like years, I let myself enjoy it. I laughed, I danced, I even let Jared drag me to the front to scream out lyrics I didn't know, just because the people around us were doing it. The music, the people, the lights—they didn't fix anything. But for one night, they gave me the freedom to not think about the weight of the world that had been pressing down on me for far too long. And maybe, just maybe, that was enough.

The night bled into the kind of crisp, moonlit silence that only came with the early hours in the city, a brief moment when everything seemed to exhale at once before the buzz started again. Jared and I had left the venue hours ago, the pounding music still ringing in my ears like a distant heartbeat, and made our way to a small late-night diner off Belmont Avenue. Its fluorescent sign flickered erratically, but I could see the soft orange glow of the neon lights bleeding through the cracked windowpanes. Inside, it was warm, too warm for my liking, the smell of greasy diner food mingling with the faintest scent of over-brewed coffee.

It was quiet except for the soft clink of cutlery and the murmurs of a few other patrons hunched over their plates of eggs and toast.

A man in a greasy apron stood behind the counter, his hands steady despite the late hour, as if his routine was what kept the world spinning. Jared slid into a booth across from me, eyes still twinkling with the sort of mischief that came from an impromptu night out with no agenda. He'd already ordered for both of us, of course, because Jared never let a detail slip.

"Okay," he said, his voice low, but with that undeniable edge of curiosity. "What was that back there? What's really going on with you?"

I stirred my coffee absently, the liquid swirling lazily in the cup, as if I could delay the inevitable. It was hard to tell Jared things—he had this way of cutting through the surface that left me feeling naked. But there was something in the way his gaze held mine, patient and steady, that made me feel like I could say whatever I needed to.

"Do you ever wonder if you're just playing a part?" I asked suddenly, the question catching even myself off guard. "Like... like you're acting out a role in some play you never auditioned for, and the lines are starting to feel like they belong to someone else?"

Jared leaned back, eyes never leaving me, his fingers tapping a rhythmic pattern on the edge of the booth. "I think you're giving this too much weight," he said finally, his voice light, but laced with something that made me stop. "You're looking for meaning in a place where maybe there isn't any. Not yet. Maybe that's the point, right? You don't have to know the full story to live in it."

I opened my mouth to argue, but the words stuck, lodged somewhere between my chest and my throat. It was as if he'd just cracked open a window in a room I hadn't realized was suffocating me.

"What if I'm tired of not knowing?" I asked softly, the confession slipping out almost without thought. "What if I need something—anything—that feels real?"

Jared was silent for a moment, his expression shifting from playful to something more thoughtful. He drummed his fingers on the table as though sorting through the words that would come next. But before he could say anything, the bell above the diner's door jingled, and a couple walked in, talking loudly, their laughter filling the empty space with an unexpected sharpness.

I watched them for a moment. A man and a woman, both in their thirties, walking like they had somewhere to be but were content enough to enjoy the journey. Their presence felt foreign against the stark quiet of the diner. The woman's hair was tied in a messy ponytail, her cheeks flushed from the night air, and she wore a leather jacket that had seen better days. The man was grinning, clearly enjoying their conversation as they slid into a booth near the corner.

"Do you think we'll ever find that?" I asked, the words out before I could stop them. I hadn't meant to ask it aloud, hadn't meant to share whatever small kernel of hope had formed in me. But there it was.

Jared followed my gaze, and for a brief moment, the world outside of the diner faded. The clink of plates, the hum of the lights—all of it disappeared.

"Find what?" he asked quietly, his voice catching just slightly, as though he already knew the answer.

"Something real," I said, my voice smaller now, almost a whisper. "Something that matters enough to make all this—the confusion, the mess, the loneliness—make sense."

Jared was still, his gaze flickering between me and the couple across the room. "What's stopping you from finding it?"

I opened my mouth to respond, but the words didn't come. Instead, my heart seemed to stutter in my chest. The question hung in the air between us, the weight of it pulling down on my shoulders until it felt almost suffocating.

Before I could gather myself, the door to the diner opened again, this time more abruptly, as if a sudden gust of wind had pushed it open. A figure stood in the threshold, tall and shadowed, their features obscured by the streetlight behind them. My heart skipped a beat, the chill that ran down my spine impossible to ignore.

For a second, I wondered if I was imagining it—if the weariness in my bones had finally driven me to the point where I was seeing ghosts. But no, this person—this stranger—was real.

The figure's eyes locked onto mine, piercing, as if they knew me better than I knew myself. And just as quickly, they disappeared into the shadow of the diner's corridor, vanishing behind a set of heavy curtains.

I blinked, trying to convince myself it was nothing, but my pulse raced in my ears. Jared didn't seem to notice. He was still watching me, waiting for a response.

But I couldn't speak. My throat had tightened, the air around me thick and heavy. Something—someone—had just entered my life uninvited, and I couldn't shake the feeling that it had everything to do with what I'd been searching for.

Chapter 21: The Dance of Shadows

I had long been told that the Court of Ebonveil was a place where shadows danced as freely as the moonlight, and I had never believed it to be true until now. The grand hall stretched out before me, its vaulted ceilings lost in a haze of gilt and candlelight, the flicker of a thousand flames reflecting off the polished marble floors. It was beautiful in a way that made your heart ache, and yet, beneath the beauty, there was an undercurrent of something darker—something sharp. I could feel it pressing in from all sides, a web of secrets spun so tightly that one misstep would make it unravel. And I would be caught in the middle.

I adjusted my mask—half black lace, half silver filigree—just enough to hide the truth of who I was, or at least, that's what I told myself. But I had never been good at hiding. It was always something in my eyes, or the way I carried myself, or how the light seemed to follow me, as if it knew the truth even when I didn't. Tonight, however, I could only pray that the mask would be enough, that it would shield me from the prying eyes of those who could see through it all.

The crowd parted as I made my way further into the hall, the laughter and music swirling around me like an intoxicating perfume. It wasn't the kind of event where you could simply stroll in and blend with the guests. Every movement had to be deliberate, every glance a careful dance. The people here were experts at wearing their masks—of both the physical and emotional variety—and they could sense weakness like a wolf senses blood in the water.

Kael appeared at my side just as I was beginning to wonder if I had made a terrible mistake. I didn't have to look at him to know he was watching me, studying my every reaction. His presence was a weight, a heavy pressure that seemed to pull at the very air between us. I could feel the heat of his gaze, even through the black silk of his own mask, and it made my pulse quicken in spite of myself. He was dangerous—more dangerous than anyone at this ball.

"We're being watched," he murmured, his voice a low, almost teasing whisper that vibrated against my skin. It sent a shiver down my spine, both for the warning and for the way it curled in my chest.

"I know," I replied, keeping my voice steady, though my heart was anything but. I could feel their eyes on me now—those who were interested, those who were suspicious, and perhaps, those who would simply find it amusing to watch my downfall.

"Keep your wits about you," Kael said, and though the words were stern, I could hear the underlying amusement in them. He wasn't worried about me, not really. He was enjoying this, the game, the tension, the unpredictability.

I could feel my pulse quicken with something else—something dangerous, something that wasn't just the buzz of the evening or the constant hum of uncertainty in the air. The music shifted, becoming deeper, more sinister, as the guests began to sway in time with the melody. I stepped forward, my feet moving on their own accord, pulled by the rhythm. A waltz, slow and languid, but with a sharp edge beneath it, like the promise of a blade just beneath silk.

Kael's hand found mine, guiding me into the center of the floor, and we moved as one—two figures in a sea of masks, spinning and twirling with the ease of long familiarity. His touch was a whisper of heat against my skin, and for a moment, I let myself forget the danger, let myself simply feel the beat of the music and the warmth of his presence. But only for a moment.

As we danced, I let my gaze drift over the crowd. The court was filled with faces half-obscured, eyes glittering from behind jeweled masks, lips painted in the colors of seduction and lies. I could taste the bitterness of it in the air—the sharp, metallic scent of secrets kept too long. And then, I saw her.

Selene.

She was a vision of dark elegance, stepping into the room as though she owned the very night itself. The crowd parted for her as if by command, and even the music seemed to still in reverence to her arrival. Her mask was crafted of midnight blue lace, her gown a cascade of black velvet that shimmered with hints of silver. It was impossible not to notice her, impossible not to feel the weight of her presence. She was everything this court represented—danger, power, and an unsettling beauty that could tear you apart without a second thought.

Kael stiffened beside me, his grip tightening just slightly on my waist. "There she is," he murmured, more to himself than to me.

I didn't need him to tell me that. I could feel it in my bones, the shift in the room as she moved. Her eyes swept over the guests with a practiced ease, pausing only when they met mine. The smile she gave me was slow, deliberate—a blade hidden behind rose-colored lips.

"Do you think a mask can hide who you are, little Raven?" she asked, her voice like silk over stone. The words slid into my mind like an arrow, sharp and cold, and I felt the chill of them even as the warmth of the room closed in around me.

I opened my mouth to respond, but nothing came out—not immediately. Her gaze, heavy with knowing, held me captive. It was as if she could see right through the mask, right through all the lies I had told myself.

"No," I finally managed, my voice thick with something I couldn't quite name. "I don't think it can."

And just like that, the air between us crackled with something more than tension—something that might very well tear us apart.

I swallowed, the taste of her words still hanging in the air, thick and acrid like smoke from a fire you couldn't quite escape. My fingers tightened against Kael's, the only tether to reality in a room that felt more like a fever dream with each passing second. His grip was steady, unwavering, a silent reassurance that I wasn't in this alone. But the way his eyes glinted—dark, dangerous, with an edge of something like amusement—told me that he was just as enmeshed in this game as I was. We were two pieces on a board, but the rules were constantly shifting, and I wasn't sure if we were playing checkers or chess—or something even more sinister.

Selene's smile lingered, a cruel twist that didn't reach her eyes, as though she found the entire scene beneath her. The crowd around us continued their dance, oblivious to the quiet tension spiraling out of control in the center of the room. The laughter, the music, the flickering candlelight—it all felt distant now, like I was seeing it through a fog. Only Selene, and her eyes, and her words, were clear.

"You're far too good at this game, little Raven." Her voice was low, and there was a certain satisfaction in the way she said it, as if she were the cat and I was already in her claws, struggling to break free.

I let out a breath I hadn't realized I'd been holding, forcing a smile that I hoped masked the unease creeping up my spine. "It's not about being good," I replied, the words leaving my lips before I could reconsider them. "It's about knowing when to move."

Selene's lips curled, but she said nothing more. She simply tilted her head, acknowledging my challenge with a slight narrowing of her eyes, before turning away to address another guest. I watched her go, the faintest shiver crawling over my skin. This dance was far from over.

Kael leaned in, his lips brushing my ear. "You're playing with fire, you know that?" His voice was a soft murmur, but I felt the weight of it. He wasn't warning me so much as observing, as if he found the whole thing a bit too... entertaining.

I gave a small shrug, trying to mask the tightness in my chest. "And you're the one who led me into the fire, Kael."

A dark laugh rumbled from him. "True. But it's never about the fire, is it? It's about who controls it."

I couldn't argue with that. There were too many people here who would burn the world down just to watch it smolder. And yet, I couldn't shake the feeling that I wasn't just another pawn in a game too complex to understand. The more I learned about the Court of Ebonveil, the more I realized that every person here had a story that had been carefully crafted, each word, each action, a deliberate step toward something greater—something more dangerous. And I had walked right into the middle of it.

The music shifted again, a slow, mournful tune that seemed to swirl like smoke around us. It was as if the entire room, even the chandeliers, were holding their breath. I looked up at Kael, his face hidden behind his mask, but I could feel the weight of his gaze, the intensity of it pulling at me. He was a master of this world, of the court's unspoken rules. I, on the other hand, was still trying to find my footing in the labyrinth they called a ballroom.

And then I saw him—another figure, standing just beyond the crowd, a lone silhouette that seemed out of place in the sea of opulence. His mask was simple, nothing like the elaborate creations surrounding us, just a single piece of dark cloth covering his eyes. He wore a suit of dark leather, cut to perfection, with none of the glittering embellishments of the others. He was watching me, his stance relaxed but intent. I couldn't explain it, but there was something about the way he observed me that sent a jolt of recognition through my chest.

"Who's that?" I asked Kael, my voice barely above a whisper.

Kael's gaze followed mine, his expression tightening. "Don't look at him. Don't even think about it."

I was already thinking about it, of course, and I didn't like the way his words landed. There was something about this stranger that Kael wasn't willing to explain, something that pulled at the edges of my curiosity like a thread I couldn't ignore.

"Why?" I pressed, my gaze still fixed on the mysterious figure. "Who is he?"

Kael's eyes darkened, and his grip on my hand shifted, pulling me closer. "Someone you don't want to know."

His tone was final, and I couldn't help but notice the way his jaw tightened as he spoke. There was a history here, a shadow that stretched long between them, and I was beginning to wonder just how deep Kael's entanglements ran. The thought made my stomach churn, but I swallowed it down. I wasn't here to ask questions—I was here to survive.

But survival was becoming more complicated by the second.

I glanced back at the figure, only to find that he had vanished, as though the shadows had swallowed him whole. I blinked, disoriented, trying to trace where he might have gone, but the crowd had shifted again, and he was lost among the masks.

"What just happened?" I muttered under my breath, half to myself.

Kael's lips brushed my ear again. "Nothing. Forget about him."

That was easier said than done. But I nodded, and we continued to dance, my body moving on autopilot as my mind spun with a thousand thoughts. It wasn't just Selene's warning that haunted me now. It was the feeling that I was caught in the middle of something far larger than I had ever anticipated, a storm that was about to break and sweep us all away.

And I had no idea where I stood in it—only that I would have to find my place, or risk being crushed by the weight of it all.

The music shifted, its melancholy rhythm pulling at my chest in a way that had nothing to do with the melody itself. It was as though the notes were threading themselves into the very fabric of the room, knitting tension into every corner, every glance, every breath. I glanced over at Kael, hoping for some sign, some reassurance that we were still in control. His face was a mask of impassivity, but the way his jaw clenched told me all I needed to know: the game was on, and neither of us had any idea how it would end.

"We should leave," I murmured, the words slipping out before I could stop them. I felt the pressure of the crowd around us, like a living thing, squeezing tighter with every passing moment. Selene's gaze was a weight I couldn't shake off, a presence that hovered just out of reach but was always there, watching, calculating. Her challenge hung in the air between us, daring us to reveal more, to show our hand.

Kael's lips curved upward in a semblance of a smile, but it didn't reach his eyes. "You think she's the only one watching us, Raven?" he asked softly, the words laced with amusement and something darker, a warning hidden beneath the playful tone. He tugged me closer, his fingers pressing into my back with a gentle but insistent force, guiding me through the crowd.

"I wasn't worried about her," I admitted, my voice low, almost too quiet for anyone but him to hear. "It's the others. The ones lurking in the shadows. I can feel them, Kael. They're waiting for something."

His eyes flickered toward the periphery of the room, where the shadows seemed to gather, coiling like smoke around the pillars and velvet-draped alcoves. "Then we'd better give them something worth waiting for," he replied, his tone light, but his body stiffened as he scanned the crowd. I caught the subtle shift in his posture—he was no longer the carefree charmer, the confident man who navigated the undercurrents of this world with ease. In that moment, I saw something raw, something dangerous, and I wasn't sure if it was directed at me or at the forces closing in around us.

The next song began, slow and sultry, and the dance floor seemed to exhale, the tension easing just enough to let the guests slip into the rhythm of their well-rehearsed movements. I was barely aware of our steps, moving through the crowd like two ghosts weaving between dancers, but I couldn't ignore the prickle on the back of my neck. Something was wrong—something more than the quiet game we were playing, something I wasn't seeing but could feel in my bones.

"We're being followed," I whispered, the realization coming in a flash, sudden and sharp. My pulse spiked, and I could hear the rush of blood in my ears as my gaze flicked over the crowd. I had always trusted my instincts, but I couldn't tell if this was fear or something else—a premonition, perhaps, or just the weight of the night settling on my chest.

Kael didn't respond at first, his face a mask of concentration. Then, just as I was about to speak again, his fingers tightened on my waist, and he turned me slightly, positioning me so I could no longer see the entrance. A subtle move, but I felt it—the shift in the air, the tension that rippled through the crowd. Someone was approaching, someone who wasn't part of the game, someone who didn't belong here.

I didn't need to look to know it was him.

The figure from earlier—the man in the simple dark mask—had returned, and this time, he was walking directly toward us. His presence was like a ripple in the crowd, unnoticed by most, but unmistakable to me. I could feel the weight of his gaze even from this distance, his eyes hidden, but his intent clear. There was no more pretense of subtlety. He was here, and he was coming for us.

Kael stiffened, his body going rigid, and I caught the brief flash of something like recognition in his eyes. This wasn't just a chance encounter. This was a meeting, one that had been planned—one that neither of us had anticipated.

"Stay close," Kael murmured, his voice like steel wrapped in velvet. "Don't make a scene."

I barely nodded, my heart pounding in my chest as I tried to keep my face neutral, my gaze averted. But the figure's approach was impossible to ignore, and every instinct I had screamed at me to run. I didn't know who he was, what he wanted, or how he was connected to Kael, but I could feel the danger in the air, thick and suffocating. It wasn't just the atmosphere of the court anymore. This felt personal.

I tried to move closer to Kael, but before I could, the man was upon us. He was taller than I had initially thought, his presence commanding, and his mask, though simple, seemed to draw the eye with its stark contrast to the others around us. It was a dark, unadorned cloth, fitted perfectly over his features, leaving only his lips visible.

His voice, when he spoke, was smooth and low, just above a whisper. "Kael," he said, the name slipping from his lips like a warning.

Kael's gaze met mine for the briefest of seconds, and in that instant, I saw it—a flash of something dark, something I hadn't seen before. It was an unreadable expression, a mixture of anger, regret, and... fear?

"Dorian," Kael finally responded, his voice betraying none of the emotion I had glimpsed. "I wasn't expecting you tonight."

The man named Dorian didn't smile, but there was a sharpness in his gaze that suggested he found this all a little too amusing. "No one expects me." His eyes shifted to me, the look lingering just long enough to make my skin crawl. "But you must be the infamous Raven."

I met his gaze without flinching, but inside, my heart was hammering in my chest. The room felt colder suddenly, and I wasn't sure if it was the music or the way Dorian's presence seemed to freeze the air. Whatever it was, it was clear—this moment wasn't just an encounter. It was a beginning.

Chapter 22: The Tether Breaks

The hum of the city outside filtered into the loft through the cracked window, muffling the usual symphony of car horns and distant voices. In the apartment, though, there was nothing but stillness. I paced, hands shaking, the sudden coldness in my chest a jagged reminder of how quickly the bond between Kael and I had unraveled. It was as if the universe itself had conspired against us, weaving a web of doubt and confusion with every passing hour. The tether—our connection, the one I had once believed to be unbreakable—was no longer something I could rely on.

New York felt different today. It wasn't the city that had changed—it was me. I stood in front of the mirror, studying my reflection. My hair, which once fell in thick waves down my back, now hung lifeless, a reminder of the sleepless nights and the relentless stress that had started to gnaw away at my resolve. My eyes were bloodshot, the remnants of a sleepless rage that hadn't found its target. In the reflection, I saw a stranger. I didn't know who she was anymore, didn't know what she wanted or if I was even capable of getting it back.

A knock at the door.

I didn't need to look through the peephole. Kael's knock was unmistakable—sharp, insistent, like the sound of a storm breaking. My fingers hovered over the door handle, but for a moment, I simply stood there. What was I supposed to say to him? After everything? After all the things we had hurled at each other in the citadel, things I knew neither of us would ever be able to take back? There was no undoing the words. No undoing the hurt.

I opened the door.

Kael stood there, his dark eyes scanning my face like he was trying to figure out whether I was still the person he had once known. His jaw was tight, his brow furrowed in that way I had come to recognize as the precursor to an argument—a fight he was already winning in his mind. But for the first time, I didn't feel that urge to fight back. I didn't want to yell. I didn't want to make him see things my way. I was tired.

"You left," he said quietly, and despite everything, I felt a stab of guilt. His voice was raw, like he hadn't slept either, like the same hollow ache gnawed at his insides too.

"I had to," I replied, trying to hold my ground. I couldn't let him see how deeply his silence from earlier had shaken me, how his indifference had cut me in places I hadn't known could bleed.

"Because I don't need you?" The bitterness in his words stung, but I didn't flinch.

"You've never needed anyone, Kael," I shot back, the words sharper than I had intended. "I've been a distraction to you. A complication."

He stepped forward, and I instinctively took a step back, my heart pounding in my chest. "Is that what you think?" His voice was soft, almost too soft. "That I don't need you?"

I wasn't sure what to say. The truth—well, the truth was far messier than I could explain. I wasn't sure I even knew the truth anymore. The secrets we had kept from each other were so thick between us, so suffocating, that all I could do was hold my breath and wait for one of us to crack.

"You lied to me, Kael," I said instead, my voice trembling. "About Selene. About everything. And I... I can't keep pretending like I don't feel it. Like I don't feel... used."

His face hardened, and for a moment, the mask slipped. He didn't look like the man I had trusted—he looked like a stranger. "I never meant to use you," he said, his voice low, almost dangerous. "But I don't have the luxury of being honest. Not when so many lives are at stake."

I wanted to scream at him. To throw the truth in his face like it was a weapon, something that would pierce through the veil of his carefully constructed lies. But something in me—something that was tired and broken—stopped me.

"What's at stake, Kael?" I whispered, more to myself than to him. "What's worth all this? All the hurt? The lies? The distance between us?"

He was silent for a long time, his eyes flicking away, staring out into the night like the answers lay hidden somewhere out there, in the vastness of the city. But I knew better. I knew that the answers were right here, between us, just out of reach. If we could stop pretending, stop lying, maybe—just maybe—we could salvage something.

But then he looked back at me, and in that moment, I saw something. Something fleeting. A crack in his armor. A brief flash of vulnerability that sent a chill down my spine.

"I don't know anymore," he admitted, his voice barely above a whisper. "I thought I was doing the right thing. I thought I had control of this... but now, I'm not sure what to believe. Or who to trust."

I swallowed hard, my throat tight, every instinct screaming to pull him closer, to tell him that I would help him, that I could fix it. But I knew that I couldn't fix anything. Not anymore.

"Maybe," I said, the words feeling foreign on my tongue, "Maybe we need to stop trying to fix each other."

The silence between us was unbearable, the space growing wider with every heartbeat. And then, without a word, Kael turned and walked away, leaving me standing in the doorway, empty-handed and full of regret. The tether was gone. For good this time.

I closed the door slowly, the click of the lock echoing in the quiet apartment. And as the city continued to pulse beyond the walls, I was left alone with the remnants of a bond that had once meant everything.

The morning light filtered through the blinds in sharp slants, casting thin, angled shadows on the floor. I hadn't slept—again. Not really. There had been moments of half-dreams, scattered thoughts, and a pervasive hum in my mind that kept time with the city's pulse outside. A quiet agitation. It wasn't just the silence Kael had left behind in the apartment that kept me up. It was the weight of the choice I had made. To walk away. To let the tether snap, even if it felt like the only option.

I stood in front of my kitchen counter, staring at the half-empty mug of coffee, the steam rising in soft, curling tendrils. The bitterness of the brew mirrored the taste in my mouth, thick and acrid. I could hear the usual sounds of the city—dogs barking, a distant conversation on the street below, the sharp crack of someone's heels tapping against the pavement—but it all felt distant, muffled by the hollow space inside me.

There was a knock at the door.

I didn't have to wonder who it was. No one else ever came by this early. And no one else had the guts—or the audacity—to show up after everything that had happened. I set the coffee down with a decisive thud and made my way to the door, every step heavier than the last.

When I opened it, there he was. Kael, standing on the other side, still in the same clothes from the night before, his hair tousled in that way I had once found endearing. But now, it just looked like a mess—like everything between us. His eyes locked with mine, searching, unsure. He hadn't even knocked this time; his hand just hovered, poised in midair like he was afraid to reach for the doorframe.

"You're still here," I said, my voice low, almost too quiet.

"Yeah," he said, his voice rough, like it had been dragged through gravel. "I wanted to make sure you were okay."

I didn't let myself react. Didn't let myself feel that brief, foolish flutter in my chest. I had been angry with him yesterday—furious even—but now, in the cold light of morning, that anger felt like something foreign, something that didn't belong to me. I had nothing left to fight for. Nothing left to hold onto.

"You should go, Kael," I said, stepping back, pressing my palm flat against the door. "I can't do this anymore."

He didn't move. Instead, his gaze softened, his jaw tightening. I could see the weight of the words he was holding back, the way they sat heavy in his throat, threatening to spill out if he just gave them permission. "I don't want to leave you like this."

"Then what do you want?" I demanded, my frustration slipping through the cracks in my composure. "You're the one who walked away. You're the one who shut me out."

His breath caught, and he closed his eyes for a second, like he was fighting something inside him. "I never wanted to shut you out."

"Then why did you?" I challenged, folding my arms across my chest. "Why all the lies, Kael? Why the secrets?"

He looked at me then, and there was something in his eyes—something raw, something broken—that made my heart twist. It wasn't the fierce, confident man I had once known. It wasn't even the man who had manipulated me into trusting him. No. It was something more vulnerable. More human.

"I was trying to protect you," he admitted quietly. "From Selene, from everything. I thought... I thought if I kept you at a distance, kept you safe, that you'd be better off. That I'd be better off."

"Better off?" I repeated, a bitter laugh escaping me. "Is that what this has all been about? Protecting me?"

"I'm not a good person," he said, voice hoarse, the words like they were tearing him apart. "I never was. I don't know how to do this... any of this. I don't know how to fix it."

I wanted to shout at him, to tell him that the only thing that needed fixing was the mess he had created. That I had been a pawn in his game of control and manipulation, and he had used me like a tool, like a piece on a board. But when I opened my mouth, nothing came out. The rage—the fury that had felt so right last night—was gone, replaced by something softer, something that felt like grief.

"Do you even know what it's like, Kael?" I whispered, my voice barely a breath. "To feel like you're always the second choice? To always wonder if the person you're with actually wants to be with you, or if they're just settling because it's easier?"

He flinched, the accusation hitting him like a blow to the chest. For a moment, I thought he might speak. Apologize. But the words never came. Instead, his eyes lowered to the floor, and I saw a flicker of something like shame.

"I never meant for you to feel like that," he said, his voice tight, rough with regret. "But I've never known how to be what you need."

"You've never known how to be what anyone needs, Kael," I said softly, stepping back and closing the door between us. "And I think... I think that's the problem."

There was a finality in the click of the lock that I couldn't ignore. It was the sound of an ending, and as much as I wanted to deny it, I knew in my bones that this time, we were done. The tether was gone. And no amount of words, no amount of regret, could bring it back.

I leaned against the door, feeling the weight of everything that had happened settle in my bones. The silence stretched on, thick and heavy, as if the city outside had suddenly fallen asleep.

And for the first time in what felt like forever, I let myself breathe.

The room was silent, save for the muffled hum of traffic from the streets below. My phone lay on the coffee table, face down, as though it too had given up trying to bridge the distance between me and the world outside. I could hear the faint whispers of life beyond my apartment—sirens in the distance, the occasional honk of a car, the murmur of voices in the stairwell. But none of it mattered. The city, my life, the noise—none of it filled the empty space Kael had left behind. The tether was gone, and it felt like a wound that refused to heal.

I wasn't even sure where to go from here. I should've been angry, I should've been packing my things, putting distance between myself and everything that had happened, but instead, I was... exhausted. So, I sank into the couch, my gaze fixed on the rain streaking down the windowpane, blurring the skyline in the distance. The storm outside was a reflection of the one brewing inside me, violent and unrelenting.

A knock at the door.

I couldn't remember the last time anyone had visited me uninvited. Not since Kael. And now—now, after everything, I wasn't sure I wanted to face anyone else. But curiosity, that insistent little voice, won out. I dragged myself to the door, each step dragging through the thick air of my own confusion.

I didn't look through the peephole this time. The knock had been soft, almost tentative, but I knew who it was before I even opened the door. There was no surprise, no disbelief. Just... inevitability.

"Not you again," I muttered, the words barely escaping before I'd even fully opened the door.

Standing in the hallway, dressed in a leather jacket that looked far too well put together for this early hour, was Dylan. Of course it was Dylan. Who else would it be? The very last person I wanted to see, and yet, here he was, his casual smile doing nothing to disguise the weariness in his eyes.

"I'm starting to think you're stalking me," I said, stepping back to let him in, though the invitation felt more like an accusation than an offer.

Dylan smirked, his signature charm sliding into place like armor. "Oh, come on, I wouldn't call it stalking. You've just got an aura about you, and I'm a sucker for complicated women."

I rolled my eyes, but there was no heat behind it. "If you're here to lecture me about Kael—"

"I'm not here to talk about Kael," he interrupted, stepping into the apartment like he owned it. "I'm here to talk about you. Or, more specifically, the look on your face when I passed your apartment this morning. Not the same confident woman I saw a week ago. Something's off."

"Nothing's off," I said, though I was already regretting the words. Who was I trying to fool? Certainly not Dylan, who had seen through my defenses long before Kael had.

He raised an eyebrow and leaned against the kitchen counter, arms folded. "Really? Because I've been around long enough to know that you don't wear that face unless you've been hit with something harder than just a little bad luck."

I exhaled sharply, rubbing my temples. "It's complicated."

"Well, that's convenient," Dylan quipped. "I'm a man who thrives on complications."

"I'm not in the mood for games," I snapped, my patience thinning. But the words barely left my mouth before Dylan's expression softened, and I realized, with a sudden clarity, that this wasn't the same cocky, flirtatious Dylan I'd known. No. Something had shifted.

"You don't have to explain anything to me," he said, his tone uncharacteristically gentle. "But you might want to consider talking to someone. Because if you don't, you'll end up doing what you always do. Pushing people away when they're trying to help."

My eyes flicked up to meet his, surprised by the seriousness in his voice. Dylan wasn't the type to play the role of the concerned friend. Hell, I wasn't even sure I had any friends left after everything with Kael, but Dylan... Dylan was different. Maybe it was because he wasn't involved in the mess. Maybe it was because he had no stake in whatever had happened between Kael and me.

I didn't say anything. Instead, I walked over to the window and stared out at the city below. The rain had stopped, but the ground was still slick with water, reflecting the neon lights of the city like a warped mirror.

"Do you ever wonder, Dylan," I said slowly, "if everything we've been doing... is just one big, long mistake? That maybe we've been so busy trying to make sense of things, we never stopped to ask if we should be doing any of it in the first place?"

He was silent for a moment. Then, "Maybe," he said, voice quiet. "But that doesn't mean you stop trying."

I laughed—softly, bitterly. "Trying what, exactly? To fix something that was never ours to begin with?"

The air between us crackled with the weight of unspoken truths. I could feel the walls I'd spent so long building up begin to crumble, and it made me feel vulnerable, exposed. I didn't like it.

Before I could say anything else, there was another knock on the door. But this one was different—urgent, sharp, demanding. It was followed by the unmistakable sound of a voice calling my name.

"Diana, open the door. It's important."

Kael. My heart stopped in my chest. I didn't move.

Dylan, who had been leaning casually against the counter, suddenly stiffened. "That's him, isn't it?"

I didn't answer. Instead, I stared at the door like it was some kind of test. A test I didn't know if I was ready to face.

And then, as if the universe were just waiting for the right moment to shatter whatever fragile peace I'd managed to scrape together, the door swung open—just a crack—and I saw his face. And everything I thought I knew, everything I had decided was true, came crashing down.

But before I could speak, before I could even process what was happening, Kael stepped inside.

And in that moment, I knew: Nothing would ever be the same again.

Chapter 23: A Shattered Alliance

The sun hung low over the skyline of Chicago, casting an amber glow across the city like a slow-burning fire. I leaned against the railing of my apartment's balcony, watching the rush of traffic below. The hum of the city felt distant now, muffled, as though a veil had descended between me and everything I once knew. It had been three days since Kael walked out, leaving nothing behind but the soft echo of his footsteps. And yet, every inch of me still held on to the memory of his voice, the warmth of his touch. I had convinced myself that I could fight without him. But the truth was far harsher.

Inside, Seraphina's words still hung in the air like a curse. "We cannot win if we stand divided." The city seemed to close in on me as if it were pressing down, suffocating any hope I had left. I could still see the battlefield in my mind, the chaos of that final moment before Selene's forces overwhelmed us. We had been unprepared. The citadel had been nothing but a crumbling foundation, and in the end, we were left with nothing but ash and broken promises.

There was a knock at the door, soft but insistent. I didn't need to check the peephole to know who it was. No one else would dare disturb me in this fragile state of mind. I opened it with the kind of resignation that had become second nature, and there he stood—Marcus. His broad shoulders filled the doorway, his dark eyes as unreadable as ever. He didn't speak at first, merely regarded me with that odd mixture of concern and detachment that I had never quite figured out.

"Still pretending to be alone?" he asked, his voice a low drawl that, in any other context, would have felt teasing. But now, it only served to remind me of the weight of the silence that had settled between us all.

I shrugged, stepping aside to let him in. "If I can't trust my own allies, I'm better off in solitude."

Marcus didn't flinch at the bite in my tone. Instead, he made his way into the apartment, his eyes scanning the room before landing on me once more. "You're making this harder than it needs to be," he said, folding his arms across his chest.

I narrowed my gaze at him, refusing to be intimidated. "And you're here because...?"

"Because the city's falling apart, and whether you like it or not, we need you back in the fold," he replied, his voice steady but laced with the subtle urgency of someone who had already seen too much destruction. "We've been keeping it together as best as we can, but that doesn't mean much when half our forces are scattered, and the other half is wondering if we'll be able to survive the next wave."

His words hit me like a slap, but I refused to acknowledge the sting. "Surviving isn't enough," I muttered, my voice barely above a whisper. "What's the point of survival if we're just waiting for the next blow to come?"

Marcus took a step toward me, his expression softening ever so slightly. "You know better than anyone that sometimes survival is all you've got left. You don't get to choose the battles. You just fight until you can't anymore."

I turned away from him, the words twisting in my chest. I had fought, I had bled, and for what? To watch it all crumble into dust? Kael's betrayal, or whatever it was, had left a void I wasn't sure I could fill. I could still hear his voice in my head, the cold finality with which he'd said goodbye.

"We need you, Aisling," Marcus pressed, his voice growing softer now. "But not just as a soldier. We need you because you're the one who can hold us together, whether you believe it or not."

I closed my eyes, trying to fight back the overwhelming sense of failure that gnawed at me. I wanted to tell him that he was wrong. That the weight of our failure wasn't mine to carry. But the truth was, I couldn't lie to myself anymore. There was too much at stake. And if I didn't step up, who would?

"You're right," I finally said, my voice a faint echo of the determination I once had. "But I can't do it alone. I can't fix what's been broken."

Marcus didn't answer right away, and I wondered if he was calculating whether my words were an admission of defeat or a plea for help. After a long pause, he spoke again, his voice quiet but resolute. "You don't have to. But you can't do this by pushing everyone away, either."

I looked at him then, really looked at him, and for the first time, I saw the cracks in his own facade. The walls we had all built around ourselves were crumbling, piece by piece. In this city, in this war, none of us were untouched by the chaos. Not even Marcus, the ever-cool strategist.

"There's no going back," I said, my voice barely above a whisper, the weight of my words heavy in the air between us. "The lines have been drawn. The alliances have been shattered. It's over."

Marcus shook his head, a small, wry smile tugging at the corner of his mouth. "Maybe you haven't noticed, but the world doesn't quite work that way. It never has, and it never will. Not as long as people like you are still standing."

His words lingered in the silence, and for the first time in days, I allowed myself to believe that maybe, just maybe, there was still a chance.

The nights in Chicago had always held a certain magic, the kind that made you feel like anything was possible, as though the city itself could cradle your dreams or shatter them in a single breath. Tonight, however, the skyline felt more like a warning—bright lights that flickered in the distance, taunting me with the life I was no longer certain I could return to.

I should have been asleep, should have been gathering what little strength remained, but the thoughts in my head were too loud. Too heavy. Kael's absence had hollowed out every corner of my mind, each thought a reminder of the fracture that now defined everything. The city outside seemed like a distant world, one that had nothing to do with the ruins we had left behind at the citadel. But the city was, in its own way, a reflection of that very destruction. We all lived in the cracks, pretending we could fill them in with busy work and small comforts.

There was another knock at the door, though this one wasn't soft like Marcus's. It came with the kind of force that made the whole apartment seem to shake. I didn't have to check the peephole again. The sound of heels on the worn wood floor was unmistakable.

I stood slowly, my legs still feeling the remnants of last night's exhaustion, and walked to the door. Seraphina stood there, her dark coat pressed tight against her frame, her hair pulled back in a perfect knot that only served to emphasize the weariness behind her sharp eyes. The walls that always seemed to separate her from everyone else were gone now, and I could see the vulnerability she had tried so hard to hide. I hadn't expected her to come here, not like this.

"I didn't think you'd come," I said, my voice thick with disbelief, though the words felt right. I hadn't expected anyone to make the effort.

Seraphina didn't reply immediately. She stepped into the apartment, not waiting for an invitation. "You're making a mistake," she said, her voice tight, but sharp as always.

"I'm not making a mistake," I replied, though even as the words left my mouth, I wasn't entirely sure I believed them. "I'm just... tired."

"Tired of what?" she asked, her gaze unwavering. "Tired of fighting? Tired of losing?" She paused, letting her words hang in the air between us, as though daring me to respond. "This isn't about you, Aisling. Not anymore. We're past that."

I shook my head, bitterness creeping into my veins like poison. "You don't understand. You weren't there. You didn't see what happened when—" My words trailed off, the memory of that final, desperate stand still too fresh. Too painful.

She exhaled slowly, taking a step closer, the light from the lamp casting shadows across her face. "Kael left. And you're still standing here, letting that define you." Her words were like a slap, quick and clean, but they left a sting that I couldn't ignore.

"Don't," I whispered, my breath catching in my throat. "You don't know what it was like."

"I don't?" She gave a single, sarcastic laugh, but it had no warmth in it. "I'm not the one who let our army fall apart. I'm not the one who chose to walk away."

I flinched at the accusation, though I knew it was true. I had let this happen. I had let my emotions fracture what little strength remained in our cause. I had believed in something that had, in the end, turned to ash.

"I don't need your judgment, Seraphina," I snapped, stepping away, needing to put distance between us. "You don't know what it's like to fight alongside someone and then lose them—not just in the physical sense, but in every other way. You didn't see his eyes when he turned away from me. You don't understand how that feels."

She took a deep breath, the lines around her eyes softening ever so slightly. "I'm not judging you, Aisling," she said quietly. "I'm telling you that we're at a crossroads. You can stay in this grief, in this pit where Kael's betrayal is all you have, or you can look around you and see that the people who still need you are here, waiting. We've all been broken. Every single one of us. But we're still here. We're still fighting."

There was a long silence, the weight of her words heavy in the room. I couldn't deny the truth in them, but the wound she'd uncovered was raw. "I'm not sure I can fix this," I murmured, finally turning back to face her.

"You don't have to fix it," she said, the edges of her tone softening. "You just have to stop pretending you're the only one carrying it."

I closed my eyes, the truth settling over me like a suffocating blanket. What was I holding onto, anyway? The memory of Kael? The ideal of him? The promise of something we had never truly had?

"I can't do this alone," I whispered.

Seraphina's expression softened, her walls momentarily coming down. She stepped toward me and placed a hand on my shoulder, the touch unexpectedly warm. "You don't have to," she repeated. "But you do have to stop running. We're still here. And we're going to need you, Aisling. More than ever."

I nodded, though the tightness in my chest threatened to undo me. For the first time in days, I allowed myself to believe, even if only for a fleeting moment, that there might be a way out of the wreckage. That maybe—just maybe—there was still a place for me in all of this.

"I'll be there," I said finally, my voice steadier than it had been in days. "But I won't do it alone."

Her lips quirked into the faintest of smiles, a flicker of something between us, and I realized then that she had been just as lost as I had. Just as desperate.

Together. That was the only way we stood a chance.

The morning light filtered through the half-open blinds, casting slanted stripes of gold across the room. It was early—earlier than I should have been awake—but I couldn't seem to stay asleep for long. My body was used to the rhythm of late nights, but my mind refused to cooperate. Every time I closed my eyes, I saw the battlefield again. The sound of the walls cracking. The weight of Kael's absence. It was like I could still feel him there, in the space we had shared. But it was empty now.

I stood and walked to the small kitchen, the harsh light of the morning illuminating the disarray of my life. The sink was filled with dishes I hadn't bothered to clean, a forgotten cup of coffee growing cold on the counter. I was never one to care much for cleanliness when the world around me felt like it was falling apart, but today I found myself wanting to clear the clutter, to pretend that something could be set right in this world.

There was a knock at the door, and I froze. The sound was soft but unmistakable, and something about it made my stomach twist. Not Marcus. Not Seraphina. This was different. I opened the door to find a tall, unfamiliar figure standing in the hallway. His features were sharp, almost sculptural in their precision, and his eyes were a dark shade of green that reminded me of the dense, shadowed woods outside of town—impenetrable, dangerous.

He smiled, a cold, unsettling thing. "Aisling," he said, his voice smooth and calm. "We need to talk."

I didn't invite him in. There was something about him that immediately set off warning bells in my head. "I'm not interested in talking," I replied, keeping my tone steady, but I could feel my pulse quickening.

"Oh, I think you are." He took a step forward, his presence suddenly imposing in the narrow hallway. "I'm not here to waste your time. I'm here to offer you a choice."

I stepped back instinctively, my hand on the doorframe. "A choice?"

He nodded, his eyes never leaving mine. "The people who are leading this city into chaos? They're getting bolder. Stronger. I can help you, Aisling. I can give you the power to fight back, to regain what's yours. But only if you come with me."

I narrowed my gaze. "Who are you?"

"My name is Elias." His lips curled into a smile that didn't reach his eyes. "And I'm here to offer you an alliance. A real one. Not the broken pieces you've been clinging to. Not that... fractured excuse for leadership."

His words were like ice-cold water splashing against a flame, each syllable dousing the small ember of hope that had started to kindle within me. Alliance. That word—so easily spoken, so hollow now—felt like a lie in the pit of my stomach. The last alliance had already been shattered. The one I'd trusted. The one that had promised everything only to leave me holding the shards of what was left.

"You think I'll just follow you?" I scoffed, not bothering to hide my disbelief. "You've got the wrong person. I don't trust anyone who walks in here uninvited, offering 'choices.'"

Elias didn't flinch. His expression remained carefully neutral, as if this was all part of some grand script he had rehearsed. "I'm not asking for your trust," he said simply. "I'm asking for your decision. Will you join me, or will you continue to play at being the last hero standing in a city that's already given up on you?"

I felt the pressure in my chest tighten, the weight of his words sinking in. Chicago had always been a city of contrasts. A city that could break you or make you. A city that had built itself on the backs of the broken, the bruised, and the betrayed. But the city had become something else, something darker, ever since the rift had formed. The air crackled with tension, with whispers that nothing would ever be the same.

"I don't need your help," I said firmly, though my voice wavered slightly. "I'm not some pawn you can move around the board. And I'm not stupid enough to trust someone who's only here because it suits his interests."

Elias didn't react the way I expected. Instead of anger or frustration, there was an eerie calmness to him, an assurance that made my skin crawl. "You'll come around," he said, his voice soft but certain. "I'll give you time. But remember this, Aisling: time is something you're running out of. Every day you wait, someone else makes a move. Someone else gains power. And the longer you refuse to act, the harder it will be to take back what's yours."

Before I could say another word, he turned on his heel and walked away, his footsteps soft but deliberate as he disappeared down the hall. I watched him go, the quiet hum of the apartment filling the space where his presence had been, the silence somehow louder than the conversation itself.

I stood in the doorway for a long time, my mind whirling. His offer—his ultimatum—had been tempting in a way I hadn't expected. But something about him felt off. The easy charm, the polished exterior, the promises of power—those were the things that made me want to turn away and never look back. But I couldn't help but wonder, if the city was really slipping further into chaos, could I afford to ignore him?

The question gnawed at me as I closed the door, the echo of his voice lingering like an unwelcome guest in my mind.

Later that day, Seraphina found me again. This time, she didn't knock. She walked right in, her eyes narrowed as if she'd already made up her mind about something.

"You met him, didn't you?" she asked, her voice a low murmur.

I didn't have to ask who she meant. "Elias," I said, the name tasting bitter on my tongue.

Seraphina's eyes flickered, and for the first time, I saw a trace of hesitation in her gaze. "He's dangerous," she said quietly, as if speaking his name aloud might summon something dark and untamable. "But you already know that."

I opened my mouth to reply, but a sound from the hallway froze me mid-word—a sharp crack, like the shattering of glass. A shrill scream echoed through the building, followed by another, then more. I rushed to the window and looked down below, my heart skipping in my chest.

The street was a frenzy of motion, people running, screaming. Something was happening. Something far worse than we could have imagined.

And then I saw him. Elias. Standing in the midst of it all, a smile playing at the edges of his lips.

I didn't have to wonder anymore. He wasn't here to offer help. He was here to watch it all burn.

Chapter 24: Echoes of the Past

The city of Arklight had always been a place where shadows stretched long into the evening, where even the sun seemed reluctant to fully claim the sky. Its name, a lingering relic of a forgotten past, was spoken in hushed tones by those who knew better than to ask questions. Once a thriving metropolis, brimming with the promise of progress, it had crumbled into a hushed ruin, overtaken by the slow march of time and nature. The very ground beneath my feet felt alive with the weight of history, and I couldn't shake the feeling that something was watching, waiting for me.

I stood at the edge of what had once been the grand courtyard, now a fragmented puzzle of broken stone and curling vines. The Ravenmarked had gathered here in times long past—mages and seers whose names had been swallowed by the pages of forgotten books. Their power had once been a beacon, a light cutting through the darkness of a world on the brink of change. But now, all that remained were the crumbling walls and the eerie silence that hung in the air like a curse.

I had come here in search of answers, though whether I was ready for them, I couldn't say. The journal I had found in the heart of the ruins wasn't much, just a few tattered pages, the ink faded and smeared with the passage of years. But it had drawn me in, the words of a mage who had once walked the same path I now found myself on. "To wield this power is to walk a path of sacrifice," she had written, her handwriting looping gracefully across the page like an intricate spell. The words seemed to breathe life, their meaning twisting in my mind with every passing moment.

Sacrifice. It was a word I had heard too often in the last few weeks, a word that seemed to follow me like a shadow, lurking just behind me, waiting to catch me when I faltered. What would I have to give up? My freedom? My humanity? A piece of my soul? Or something even worse, something I couldn't yet comprehend?

I sat down on a fallen stone, the sharp edges digging into my legs, and opened the journal once more. The mage's words continued to haunt me, her struggle mirroring my own. She had faced the same decision, the same gnawing doubt that had eaten away at my resolve. "Power is never without cost," she had written, her words more like a warning than a lesson. And I felt it in my bones, that same pull, the same temptation that had been gnawing at the back of my mind for days. But could I trust her? Could I trust anyone? Was this path truly mine to walk, or was I simply a pawn in someone else's game?

The wind stirred around me, rustling the pages of the journal, the soft rustle reminding me of the fragility of this world. I closed my eyes for a moment, letting the sounds of Arklight wash over me—the distant cry of a hawk, the soft swish of the trees swaying in the wind, the deep hum of the earth itself, as though it were alive with secrets.

There was a choice to be made, one that would shape the course of my life, and yet, I found myself torn between the desire to continue down this path and the overwhelming urge to turn back, to leave the past where it belonged and never look back. But that wasn't an option anymore. Not when I had already walked so far.

I stood, brushing off the dust from my clothes, and surveyed the ruins before me. The stone pillars loomed like ancient sentinels, their surface etched with symbols that had long since faded into obscurity. The Ravenmarked had once gathered here to share knowledge, to exchange wisdom, and to bind themselves together in a covenant of power. But now, those very pillars seemed to sag under the weight of time, their once-proud architecture reduced to little more than a shadow of what had once been.

And yet, despite the decay, despite the desolation, I could sense it—the faintest stir of something deep beneath the earth, something ancient and powerful. It was as if the land itself had been waiting for me, waiting for the moment when I would finally understand.

The journal clutched tightly in my hand, I began to walk through the ruins, each step deliberate, as if I were treading carefully on sacred ground. I didn't know what I was looking for. The mage's words had set something in motion, but I wasn't sure what it was. All I knew was that I couldn't leave yet. Not when there was more to uncover.

As I passed a broken archway, a sudden chill swept over me, the kind of chill that crawls beneath your skin, makes your breath catch in your throat. I froze, my heart pounding in my chest as I scanned the shadows. The air felt thick, heavier than it had moments before. And then, through the haze, I saw her.

She was standing just beyond the archway, a figure draped in shadows, her eyes glowing faintly with an otherworldly light. Her presence was undeniable, like a force of nature, yet she stood still, watching me with an intensity that made my skin prickle. My first instinct was to run, to flee from whatever this was, but my feet were rooted to the ground, as though the very earth was holding me in place.

"You came," she said, her voice soft, yet carrying with it a power that made the air hum. "I wondered if you would."

I took a cautious step forward, my heart racing. "Who are you?"

She smiled then, a slow, knowing smile that sent a shiver up my spine. "I am the one who has been waiting for you to understand. The one whose path you follow."

The woman before me seemed to shimmer with an almost unreal quality, like a figment of a dream clinging too tightly to reality. Her skin had the smooth pallor of marble, but it wasn't cold—no, there was something alive about her, something warm that hummed beneath the surface, barely perceptible. The glow of her eyes, dim as it was, seemed to echo against the ruins, reflecting back a thousand forgotten stories. She didn't move as I took another step forward, though the silence between us thickened, as if the very air was holding its breath, waiting for something to break it.

"You came," she repeated, her voice lilting in a way that almost sounded like a question, though I could hear the certainty in it. "I wondered if you would."

I swallowed, caught between wanting to run and the overwhelming pull to understand what was unfolding in front of me. "You keep saying that. What do you mean, 'I came'?"

Her gaze flicked to the journal still clenched tightly in my hand, the pages now crinkled from my grip. A slight smile tugged at her lips, though it wasn't a comforting one. It was the kind of smile that hinted at secrets only she knew, at pieces of a puzzle I wasn't yet capable of seeing.

"Do you know what you're holding?" she asked, her voice dropping an octave, each word dripping with layers of meaning.

I glanced down at the journal, the weight of it suddenly more apparent, as if the parchment itself were aware of the shift in the air. "A mage's journal. It belongs to someone who was here before me, part of the Ravenmarked."

She inclined her head, as though acknowledging my words without truly hearing them. "Yes, she was one of us. One who made the same choices you now face. The same sacrifices." Her gaze locked onto mine, and for a moment, I felt as if the ground had slipped beneath my feet. She was no longer just an observer, no longer a stranger. She was a part of the fabric of this place, and I—however unwittingly—had become part of it too.

"I don't understand," I admitted, my voice betraying the unease that was rising in my chest. "What do you want from me?"

"Nothing," she said simply, though the word held a weight that made my stomach twist. "But I can offer you something. An understanding, if you're willing to listen."

"Listen to what? Another cryptic prophecy? More riddles? Because I'm starting to think this whole damn place is made up of riddles."

The woman chuckled, the sound light and musical, but there was something dark underneath it. "You're right. Riddles, yes. But they're not mine to give. They were here long before you and I. This place... it does things to people. Makes them think they're in control when they're anything but."

I took a hesitant step forward, the journal pressing into my palm like a living thing, pushing me toward something I wasn't sure I was ready for. "I'm listening. So, tell me what's next."

Her gaze softened, just a fraction, and she gestured toward the ruins behind her. "Walk with me."

I didn't question it—didn't have the energy to. If there was one thing I had learned about the world in the last few weeks, it was that nothing ever made sense unless you were willing to dive in headfirst, even if the water felt like it was going to swallow you whole.

We moved through the crumbling ruins, the earth beneath our feet giving a strange, uneven groan as we walked. The stones seemed to shift with every step, as though they were breathing, the remnants of the Ravenmarked past still seeping into the present. There were no more words for a while, just the sound of our footsteps and the quiet rustle of leaves in the wind.

"You asked what it means to sacrifice," she said after a long pause, her voice cutting through the stillness like a blade. "But you already know the answer."

I didn't. Not really. How could I know when every part of me wanted to deny the very idea of sacrifice? But there was no denying the feeling that had been gnawing at my insides since I first set foot in this place—the feeling that the world I thought I knew was slipping through my fingers, and I wasn't sure I could hold on to any of it.

"Power always comes at a price," she continued, her gaze fixed straight ahead, as though seeing something beyond the ruins, beyond even time itself. "You want to know what it costs? It costs more than you're ready to give."

I stopped walking, the words hanging in the air like a thick fog. "And what if I'm not ready? What if I don't want to pay the price?"

The woman turned to face me then, her expression unreadable, her eyes still glowing faintly in the dim light. "That's the question, isn't it? What will you do when the time comes? When you have no choice but to choose?"

I stood there, rooted to the spot, the journal trembling in my hands as if it too felt the weight of the decision hanging in the air. Could I truly walk away from this? Could I ignore the pull of power that had already started to sink its claws into my soul? The idea of turning back—of walking away from the Ravenmark, from everything that had been set in motion—felt impossible.

And yet, I knew there was a risk, a danger that came with embracing the power that was calling to me. I had seen it in the mage's journal, in the stories she had left behind. Those who had walked this path before me hadn't come out unscathed. No one ever did.

I glanced up at the woman, her gaze unwavering, as though she could see the storm raging inside me, the indecision that was threatening to tear me apart. "I don't know what to do," I whispered, my voice small despite the enormity of the question.

She smiled then, a smile full of knowing. "That's the beauty of it. You don't have to know yet. You just have to decide when the time comes."

And as her words settled into my mind, I realized that the hardest part wasn't making the choice—it was accepting that, when the moment came, there would be no turning back.

The woman's words lingered in the air long after they left her lips, each syllable weighted with something ancient and unfathomable. I stood frozen, my heart pounding against my chest, my mind struggling to grasp what she was offering—or warning me about. She was right, though. I didn't have to know what to do yet, didn't have to decide in this moment. But the pressure was there, thickening the air around us. It was the kind of pressure that made every breath feel heavier, as though the very weight of the ruins was pushing down on me, urging me toward something I was too scared to confront.

"So, what happens now?" I asked, my voice more steady than I felt. "Do we just stand here, waiting for the world to end or for some cosmic revelation to drop from the sky?"

Her smile didn't falter, though the slight tilt of her head made it clear that she wasn't fooled by my bravado. "The world doesn't end until you decide it does." She raised a hand, her fingers brushing the air as though conducting some invisible orchestra. "I'm not here to show you the future, or to make the choice for you. I can only show you what lies beneath the surface."

I frowned, irritation bubbling up. "That's helpful."

She let out a small, amused breath. "You would be surprised how many come here looking for answers and walk away with more questions."

I had no doubt that she was right, but that didn't make it any easier to stomach. "What exactly is it you want from me?" My words felt heavy, tinged with something I couldn't quite identify, some unspoken dread creeping into the corners of my mind.

The woman seemed to consider my question for a long moment, as though weighing her answer carefully. "What do you think I want from you?" she asked, her voice oddly soft, but there was a steeliness beneath it, like the calm before a storm.

I took a step back, suddenly aware of how close I had gotten to her—close enough that I could almost feel the pull of the strange energy radiating from her. "I don't know. You keep saying things that make no sense. You've led me here, made me believe that this—" I gestured vaguely at the ruins around us, "—means something. But it's all just so... vague. You've got me on the edge of something, but I can't see it."

The woman tilted her head, her expression shifting, a glint of something unspoken dancing in her eyes. "It's not about seeing, not yet. It's about feeling." She extended her hand toward me, palm open, as though offering me something I couldn't quite comprehend. "You are already feeling it. You've felt it for days, maybe longer. The pull. The hunger. The part of you that wants to step into the dark and claim what it offers."

I glanced down at the journal in my hands, the cover worn from my constant grasp. The words inside had unsettled me more than I cared to admit. "And if I don't want to claim it? What if I choose to walk away from all of this?"

Her smile deepened, and for a split second, I thought I saw something like pity flicker in her eyes. "You can walk away, but only for a while. The path doesn't let you forget. It's always waiting for you to return."

A sudden gust of wind swept through the courtyard, scattering dried leaves across the stone floor, and for a moment, it felt as though the ruins themselves were alive, their very bones creaking and shifting in a way that made the hairs on the back of my neck stand on end.

"Why me?" I found myself asking before I could stop it, the question slipping out, raw and desperate. "Why am I the one who gets to decide? Why not someone else? I'm not special, not some chosen hero. I'm just me."

The woman's eyes softened, and for a moment, there was a flicker of something almost human in her gaze. "You are not just anyone. You are the one who found the journal. You are the one who came here, even when the world was telling you not to. You were always meant to be here."

I opened my mouth to argue, but the words caught in my throat. Maybe she was right. Maybe I hadn't been running from this. Maybe I'd been running toward it all along, even when I didn't fully understand what it was.

But before I could speak, a distant rumble echoed through the air, a deep, resonant sound that seemed to vibrate beneath my feet. My first thought was that it was thunder, but the sky above remained clear, unmarred by a single cloud. The rumble grew louder, sharper—like the groan of an ancient beast awakening after a long, uneasy sleep.

I turned, searching the horizon for the source of the sound, my heart racing as the ground trembled beneath me. It was as though the ruins themselves were reacting, their once-still stones vibrating with an energy that felt almost... alive.

"What is that?" I demanded, my voice rising above the sudden noise.

The woman's expression had shifted again, her serene composure cracking, her gaze sharp and focused. "You're not the only one drawn to this place," she said quietly, her tone grim. "The question is, what will you do when they come?"

I didn't need to ask who they were. I could feel it now, the presence of something—or someone—approaching, something that made the air thicken with foreboding.

A figure emerged from the shadows of the ruins, tall and cloaked in dark fabric, moving with an unnatural grace. My pulse quickened. The moment I saw them, I knew: they were not human. And whatever they wanted, it wasn't going to be good for anyone involved.

The woman stepped forward, placing herself between me and the newcomer, her face now hard with determination. "You need to make your choice, and quickly."

But before I could move, the ground beneath us cracked with a deafening sound, the very earth splitting open as if it were unwilling to hold whatever was coming. And in that moment, I realized: this was only the beginning.

Chapter 25: The Pact Renewed

The sun was beginning its slow descent over the city, casting a honeyed glow across the crumbling buildings that had once been grandiose but now stood as monuments to another time. The streets were quieter than usual—just the hum of distant traffic and the soft whispers of the wind. I stood at the edge of the ruins, my boots sinking slightly into the overgrown grass, its wild green tendrils curling around my ankles like a forgotten secret. The remnants of old stonework crumbled beneath my fingers as I absentmindedly traced the jagged lines of a broken wall. There had been a fire here, once, years ago—one of those fires that didn't just scorch the earth but seemed to eat away at the very fabric of the place. As I stood there, I wondered if this was what we were becoming. Something half-done, abandoned, waiting for the inevitable.

My mind flickered back to him. Kael.

He had been a force of nature in my life, like a thunderstorm that swept through without warning, leaving chaos in its wake. But this time, when he appeared at the edge of the ruins—his silhouette outlined by the fading sunlight—I felt a strange calm wash over me. It wasn't the panic I had expected or the anger that usually flared when he showed up unannounced. No, today, something inside me shifted, and I didn't know whether I wanted to run toward him or away from him. But I stayed rooted to the spot.

"You're here," I said, my voice surprisingly steady considering the weight of everything that had transpired between us.

He didn't answer right away. Instead, he took a step closer, his eyes dark with something that looked like regret, though he didn't quite seem the type for such feelings. Kael always wore his emotions like armor—sharp, cold, and unyielding—but today, his gaze was stripped bare, almost vulnerable. It threw me off balance.

"I was wrong," he said, and there was a rasp to his voice, like it hadn't been used in a while. Like he had forgotten what it was like to apologize—or maybe, simply, to admit he was flawed.

I didn't know how to respond. The words had been waiting to spill out of me for so long, the grievances, the betrayals, the hurt—but now, they felt hollow. The truth was, I had been waiting for him to come back, to face me, to own up to the mess he had made. But there was something else—something unspoken—that kept me from lashing out.

"I can't do this without you," Kael continued, his voice softer now, and the words carried a weight they hadn't before. He reached a hand out, hesitant, as if he feared I might recoil. But I didn't move, not even a little, as his fingers brushed against the sleeve of my jacket. The coolness of his touch sent a ripple through me, but I didn't pull away. Not yet.

I studied him for a moment, watching as the setting sun bathed his face in a warm, golden hue. He looked different, somehow. Less certain, more human.

"You always think you can do it alone," I finally said, my tone sharper than I intended, but it was hard to keep the edge from creeping in. "That's been your problem from the start, Kael."

He let out a breath, running a hand through his dark hair, the gesture somehow making him seem more like the person I once knew. Before the secrets, the lies, the betrayal. Before I had learned that love wasn't enough to bridge the gap between who we were and what we had become.

"I know," he admitted, his eyes meeting mine now with an intensity that made my breath catch. "But I don't want to do it alone anymore."

The silence between us stretched, thick and uncomfortable. I wanted to argue with him, to tell him that it was too late, that the damage was done. But I couldn't. Because in the quiet that followed, I realized something—something I hadn't allowed myself to understand until now. I still needed him. As much as I hated it, I did.

"Why now?" The question slipped from my lips before I could stop it. "Why after everything? After we—" I couldn't bring myself to finish the sentence. We had been through too much, and the wounds were still fresh.

Kael took another step forward, and this time, I didn't back away. "Because I made a mistake. A big one. And I've been living with it, carrying it like a weight around my neck. But I've been wrong about so many things. About us. About the choices I made." He swallowed hard. "And I can't do this without you, Tess. I need you. You were always the one who kept me grounded. You're the reason I could even think straight, the reason I was able to make it through the storm."

His words were both a balm and a knife to my heart. They made me want to trust him, to believe that the man standing before me was the same one who had once promised me the world, only to watch as he shattered it. But they also reminded me of all the ways he had let me down. How do you trust someone who has burned you before? How do you pick up the pieces of something so broken?

But there was something about his sincerity, something that pulled at the raw edges of my heart. Maybe it was the fact that, for once, he wasn't hiding behind a mask of arrogance. Maybe it was the way he looked at me, like I was the only thing that mattered in the world. Or maybe it was the desperation in his eyes that made me realize just how far he had fallen. And I didn't want to see him fall any further.

"I don't know if I can forgive you," I said quietly, my words soft but firm.

"I'm not asking for forgiveness," Kael replied, his voice steady now, like he had made peace with that fact. "I'm asking for a second chance. For us."

I met his gaze, the weight of his plea pressing down on me. The city stretched out behind us, the ruins now seeming less like destruction and more like the beginning of something new. Maybe that was what we were—ruins in need of rebuilding. Maybe it was time to try, again.

Slowly, I extended my hand, my fingers brushing against his. The touch was tentative at first, but as soon as our palms met, the weight between us seemed to lift. There was no grand declaration, no promises of forever—just an unspoken understanding that we were both ready to face whatever came next. Together.

The light was fading fast, the amber glow of the sunset slowly retreating, as if even the sky were retreating into the safety of darkness. We stood in the silence, two people whose worlds had collided and shattered, only to find themselves inexplicably tethered once more. I could feel the weight of his hand in mine, like the slow, steady pressure of something unspoken, something that had always been between us but had never been named. For a moment, I simply watched him, unsure of where this was going, or even if I was ready for it. The last time Kael had pulled me in like this, it had been a tidal wave, pulling me under, drowning me in his charm and promises. This time, it felt different—calmer, but with an edge. A warning, perhaps. Or maybe just the quiet acknowledgment of everything that had happened.

"Are we really doing this?" I asked, my voice barely above a whisper, more to myself than to him. It was strange, this need to question everything again, to make sure I wasn't just running on instinct, as I had done so many times before.

Kael hesitated, his brow furrowing slightly, the lines of his face softening as he thought. "Only if you're ready."

My breath caught at the uncertainty in his voice. Kael had always been the one who was sure of himself—too sure, sometimes, but now there was a hesitation that mirrored my own. It was like we were both standing on the edge of something new, unsure if the ground beneath us would hold.

"I don't know if I am," I admitted, my eyes falling to the ground between us. There was so much we had to untangle, so much I didn't know if I could ever forgive. Yet the thought of walking away from him—again—wasn't something I was sure I wanted either.

"Then let's just… take it slow," he suggested, his voice gentle, but firm. "One step at a time. No rush."

I nodded, though the words left a strange taste in my mouth. We had been rushing for so long, chasing something we both thought we needed. But now, standing here, the realization that maybe I didn't need to rush was something I wasn't sure how to embrace. My heart was still too battered, too bruised from everything that had come before.

But as we stood there, the last of the sunlight sinking beneath the horizon, a quiet, unspoken agreement passed between us. Kael had made his peace, and I, for the first time in months, felt like I could begin to make mine. We had been so focused on the past, on everything we had lost, that we hadn't realized how much we still had. Not just together, but individually.

"I don't want to fight anymore," I said, more to myself than to him.

He nodded, a quiet understanding in his eyes. "Then don't."

I could hear the sincerity in his voice, and I realized that maybe, just maybe, we could find a way forward. Not by forgetting the past, but by learning from it—by recognizing the flaws in both of us, and instead of letting them tear us apart, using them to rebuild something better. Stronger.

As if on cue, the soft hum of the city's nightlife began to trickle back into the silence around us. The distant sound of car horns, the low murmur of voices, the soft clink of glasses in a bar nearby. It was the heartbeat of the city, and for the first time in a long while, it felt like we were part of it again. Like we weren't just drifting through life, waiting for something to happen, but instead, we were here. Together.

It wasn't perfect—nothing ever was, with us—but it was real. The kind of real that both terrified and comforted in equal measure.

Kael squeezed my hand lightly, breaking the momentary spell of quiet reflection. "You know, I never could have done this without you. Not in a million years."

The words landed in the air between us like a soft promise, and I found myself smiling—despite everything. Despite the ache that still lingered in my chest, despite the countless nights I had spent wishing for things to be different.

"You always say that," I said with a wry smile, leaning against the crumbling remnants of the old wall beside us. "Like you're some kind of tortured hero who can't function without me. You're such a melodramatic mess, you know that?"

He chuckled, a low, almost embarrassed sound. "You're one to talk. You always act like you've got it all figured out, but we both know you're just as much of a mess as I am."

"Oh, I know," I said with a raised eyebrow, tilting my head to look at him more fully. "I'm a complete disaster. But at least I'm an honest one."

His smile softened, the corners of his mouth curving upward in that way that made everything inside me ache with a mix of nostalgia and hope. "Maybe we both are."

For a moment, the distance between us seemed to shrink, and I felt the first stirrings of something that wasn't just fear or anger.

It was a quiet, tentative hope. Hope that maybe this time, we could get it right. Not perfect. But better.

"I'm still not sure about this," I said, the uncertainty creeping back in. "About us. About what comes next."

Kael's eyes never left mine, his voice steady. "We'll figure it out. Together. You don't have to have all the answers. Neither do I."

I opened my mouth to protest, but his finger pressed gently to my lips, silencing me. "No more questions. Just... trust me."

It was impossible to resist. I couldn't explain why, but for the first time in so long, I wanted to believe him. And maybe that was enough—for now. For this moment.

As the night settled in around us, the city buzzing softly with its usual rhythm, I allowed myself to trust. To believe that maybe we had a second chance at this, a chance to rebuild, to not just survive, but to actually live. Side by side.

The streetlights flickered on one by one, casting long shadows across the cracked pavement as we walked side by side. The evening air was cool but not quite cold, a reminder that fall had barely begun to settle in, yet there was already a heaviness to the breeze, like the city was holding its breath. It was the kind of night that made everything feel suspended—like time was stretching its arms lazily and waiting to see if it should continue, or if we had already lingered too long.

I could hear Kael's footsteps behind me, his presence just close enough that I felt the heat of him but not enough to touch. There had been a time when his mere nearness had made my heart race, when every brush of his arm had felt like a promise. But now, each step we took together felt more like an agreement. A truce.

"I'm not going to lie and say this feels like we're picking up right where we left off," I said, breaking the silence, my voice a little sharper than I intended. "Because it doesn't. It feels like we're two people who have to start over from scratch."

Kael's laugh was a dry, almost bitter sound. "I know," he said. "I think I'd be worried if it did."

I stopped walking, turning to face him. The city stretched out before us, with all its noise and energy, but right here, in this moment, everything felt quiet. Like the world was waiting for us to decide what we would do next.

"I don't even know what that means," I admitted, the words spilling out before I could stop them. "Start over. How do you even begin to fix something that's broken so badly?"

His eyes, dark and unreadable in the dim light, met mine. "I think you just... start. You don't try to fix everything all at once. You just start with one thing. One step."

I sighed, running a hand through my hair. "And if that step leads to a cliff?"

"Then you jump," he said, his voice low but steady. "Together. I'm not asking for you to trust me again right now. But trust me enough to walk beside me."

I didn't answer immediately. The words hung there in the air between us, as if he had just offered me a lifeline I wasn't sure I could reach for. Trust had always been a luxury, something we couldn't afford. Not with the way we had been, the things we had done. But maybe, just maybe, trust was the only thing we had left.

I nodded slowly, the tension between us easing just a fraction. "Okay," I said, the word tasting foreign on my tongue. "One step."

We resumed walking, this time with a silent understanding between us, the kind that only comes from the realization that words don't always hold the weight of what you truly mean. We didn't need to speak of everything that had come before, the fights and the misunderstandings, the lies we'd told each other and the truths we had kept hidden. It felt like the city was doing the talking for us—its thrum of life surrounding us, filling the space with noise we could both hide behind.

As we approached the corner, where the lights from a diner flickered in the distance, I noticed something shift in the air. A subtle change, a shift in energy. It wasn't Kael—he hadn't moved, hadn't said anything that would make me feel like the tension between us had cracked wide open. No, it was something else. Something deeper.

I stopped again, my gaze scanning the street. Something didn't feel right.

Kael's voice broke through my thoughts. "What is it?"

"I don't know," I said, my heart picking up speed for reasons I couldn't quite explain. "I feel like we're being watched."

The words sounded ridiculous even to me, but I couldn't shake the feeling that something—or someone—was out there, just beyond the edge of the streetlights, lurking in the shadows.

"Don't be paranoid," Kael said, a small chuckle in his voice, but there was an edge to it now, something that suggested he was feeling it too.

I turned, my eyes scanning the darkened alleyway that ran beside us. The neon lights from the diner cast a sickly pink glow against the brick walls, but it only made the shadows deeper, more menacing. I could swear I saw movement, a flicker at the corner of my vision. But when I blinked, it was gone.

"Maybe we should—" I began, but before I could finish my sentence, a sound interrupted us. A soft rustling. Then a sharp, unmistakable crack.

Something—or someone—was coming our way.

Kael moved instinctively, his body shifting to place himself between me and the alley. His hand was already at his side, where I knew his gun was holstered. But there was a tension in his movements, a hesitation I couldn't ignore.

"It's not a random junkie," he muttered, his voice tight. "Someone's coming for us."

Before I could respond, the sound came again, louder this time, closer. Footsteps, deliberate and slow. But it wasn't the footsteps of someone rushing toward us in a panic. No, these were measured, almost too calm.

I could feel Kael's muscles tense beside me, ready to react. But I was frozen. There was something about the way those footsteps echoed in the empty space, the way they seemed to wait just long enough to make you second-guess everything, that kept me rooted to the spot.

"You hear that?" I whispered, barely able to breathe.

Kael nodded, his jaw clenched. "Get behind me. Now."

I took a step backward, my pulse pounding in my ears, but before I could move any further, the alleyway was filled with a shadow—a figure emerging from the dark, too tall, too silent to be anything other than trouble. The streetlights flickered again, as if the city itself were holding its breath.

"Kael," I breathed, a tremor in my voice, my eyes widening in recognition.

The figure stepped into the light.

And for the first time in a long time, the ground beneath me seemed to tilt.

Chapter 26: The Blade of Truth

The smell of rain was in the air, thick and earthy, clinging to the asphalt like an old secret. A few streets over, a bus groaned its way through a fog of smog and headlights, its yellow body sputtering like it knew it was past its prime. But me? I was standing on the edge of a rooftop in downtown Chicago, staring at the glowing lights of the city below, my heart a tangled mess of hope, fear, and something dangerously close to love.

Kael was beside me, a solid presence in the murk of the storm clouds. His eyes flickered with the dim glint of the distant skyline, reflecting the light as if he'd spent a lifetime battling shadows and making them bow to his will. The wind tugged at his dark coat, and his jaw was tight, the unspoken thoughts churning beneath the surface. I'd gotten used to his silence, but that didn't make it any easier to figure out what he was thinking.

"I never thought we'd be here," he muttered, more to himself than to me. His voice was low, gravelly, like he hadn't used it for anything other than ordering people around in far-off places. He turned his head, just enough to catch my eye. "This... whatever this is. I didn't think you'd be the one I'd end up trusting."

I raised an eyebrow, stepping closer to the edge, my fingers curling around the cold metal railing. The city sprawled out before me, the streets glowing faintly under the rain-soaked sky, but none of it felt real. Not the blade, not the trials, not the strange bond between us that had grown as we fought our way through them. I didn't know what to make of it anymore, but I sure as hell wasn't going to be the first to admit it.

"You didn't trust me?" I asked, the question coming out sharper than I'd intended. He didn't flinch, though. Kael never did.

"No," he said, a small smirk playing at the corner of his mouth. "I thought you were just a distraction. A complication."

I smirked back, the rain hitting my face, cold and biting. "Well, you're welcome for that." I shrugged, feeling my pulse quicken. "I'm a complication, but I'm still standing here. The Blade of Truth isn't going to claim itself."

"Truth," he repeated, as if the word had a weight that needed to be savored. He stepped closer, his eyes narrowing, studying me. I could feel the invisible thread between us pulling taut, like some sort of invisible tether. "And you think it will be that simple? You really believe it will give us what we need?"

I looked at him, really looked at him, for the first time in days. His face was carved with lines of exhaustion, his eyes weary, but there was something else in the depths of them, something that made me pause. Something that made me think that maybe Kael didn't want this fight to be over as much as I did.

"I don't know," I said honestly. "But I don't see any other way." I leaned forward, bracing my hands on the edge of the roof, feeling the slickness of rain beneath my fingertips. "I'm not letting Selene win. Not now. Not ever."

Kael exhaled through his nose, a low sound that almost bordered on a laugh. "You're stubborn. I'll give you that." He stepped back, taking his eyes off me and turning toward the darkened street below. "And you're right about one thing. We don't have a choice. It's all or nothing now."

I swallowed hard. The weight of the Blade of Truth in my mind was growing heavier with every second. I could feel it, just beyond the horizon, waiting for us. If we could just survive the trials, claim it, then maybe we could stop Selene. Maybe.

"But do you trust yourself enough?" Kael's voice cut through the rain, softer now. Almost intimate.

I didn't want to admit the truth, didn't want to say it aloud, but the words slipped out before I could stop them. "No. But I trust you."

There was a long pause, one that stretched between us like a taut rope, ready to snap. His eyes found mine again, and for a split second, I saw something flash there. Something more than just the remnants of a battle-hardened man. His lips parted, but he didn't say anything, just took a step back and motioned toward the dark alleyway that led to the entrance.

"Then let's get this over with," he said, his voice low, but resolute. "We don't have much time."

I nodded, following him into the shadows. As the first drops of rain hit the back of my neck, I knew we were walking toward something more than just the blade. Something I couldn't name. Something I didn't understand. But I trusted him—enough to face it with him. And maybe, just maybe, that would be enough to survive what was coming next.

The trials had already begun, and I could feel it.

The alley was narrow, almost claustrophobic, the kind of forgotten space that only the desperate or the dangerous would venture into. Graffiti-covered walls, slick with moisture, shimmered faintly under the glow of distant streetlights. I could hear the occasional thrum of a passing car, the hum of the city beyond us, but here, in this forgotten corner of Chicago, there was only silence—cold and oppressive. It made me uneasy in a way I hadn't expected.

Kael moved ahead, his long strides eating up the distance with that effortless grace that made him seem more ghost than man. I tried to keep pace, but his intensity, the way he seemed to anticipate every shift in the shadows, made me feel like I was lagging behind. Still, I wasn't about to let him leave me in the dust—not with everything on the line.

"Stay close," Kael murmured, his voice a little more than a breath, like he didn't want to disturb the fragile peace of the night.

I wasn't sure if he meant it for the danger we were about to face or for the distance that had quietly crept between us in the last few weeks. Either way, I wasn't going anywhere. Not now.

The closer we got to the entrance of the building, the heavier the air felt. I could almost taste it—metallic and sharp, as if the city itself had been waiting for us. Waiting for something to break. The blade was close. I could feel its pull in the pit of my stomach, like a siren song that made my head spin and my heart race.

"Do you think it's real?" I asked, breaking the silence as we reached a rusted steel door. I tried to steady my breath, tried to stop my pulse from betraying my nerves. "The Blade of Truth? I mean, do you believe it's really the answer to all of this?"

Kael didn't answer right away. Instead, he pressed his palm to the door, his fingers brushing lightly across the surface, as if testing for something unseen. The faintest of cracks appeared beneath his touch, and the door groaned open with a reluctant, mechanical sigh.

"I believe it's our only shot," he said at last, his voice low but sure. His gaze flickered toward me, that intensity burning in his eyes again. "Whether it's the answer or not, that's something we'll find out together."

I swallowed. Together. The words meant more than they should. There was something about them, about this bond we had formed through blood, sweat, and magic, that made me feel like I couldn't breathe. I wasn't sure if I was ready for whatever that might mean—but I wasn't about to turn back now.

Inside the building, the air was thick with dust, the faint echo of our footsteps bouncing off the old brick walls. The floors creaked beneath our weight as we moved deeper into the building, each step a reminder of the centuries of history that had been buried here. I could feel the weight of it pressing down on me, a quiet urgency that made my hands tremble, even though I knew I couldn't afford to show fear. Not now.

"Tell me again," I said, the words tumbling out before I could stop them. "How do we even know that we'll survive this? Survive the trials?"

Kael's lips twisted into something that might have been a smile, though it was more a ghost of one than anything else. "We don't. That's the fun part."

I shot him a sideways glance, not entirely convinced that he was joking. "Fun, huh?"

"Isn't that what you're into?" he asked, voice dripping with the kind of sarcastic amusement I'd come to expect from him. "A little danger? A little chaos?"

I rolled my eyes. "You know, for someone who's always pretending to be the brooding, mysterious type, you're surprisingly annoying."

"I'm not pretending," Kael shot back with a quick, glinting look over his shoulder. "I am the brooding, mysterious type."

"You're lucky I haven't stabbed you yet," I muttered, but I couldn't help the smile that tugged at the corners of my lips.

Kael raised an eyebrow, and I couldn't tell if he was daring me or just indulging me. Either way, it was a challenge I didn't intend to back down from.

The building grew colder as we ventured deeper into its bowels, the kind of cold that settled into your bones. I pulled my jacket tighter around my shoulders, wishing for something warmer than the thin fabric between me and the chill. As we reached the heart of the building, I noticed something strange. The walls, once slick with age and grime, had started to change. There were carvings now, deep and ancient, etched into the stone like a language I couldn't quite decipher.

"I think we're here," Kael said, his voice suddenly serious, his gaze scanning the room with a precision that was almost unnerving. He stepped forward, his eyes narrowing as he reached out to touch one of the carvings. A low hum filled the air, and the ground beneath our feet seemed to tremble, as if the building itself was waking up after centuries of slumber.

"This is it," I said, my voice a little breathless as I took in the sight before me. A pedestal stood in the center of the room, bathed in an eerie, dim light. And there, on the pedestal, was the Blade of Truth.

Its blade shimmered with an otherworldly glow, the metal itself reflecting every flicker of light like it was alive. I felt its power like a jolt of electricity running through my veins, and for a moment, I thought I might actually be sick.

Kael stepped toward the blade, but before his fingers could touch the hilt, a deep, rumbling voice echoed through the chamber.

"Only the worthy may claim the blade."

I froze, my pulse thundering in my ears. The trials were about to begin.

The voice that echoed through the chamber wasn't human. It was ancient, the kind of sound that seemed to vibrate in the very marrow of your bones. It reverberated through the stone walls, making the air feel thick, oppressive, as if the room itself had been waiting, watching, for us to arrive. I didn't dare move. Didn't dare even breathe. The weight of the moment pressed down on me, heavy and suffocating.

"Only the worthy may claim the blade," the voice repeated, its tone deepening, the words laced with a challenge that hung in the air like a dare.

I turned to Kael, his expression unreadable as he stood beside me, his eyes locked on the pedestal. The blade gleamed under the dim light, a tantalizing promise of power and truth, but I could feel the danger crawling up my spine. This was it. This was the moment that would either make or break us.

"Are we worthy?" I asked, my voice barely a whisper, the question more of an affirmation than anything else. I already knew the answer, or at least, I thought I did. But Kael had never been one to give me easy answers.

"We'll find out," he said, his gaze hardening, determination sweeping over his features. His jaw clenched, his fingers twitching as if reaching for something just beyond his grasp. He was always like this—so sure of himself, so locked in. The kind of man who never wavered, even when the world around him was about to collapse.

The room seemed to hum with anticipation, the air charged with a strange, electric energy. I could feel my heartbeat in my throat, each beat more frantic than the last. I was scared. I'd never admit it aloud, but the truth had a way of forcing you to face things you weren't ready for. And this—this was the truth in its most brutal form.

"What happens if we're not worthy?" I asked, glancing toward the door behind us, already half-tempted to bolt. A part of me wanted to run, to escape the weight of it all. But there was no escape from this, not anymore.

Kael's lips curled into something that was almost a smile, though it didn't quite reach his eyes. "I guess we'll find out that, too."

I hated how calm he was. It made my insides twist in a way I wasn't used to. I was all chaos and nerves, barely holding it together. Kael, on the other hand, was the picture of controlled chaos, a storm in human form. He was always the one who jumped first, always the one who led. And I had no choice but to follow.

"I'm not ready for this," I said before I could stop myself, the words rushing out like they'd been trapped for too long. "I don't even know if I can do this, Kael. What if—what if I fail?"

His gaze softened for just a moment, the first time I'd seen any hint of vulnerability in him. It was gone before I could process it, replaced by that same cold steel, the mask he wore so well. "You won't fail. Not with me by your side."

His words sent a flicker of something through me, something warm that battled the cold dread swirling in my gut. The part of me that wasn't afraid, the part that had never been afraid of anything, no matter how impossible the odds. That part of me wanted to believe him. To believe that together, we could take on the world.

I wanted to believe that we could take on Selene.

But something inside me hesitated. A voice, small but insistent, whispered that I was about to do something far beyond my control. Something that would change me, change everything.

Kael stepped forward, and with a single motion, he reached for the hilt of the blade. The air in the room thickened, charged with an energy I couldn't quite place. As his fingers brushed against the metal, the ground beneath us shuddered, sending a shockwave of magic rippling through the room. The lights flickered, and the walls seemed to close in, as if the room itself was alive, testing us, pushing us.

"Let's see if we're worthy," he muttered, more to himself than to me. The words hung in the air, heavy with the weight of the moment.

His hand tightened around the blade's hilt, and for a brief, terrifying second, I thought I saw the faintest crackle of light dance across the surface. But then—

Nothing.

The blade didn't move. It didn't shift, didn't pulse with the energy I expected. It simply sat there, waiting.

I felt a knot of frustration twist in my chest. "Why isn't it—"

A sharp, guttural laugh echoed through the room, not from Kael, but from the shadows themselves. It was dark, mocking, and far too familiar. My skin prickled as the voice spoke again, this time filled with venom.

"You think it's that easy?"

I froze. The voice was unmistakable.

Selene.

Her name clung to the air, sour and bitter, the taste of it lingering in the back of my throat. The blade had been a lie. The trials had been a lie. And the real trial—was standing right in front of us.

I felt the ground beneath my feet shift, the stone trembling as if some great force was pushing against us. The walls seemed to stretch, warping, bending, until they collapsed inward, revealing a dark figure shrouded in a cloak of shadows.

"You've come too far," Selene said, her voice a sweet, sickly whisper. "And now, it's time to face the truth."

Before I could react, the shadows swallowed the room whole, plunging us into darkness. My heart pounded in my chest, my breath coming in ragged gasps. I reached out for Kael, but I couldn't find him in the blackness.

And then, in the distance, I heard her laugh.

Chapter 27: The Siege of Shadowspire

The city was a tapestry of contradictions, a mishmash of old-world charm and modern chaos, its pulse quickening with each passing day. I hadn't meant to be here, not like this, not amidst the swirling din of traffic and the constant hum of a city that never quite shut down. But here I was, having come to grips with the fact that I was living in a perpetual state of near-crisis. The kind of crisis you don't always recognize until it hits you full force—like the heat that wraps around you in an oven when you're least prepared.

The sticky summer air clung to my skin, the scent of asphalt and stale pretzels drifting through the air. I wiped a stray lock of hair from my face, the breeze too stubborn to comply with my attempts at taming it. New York was alive, yes, but it wasn't kind. The kind of city where people came to find themselves, only to realize that finding yourself in the chaos meant you had to fight for every inch of peace you could scrape together. I had learned that the hard way.

My apartment was a relic of the 1970s, complete with peeling wallpaper and a view that looked straight into the neighbor's unkempt balcony where a pigeon family had taken residence. Still, it was mine. Every creaky floorboard was a reminder of my resilience, my refusal to leave, no matter how much it tried to break me. I could've moved to the suburbs, settled into a quieter existence with less of the relentless urban sprawl, but something about the constant buzz of this place felt like the soundtrack of my own restless heart.

And then there was him.

I hadn't been expecting him—especially not like this. Not with the kind of intensity that made the rest of the world blur, his presence cutting through the mundane like a jagged knife through silk. If you'd asked me six months ago, I would have told you that I wasn't the kind of woman to fall for a man like Kael. Too brooding, too enigmatic, too...dangerous. But life doesn't ask you what you want; it simply delivers.

He wasn't the sort of man you could ignore. Or even the kind you wanted to ignore. In fact, I'd tried—more than once. But no matter how I turned the page, his dark eyes, the kind that could see straight through you, were there, never judging, only observing. He had that magnetic quality, the kind that made you feel like you could never escape, even if you tried. Not that I wanted to.

We hadn't spoken for two days—two long days that stretched into eternity, each hour a test of my restraint, my will. Kael had a way of making silence feel like an active thing. It wasn't comfortable. But it wasn't unpleasant either, in its own strange way. It was the sort of silence that demanded something, yet left you wondering whether it was something you could ever truly give.

I leaned against the kitchen counter, trying to ignore the smell of burned coffee that clung to my shirt. The city hum outside my window was a constant reminder that there were more urgent matters at hand, but still, I couldn't push him out of my mind. Maybe that's the thing about Kael. He had a way of existing in the spaces you didn't want him to, forcing his way into your thoughts like a storm you couldn't outrun.

I heard the familiar shuffle of his boots on the hardwood floors behind me, that unmistakable sound of a man who moved through the world with a quiet kind of strength. It wasn't so much that he was physically imposing—though, of course, he was—but more that he exuded this certainty, this confidence that could bend reality. And even though I hated to admit it, I knew I was under his spell.

"Burned your coffee again?" he asked, his voice low, carrying that familiar hint of amusement.

I shot him a look, half-annoyed, half-amused myself. "Funny, I don't remember asking for your opinion."

He chuckled, stepping further into the room, his presence suddenly filling the space. "I wasn't giving it, just stating a fact."

I turned, leaning back against the counter with an exaggerated sigh, trying not to let my heart betray me. "You're relentless, you know that?"

He stepped closer, his lips curling in that devil-may-care grin that made my stomach flutter in a way I didn't want to acknowledge. "I'm persistent, not relentless," he said, his voice lowering with each word. "There's a difference."

His proximity was making it harder to concentrate, and I hated that. I hated how easily he seemed to invade every part of me, from my thoughts to my very breath. "Persistent about what?" I asked, suddenly aware that the air between us was thickening, as though something was about to change.

He paused, his gaze narrowing in that way that made it feel like he could see the deepest parts of me, parts I hadn't even shared with myself. "About you," he said simply, as if it were the most natural thing in the world.

I didn't know how to respond. I never did. With Kael, words always felt inadequate, as though anything I said would be swallowed by the intensity of what hung between us. So instead, I did what I did best: I deflected.

"Maybe I'm just not the kind of woman you think I am," I said, crossing my arms over my chest, though I wasn't entirely sure why I was suddenly defensive.

His gaze softened, a fleeting moment of vulnerability that almost broke through his carefully constructed walls. Almost. "I don't need you to be anything but yourself," he said, and for a second, I almost believed him.

The knock at the door felt like a shot to the chest, sudden and loud enough to shake me out of the moment. I barely had time to steel myself before the door swung open, revealing him. Kael.

Of course. Of course, he would be the one to shatter the quiet, the stillness that I had clung to all day. His tall frame filled the doorway, leaning against the wood with that effortless grace of his, like he had all the time in the world. If only I could say the same. His eyes searched mine for an answer to a question I hadn't even realized I was asking—did I want him here? Did I need him here? It wasn't a simple question, and it certainly wasn't one I could answer with a neat little bow.

"Need a hand?" he asked, his voice dipping into that familiar, comforting lilt. The kind of voice that could either be an invitation or a command, depending on which way the wind blew.

I couldn't help but roll my eyes, though there was a small flicker of something warmer inside. Maybe it was because he had been so effortlessly right, or maybe because he always knew exactly when to show up. "You've been keeping track of me, huh?" I asked, pretending to sound indignant even though I was far from it.

He smirked, walking in without waiting for an answer. "I've got my ways," he said, as if it were no big deal, like his presence here was the most natural thing in the world. And maybe, for him, it was.

My apartment suddenly felt smaller with him in it, like the walls were shrinking with every step he took toward the counter, his eyes flicking over the kitchen as though he could read the disarray better than any map. And maybe he could. It wasn't that he was some sort of mind reader, but he had an uncanny knack for seeing through the layers, like he could sift through the noise and get straight to the truth. Which was dangerous, considering the truth was something I wasn't always ready to face.

"What's your game, Kael?" I asked, half to myself, half to him. I didn't want to be vulnerable. Not now. Not with him. The thing was, though, when it came to Kael, vulnerability was never something I had much say in.

He paused at the sink, his fingers lightly brushing the edge of an empty coffee mug, his expression unreadable. For a moment, I almost thought he hadn't heard me. But then his gaze lifted, and for a heartbeat, everything stopped. He stepped closer, his hand brushing mine, so lightly that it sent a shiver down my spine. It was as though his touch had some kind of invisible weight, enough to stir something deep inside me, something I had no intention of acknowledging.

"You think I'm playing a game?" he asked, his voice a whisper now, closer to a question than a statement. "I'm not the one who keeps running."

I winced, though I quickly masked it with a defensive laugh. "Running? I don't run. I just...prefer to think things through."

His lips curved into a smile that was more a challenge than anything else. "Is that what you call it? Thinking things through? Because from where I'm standing, it looks a lot like avoidance."

My stomach twisted, but I didn't back down. "And what if I don't want to be anyone's...project?" I asked, the words slipping out before I could stop them. It was a low blow, one I didn't even believe, but sometimes you said things you didn't mean when the tension in the room got too thick, when everything you wanted to say felt too dangerous to say aloud.

Kael took a step back, as though my words had struck him. For the first time in weeks, there was something distant in his eyes. Maybe it was the faintest trace of hurt, or maybe it was something else entirely. But whatever it was, it made my chest tighten.

"You think I see you as a project?" he asked, the words heavy with something I couldn't name. "You've got it wrong. I don't need to fix you, Quinn. And I'm not the one who needs saving here."

It was strange, hearing that from him. Kael had never been the kind of man to say things without expecting something in return. But in that moment, his words hung between us, raw and unspoken, like a thread that had been pulled too tight and was threatening to snap. The silence stretched on longer than I expected.

I opened my mouth to speak, but the words wouldn't come. There was a weight in the air now, a pressure building that I hadn't anticipated. Not from him, not like this.

Finally, he broke the silence, his voice quieter but no less certain. "You don't have to do this alone, you know," he said, his gaze steady as he met mine.

I shook my head, feeling something in me stir—a warning, or maybe just fear. "I don't need anyone to save me."

He didn't argue. Instead, his hand brushed against mine again, this time lingering, as if the contact itself was meant to convey more than words ever could. And for the first time, I let myself feel it. The way the tension between us thrummed, like a string pulled taut, ready to snap if either of us made the wrong move.

"I'm not trying to save you, Quinn," he said softly. "I just want to stand beside you."

The words settled into the space between us, heavy and profound, yet somehow tender. It was almost too much. Almost.

"I'm not sure how to stand beside you," I whispered, my voice barely audible, as though saying it aloud would make it real.

Kael's fingers tightened around mine for a brief moment, his touch grounding me, reminding me that we were no longer two separate forces in the world but something more. Something that neither of us had fully grasped yet, but something undeniable, nevertheless.

We stood there for a long time, the air between us thick with unspoken things. Neither of us had the courage to move first, so we simply existed in the silence, each of us figuring out whether we were ready to let the other in.

The phone buzzed on the countertop, its shrill ring slicing through the thick silence of the apartment. I jumped, startled out of the moment I had spent trying to convince myself that everything was fine, that nothing was more pressing than this, than us. Kael glanced at the phone with an eyebrow raised, and something passed between us, unspoken but understood. It was a look that said everything I was trying not to say.

I didn't move to answer it. Instead, I stared at the flashing screen. His name was unfamiliar, but the number felt heavy, like it belonged to someone I didn't know yet but whose presence was already embedded in the corners of my mind. I hated that. Hated how everything seemed to be happening without my permission, like I had lost control somewhere along the way.

"Go ahead, answer it," Kael said, his voice as casual as ever, but there was something in his tone that made me pause, something like he was testing me, waiting for me to make the wrong move.

I shook my head. "I'm not in the mood for surprises," I muttered, picking up the phone and sliding it into my pocket. There was no telling what the caller wanted, but something told me it wasn't good.

A silence fell between us then, the kind that sat uncomfortably, as though the air had thickened with an invisible weight. Kael didn't move, didn't speak. He just watched me, his gaze fixed in that unnerving way of his, like he was trying to figure me out, or maybe just waiting for me to crack.

"You know, you're not fooling anyone with this 'I've got it all figured out' act," he said finally, his words a gentle prod. "You can't always handle everything on your own. And you know that."

I stiffened. "You don't get it."

Kael's lips quirked into a half-smile, that mix of confidence and mischief that made it impossible to decide whether I wanted to kiss him or slap him. "I get more than you think," he said, stepping a little closer, his voice lowering. "I'm not going anywhere, Quinn."

I looked up at him, searching his face for any sign of doubt. But there was none. He was serious. Too serious. And that terrified me more than anything else.

I had never been good at trusting people, especially not with pieces of me I wasn't ready to part with. But Kael... Kael had a way of making you forget yourself, of erasing the lines between where you ended and where he began. It was dangerous. It was reckless. And yet, I couldn't stop myself from wanting more.

"Why are you here, Kael?" I asked softly, my voice quieter than I'd intended, as if somehow that would make the question less loaded.

His gaze softened, his hands now hanging loosely by his sides, as if he were trying to resist the temptation to reach for me. "Because I want to be."

My heart skipped. He didn't say it like he wanted something from me, but like it was an inevitability, like he'd always known that this—us—was where we were meant to be. It made me want to run, to bolt out of this room and never look back, but something else held me there, tethered to him.

The sound of a knock at the door interrupted the moment, the sudden intrusion both a relief and a curse. Without thinking, I walked over to open it, almost hoping it was anyone but the person on the other side. But when I pulled the door open, I froze. Standing there was a man I'd never seen before, wearing a sharp suit, his expression all business, but there was a flicker of something dangerous in his eyes.

"Are you Quinn Edwards?" he asked, his voice smooth, but his words carrying an edge.

I frowned, suddenly wary. "Who's asking?"

The man didn't answer right away. Instead, he reached into his coat pocket and pulled out an envelope, which he handed to me with a quiet nod. "This is for you. It's important."

I stared at the envelope, the thick paper stark against my palm, a weight that felt heavier than it should. "I didn't ask for anything," I said, my voice more clipped than I intended.

He didn't say a word. Just turned and walked away, his footsteps fading as quickly as they had come.

I stood there for a moment, the envelope still in my hand, my heart hammering against my chest. Something about the way he'd handed it over—so detached, like it was part of a greater plan I wasn't yet privy to—made every instinct in me scream that I wasn't safe.

Behind me, Kael shifted, his presence closing in as he read the tension in my body. "What is it?" he asked, his voice barely above a whisper.

I swallowed hard, looking down at the envelope. The seal was unbroken, the gold wax glistening ominously under the dim kitchen light. I hesitated for a moment, then slowly broke the seal, pulling out the letter inside.

The words were simple. Too simple.

"Your time is running out. There's only one way out now. Trust no one."

I felt a chill run down my spine, a sense of dread creeping up my limbs like cold fingers. The letter was unsigned. No clues, no directions. Just those chilling words. My breath caught in my throat as I felt Kael's presence behind me, his body taut with the same unease I was trying to suppress.

"What does it mean?" Kael's voice was low, tense. "What does it want from you?"

"I don't know," I whispered, feeling the air around us thicken. I turned to face him, the question hanging between us, unanswered. "But I'm about to find out."

Just then, a distant sound reached my ears—soft, but unmistakable. A siren. The kind of siren you only hear in the dead of night, the kind that signals something is coming, something worse than you can imagine. I didn't know what it meant. All I knew was that whatever was happening, we were right in the middle of it—and there was no going back.

I turned, half-expecting Kael to be right behind me. But when I looked, he was gone. The space where he had stood was empty.

And then, I heard it.

A knock at the door. Again.

Chapter 31: The Broken Crown

The world had never felt so silent. The remnants of the crown, broken and disheveled, littered the stone floor of the ancient hall like the bones of forgotten gods. My fingers still burned from the touch of it—its once-glorious edges now fractured, each shard holding the echo of a power I could barely understand. I stepped back, my boots leaving smudges on the dust beneath me, the weight of the moment pressing against my chest like a storm on the horizon.

Selene had always been dangerous, but in her last moments, she'd become something else—something darker, more cunning. Her parting words lingered in the air like the sharp sting of a bee's last strike. The prophecy. That cursed prophecy. I'd thought we had finally broken its hold over us, thought we had won. But here I was, standing among the pieces of a crown that was supposed to herald an end, only to realize it had been but the first page of a much darker story.

Beside me, Kael's breath came in slow, steady exhales, his grip on my hand firm and comforting. His presence was like an anchor in the midst of the storm, but even he couldn't pull me from the whirlpool of questions that threatened to drown me. I could feel his gaze on me, the heat of his stare like a brand against my skin, but I couldn't bring myself to look at him just yet. There was too much to unravel in my own mind, too much that didn't add up.

"We didn't win," I muttered, mostly to myself, the words tasting bitter on my tongue. I was never one for the easy wins anyway.

"Not yet," Kael answered, his voice low, his hand squeezing mine. "But we're closer. She wouldn't have fled like that if she didn't feel cornered."

I could almost hear the trace of hope in his voice, but it was the kind of hope that felt like it was running out of breath. It wasn't like him to be this careful with his optimism, but then, we'd both seen enough of the world to know that hope was often the most fragile thing of all.

I took a step closer to the broken crown, my boots scraping against the stone with a hollow sound. My fingers hovered over the shards, but I pulled them back quickly, as if the crown might bite me. I could feel the cold, ancient energy still radiating from it, seeping into the cracks of the room, into my skin, making my heart race with a strange urgency. The air was thick with the scent of old magic, iron, and something far more elusive—a fragrance I couldn't place but felt deep in my bones.

"I don't understand," I said quietly, more to the emptiness than to Kael. "What was she trying to do? Was this... Was it all part of her plan?" My voice cracked as I spoke the words aloud, finally giving them shape. I could hear my own doubt, but there was something deeper. Something gnawing at me like a distant memory I couldn't quite touch.

Kael's voice was steady, but there was a flicker of something in his eyes, something I couldn't read. "Maybe. But she wasn't expecting you to have the crown. Not like this."

The way he said it made me pause. The crown. It was the one thing Selene had coveted above all else. Her obsession with it had been consuming, blinding even. She had believed the crown held the key to her ascension—to power beyond anything I had ever seen. But now it was shattered at my feet, and the world seemed no closer to peace than it had before.

I bent down, careful this time, my fingers brushing against one of the broken pieces. The shard felt almost warm, pulsing with a strange rhythm that seemed to beat in time with my own heart. For a moment, I was tempted to pick it up—to hold it in my palm and let whatever magic still lingered within it course through me. But something held me back. The power felt wrong, like a dangerous temptation that had no place in the hands of anyone who still had a soul to lose.

"Do you think she'll come back?" I asked, more to break the silence than to seek an answer. But Kael's face was unreadable.

"I don't think she ever really left," he said softly, his voice carrying an edge of something like resignation. "She's been a shadow for too long. Shadows don't disappear. They just wait for the light to weaken."

The air around us seemed to grow heavier with his words, the walls of the hall pressing in as though they, too, were waiting for something to shift. I swallowed hard, my thoughts tangled in a web of confusion and dread. If Kael was right, if Selene was more than just a woman defeated in battle, then there was no telling what we had truly unleashed. The crown—broken as it was—wasn't the end of her. It had only been the beginning of something worse.

I stood up, my knees creaking with the movement, and turned toward the narrow window that looked out over the city beyond. The view was always the same—a city of stone and steel, alive with the bustle of countless lives, unaware of the dark forces that lurked just out of sight. It was strange, how normal it all seemed, how unaware the world was of the chaos just beneath the surface.

I could feel Kael's gaze on me, but I didn't turn to meet it. Not yet. I needed to think. I needed to understand what it all meant. The crown, the prophecy, Selene's parting words. I needed to piece it all together before the world—our world—was consumed by whatever she had set in motion.

And yet, for all my uncertainty, one thing was crystal clear: this was far from over.

I stood there, the broken crown at my feet, its once-pristine metal now a scattering of jagged edges and hollow promises. A few glimmering sparks still flickered from it, like the last flickers of a dying flame, but I knew better than to think there was any comfort to be found in those embers. Whatever power Selene had been after, it wasn't the crown itself—it was something deeper, something hidden beneath its fragile surface. Her departure had left a trail of smoke and doubt in its wake, and with it, the unsettling feeling that the battle was far from over.

Kael shifted beside me, his body pressing against mine, his warmth a small but steady anchor in a world that suddenly felt unrecognizable. I could feel his breath, shallow with restraint, though his hand still held mine with a reassuring firmness. We hadn't spoken since Selene disappeared in a cloud of smoke, but I could sense the question that loomed between us. Was this victory? Had we really done enough?

"I've got a bad feeling," I murmured, more to the empty hall than to Kael. The silence pressed in around us, thick and oppressive, as though the very walls of this forsaken place were holding their breath.

"Can't say I blame you," he replied, his voice a low rumble, like a thunderstorm on the horizon. "This doesn't feel like closure. It's... incomplete."

That was the word. Incomplete. It had taken us everything to shatter Selene's hold over the crown, but in the end, she'd slipped away like smoke through our fingers, leaving behind only an echo of her words. The prophecy. That blasted prophecy. She'd left us with more questions than answers, and it was enough to make my blood run cold.

I took a step back, my feet dragging against the stone, as I surveyed the room. The ancient hall, which had once been a place of power and celebration, now felt like a tomb. The cracks in the walls seemed to stretch further, reaching for me, as though they were trying to pull me into the shadows. There was something strange in the air, a heavy, tangible tension that I couldn't shake. It pressed against my chest, making it harder to breathe.

"We should leave," I said, my voice hoarse. I didn't wait for Kael's response before I turned and walked toward the exit, my boots echoing on the cold stone floor. The sudden movement seemed to break the stillness, and Kael followed without a word.

We stepped out into the night, the cool breeze carrying with it the scents of rain and earth, the familiar smells of the city that had once been my home. The lights of the skyline shimmered in the distance, like a thousand little stars just waiting to snuff themselves out. But I wasn't thinking about the city's beauty right then. I was thinking about Selene. About what she had said before she vanished.

"You've only begun to unravel the prophecy, little Raven," her voice still rang in my ears, mocking and cold. I stopped at the edge of the street, the neon lights casting a sickly glow on the pavement. The city was alive, buzzing with the usual noise, but the hum of it all felt distant, like the sound of a drumbeat heard through thick glass. Nothing felt quite right.

Kael stepped up beside me, his face serious, his dark eyes studying me with a mixture of concern and understanding. He knew what was eating at me, even if I couldn't put it into words.

"We don't know what she meant," I said, though the doubt in my own voice betrayed me. "But she's right about one thing: this isn't over."

"Not by a long shot," he replied, his voice low and steady, like a man who'd seen the darkness and was already bracing for the next round.

I let out a breath, one I hadn't realized I'd been holding. "I can feel it, Kael. Something's coming. Something worse."

His gaze shifted to the city beyond us, his expression darkening as if he, too, could sense it—the shift in the air, the unsettling quiet that had settled over everything. The calm before the storm, I realized. We were standing on the edge of something far more dangerous than we'd ever prepared for.

"Whatever it is," he said, his voice sharp and resolute, "we'll face it together. We always do."

His words, simple as they were, settled something in me. The weight of everything that had happened, all the lives lost, the choices made, still hung over us like a shadow, but I wasn't alone in it. Not now. Not ever again.

"I hope you're right," I muttered, pulling my jacket tighter around me as the wind picked up, sending a chill through my bones. The city had a way of making you feel small, insignificant, but tonight it felt like we were part of something bigger, something that could tip the balance of everything.

We turned and started walking, the rhythm of our steps in sync as we made our way through the streets. The neon signs flickered above us, their garish colors a sharp contrast to the darkness that lingered just beyond the edges of the city's light. The streets were bustling with the usual crowd—people oblivious to the fact that the world was changing beneath their feet. They were too busy to notice the dark storm gathering in the distance, too wrapped up in their own lives to care.

But I cared. I had no choice but to care. Whatever Selene had set in motion, it was going to affect all of us. And I was going to be damned if I let it take me down without a fight.

As we walked, I couldn't help but glance up at the sky, the stars barely visible behind the city's haze. I used to think that the night sky was full of answers, that if I stared long enough, I'd find something in the constellations that would tell me where I was supposed to be. But tonight, the stars felt like a lie—a reminder that some answers were never meant to be found.

Kael's voice broke through my thoughts, as he nudged me with his elbow, a rare grin tugging at the corner of his mouth.

"You know, I'm starting to think we're good at this whole 'facing impossible odds' thing," he said, his tone light despite the gravity of our situation. "Maybe we should make it a career."

I chuckled, though it was hollow. "Oh, sure. 'Supernatural crisis management' has a nice ring to it."

"We'd be good at it," he said with a smirk. "If nothing else, we're persistent."

And with that, the weight of everything didn't feel quite as heavy, though I knew it wasn't over yet. There was a long road ahead. But as long as I had Kael at my side, maybe, just maybe, I'd make it through.

The city felt different that night, like the air itself had shifted, as though the very atmosphere had caught wind of something ominous stirring. The usual hum of streetlights and the clamor of tired city workers had been replaced by a strange, unnerving silence, a pause between breaths. I could hear every footstep echoing in the alleyways as we walked, the sound sharp in the otherwise quiet world. Kael's presence beside me was grounding, but even he couldn't shake the sense that something was circling us, just beyond our reach.

We moved through the streets, the night cool against my skin, the kind of cold that gets inside your bones and makes you long for warmth. But no matter how much I pulled my jacket tighter, it wasn't enough. There was something else pressing in—something that clung to the edges of my thoughts. Selene's last words echoed in my mind, each syllable laced with a promise of danger.

"You've only begun to unravel the prophecy, little Raven." Her voice still sent a shiver down my spine. The words were a thread, unraveling, dragging us into a labyrinth of uncertainty. We had thought we were so close. The crown, the prophecy, Selene's twisted game—it all seemed like it had been leading to this moment, to the shattering of the crown and the end of her reign. But now? Now I wasn't so sure.

Kael's hand brushed mine as we walked, his touch small but steady. "It's not over yet," he murmured, as though trying to convince both of us.

I glanced at him, raising an eyebrow. "You think?"

He chuckled softly, a sound that seemed almost too bright for the weight of the night. "You've got that look in your eyes—the one you wear when you're about to charge headfirst into trouble."

"Trouble doesn't quite cover it," I muttered, adjusting my grip on the straps of my bag. The city lights flickered above us, casting long shadows on the ground. They felt like sentinels watching us, silently judging the way we moved, the way we tried to outrun whatever had been unleashed with the breaking of that damn crown.

Kael stopped walking abruptly, his gaze focused on something far down the street. I followed his line of sight, my heart skipping a beat when I saw what had caught his attention. A figure in a long coat stood under the flickering light of a streetlamp, the silhouette of their form sharp and unnatural in the night.

We both froze.

"What do you think?" I whispered, barely able to move the words past the lump in my throat.

"Don't know yet," Kael replied, his voice low. He hadn't drawn his blade, but the tension in his posture was enough to tell me he was ready for anything.

The figure didn't move, their gaze unshifting, like a statue frozen in place. A streetcar rumbled by, its wheels clattering along the tracks, and when it passed, the figure was still there, but closer. Too close. A knot formed in my stomach, cold and tight.

"I don't like this," I said, more to myself than to Kael.

Kael's eyes met mine, his expression unreadable. "Stay behind me."

Before I could protest, he started walking toward the figure, his stride purposeful, confident. I followed, reluctantly, my pulse quickening. The figure had no obvious weapon, no visible threat, but there was something in the air that made my skin prickle.

As we got closer, the figure finally spoke, their voice smooth and calm, almost too calm for the situation. "You're not the first to seek answers, Raven. And you won't be the last."

The words made the world around me tilt, like I had stepped off a solid surface and into a void. My heart pounded in my chest as I stopped dead in my tracks, Kael turning slightly, his stance more defensive now.

"Who are you?" I asked, trying to mask the unease that crept into my voice.

The figure took a small step forward, their coat fluttering slightly as they moved, their face still hidden in shadow. They wore a hood that obscured their features, but I could see the glint of something metallic hanging from their neck, a symbol I couldn't place.

"My name doesn't matter," the figure said. "What matters is the path you've started down. The prophecy you think you've unraveled is just a whisper of the storm. The real game begins now."

The words hit me like a splash of cold water, each one heavier than the last. I glanced at Kael, whose jaw was set in that familiar line, his eyes never leaving the figure.

"What do you mean?" I demanded, stepping forward, trying to meet the figure's shadowed gaze. "What game are you talking about?"

A soft laugh echoed from the figure, dry and without humor. "You've broken the crown, yes. You've broken the first seal. But the crown was never the heart of it all, Raven. It was merely a key. And there are more. Much more."

I felt a shiver race down my spine. "More keys? What are you talking about?"

The figure didn't answer immediately. Instead, they raised their hand, and for a brief moment, the air around us grew heavier, darker. I could feel it—the pressure building, as though the ground beneath us was shifting, sliding, revealing something ancient and dangerous just beneath our feet.

"Your enemies are closer than you think," the figure said, their voice a mere whisper now, "and you're running out of time."

A sound, sharp and quick, rang out from the alley beside us. I whirled around, my hand instinctively reaching for the dagger at my waist, but there was nothing there, nothing to see. The street was empty, too empty.

When I turned back, the figure was gone. No trace. No sound of footsteps. Just the hollow emptiness of the street, and the growing sense that we were being watched.

Kael cursed under his breath. "This doesn't feel right."

I swallowed, my throat dry, my heart beating erratically. "No," I said, my voice tight, "it doesn't."

A sudden rustling behind us caught my attention—too close, too fast. Before I could react, a sharp voice pierced the air.

"Raven."

I spun around, adrenaline spiking, but there was no one there. Just shadows, stretching long and cold in the moonlight.

"Raven..."

The voice came again, this time from within my own head.

And in that instant, I understood. This was only the beginning.

Chapter 32: The Prophecy Unbound

The morning air was thick with the scent of rain, a promise hovering just beyond the horizon. I stood at the window, watching the city below me as its veins pulsed with life. New York. The only place I knew where the streets never seemed to sleep, even when they should. The hum of car horns, the distant chatter of pedestrians, and the steady march of time made the city feel like a living, breathing entity. The hum in my chest matched it. It always had. But today, there was an unsettling kind of silence. An ominous stillness that clung to my bones like a wet wool sweater.

I turned away from the view and took a deep breath. The smell of freshly brewed coffee, dark and rich, was the only comfort in this room. The kitchen behind me had a pile of dirty dishes from a meal I couldn't remember cooking. The sink, however, was silent. Almost too silent.

It wasn't a coincidence that I found myself back in this space today. The apartment I had once called my own, the place where I used to write late into the night, where I crafted narratives out of my own dreams. But now, it felt like a place of waiting. And waiting, I had learned, could be as dangerous as any other kind of uncertainty.

A knock on the door echoed through the hallway, jolting me from my thoughts. I knew who it was before I even opened it. Kael. He had a habit of knocking just once, like he didn't want to intrude. As if the world outside didn't demand enough of him. He never understood that my life had always been about intrusion—into my thoughts, my space, my soul. But Kael, with his worn leather jacket and his ever-so-carefully tousled hair, was never an intrusion. He was a tempest I had learned to survive.

"You look like you've been here for days," he said, stepping inside and glancing around. His voice was soft, a reminder that even in the chaos, he could be a source of calm.

"More like months," I muttered, my gaze falling back to the window. "Time doesn't really make sense here."

He laughed, but there was an edge to it. "Well, that's what happens when the prophecy starts pulling at your strings, Evanna. Time's the least of your problems."

I turned to face him, crossing my arms. "So, what now? We wait for the other shoe to drop?"

Kael's eyes flickered with the sharpness of someone who had seen too many shoes drop. "Something like that. Except it's not a shoe. It's a bomb. You know that, right?"

I felt the sudden weight of his words settle over me, thick and suffocating. Of course, I knew it. I had always known that the Ravenmark wasn't some mere symbol of power or an abstract threat. It was a ticking clock. And I was the one who had wound it.

"You're sure about this?" I asked. I didn't want to hear the answer. I didn't want to know the truth.

He didn't flinch, his gaze never leaving mine. "I'm as sure as I can be. Seraphina said it's not just about you being the key—it's about what you unlock when you turn it. But the lock? That's something else entirely."

I swallowed hard, my throat dry. "And what happens if I don't unlock it? If I walk away?"

Kael's lips tightened, his jaw clenching. "Then we all pay the price for your hesitation. There's no walking away from this, Evanna. There never was."

I could feel the pulse of the city beneath my feet, a silent drumbeat that carried the weight of fate. My fate. I didn't want to face it. I didn't want to be the one who had to make that choice.

But deep down, I knew I didn't have a choice. The prophecy was already unfolding, and no matter how far I ran, it would find me.

I let out a slow breath, turning back toward the window. The rain had started to fall now, soft and steady, washing the streets in a blur of grey and silver. I watched the droplets trace patterns on the glass, feeling a strange sense of calm in the chaos. It was a moment of peace before the storm. Before everything changed.

"So," Kael said, breaking the silence, his voice teasing but laced with something darker, "when are we going to face it?"

I turned back to him, forcing a smile that didn't reach my eyes. "I'll face it when I'm ready. Not a moment before."

He didn't argue. He never did. He understood, perhaps better than anyone else, that facing this was a decision I had to make on my own. Even though we both knew the clock was ticking. The Ravenmark was a legacy, something that had waited for me, just as much as I had waited for it. And now, I had to step into it, unknowing and unwilling, but undeniably bound.

Kael's eyes softened, and for a moment, he didn't look like the soldier, the man with the weight of the world on his shoulders. He just looked... human. "I'll be here, Evanna. Whenever you decide to move."

"Good," I said, my voice a little more steady than I felt. "Because I'm going to need all the help I can get."

The city felt different that night—quieter, like the air itself was holding its breath. The neon lights of the Lower East Side flickered overhead, casting an almost surreal glow on the wet pavement. I'd found myself here, standing at the entrance to a dive bar I'd once frequented on my worst days. It had been a while since I'd let the weight of the world press me into a seat, nursing something strong enough to burn. Tonight, though, I wasn't just here for the whiskey.

I walked in, the heavy door swinging shut behind me with a thud, and the familiar scent of stale beer and old wood settled around me like a second skin. It wasn't the kind of place you brought anyone home to meet your mother. But for me, it was home, in its own way. A strange sort of solace in the chaos of New York's never-ending buzz.

Kael was already at the bar, perched on one of the high stools like he belonged. He had that air about him—always poised, never entirely out of place, no matter where he went. His jacket was unzipped now, a hint of the faded tattoos beneath it visible as he spun his drink idly in his hand. His eyes caught mine the moment I stepped inside, a brief flash of something unreadable passing between us.

"Couldn't stay away, huh?" His voice was smooth, with that lilt that told me he found more humor in this situation than he should.

I slid onto the stool next to him without answering, nodding toward the bartender to order my usual. The whiskey burned its way down my throat, leaving the heat of it lingering like a small rebellion. "I needed the noise," I said finally, running a hand through my hair. "The city's quieter than it's ever been."

Kael didn't respond right away. Instead, he picked up his drink and leaned back, a small smile curling on his lips. He was always good at reading me—probably too good. The kind of good that made me question how much he knew before I did. "You think you're the only one feeling it? You should see the looks people are giving me on the street. Like they're waiting for something to happen."

The words hit harder than they should have. That damned prophecy hung over everything, no matter how much I tried to outrun it. The Ravenmark. The balance. The reckoning. It had started to make the world feel smaller, more confined. Like the walls were closing in, slowly but surely, and I was too busy chasing shadows to see it.

"Yeah," I muttered, swirling my glass. "But you always liked waiting for things to blow up, didn't you? You're the kind of guy who thrives in chaos."

Kael didn't react, his eyes locking onto mine with that intensity I couldn't quite shake. He leaned forward slightly, his voice dropping. "You think I want this? Want you caught in the middle of it all? I didn't sign up for this either, Evanna. But here we are. And if you think you can fix it by running, you're wrong. This is bigger than either of us. And you're the one who's going to have to decide which side you're on."

I hated that he was right. Hated how he always seemed to see through me, strip away the layers I'd worked so hard to build. But there was something else, too—something that gnawed at me. His words, they weren't just about the prophecy. They were about me. About us.

"Don't act like you're some saint, Kael," I said, my voice sharper than I meant it to be. "You've made your choices. You've been playing both sides from the beginning. And now you want me to jump into the fire with you?"

For a long moment, he didn't answer. Instead, he stared at me, his face unreadable, but I could see the conflict in the twitch of his jaw, the tightness around his eyes. "I never asked you to follow me into the fire," he said finally, his voice softening, the anger fading just as quickly as it had appeared. "But you're not the only one with a choice to make. And neither of us can outrun it. Not anymore."

I turned away, staring into my glass, the amber liquid swirling with the same sense of indecision I was drowning in. The weight of the world, the weight of the prophecy, pressed down on me, but it wasn't just the burden of what I was supposed to do. It was the knowledge that whatever decision I made, it would change everything. And the idea of living in that kind of uncertainty was worse than the thought of facing the unknown.

The sound of the door opening pulled me from my thoughts, and I glanced up just in time to see a woman enter, a sleek figure dressed in black. Her heels clicked sharply on the hardwood floor, the sound echoing through the dim room. She was a stranger to me, but the way she moved—carefully calculated, deliberate—was unmistakable.

I saw Kael's eyes narrow as he took in the woman, his entire demeanor shifting in an instant. "This should be interesting," he muttered under his breath, more to himself than to me.

The woman made her way toward us, her gaze fixed on Kael. I didn't recognize her, but there was something unsettling about the way she carried herself—like she knew exactly who she was, and she expected everyone else to know it too.

"Kael," she said, her voice smooth, cold, and almost rehearsed. "You've been busy. I trust you haven't forgotten about our... arrangement."

Kael's expression darkened, and I could feel the tension rising between them, thick as smoke. "You should've stayed away," he said quietly, his words clipped. "This isn't the time."

The woman smiled, and it was all teeth. "I think it's exactly the time, Kael. Don't you?"

The atmosphere in the room shifted. All at once, the hum of the city outside felt like a distant memory, the energy inside the bar crackling with the promise of something more dangerous than either of us had anticipated. I didn't know who this woman was, but I had a sinking feeling that she wasn't just a random player in this game. She was a threat. And in the world I was about to step into, threats came in all shapes and sizes.

The woman's smile remained, frozen and too wide. It was a knowing kind of grin, one that suggested she wasn't waiting for us to react—she had already seen the ending. I could feel my pulse quicken as I studied her, searching for any hint of vulnerability, any crack in the polished façade. There was none. If anything, her presence seemed to make the room shrink, the air itself turning a shade darker.

Kael, on the other hand, didn't seem remotely surprised. His body was still, his posture unyielding, but I could feel the subtle shift in him—the way his shoulders squared, his jaw tightening. The tension that bloomed between them was thick, palpable, and I found myself wondering how much history they shared, and whether that history was one I was going to regret learning about.

"You," Kael muttered, a single word laced with a hint of something—anger? Resentment? It was hard to tell. "What do you want, Alessandra?"

Her laugh came out like a low, dangerous hum, almost musical. "What do I want? Oh, Kael. I think the better question is, what do you want?" She shifted her gaze to me then, her eyes sharp and assessing. "I didn't expect you to be the one standing beside him. How quaint."

I bristled, irritated by the undercurrent of condescension. "And who are you to make assumptions?" I shot back, my voice sharper than I intended, but my fingers curling tightly around the glass in my hand. If this woman was going to be a problem, I wasn't going to let her walk all over me.

Her lips twitched, like she was enjoying the exchange more than was reasonable. "You must be the one he's been avoiding. Evanna, right? Funny. I would have thought he'd have more tact than to bring someone so… unpredictable into his affairs."

I met her gaze with equal intensity. "I can be as unpredictable as I need to be."

Kael stepped between us then, his body turning slightly to shield me, and I couldn't help but notice the slight tremor in his shoulders. It wasn't fear—no, not him. But it was something close. Regret, maybe? Or maybe it was just the weight of something long overdue. "What do you want, Alessandra?" he repeated, his voice colder now.

She sighed, almost theatrically, and pushed a lock of her dark hair behind her ear, the movement languid. "You know what I want, Kael. You've known for a long time. But now that she's here, I suppose I'll have to spell it out for her, too."

My gut twisted in suspicion. I had no idea what she meant, but I didn't like it. I wasn't in the mood for more cryptic conversations, especially not from someone who made me feel like I was standing on the edge of a cliff. I wanted answers, not more riddles.

"You're wasting my time," I said, standing up abruptly, the chair scraping harshly against the floor. "Get to the point."

Alessandra didn't flinch, not even when I cut her off. Instead, she seemed to enjoy the discomfort in the room, the air thick with tension. "You know," she said, her voice dripping with mock sympathy, "the Ravenmark isn't just a prophecy, is it? It's not something that can be ignored or dismissed with a quick prayer to whatever gods you think will save you. The Ravenmark is the legacy you've been born into, Evanna. It's in your blood. And soon, it will be in your hands."

I shook my head, the words ringing through me like a gong that refused to stop echoing. "What are you talking about? I'm not some chosen one in a fairy tale. I'm just trying to live my life."

"How sweet," Alessandra said, her smile stretching further. "How naïve. But that's the beauty of it, isn't it? You think you have a choice, and yet you're the one who's been chosen all along. The Ravenmark demands its reckoning. It's always been about you, Evanna. Always will be."

The realization hit like a slap, the gravity of it sinking in, dragging me under. I wasn't here because of some twist of fate. I wasn't just caught in the crossfire of a prophecy. I was the prophecy.

And that thought was both the most terrifying and the most liberating thing I'd ever known.

I felt the room shift again, the sudden weight of it too much to bear. My heart hammered in my chest as I turned to Kael. "Is this true?" My voice was tight, like I could barely get the words out. The cold edge in his eyes softened for a brief moment, but it wasn't enough to soothe the storm that was building inside me.

Kael was silent for a beat too long, and in that moment, I felt a strange pull—a tugging sensation deep within, as though something invisible was pulling me toward a future I couldn't quite understand, couldn't quite control.

When he finally spoke, his voice was low and resigned. "It's true."

The weight of those two words hit me harder than I expected. I thought I had prepared myself for the truth, but nothing had quite prepared me for this. The Ravenmark, the prophecy, the reckoning—it had all been a slow burn, a story unfolding whether I wanted it to or not. And now, I realized I wasn't just waiting for something to happen. I was the one who had to make it happen.

Alessandra didn't seem interested in my moment of realization. Instead, she took a slow step forward, her heels clicking against the floor with a finality that made my breath catch. "You think you're in control here? Think again, Evanna. The key may be yours, but the lock? That's something even you can't unlock on your own."

Before I could respond, she reached into her jacket and pulled something out—a small, gleaming object that caught the dim light of the bar. It looked innocuous at first, just a shard of crystal, but the way her fingers tightened around it made my skin prickle with warning.

"I'll be back," she said softly, her eyes glinting with something darker than malice. "And when I return, we'll see if you've figured out the rest of the puzzle."

And with that, she turned and walked out the door, leaving me with more questions than answers—and with the terrifying realization that the clock had already started ticking.

Chapter 33: A Kingdom Divided

The capital was a city in the throes of change. You could almost taste it in the air—sharp, electric, as though the skyline itself had shifted overnight. I had walked these streets a thousand times, each step worn into the cobblestones like a memory made flesh. But today, the city felt different. There was a hum beneath the usual chatter, a low vibration that clung to every corner, every whisper of conversation that fluttered through the market stalls and the alleys.

It wasn't just the news of Selene's return, though that had struck like a spark in dry tinder. The people were uneasy, and it wasn't just fear of her—it was something more. It was uncertainty. It was the tension of knowing that the world had been turned upside down, and no one quite knew where the pieces would land. We had won, or at least, we thought we had. But the victory had left us fragmented, and no amount of polished speeches or public celebrations could erase the cracks that had formed between us.

Kael's voice cut through my thoughts, his tone a mix of quiet concern and determination as we stood on the balcony of Seraphina's quarters, watching the city spread out beneath us like a map of uncertainty.

"We can't keep pretending everything is fine," he said, his eyes scanning the streets below, where the citizens moved with a mixture of hurried steps and cautious glances, as if they were all waiting for something to happen. "The factions are tearing themselves apart. Seraphina can't hold this together alone."

I nodded, not needing to answer. It was obvious. I had seen it in the meetings, in the dark corners of the council chambers where murmurs of dissent had begun to replace the once-unified calls for progress. Each faction, once aligned in its desire for a shared vision of the future, had splintered into something else—something darker. There were those who believed that Selene's return was a sign of divine retribution, that the old order was meant to be restored, even if it meant sacrificing everything we had built. Then there were those who thought we should double down, fortify our positions, press ahead with the momentum we had gained. Neither side trusted the other, and the space between them was widening by the hour.

"Tell me something, Mara," Kael's voice shifted, quieter now, more personal. "Do you ever wonder if we're doing the right thing?"

I hesitated, the question stirring something deep inside me, something I wasn't sure I wanted to confront. The right thing. What was that, anyway? Was it victory? Was it power? Or was it something else entirely, something that couldn't be defined by the language of politics or war?

"I wonder," I said at last, my words low but steady, "if anyone truly knows what the right thing is anymore."

He didn't respond right away, and I knew he was thinking, weighing his options. Kael always thought too much, always saw the paths ahead like a chessboard where every piece was a risk. I envied that sometimes, his ability to see everything in shades of strategy, even if it made him distant. But I didn't want to go down that road now. Not with him.

"Let's just survive today first," I added, my voice sharper than I intended, more a command than a suggestion. "Then we'll figure out what happens next."

Kael chuckled, the sound warm and easy, and for a moment, I could forget the weight of everything pressing down on us. "You always did have a way of keeping me grounded, Mara," he said. "A gift, really."

Grounded. I let the word hang in the air between us. I had never felt grounded. Not in this world, not in this city, not in this life. Not even with Kael beside me.

The door to the balcony opened behind us, and Seraphina stepped into the room, her presence filling the space with that quiet authority she carried like a mantle. Her silver hair, usually sleek and controlled, was tousled from a long day of dealing with the chaos outside. She had been doing this longer than any of us, but the strain was starting to show. I could see it in the lines beneath her eyes, the way her shoulders were slightly hunched, as though the burden of leadership had begun to bend her.

"We need to talk," she said, not a question but a command.

I turned to face her, giving Kael a quick look that conveyed everything I needed to say. He nodded once, the line of his jaw tightening. He didn't need to ask what we were about to discuss. We had all known it was coming.

She motioned for us to follow her into the chamber, where the maps and letters had been spread out across the long table. The room was cold, the air thick with the weight of decisions made and the ones still to come.

"The unrest is growing," Seraphina said without preamble, sweeping a hand over the map that was covered in ink-streaked lines, symbols of movement, of uncertainty. "We can't control the factions anymore, not the way we did before. If Selene moves against us, if she gathers the right support…"

I didn't need her to finish the sentence. It was clear enough. If Selene moved against us, the city would fall into open rebellion. And we'd be left scrambling to pick up the pieces, even as we watched the ashes of everything we had fought for burn to the ground.

"What do we do?" Kael asked, his voice edged with frustration, the cracks beginning to show through his calm exterior.

Seraphina paused, as if weighing the question. Then she leaned forward, her eyes sharp and unyielding. "We act first. We don't wait for her to strike. We take control of the narrative. We make sure the people know where our strength lies. And we show them that we won't bend. Not to Selene, and not to anyone else."

Her eyes flicked to me then, and I could feel the weight of her gaze like an anchor around my neck. "Mara, I need you to rally the people. They trust you. They always have. You need to remind them why we fought."

The words settled on me like a sentence, as though I were being drawn into a battle I hadn't yet fully understood. But I could feel the storm building, the need for action pressing down on me. And in that moment, I realized—no one else would step forward. Not now. It had to be me.

The day stretched long, its heat heavy with the weight of unspoken things. I had always found comfort in the rhythm of the city—the bustle of street vendors selling their wares, the clamor of hawkers calling out for customers, the comforting murmur of life. But today, it was different. Today, the sidewalks were full, and yet they seemed empty. People walked with their heads down, their eyes shifting as if expecting someone to jump out from the shadows, ready to take advantage of their vulnerability. It wasn't just the news of Selene's return that hung in the air. It was something more. It was the slow realization that everything we had fought for—everything that had felt solid—was slipping through our fingers.

I wasn't sure if it was the oppressive heat or the sheer weight of what was at stake that made my chest tight. Or maybe it was the pressure from every direction, like the city itself was collapsing in on me. Kael and I had been working nonstop for days, trying to piece together the fractured alliances, to figure out who could be trusted, and who was already making their own play for power. Some days, it felt as though every word spoken in these meetings was a delicate dance, a test to see where loyalty truly lay.

"Are you sure you're alright?" Kael's voice broke through my thoughts as we turned down a narrow alley, the shadows offering a momentary respite from the sun's punishing heat.

I wasn't sure if I was alright. But I didn't want to admit that even to myself, let alone Kael. So I smiled, a sharp little curve of my lips that I hoped looked convincing enough.

"I'm fine," I said, though the words felt foreign as they left my mouth. "Just tired, I suppose."

He didn't buy it, but he didn't press. Kael had a way of knowing when to push and when to pull back. If I said I was fine, that was the end of it.

We walked in silence for a few moments, the crunch of gravel beneath our boots the only sound in the otherwise still street. I'd grown up in the capital, and I knew every crevice of this city—each corner where trouble could spring up, each building that had witnessed a hundred years of power struggles. But there was a new undercurrent now, something dark and unpredictable. A sense of urgency thrummed beneath every step, like the city itself was holding its breath.

Ahead, the door to a modest tavern swung open, and a voice called out to us. "Mara, Kael. Thought I might find you two skulking around here."

We turned in unison, instinctively reaching for the weapons we carried, though we both knew it was just Ezra leaning against the doorway, his usual grin plastered on his face. I hadn't seen him in days, and his presence, though familiar, felt oddly out of place right now, like a reminder of a simpler time before all of this madness had begun.

"What is it with you?" I said, half-laughing, half-exasperated. "Don't you have a more important place to be?"

"Isn't it the most important thing, finding you two when the whole city's on edge?" Ezra shrugged, stepping out of the shadows and into the light, his broad frame filling the doorway. "I've heard the whispers. People are starting to lose their faith. They want someone to stand up and lead them. They want answers. And they're looking at you two."

Kael and I exchanged a look. We'd already had enough conversations about the way people were turning toward us, expecting us to hold the threads of power together. The pressure was relentless, gnawing at us from all sides. But there was no way out, no simple solution.

"What do you want, Ezra?" Kael asked, his voice flat but sharp, his hand still on the hilt of his blade. He'd never fully trusted Ezra, even though the man had been a loyal ally when the stakes were high. And right now, loyalty seemed like a fragile thing, harder to come by with every passing day.

"Just offering a little perspective," Ezra said, a devilish gleam in his eyes. "You both think this is about winning battles, but you've forgotten the most important thing: perception. You need to make the people believe in you. If you don't, everything you've fought for will crumble, no matter how many speeches you give or how many treaties you sign. Trust me, I've seen it before."

I took a breath, trying to ground myself in the moment. Ezra's words rang too true. Perception. It was a currency more valuable than gold in these times. The people were restless, afraid of what Selene's return meant for their future. And there was no way to predict how they'd react if we didn't deliver a decisive answer soon.

"Are you suggesting we just start acting like we've already won?" Kael asked, the edge in his tone unmistakable. "That we lie to the people?"

"Not lie," Ezra said, his grin widening. "Just... frame things in a way that keeps them on your side. Give them a reason to believe that everything you've worked for is worth fighting for. If you can't do that, then it doesn't matter who's in power. They'll tear you apart from the inside out."

I took a long look at him, weighing his words. There was truth in them, but that truth felt like quicksand—slippery and dangerous. What if we sold a vision that wasn't real? What if, in the end, the people rejected it, rejected us?

"We're not selling lies," I said, the words firm as I met his gaze. "We're offering them hope. If that's not enough, then we don't deserve their trust."

Ezra raised an eyebrow, his grin faltering for a fraction of a second before it returned, even wider than before. "Well then, it's good to know you haven't forgotten what this is all really about." He pushed off from the doorway, stepping closer to us. "But don't forget this, Mara. You're walking a razor's edge. One wrong move, and you'll be the one they turn on next."

With that, he turned on his heel and disappeared into the tavern, leaving us with more questions than answers. The weight of his words pressed down on me, making it harder to breathe, but I knew there was no time to dwell on them. We had decisions to make, alliances to solidify, and a city to save. The game had begun, and I had no choice but to play it to the very end.

The night came with a chill, a biting breeze that twisted through the streets, carrying with it the faint scent of rain and uncertainty. The city felt different under the cover of darkness—quieter, but more dangerous. The lamps lining the streets flickered erratically, casting long, stretching shadows that seemed to shift with the movement of the few souls brave enough to venture out. The alleyways were still. There was an unspoken tension in the air, the kind that makes your skin crawl, as if something unseen, something insidious, is waiting just beyond the corner.

I had grown used to the strange quiet of nightfall in the capital, but tonight it felt like a warning, a prelude to something I couldn't name but knew was coming. I wasn't the only one feeling it. As we walked down the cobblestone street toward the city's heart, Kael's hand lingered close to his sword, his pace slower, deliberate. His silence spoke louder than any words could have. He had always been one to hide his thoughts behind a cool exterior, but I knew him well enough to understand when something gnawed at him. He was always the first to spot danger—too quick to see it sometimes, but I trusted his instincts.

"Do you think we're doing the right thing?" I asked him suddenly, the question slipping out before I could stop it. It wasn't like me to doubt, especially not in the middle of this mess. But the weight of Seraphina's request still hung heavy on my shoulders. She had been right when she said we needed to unite the people, to make them believe in us. But how? The city was fractured, its very core shifting beneath our feet, and I didn't know if we could hold it together.

Kael paused, his face lit only by the dim glow of the lamplights. He didn't look at me immediately, his eyes scanning the streets around us, taking in everything, missing nothing. He was still weighing the question, as if turning it over in his mind before offering an answer.

"Right and wrong are luxury items in this world," he said finally, his voice low and rough. "Sometimes you just do what needs to be done, even if it doesn't feel good."

I let his words settle between us, my gaze on the flickering streetlamp ahead, its light swaying with the wind. He was right, of course. The luxury of moral clarity had always been reserved for those who hadn't been forced to make impossible decisions, those who hadn't seen the way power twisted good intentions into something unrecognizable.

Just then, a noise broke the stillness—a sharp, discordant sound of footsteps too hurried, too panicked to be anything but trouble. We both froze, instinctively reaching for our weapons. The tension in the air thickened, and the city seemed to hold its breath.

A figure appeared in the distance, moving fast, their face hidden in shadow. Whoever they were, they were coming straight for us. I instinctively took a step back, my heart pounding in my chest. This wasn't a time for mistakes. I reached for the dagger hidden beneath my cloak, my hand steady despite the sudden surge of adrenaline.

The figure slowed as they neared, and when the dim light caught their face, I recognized them immediately. It was Elias, a low-ranking member of the guard, but one who had been with us through everything. His eyes were wide with panic, his breath coming in ragged bursts.

"Mara," he gasped, barely able to catch his breath. "You need to come quickly. There's—there's been a betrayal."

I felt the air around us shift, the realization sinking like a stone in my gut. Betrayal. The word itself was a poison, and hearing it from Elias made my heart race. He wasn't the kind of man to panic, not unless there was something truly wrong.

"What's happened?" Kael's voice was steel, his posture already shifting into the stance of someone prepared for anything.

"The council," Elias gasped again, his hands trembling. "They've made a move. They've sided with Selene. They're planning something tonight. You need to come now, before—"

The sound of a horn blasted through the city, low and mournful, a warning. I froze, my blood running cold. That was the signal—the one we had all agreed upon for when things had gotten out of hand. The one that meant the rebellion had begun. There was no time to waste.

"Come on," Kael said sharply, his voice now full of urgency as he grabbed my arm, pulling me into motion. "We need to get to the council chambers, now."

We ran, the cobblestones beneath our feet echoing in the stillness of the night, the wind biting at our skin. The path to the council wasn't far, but every step felt like an eternity. I could feel my pulse pounding in my ears, my body moving on autopilot. Betrayal had always been a possibility, but to hear it so plainly—to know that it was happening now, in this very moment—was a blow to the gut I hadn't been prepared for.

As we neared the grand building that housed the council, the streetlights seemed to dim, as though the city itself were retreating into the shadows. The doors to the council chambers were wide open, and the sound of muffled voices drifted out into the night, harsh and low. There was no more pretending, no more time to delay.

We pushed through the door, weapons drawn, our movements synchronized. Inside, the council chamber was a blur of faces—some familiar, some not—but all with the same tense, determined expressions. In the center of the room stood Seraphina, her back straight, her hands clenched at her sides as she faced off with a group of men and women who had once been her closest allies.

"Traitors," she spat, her voice venomous as she turned toward us. Her eyes met mine, and in them, I saw a mixture of defiance and fear, an unspoken plea for help.

And then, from the shadows, a voice cut through the room, icy and cold.

"It's too late for that, Mara. The city is ours now."

I turned, my heart hammering in my chest, to see the figure step into the light. The last person I had expected to see standing there, his eyes gleaming with the confidence of someone who had just seized everything he had ever wanted.

"Marcus."

Chapter 34: The Ashen Gate

The heat from the Ashen Gate lingered on my skin, clinging like the weight of a secret. The dark energy pulsed in the air, vibrating through the soles of my boots, creeping into my bones. This was not just any world we had entered—it was a place where time didn't bend so much as it snapped and cracked like dry twigs underfoot. The air itself felt heavy, laden with the taste of burnt metal and ash, the very air suffocating in its intensity.

I blinked hard, trying to clear the haze from my vision, but nothing changed. The world was a blur of shadowed outlines and shifting edges, a painting that had been smeared just beyond recognition. I felt Kael beside me, the warmth of his body the only solid thing in a landscape that seemed to shift and breathe with its own intent. His presence was a tether, a lifeline in the chaos. But there was something else in his eyes, something raw, something that hinted he had already known what this place would feel like.

"It's worse than I imagined," I whispered, my voice sounding foreign in the thickness of the air.

Kael didn't answer immediately. Instead, he reached out and grasped my wrist, his grip firm but not painful. The heat of his touch grounded me, pulled me back from the edge of panic that threatened to swallow me whole. He didn't need to say a word. His touch was an unspoken promise, a quiet agreement between us that whatever this place was, we would face it together.

"Stay close," he murmured.

I nodded, not trusting myself to speak further. The shadows were shifting in ways that felt deliberate, as if they were waiting for us to make the first move, to make a mistake. The sense of being watched was overwhelming, crawling beneath my skin like the tickle of a thousand unseen eyes. I felt the pressure of the dark magic, pressing against my chest, trying to find a way in.

But it was when I looked beyond the gate itself that the real weight of our situation hit me. The land before us was nothing more than a sea of blackened stone, jagged and twisted in unnatural ways. The horizon, if you could even call it that, was blurred by the weight of thick, swirling clouds. The sky was the color of bruised fruit, a deep purple-black, and it looked as though it had never known sunlight. The ground beneath our feet cracked and groaned with every step, as though the earth itself was shifting, uncertain of our presence.

And yet, amid the oppressive stillness, there was a hum. It was faint at first, like the vibration of a far-off bell, but it grew louder, vibrating in my bones. It was the pulse of the world itself—alive, and angry. A place that resented our intrusion.

"Selene has spent too much time here," Kael muttered, his voice thick with an emotion I couldn't place. Fear? Regret? I couldn't tell. "The magic has... it's taken a toll on her."

I stole a glance at him, catching the flicker of something dark in his eyes. He was trying, unsuccessfully, to mask it with stoic resolve, but there was something more. Something unspoken between us. The thought of Selene, that elusive figure who had lured us here, twisted my gut in ways I hadn't expected. She had drawn us into this place with the promise of refuge, a salvation from the looming darkness that was taking over our world. But what if she had been running from something darker still?

"What do you mean by that?" I asked, my voice barely above a whisper. The question felt too heavy to speak aloud, as though the world itself might hear me and answer in a language I wasn't prepared to understand.

Kael glanced down at me, his lips tightening as though he had bit back a curse. "The Ashen Gate doesn't let go of those who pass through it. Not completely. Not without a price." His gaze drifted toward the horizon, where the shadows seemed to reach for us, fingers made of smoke and malice. "I've seen what it does to people."

I didn't ask what he meant. I didn't need to. The silence between us spoke volumes, and I could hear it now, in the way the wind howled and the ground shuddered beneath our feet. Something was waiting for us here, something ancient and hungry.

A sudden movement in the distance caught my attention—a flicker of light, almost too quick to register. I turned toward it instinctively, my breath catching in my throat. The shadows parted just slightly, revealing a figure—tall and draped in flowing black robes, their face hidden beneath a hood. For a moment, I thought it might be Selene, but something told me it wasn't. The figure stood still, watching us from afar, as if waiting for us to make the first move.

"Who's there?" I called out, my voice more defiant than I felt.

The figure didn't answer. Instead, it raised a hand, fingers long and delicate, and in that moment, the world seemed to hold its breath. The shadows thickened around us, drawing in close. The temperature dropped sharply, and I felt the chill press against my skin. Kael stiffened beside me, his hand moving to the hilt of his blade.

But before either of us could act, the figure was gone. Vanished into the dark, as though it had never been there at all.

I turned to Kael, my heart hammering in my chest. "Who was that?"

His expression was unreadable, but there was something darker in his eyes now. "That," he said slowly, "was no friend."

The silence that followed the disappearance of the figure hung in the air like a thick fog. I could feel the weight of it pressing against my chest, suffocating and relentless. Kael remained still, his gaze locked on the spot where the figure had been, though I suspected he had already known it would vanish. It wasn't the first time something elusive had slipped through his grasp, but that didn't make it any easier to bear. I couldn't help but wonder just how many times Kael had stared down into the abyss, only to find it staring back.

"You're not surprised," I said, more to break the tension than to elicit an answer.

His mouth twitched, a brief, dry smile that barely softened the hardness in his eyes. "You're a quick learner."

I hated how much that statement stung. Of course, he was right. I had seen enough of this world, of these realms, to know that nothing was as it seemed. Magic didn't just bend reality here—it tore it apart and stitched it back together, piece by piece, like a patchwork quilt made of nightmares.

"You're wrong," I said, my voice louder than I intended, betraying a hint of defiance I hadn't expected to feel. "I'm not here to learn. I'm here to stop this. To stop whatever's going on between Selene and this place."

His gaze softened slightly, but it was fleeting. "You've never met Selene. Not really."

I bristled at the implication, but before I could respond, he held up a hand, signaling for quiet. His eyes darted around the horizon, scanning the shifting shadows that loomed like specters. I followed his gaze, feeling a creeping unease inch down my spine. The figure had disappeared, but that didn't mean we were alone.

"It's not her," Kael said, his voice low. "This is a place of power, yes. But it's also a place of temptation. A place that twists people, makes them forget what they wanted in the first place."

My stomach twisted. The Ashen Gate, an ancient symbol of power and refuge for Selene, had already begun to feel less like a sanctuary and more like a trap. Every instinct I had screamed at me to turn back, to leave this forsaken land behind. But it was already too late.

"I don't like it here," I admitted, my voice almost a whisper, as though the very act of speaking the words might make the land itself react.

Kael turned to face me, his features unreadable. "No one does. Not after you've crossed through the gate."

He didn't need to elaborate. The warning was clear. The Ashen Gate was a threshold. Once you crossed it, there was no easy way back.

I glanced around, trying to ground myself in the present, trying to ignore the fact that every step seemed to lead us deeper into the heart of darkness. The shadows, though distant, seemed to press closer with each passing moment.

"What's our plan?" I asked, forcing my voice steady.

Kael looked at me, a ghost of a smile curving his lips. "Survive. For now."

As we moved forward, the ground beneath us seemed to change. No longer was it just blackened stone, jagged and unforgiving. Now it was like walking on the remains of something long forgotten, a graveyard of twisted metal and shattered stone, relics from another time. Some of the remnants were familiar—torn banners, broken weapons, half-collapsed archways—but they had been warped, altered by whatever dark forces lived here.

I could almost hear the whispers of the past in the wind, like echoes that didn't belong, murmuring warnings too soft to be fully understood. The silence between us grew heavier, as if the land itself was alive with a consciousness of its own, watching and waiting for us to slip up.

I stumbled over a jagged rock, my foot catching on the uneven ground. Kael reached out, steadying me with a hand on my arm. His fingers were colder than I expected, as though the Ashen Gate had already claimed a part of him.

"You're too reckless," he murmured.

"Funny," I retorted, brushing myself off, "I was just thinking the same thing about you."

Kael didn't respond, but the corner of his mouth twitched again, the briefest of smiles that vanished as quickly as it came. The tension between us was palpable, but there was a comfort in it, a familiarity, like two people who had long ago accepted their mutual distrust yet relied on each other in ways they couldn't admit.

As we pressed forward, the darkness shifted, and in the distance, I saw a flicker of movement. This time, it wasn't a shadow but something more substantial—a figure, standing tall and straight, watching us with an intensity that made the hairs on the back of my neck stand on end. I could tell from the way it moved—or rather, didn't—that it wasn't human.

"Is that her?" I asked, my voice barely above a breath.

Kael's gaze never wavered. "No. That's something else."

The figure did not approach. Instead, it stood motionless, almost in waiting, like a sentry on guard. The longer we stared, the more I felt the weight of its presence press against my chest. It wasn't just the figure I feared—it was the feeling of being drawn into something much larger, something much darker.

"Are you sure we should keep going?" I asked, more to myself than to Kael.

But his expression had hardened, his gaze fixed on the figure. "It's our only choice."

Before I could respond, a strange, unearthly sound filled the air—an echoing chime, like the tolling of a bell from far away. I froze, my heart hammering in my chest. The figure, still unmoving, raised its arm, and the chime rang louder, reverberating off the jagged walls of the broken landscape.

"It's a warning," Kael muttered under his breath. "But it's also an invitation."

I didn't need him to elaborate. We had crossed the threshold. Now, there was no turning back.

The echo of the bell reverberated in my chest, a constant thrum beneath the surface, its resonance wrapping around us like a tightening noose. The figure did not move, but I could feel the pull of its gaze, even from this distance. There was no warmth here, no comfort, just a chilling sense that the world itself was watching us, calculating whether we were worth the trouble of devouring.

"We're not alone," I said, trying to steady my voice.

Kael gave a tight nod, his eyes narrowing on the shadowed figure. "Not by a long shot." His hand instinctively brushed the hilt of his sword, a motion so familiar, so practiced, that it almost seemed like a reflex, an automatic response to danger.

I followed his lead, my own senses on high alert. Every step felt like it might be our last, but we moved forward, the shadows licking at our heels like flames at the edge of a bonfire. There was no sense in waiting for the figure to approach. It was already in our midst, its presence so tangible that I could almost reach out and touch the cold, oppressive air it carried with it.

As we neared the figure, it remained perfectly still, as though frozen in time. The longer I looked at it, the more I felt the unmistakable presence of something ancient, something so old that even the shadows around it seemed to bow in respect. This wasn't just a watcher. It was a sentinel.

"We need answers," I muttered under my breath, hoping Kael could hear me over the low hum of the landscape. My heart was racing, but I refused to let fear take hold. Not yet.

Kael didn't answer at first. Instead, he stepped forward, his boots crunching softly on the ground. The moment his footfall broke the silence, the figure moved, its long arm rising with a slow, deliberate motion. It pointed toward the horizon, a gesture that sent a ripple of dread through me.

"What's that?" I asked, squinting into the distance where the figure's finger had pointed. The ground was cracked and barren, a wasteland of ash and bone, but beyond that... there was something. A faint glow. A flicker of light in the distance, too bright to ignore.

"It's a beacon," Kael said, his voice a low growl, like the promise of a coming storm. "An invitation—or a challenge."

I could feel the weight of his words settle in my chest like a stone. We weren't just walking through a forgotten world. We were being drawn into something, something far larger than Selene's escape, far older than either of us could understand. Whatever this place was, whatever Selene had unleashed, it wasn't just the ruins of a forgotten kingdom. It was alive.

"We don't have much of a choice, do we?" I said, more to myself than to Kael. The harsh winds that swept through the broken landscape only heightened the feeling that we were on the precipice of something far darker than I had imagined.

"No," he replied simply, his tone a mixture of resignation and determination. "We don't."

Without another word, we began walking toward the glowing light. Every step felt weighted, as though the ground itself was trying to suck us back into the earth, to keep us from moving forward. The shadows thickened with each passing second, the temperature dropping to a bone-chilling cold that seeped into my skin. I could feel the familiar prickling sensation at the back of my neck, the one that came right before something went horribly wrong. I wasn't sure if it was the magic of the land or something more sinister, but I knew one thing for certain: something was coming for us.

I glanced over at Kael, trying to gauge his reaction, but his face was a mask, the same unreadable expression that had shielded his thoughts from me for as long as I had known him. If he was afraid, he wasn't showing it. That, in itself, was both comforting and unsettling.

The further we walked, the closer the light became. It flickered like a candle flame caught in a restless wind, and just as I thought we might finally reach it, it vanished, disappearing into the horizon as though it had never been there at all.

"Damn it," I muttered, stopping in my tracks. The sudden emptiness left me feeling exposed, vulnerable.

"We're being tested," Kael said, his voice barely above a whisper. "Whatever is waiting for us, it's watching."

Before I could respond, the ground beneath our feet rumbled, a deep, earth-shaking tremor that nearly knocked me off my feet. The shadows around us swirled like a storm, twisting and bending in impossible directions. A low growl reverberated through the ground, the sound so deep and guttural that it felt like it was coming from within the earth itself.

And then, from the darkness, something moved. A shape, larger than any living creature I had ever seen, its eyes glowing a fierce, unnatural red. I could feel the intensity of its gaze on us, its hunger palpable in the air.

I drew my sword instinctively, the cold steel of it a familiar weight in my hand, but even as I braced for whatever was coming, I knew it wasn't enough. Whatever this thing was, it was more than a mere creature. It was a force.

Kael stepped in front of me, his posture stiff and resolute. "Stay behind me."

I opened my mouth to protest, but before I could say anything, the beast lunged. Its massive form moved with terrifying speed, its claws tearing through the air as it slashed toward us.

The ground cracked open with a deafening roar, and the world itself seemed to twist and warp around us.

I barely had time to react. The darkness engulfed us, and everything went black.

Chapter 35: The Labyrinth of Dread

The city was alive, its heartbeat steady beneath the thrum of city traffic and the murmurs of gossip in every café, bookstore, and street corner. On this particular autumn afternoon, as I walked through the vibrant streets of New Orleans, the air tasted of sweetness and decay, the kind of air that promised mystery and, if you weren't careful, a bit of danger. The sun hung low, casting a golden glow on the wrought-iron balconies and the moss-draped oak trees, making the streets look almost otherworldly, like a scene lifted from a forgotten dream. But I didn't believe in dreams anymore.

I had learned long ago that no matter how beautiful the world might appear on the surface, it had its undercurrents, its hidden corners where darkness swam just below the light. And sometimes, you didn't have to go far to find it—sometimes, it came to you.

Kael's hand was still in mine, though it didn't feel as secure as it had that morning. There was something in the way his fingers tightened around mine, a subtle shift in his grip, like he was testing whether I would slip away. We were on our way to the heart of Selene's lair, a place she had constructed in the fabric of reality itself, a twisting maze of shadows and enchantments that had the power to pull at your deepest fears. I could feel the magic now, the pull of it on my skin, like the air itself was charged with electricity, alive in ways that it shouldn't be.

I had never been one to believe in magic, not really. But there was no denying the strange sensations that filled me, the pull in my chest that made my breath catch when I stepped too close to the walls, the way the world seemed to shift just when I thought I understood it.

"We'll make it through this," Kael's voice cut through the thick tension, rough, but steady. I wasn't sure whether he was trying to convince me or himself, but I held onto his words like a lifeline. The labyrinth stretched ahead, its entrance obscured by tendrils of mist that swirled in dizzying patterns, too quick to follow with the eye.

I wasn't sure how we'd found our way here. Selene's power was vast, and yet, it had been as if the city itself had guided us, the streets weaving together, leading us toward her. There had been signs—little things at first: a bird that had perched on a windowsill when Kael wasn't looking, its feathers glistening in the evening light, or the subtle tug of my name whispered through the breeze, though no one had spoken it aloud. And yet, I didn't feel prepared.

I had always thought myself strong, unyielding in the face of hardship. But as we stepped into the labyrinth, with its twisting pathways and ever-shifting walls, I felt small, like a child lost in a storm.

The first change came without warning. The air grew colder, and I felt a shiver skitter up my spine. The walls of the maze seemed to close in around us, though the space remained large enough to walk through. I looked at Kael, and his face had gone pale, the warmth of his usual confidence replaced with something darker.

"Do you see that?" I whispered, pointing to the flickering shadows that moved along the edges of the maze. They were subtle at first, just shifting forms, but then they started to take shape—people, faces I recognized.

My mother, standing in the distance, looking at me with a sorrowful expression. My father, his face as cold and hard as I remembered it, his eyes accusing. And then, there was me—no, not me, but a version of myself I barely recognized.

"Is this what you've become?" the shadow-self taunted, her voice sharp and cutting, like a knife through the air. Her eyes gleamed with something far colder than I'd ever felt, and my breath hitched in my throat.

Kael stepped closer, pulling me against him, his arm steady around my waist. "Ignore them," he muttered, his voice strained. "They're just illusions."

But it was hard to ignore when they weren't just illusions. They were pieces of me, pieces of the life I had lived, the failures I couldn't outrun. The walls whispered, the floor shifted beneath us, and the shadows stretched longer, darker. My heart raced, and I couldn't help but reach out, hoping to touch something real, something solid, but the fingers that grazed my own were not Kael's.

I spun around, panic rising in my chest. "Kael?"

He was still there, but his eyes were different now. Cold, like the shadows. He was no longer the Kael I knew, the one who stood tall against the world, the one who held my hand like he could face anything, everything, with me by his side. His face was distorted, shifting like smoke, the warmth replaced with something darker, something dangerous.

"Do you think you can save him?" the voice mocked, a twisted echo of my own. "Do you think you're strong enough to hold him when even you can't hold yourself together?"

I stumbled back, my breath shallow, heart hammering. The labyrinth wasn't just a test of strength; it was a test of everything I'd ever feared, every insecurity I'd buried deep. And it was going to make me face them, one by one, until there was nothing left of who I had been.

But then, through the haze of fear and doubt, I felt Kael's real presence again, his hand curling around mine, firm, like an anchor in the storm.

"We'll face this together," he said, his voice raw but steady. "No matter what comes."

And in that moment, as the labyrinth twisted and warped around us, I knew that no matter how dark things got, I wasn't going to face them alone.

I hadn't expected the mirror to be so brutal. Not after everything I'd endured. But the figure in front of me—this version of myself, cloaked in shadows and staring with a kind of knowing, hungry power—was no stranger. She wasn't the girl who had run through the rain, crying over broken dreams, nor was she the woman who had laughed at silly jokes over a glass of wine, her heart light with hope. No. She was a far darker reflection, one born of my deepest doubts, my darkest insecurities.

The darkness in her eyes felt like a weight, crushing the air in the labyrinth around us, pushing me back toward the walls, pulling me into the very shadows from which she'd emerged. I hadn't realized until that moment how much of her had been hiding in the recesses of my own mind. The woman who feared being too much and, at the same time, not enough. The one who had wondered if the world would ever see her as anything other than a quiet echo of what others expected.

I glanced at Kael, his grip tightening around my hand, as if he could feel the struggle within me. His face, though strained, was still etched with determination. But there was a flicker of uncertainty in his eyes—just a hint—that unsettled me more than any labyrinth ever could. The reflection of me, that woman I could have become, stepped forward, her lips curling into a smile that was equal parts seductive and terrifying.

"Do you think you can outrun your own darkness, darling?" she asked, her voice a twisted version of my own. It echoed through the labyrinth, rattling the walls. "Is this really the life you want? Full of messy love, constant failure, disappointment? Or is it easier to give in, to let the darkness take you entirely, like you've always known it would?"

I shook my head, taking an instinctive step back. Her words, like the weight of a thousand whispered secrets, stung, digging deep under my skin, where all the hidden fears lay. Could I outrun it? Could I outrun myself?

But Kael squeezed my hand, a silent anchor in the storm. "She's not real," he said, his voice calm but firm. "Don't listen to her."

I wanted to believe him. I wanted to believe that the darkness before me was a mere illusion, a trick of the labyrinth's cruel magic. But the longer I stared at that reflection, the more real she seemed. Her hair, darker than mine, flowed like midnight around her face, and her eyes...those eyes. They were the eyes of someone who had accepted their fate, who had embraced the power of the Ravenmark, someone who had stopped fighting for goodness or light. It was the version of me I had feared—no, the version I had feared becoming.

"I've seen the way you hesitate," the dark me continued, her gaze now piercing through me. "Every time he looks at you like he's the only one who can save you. He can't, you know. No one can. He's just as broken as you are. And one day, when it all falls apart, you'll have nothing left but this."

I felt a shiver of doubt crawl up my spine. Was she right? Could Kael and I ever truly overcome the weight of what we were up against? And more frightening still, if I couldn't hold my own darkness at bay, would I become like her?

Kael's grip on my hand shifted. His voice broke through my spiraling thoughts, steady, almost like a beacon in the storm. "You are not this. This isn't you. We've made it this far together, haven't we?"

I blinked, his words washing over me like cold water, snapping me out of the daze I had fallen into. Yes. We had made it this far. Despite everything, we had fought together, endured together. It hadn't always been easy, and it hadn't always been clean. But we had survived. And in this twisted, dark reflection of myself, I saw the truth: the only way out of the labyrinth was to face it head-on, no matter how impossible it seemed.

"I'm not afraid of you," I said, surprising myself with the confidence in my voice.

The reflection's smile faltered, just for a moment, and then she laughed, the sound hollow, cruel. "Afraid? Oh darling, you should be. You don't even know what you're capable of. What we're capable of."

"I know exactly what I'm capable of," I shot back, my voice growing stronger with every word. "I've faced worse than you. I've faced me."

The labyrinth around us seemed to pulse, the walls contracting in response to my defiance. The shadows grew thicker, swirling like a storm waiting to break. But I didn't flinch. I was done being afraid of myself. Of what I might become. I had lived too many years worrying about falling into darkness, trying to control the uncontrollable. It was time to embrace it—to confront the parts of me that I had locked away for fear of losing myself.

Kael's hand was still tight around mine, grounding me. "You're stronger than this," he murmured, his voice a soft promise that had nothing to do with magic or fate. It had everything to do with us, here and now.

And for the first time since we'd entered the maze, the world stopped shifting. The shadows receded, and the walls seemed to sigh, as though the labyrinth itself had heard me. The reflection—my reflection—vanished into thin air, leaving me standing there, breathless but unbroken.

Kael stepped forward, his eyes never leaving mine. "You did it," he said, his tone gentle but laced with awe.

I didn't know how, but I had. I had faced my own fear, and it hadn't consumed me. And for the first time, I believed what Kael had said all along: I didn't need saving. I had always been the one I was waiting for.

The silence that followed my words hung in the air like smoke, thick and suffocating. The labyrinth, as if sensing the shift, seemed to breathe with us—its walls exhaling a slow, echoing sigh, pulling away the darkness that had once threatened to swallow me. For the first time, I felt like I had found my footing, like the illusions were no longer capable of bending me to their will. But the price of clarity came with a bitter aftertaste, and as Kael and I continued down the winding corridors, the familiar sense of unease clawed its way back.

I could feel the weight of the walls closing in again, though the space remained the same. They weren't just pushing in physically, but pressing against something deeper within me, a warning that this was not over. Not by a long shot. Kael remained by my side, his presence a steady anchor that gave me the courage to keep moving. His fingers, warm and firm, were wrapped around mine, as if tethering me to reality. It was comforting, but the discomfort in my chest—the feeling that something was about to shift—lingered.

"I don't trust this place," I muttered under my breath, my gaze flicking to the walls, as if expecting them to lunge at me any second. It was a ridiculous thought, but it was all I could hold on to as my pulse quickened.

Kael's jaw tightened, his eyes scanning the labyrinth's serpentine passages. "Neither do I," he admitted, his voice low, as though any loud sound might provoke the maze to retaliate. "But we're almost there. I can feel it."

I nodded, trying to ignore the knot forming in my stomach. We had to be close to the heart of the labyrinth by now. Selene's lair had stretched before us like some cruel puzzle, each turn promising an answer but giving only more questions. The enchantments, the illusions—they were all meant to break us, to make us doubt our path. And yet, we kept moving forward, no matter how much the walls seemed to whisper our failures back at us, or how many times the shadows tried to lure us into their grasp.

There was no sound in the maze except for the quiet shuffle of our footsteps, but I couldn't shake the sensation that something was watching us. The kind of feeling you get when you're alone in a room and can't quite place where the chill in the air is coming from. I looked over at Kael, but his focus was on the path ahead, his face set in a grim determination.

We walked in silence for what felt like an eternity, the tension between us growing heavier with each step. I opened my mouth to speak—perhaps to lighten the mood, perhaps to break the tension—but the words caught in my throat as the path before us abruptly shifted. One moment, the walls were leading us down a narrow, dimly lit corridor; the next, they twisted violently, and the world seemed to buckle beneath my feet.

"What the hell?" I gasped, stumbling as the ground beneath us swayed like a boat on the ocean. The labyrinth was shifting, changing again.

Kael reached out, steadying me. "Stay close. We don't know what's coming."

And just like that, the labyrinth began to transform in earnest. The walls cracked open, revealing glimpses of the outside world. But it wasn't the world I knew. The air was thick with the stench of something burning. The sky above was an eerie shade of red, streaked with black clouds that moved unnaturally fast. I could hear the distant sound of thunder, though no lightning followed. The city that stretched out before me—New Orleans, my home, the city I thought I knew—was distorted, twisted, and fractured.

In the distance, I saw the faint outline of a building I recognized—a café, one I'd passed a thousand times before, its neon sign blinking erratically in the haze. But there was something wrong with it, something off about the way it hung in the sky. I could barely make out the figures moving below it, but their movements seemed jerky, unnatural, like puppets pulled by invisible strings.

"Kael," I whispered, my voice barely audible over the cacophony of distant screams and strange, unearthly howls that seemed to rise from the streets. "What is this place?"

He looked around, his brow furrowing in confusion. "This is… it's not real," he said, though his voice wavered just slightly. "But it is. It's another part of the maze. A piece of what Selene's trying to show us."

I could feel it now—this strange, suffocating pressure that weighed down on everything. The buildings weren't solid, but mere projections of the real world, warped by the magic that had twisted them into grotesque imitations of what they once were. And the people—no, they weren't people at all. They were phantoms, moving in and out of the shadows, their faces stretched and distorted in ways that made my stomach churn.

"Don't look at them," Kael said suddenly, pulling me away from the shifting vision. "They'll make you lose your mind if you do."

I didn't need to be told twice. I focused on his face instead, on the strength that still radiated from him despite everything we had faced. He was my anchor in this place, the one thing that felt real in a world that had lost its sense of reality.

But the deeper we went, the harder it became to hold on to that certainty. The labyrinth, it seemed, had other plans. We reached another junction in the maze, this time with no signs of movement, no echoes of footsteps. The path was still—eerily so. And that, in itself, was the most unsettling thing of all. The stillness felt heavy, oppressive, as though it was waiting for something to break.

Then, a voice cut through the silence—a low, rasping sound that seemed to come from every direction at once.

"You've made it this far, but there's no escape." The words echoed, wrapping themselves around us like chains. "This is where you belong."

I froze, my heart pounding in my chest. Kael's grip on my hand tightened. We weren't alone anymore.

Chapter 36: The Price of Betrayal

I hadn't realized, not until that moment, how quiet the city could be. The kind of silence that creeps into your bones like a fog, the air still thick with something dangerous and unspoken. The moon hung like a delicate slice of porcelain, hanging over the skyline like a cruel reminder of what we'd been willing to fight for. I stood at the edge of the rooftop, the city lights spilling across the concrete jungle below me, a thousand secrets tucked away in its dark corners. The hum of traffic seemed too far away, as though the world beneath me hadn't yet realized the storm that was about to tear it apart.

I should have seen it coming. Should have sensed something, anything, but I didn't. The betrayal had been carefully planned, a surgical strike executed with the kind of precision I'd been trained to appreciate and yet, on that night, could not recognize in time. But the truth is, I wasn't looking for it. The calm of the night, the confidence that everything was under control—my people, our mission—had dulled my instincts. I hadn't anticipated the kind of treachery that could poison a soul so deeply, so effortlessly. And maybe that was the most dangerous thing of all: I didn't even know who to trust anymore.

I turned from the balcony, the chill air biting at my skin as I stepped back into the dimly lit room. Kael was already there, his broad frame a shadow against the heavy curtains. He didn't say anything. He didn't need to. His eyes, that electric blue I always associated with calm before a storm, were fixed on me, watching, waiting for the inevitable. If he had any doubt, it was buried deep beneath the surface, buried where only he could find it.

"Was it him?" I asked, my voice barely above a whisper, as if speaking the words aloud would make the whole thing more real than it already was.

Kael didn't answer right away. Instead, he moved closer, the soft scuff of his boots on the hardwood the only sound between us. There was something about him in this moment—something sharper than I had ever seen. It wasn't fear. No, Kael didn't fear anything. It was the look of someone who knew they'd lost before the fight had even begun. And I couldn't blame him. He had trusted the traitor too. Trusted them as much as I had. Maybe even more.

I didn't need to ask who the traitor was. We both knew. The only question left was how we were going to deal with it.

"You should sit down," Kael said, his voice unusually calm. I knew that tone. It was the one he used when he was about to say something that would tear your world apart.

I didn't sit. Instead, I stepped forward, the weight of the Blade of Truth at my hip, the steel cold against my skin, its presence almost comforting in the moment. I had used it once, on someone I'd loved. The memory of that night still haunted me, but I had learned something from it: justice wasn't clean. It didn't leave behind the kind of scars you could just forget.

I had to make a choice. We had to make a choice.

"It was him, wasn't it?" I asked again, my eyes narrowing as I met Kael's gaze.

Kael's lips pressed into a thin line, his jaw working with the weight of unspoken words. "You already know the answer."

The door creaked open behind us, and I didn't have to turn around to know who it was. The footsteps were too light, the air too heavy with the tension of what was coming next. I could feel it—the pulse of uncertainty in my veins, the weight of everything that had been building up to this exact moment.

There, standing in the doorway, was the traitor. A face I had once trusted more than my own reflection, a face that now seemed nothing more than a cruel mask hiding the truth of what had been done. Their eyes were downcast, hands clasped tightly behind their back as if they were still trying to keep some semblance of control in a situation where control no longer existed.

"I didn't want it to be this way," they said, their voice strained with the kind of regret that felt like a slap in the face. "You have to understand—"

I stepped forward before they could finish their sentence, cutting them off with a coldness I didn't know I was capable of. "No," I said, my voice low, dangerous in a way that made even Kael stiffen beside me. "I don't have to understand. You made your choice. And now you will pay the price."

The traitor flinched, but they didn't back away. Instead, they held their ground, their eyes meeting mine with a strange mix of defiance and something else—something darker. They hadn't expected this. Maybe they thought I would give them a second chance, maybe even beg for an explanation. But I was done with explanations. I was done with waiting for something that would never come.

"I don't expect forgiveness," the traitor continued, voice shaking. "But I want you to know... it wasn't personal."

"Then what was it?" Kael's voice cut through the air, hard and unforgiving. "What was it that made you turn on us, turn on her?"

The traitor's eyes flickered to Kael, then back to me. They opened their mouth, but no words came out. Maybe they realized, then, that no amount of pleading would change what had already been set in motion. The finality of their betrayal hung in the air like a guillotine, waiting for the inevitable.

"I'm sorry," they whispered, but the apology was hollow. It had no place here, not now. Not after everything.

With a swift motion, I drew the Blade of Truth from its sheath, the light from the blade reflecting in the traitor's eyes as it sliced through the air. It would be quick. It had to be. There would be no lingering doubts, no second chances. Justice would be swift, but even as the blade met its mark, I couldn't help but wonder if there was anything left worth saving in a world that had become so twisted.

The room was still, save for the soft hum of the city beyond the windows. The battle had been won, but it felt more like a quiet surrender than any kind of victory. Kael and I stood in the aftermath of the storm, surrounded by the remnants of what had been a home, a fortress, a place I thought we could rely on. Now it was nothing but rubble, the stench of smoke and blood lingering in the air like an unwanted guest. I could still hear the clang of metal and the cries of those who had fought—people I'd once believed were invincible, now just like me: broken.

I didn't want to look at the body on the floor, but it was impossible not to. There, still warm in the fading light of the room, lay the traitor—someone I had trusted, someone who had shared my dreams and fears, my plans, my life. And now they were gone, no more than an echo of their former self, an impossible contradiction between who they had been and the person they had become. I reached down, fingers brushing the hilt of the Blade of Truth, the weapon still alive with the remnants of its justice. Its light had burned bright for a moment, then faded into the darkness like everything else.

Kael was the first to break the silence, though his words didn't seem to carry the weight they should have. "It's done," he said, his voice hoarse but controlled. "You did what you had to."

Did I? I wanted to ask, but the words died on my tongue. What did any of us have left after this? Was I supposed to feel better? Was the weight of the betrayal supposed to suddenly lighten because I had made the call, had ended it with the stroke of a blade? In the quiet after the storm, the only thing that echoed in my mind was the traitor's last words, their plea that they hadn't meant to hurt me, that they had done it for a reason I would never understand. It felt like a lie. But more than that, it felt like a weight—one I couldn't carry alone.

Turning from the body, I walked to the window. Outside, the city sprawled, alive in a way that seemed almost obscene. People were going about their business, unaware that their entire world had shifted. I had never been a fan of the world of politics, but I had always known it for what it was—a game. And the higher you climbed, the sharper the stakes. But I had believed that the people closest to me, those I trusted, would never play that game. I had thought that our bond was stronger than any alliance, that it could survive anything. Clearly, I had been wrong. I should have seen it. I should have—

"You're blaming yourself," Kael interrupted my thoughts, his voice gentle, but with an edge that suggested he wasn't merely making an observation. "You're wondering if there was something you missed, something you could have done differently."

I turned, meeting his gaze, but I didn't speak. There was nothing to say. The truth was, he was right. I couldn't stop the questions from swirling in my head, questions that came with no answers, only regret. "How could I not?" I said, the words slipping out before I could stop them. "I trusted them, Kael. More than anyone else. And now I'm standing here, and I can't make sense of it."

"You don't need to," Kael said, stepping closer, his hands resting lightly at his sides, as if the mere presence of them was enough to keep me grounded. "Not right now. You've been through enough."

"Have I?" I asked, my voice quiet but sharp. "Because it feels like I'm drowning in it. Like I've lost more than just a soldier. I've lost part of myself. Maybe all of it."

There was a long pause, the tension between us thick and palpable. I knew he wasn't going to offer me false comfort, and I appreciated that. Kael never did. He wasn't the type to sugarcoat things or give you empty platitudes. But in that moment, his silence was almost a relief. It was as if, for once, he didn't have an answer either. He understood the weight of it. The weight of betrayal.

The silence stretched on, but then the distant sound of sirens cut through the quiet, drawing my attention back to the city below. "I guess we're not the only ones with blood on our hands tonight," I muttered, turning my back on the window, but not before catching a glimpse of the flashing lights.

"We've been trying to clean up the mess for a long time," Kael said, the bitterness in his tone unmistakable. "But it's never enough, is it? The deeper we go, the more tangled we get in the mess. And every time we think we're free, another thread pulls us right back in."

"And here we are," I replied, my voice steadier now, though no less heavy. "Drowning in it."

Kael exhaled sharply, his eyes narrowing as he watched me. "You're not alone in this," he said, his words cutting through the tension between us like a thread pulled taut. "Whatever happens next, you don't have to carry it all by yourself."

I didn't know if I believed him. But in that moment, his words were enough. At least for now.

The city outside was still spinning, unaware of the shift, unaware that everything had changed. But we knew. And as I stood there, staring out at the world that would never be the same, I made a promise to myself. I wasn't going to let the betrayal break me. I wasn't going to let it define who I was. Because if there was one thing I'd learned in all of this, it was that I couldn't afford to be anything other than strong. And even in the darkest moments, even when everything seemed lost, I was going to find a way forward.

The city was an orchestra of noise and light, an intricate composition of life that continued to play even as our world crumbled. Outside the window, the streets were awash in the golden glow of streetlights, the hum of passing cars a constant reminder of what remained—what had to remain. People moved without knowing what had happened in the shadows, without understanding that their safety had been bought with the price of a betrayal I had yet to fully digest.

I moved through the ruined building like someone lost in their own skin, the soft crunch of debris underfoot somehow louder than the throbbing in my head. The weight of the Blade of Truth was still with me, the steel cold against my side, the memory of its light searing through the air like a warning.

"Kael," I called out, my voice surprisingly steady as I stepped into the next room. It was empty, the furniture overturned, a bookcase in pieces. "What now?"

There was a long pause, one of those silences that seemed to stretch on forever before it was broken by the unmistakable sound of his footsteps behind me. The air shifted when Kael entered the room, and I couldn't help but notice the exhaustion etched into his features, the weariness that hadn't been there before. It was the kind of weariness you couldn't shake, no matter how many battles you fought or how many enemies you defeated. It was the weight of betrayal, the kind of burden that slowly crushed you from the inside.

"You know the answer," Kael said softly, his voice heavy with something unspoken. He wasn't talking about strategy or plans or any of the usual things we discussed. His eyes held something else—something deeper, darker. "We don't have a choice. Not anymore."

It wasn't a threat, not exactly. It was a truth, the kind of truth that left no room for debate. There was no turning back. Not for me, not for Kael, and certainly not for the people who had once claimed to be on our side. The betrayal had spread like a virus, infecting everything it touched. There were no more safe spaces, no more places where we could retreat into the illusion of safety. Not after this. Not with everything on the line.

"Maybe you're right," I replied, my voice low, the words carrying the weight of decisions I had yet to make. "But I don't know if I can do this anymore. I don't know if I can keep pretending that this world is still worth saving."

Kael was quiet for a moment, and I could feel him studying me, his gaze almost too intense, too knowing. He saw the cracks that had begun to form, saw how close I was to breaking. He'd always had a way of seeing right through me, of knowing when I was on the edge and what I needed to pull myself back. But this time, there was no quick fix. There were no easy answers.

"You're not alone," Kael said at last, his voice firm, though the vulnerability in his eyes belied the words. "And you're not broken. Not yet. But if you don't do something soon..."

I finished the sentence in my head: "I will be."

I turned away from him then, walking across the room to the broken window. I didn't want to hear any more of his reassurances, didn't want him to see how badly I was struggling. The light outside was beginning to shift, the early signs of dawn creeping into the sky, casting long shadows over the ruins of our world. It was a quiet kind of devastation, the kind that left you speechless, with nothing but memories and regrets for company.

"I need answers," I said, my voice surprisingly calm, considering the storm that raged inside me. "I need to understand why."

There was no need to explain myself further. Kael knew exactly what I meant. He was always the first one to question, always the one who saw things from a different perspective. It was his greatest strength and his greatest weakness, and it was why I trusted him.

Even now, after everything, even with the shadows of betrayal looming over us, I trusted him.

"I know you do," he said, taking a step closer. "But answers aren't always the comfort you think they'll be. Sometimes they only make things worse."

I laughed, the sound bitter and unfeeling. "You think I care about comfort right now? I'm past that. I'm past everything. I just need to know who else is out there—who else is going to turn on us. And when they do, I need to be ready."

Kael didn't say anything for a long moment. I felt the weight of his gaze on my back, and it made my skin crawl in a way I couldn't explain. Finally, he spoke, his words heavy with something I couldn't quite place.

"You're already ready," he said softly. "You always have been."

The words lingered in the air like a secret I wasn't sure I wanted to hear. I turned slowly, meeting his eyes for the first time in what felt like an eternity. There was something there, something unspoken between us, but before I could ask what it was, a noise echoed from down the hall—a sharp, shrill cry that froze the blood in my veins.

Kael's face tightened, and he moved to the door before I could react, pulling it open with a force that made it slam against the wall. I followed him, my heart racing, the weight of what was coming pressing against my chest like a vice.

We stepped into the corridor, and there, standing at the far end, was someone I hadn't expected to see. Someone whose face I had hoped to never see again.

"Don't you dare," I whispered, my voice barely audible, but the fear was unmistakable.

But there they were, smiling in the doorway like they had never left, like everything was fine. And in that moment, I realized the worst part of it all: I had been wrong. The betrayal wasn't over. It had only just begun.

Chapter 37: The Binding Oath

The air was thick with the acrid tang of sulfur, curling around me like the tendrils of some ancient, forgotten god. I could barely see through the mist, but the pressure was mounting, a palpable weight pressing down on my chest as if the very earth itself was holding its breath. Every step felt like it might be my last, the jagged rocks beneath my boots threatening to swallow me whole.

Kael was at my side, his presence as familiar as the scar that ran along his jaw. His scent—leather and the faintest trace of pine—lingered in the damp air. We moved in sync, a well-rehearsed dance that had become second nature over the past few months. He didn't need to speak, nor did I; we understood the urgency without words. There was no room for error now. Not after what we had just witnessed.

Selene's curse still clung to my skin, the weight of her words gnawing at the edges of my thoughts. "Bound by choice," she had said, her voice sharp like the crack of thunder. "Unbound by sacrifice." The chill that had settled in my bones was no mere coincidence. It was as if the universe itself had shifted, a silent agreement that we were not to leave this place unscathed.

My fingers tightened around the hilt of the dagger at my side. It wasn't much, but it had served me well in the past. I could feel the slight tremor in my hand—whether from the curse or the adrenaline, I couldn't tell. Maybe both. The echo of Selene's voice pulsed in the back of my mind, threatening to unravel me, but I pushed it down, focusing instead on the here and now. We had to survive this. And we would.

"Keep your wits about you," Kael's voice was low, his tone smooth as velvet but carrying an edge that made the hairs on the back of my neck stand up. He had a way of speaking like he was letting you in on a secret, even when the stakes were life and death. "This isn't over yet."

I nodded, my eyes scanning the path ahead. The cavern stretched out before us, a labyrinth of shadow and stone. The path we had taken moments ago seemed to have vanished, swallowed up by the shifting terrain, leaving us with no map and no clear direction. The only sound was the soft scrape of our footsteps, the distant rumble of rocks falling, a warning, or perhaps an omen.

My heart thudded against my ribs as we rounded a corner, the dim light barely revealing the next stretch of our journey. There was no telling what lay ahead. If the cavern had been treacherous before, it had grown worse since Selene's incantation. The walls seemed to pulse with an unnatural energy, their surface slick with an oily sheen that made them slick underfoot. Each breath I took tasted of metal, sharp and foul, like blood in my mouth.

Kael was ahead of me, his silhouette flickering in and out of my view as he moved swiftly, deliberately, his every step a study in precision. He wasn't waiting for me, though I didn't expect him to. Not now. Not after everything. We had been a team, once. I thought we still were. But there were cracks in the foundation, little things that had started to show in the weeks following our encounter with Selene.

I couldn't help but wonder if Kael was afraid. I didn't think he was. But in a world like this, fear was a constant companion, even for those who had never shown it. If anything, Kael's silence felt heavier than any words he could have said. It was in the way he moved, in the way his eyes darted to every shadow, every corner. In the way he looked at me.

We didn't speak of it. Not then. Not ever. But there was something between us now—an invisible thread, stretched taut, threatening to snap. A choice had been made, one I had not been prepared for, and there was no going back. The bond between us was no longer simple; it was laced with guilt, with unspoken words and unshed tears. It was the kind of bond forged in fire, but that didn't mean it wouldn't burn us both in the end.

"I don't think we're alone," Kael's voice cut through the silence like a knife. His hand came up, signaling for me to stop, his body rigid with tension. His eyes narrowed, flicking to the shadows that clung to the edges of the path. "Stay close."

I didn't need him to tell me twice. Without another word, I slipped closer to his side, my hand brushing against his, the contact fleeting but electric. If I had been anyone else, I might have felt comforted by the closeness, but there was nothing comforting about the way he held himself now. The air felt alive, charged, as if something—or someone—was watching us, waiting for the right moment to strike.

And then I heard it: a faint rustle in the distance. The kind of sound that could be dismissed as nothing, but the hairs on my neck stood up just the same. Something was out there, moving, a predator in the dark.

I reached for the dagger again, my fingers tightening around the familiar grip. Kael didn't flinch, but I saw the way his jaw tightened, the flicker of uncertainty that passed across his face before he masked it again with a calmness I knew wasn't real.

"We'll have to fight our way out," he muttered, his voice low, barely a breath.

And I knew, with a sick certainty, that it wasn't just the cavern that would try to kill us this time. It was everything.

I didn't want to look back. I couldn't, not yet. The moment we'd left the cavern behind us, the world had shifted, as though the land itself had been altered by the dark magic Selene had so carelessly unleashed. My boots slapped against the wet ground, the sound muffled by the thick fog that seemed to hang in the air, pressing down on us. The damp was pervasive, infiltrating my clothes, my skin, my thoughts. I could feel the weight of the curse still clinging to me, a presence that gnawed at my insides, as though the words Selene had spoken had etched themselves into my very soul.

Kael's movements were sure, every step calculated with the precision of someone who'd been trained to survive. But there was a flicker of doubt in his eyes now, one I couldn't shake. He had always been the stoic one between us, the silent guardian in the background, the one who'd never faltered. But something had changed since the spell had been cast. It was as if the curse had taken root in him too, though he hid it better than I did. Maybe it was the same for him—his every breath an effort to maintain control, to keep the walls from crumbling down around him.

"You're quiet," I remarked, breaking the silence that had stretched between us, thick and heavy.

Kael glanced at me, his lips tight, as if unsure how to respond. He ran a hand through his dark hair, pushing it back from his face. His eyes caught the light for a split second, a flash of something unreadable in them. "Just thinking," he said, his voice more clipped than usual.

"About what?" I pressed, although I didn't expect him to answer. He rarely did.

"About how we got here," he muttered, barely loud enough for me to hear. His words hung in the air, just out of reach, like the scent of something sweet on a breeze that disappears before you can catch it.

I nodded, though I knew he wasn't talking about the cursed cavern or the danger we had barely escaped. There was more between us now—something unspoken, something neither of us was brave enough to confront.

The fog began to lift as we walked, and I could finally see the city looming ahead of us. Chicago. The sprawling skyline rose like a jagged tooth against the darkening sky, the city I had always known yet now seemed like a foreign land. The streets, usually so alive with the hum of activity, were eerily quiet, the usual rush of cars and chatter replaced by a heavy silence that made the hairs on the back of my neck stand up. Something was wrong, and I couldn't shake the feeling that whatever had been unleashed in that cavern had followed us home.

Kael stopped abruptly, his body going still as he surveyed the city in front of us. There was a tension in the air, thick and undeniable. He wasn't looking at the city with the same sense of familiarity I had; he was studying it, calculating it, as if it were a battlefield.

"We should find shelter," he said, his voice low. "Somewhere safe. For now."

I wasn't about to argue. If there was one thing Kael had always been good at, it was knowing when things were about to go south.

We moved swiftly, blending into the shadows, the streets as empty as the spaces between our words. The bright lights of downtown felt far away, the quiet corners of the city where we used to find solace now alien and threatening. I didn't know if it was the magic still sizzling beneath my skin or the city itself, but everything seemed... wrong. The air tasted of metal, a sharp tang that stung my throat. It felt like a storm was brewing, but not in the sky. No, this one was inside me.

We ducked into a narrow alley between two old brick buildings, their surfaces worn and chipped from decades of neglect. I could hear the distant hum of the city—the muffled thrum of life that continued on, unaware of the chaos unfolding beneath the surface. For a moment, I let myself breathe, the cool air filling my lungs as I pressed my back against the rough wall.

Kael, however, didn't let his guard down. He stood watch, his sharp eyes scanning every movement in the shadows, every creak of the building around us. The man had a way of seeing the world that made him seem perpetually on edge, as if danger could leap from behind any corner. I didn't think I had ever seen him this alert. The weight of the curse wasn't just pressing on me, it was on him too.

"We're not safe here," he said after a long stretch of silence, his voice tight.

I wasn't surprised. I didn't need him to tell me; I could feel the same unease gnawing at my bones. The city was changing. We were changing.

"We need to find the source of the magic," I said, surprising myself with the conviction in my voice. "Selene's curse didn't just vanish when we left. It's still here. I can feel it."

Kael gave me a look. One of those looks that said he was weighing his options. "We don't know what it is yet. We don't know what it's capable of."

"And that's exactly why we need to find it before it finds us," I said, meeting his gaze with a fierceness I hadn't known I possessed.

For a moment, he didn't respond, his eyes narrowing in thought. And then, just as quickly as the hesitation had appeared, it was gone, replaced by that same quiet determination that I had always relied on.

"Alright," he muttered. "Let's find it."

And with that, we stepped back into the city, the streets stretching out before us like an ominous maze, our every step weighted with the knowledge that we weren't just running from a curse anymore. We were chasing it.

We moved through the city like ghosts, slipping into alleyways and weaving through the forgotten corners of downtown, avoiding the glaring lights of the streets above us. The echo of the curse still hung around me, a constant thrum in my chest, as if my heart was trying to escape. The longer we wandered, the more my thoughts scrambled, like broken glass tumbling in my mind. Each fragment of the past few hours seemed to stab at me with increasing intensity. The silence between Kael and me stretched out, uncomfortable, a reflection of everything unsaid.

Kael led the way, never asking if I was okay, though I could feel his gaze on me in the shadows. There was something about him tonight—an edge, like he was a step ahead of me, always calculating the next move while I was still stuck on the last. But that's what Kael did best. He made sense of the chaos while I floundered in it.

We had come to a dead-end alley, one I knew well—an old laundromat on one side, a boarded-up liquor store on the other, both relics of a neighborhood that had seen better days. Yet it felt different tonight. As though the streets knew something we didn't. I shivered, pulling my jacket tighter around me, though it did little to block the chill that seeped into my bones.

"I don't like it," Kael muttered, his eyes flickering toward the small laundromat's cracked windows, where a faint light seemed to pulse, rhythmically, as if the place were alive.

I'd never liked this part of the city. Not after dark. Not with the things that went bump in the night, and the ones who knew how to summon them.

"Tell me we're not walking into the belly of the beast," I said, trying to make light of the situation, though the sarcasm in my voice didn't quite match the knot in my stomach. I gave him a half-smile, the kind that never quite reached my eyes.

"We're not walking into the belly of anything," he said, his tone sharp but with that underlying calm he always carried, as though danger was just another nuisance. But I knew him too well. I saw the slight tightening of his jaw, the way his hand brushed against the hilt of his knife. The quiet ones always had the most to hide.

"And yet, we're standing here," I shot back, raising an eyebrow.

Kael didn't respond immediately. Instead, he took a step toward the laundromat, his body tense as if readying for something.

I moved with him, close but not too close. Our proximity had changed over the past few days. In the aftermath of Selene's curse, I couldn't quite find my footing with him anymore.

The door to the laundromat creaked open before Kael could knock. I hadn't seen anyone enter, but the door swung like it had been waiting for us.

I exchanged a glance with him, and he nodded once. No words were needed. We were in this together, whether we wanted to be or not.

The laundromat was a shell of its former self, the walls peeling, the fluorescent lights flickering overhead, casting an unnatural glow. The washing machines were all turned off, their metallic surfaces cold and silent. But in the far corner, something moved—too smooth, too deliberate.

My breath caught in my throat. A figure stepped out from the shadows, their silhouette tall and imposing against the dim light. A woman. Her face was obscured by a wide-brimmed hat, but the glint of silver pierced through the darkness, catching my attention. A symbol, one I recognized. The mark of a forgotten order.

Kael stiffened beside me.

"Don't move," he hissed, his voice low, tight with tension.

Too late.

The woman spoke, her voice smooth and velvety, almost too sweet to be trusted. "I wondered how long it would take for you to arrive," she purred, stepping into the light, revealing more of herself. Her lips were painted crimson, her eyes cold and calculating, like she knew far too much. The silver glinting on her clothing was from intricate jewelry, but it wasn't the adornments that caught my eye. It was the sigil, etched into the leather strap of her waist, where a dagger rested.

"What do you want?" I asked, my voice stronger than I felt.

She tilted her head, studying me with an amusement that didn't sit well. "I believe the better question is what you want. You have been... marked, haven't you?"

Kael stepped forward, his posture defensive but wary. "We don't have time for riddles."

The woman chuckled darkly, her laugh too light for someone who was about to drop the weight of a thousand secrets. "Not riddles. Not yet. But you're wrong about one thing. You do have time. You just don't have enough of it."

She waved her hand, and I felt it before I saw it—something in the air shifted, thickening, coiling like smoke, and suddenly, I was caught in the pulse of her magic. It wasn't Selene's dark storm, no, it was something different—something more ancient. It wrapped around me like a spider's web, delicate yet unbreakable.

"What are you?" I whispered, though part of me already knew.

She smiled, and it was a smile that didn't reach her eyes. "I'm the one who makes sure things don't get out of hand," she said softly, almost kindly. "And you? You're the ones who've been pulling on the threads of fate."

The air grew colder, and I could feel the pulse of power radiating from her. And then, with a flick of her wrist, I felt the sharp sting at my wrist—the unmistakable sensation of something being tethered, something I hadn't even realized I had been losing until it was too late.

Kael lunged forward, but I was already falling. Into the darkness.

And everything went black.

Chapter 38: The Raven's Ascent

The city sprawled beneath me like a twisted labyrinth, the concrete veins running through it like a map of all the decisions I'd made, both wise and reckless. Every breath I took felt like I was inhaling too much of the storm that was circling inside me. I could almost taste the electricity in the air, a sharp, crackling energy that mirrored the tension in my chest. I wasn't sure if it was the Ravenmark stirring in my veins or just the weight of everything that had happened, but I could no longer tell where the magic ended and the madness began.

Kael's eyes never left me, his gaze always a touch too intense, like he could read the very pulse of my thoughts. His dark hair, usually tousled from battle or travel, hung loosely around his face, and there was an edge to his expression that spoke of something much deeper than simple concern. The truth was, Kael had never been someone to be easily swayed, but even he couldn't mask the unease that shadowed his features as he watched me. I wasn't sure if he was worried about the Ravenmark inside me or if he was worried about what would happen if I couldn't control it.

"Tell me what it feels like," he said, his voice low but sharp. His words were almost a command, a demand for understanding. But I couldn't give him the satisfaction of an answer that would make sense, not when everything felt like it was slipping through my fingers.

The truth was, I had no idea what it felt like anymore. The Ravenmark, once a mysterious gift, had become something far more dangerous. Its power was a constant, pulsing ache that coiled around my heart and sank its claws into my mind. It was like drowning and suffocating all at once—an endless pressure that would, inevitably, crush me. I could feel it swelling up again, just beneath my skin, a surging tide waiting for the slightest push to break free.

"I don't know," I said, the words barely a whisper, even though I could feel my voice tremble. "It's like trying to hold onto a knife that's slipping through my fingers. I'm not even sure how much longer I can keep my grip on it."

Kael stepped closer, his presence like an anchor in a sea of chaos. His hand brushed against my shoulder, warm and solid. "You don't have to hold it in, you know. You're stronger than this. It's not just about control; it's about letting it flow through you. Trust yourself."

I wanted to believe him. God, how I wanted to believe him. But trusting myself had never been my strong suit. It wasn't the power that frightened me—it was what I might do with it, what I might lose in the process. The Ravenmark was a creature of its own, a tempest I had no business controlling, no matter how many times Kael told me otherwise.

We stood in the middle of the street, the world around us a blur of neon lights and the hum of distant cars. The night was alive with the sounds of the city, but it felt as if we were the only two people left. I could hear the distant laughter of someone passing by, the low rumble of an engine, the click of high heels on pavement. It all felt so far away, like I wasn't even in this world anymore. Not really.

"Look," Kael said, turning to face me fully, his eyes catching the streetlights as he did. "You've already faced worse than this. You've survived things that would have broken anyone else. This... this is nothing compared to the trials you've been through. You're not just some girl with a power she can't control. You're a force. You've been to the edge, and you didn't fall. You got back up, every time."

I couldn't meet his eyes. The weight of his words felt too much to bear, like a hand pressing down on my chest. I wasn't sure if he was speaking the truth or just trying to convince me of something I wasn't ready to believe. The city felt suffocating, like the air was too thick to breathe, and I could barely see through the haze of my own thoughts.

But then something changed. Something shifted inside me, like a snap of tension that finally broke free. The Ravenmark burned brighter, hotter, as if it recognized the moment for what it was. I could feel the magic rising to the surface, not in the gentle trickle of power that I had become accustomed to, but in a violent, untamed surge that made my head spin. For a heartbeat, I thought I might lose control completely, let the magic consume me whole.

And then, just as quickly, the sensation passed.

I gasped, my knees nearly buckling beneath me. I could feel the warmth of Kael's hand steadying me, holding me upright as I stumbled, but something had changed. The Ravenmark wasn't gone, but it wasn't as overwhelming as it had been moments before. It was still there, still thrumming beneath my skin, but it had lost the edge of madness. Instead, it was like an old friend, familiar and comforting.

Kael didn't say anything at first, but I could feel his eyes on me, as if waiting for the moment when I would say something. When I would admit that I had won, that I had finally figured it out. But there was no victory in this, no moment of triumph. There was only the quiet hum of power that I didn't fully understand.

"It's still there," I whispered, more to myself than to him. "But it's... it's different."

Kael's fingers tightened on my shoulder, a sign that he was both proud and worried at the same time. "That's the first step. And it's enough."

The night pressed in around us like a suffocating blanket, its silence broken only by the distant clamor of the city, which seemed to pulse with a life of its own. I could feel the weight of it all—Kael, the Ravenmark, the looming uncertainty of what came next—and for a brief, bitter second, I wished I could shut it all out. But there was no escaping it. The city was a reflection of everything I had to face. Its energy, the constant hum of life, was no different from the restless power swirling in my veins. I was trapped in the heart of it, and no matter how hard I tried, there was no running away.

The tension between Kael and me was palpable, thick enough that even the buzzing of a neon sign across the street felt like it was vibrating through my chest. His presence was both a comfort and a threat. He was the calm in my storm, the steady rock that kept me tethered to the world when all I wanted to do was drift away. And yet, there was something about him—his too-knowing eyes, his quiet confidence—that made me wonder if he knew more about me than I was willing to admit.

"You think I'm ready?" I asked, my voice sharper than I intended. There was a bitterness that crept in, uninvited, but I couldn't push it down. The question hung in the air between us, a challenge as much to myself as to him.

Kael tilted his head, watching me, as if waiting for something—waiting for me to break or to reveal some hidden truth that I wasn't ready to share. He always had that way about him, like he was reading a book that had already been written.

"I think you're more ready than you know," he replied, his tone soft but firm, like the steady beat of a drum. "But you have to trust it. Trust yourself."

"Trust myself?" I echoed, my laugh coming out harsher than I intended. "When everything inside me feels like it's about to tear apart? How do you even expect me to do that?"

He didn't flinch. He never flinched. Kael's patience had always been his greatest weapon. He reached out, fingers brushing my arm lightly, just enough to remind me that he was there, that I wasn't alone in this battle, even if it felt like the world had turned its back on me. "Because I've seen it before. You're a survivor, Corinne.

Every time you've been knocked down, you've gotten back up. That's what makes you stronger than this."

I didn't want to believe him. The Ravenmark wasn't just some trial I could brush off with a little grit and determination. It was a force—an ancient, insidious force—and no amount of willpower could change that. Yet, as Kael's words sank in, a small, quiet part of me wondered if he might be right. Maybe this wasn't about controlling the power. Maybe it was about learning to live with it, to accept it as a part of me rather than something that needed to be banished.

I looked down at my hands, the marks on my skin faint but unmistakable. The Ravenmark had taken on a life of its own, shifting and writhing beneath my skin, its pulse a constant reminder of the power it housed. It was a beast that wanted to break free, a shadow that lurked at the edge of my thoughts, always hungry, always waiting.

But I wasn't sure I could tame it. Every time I tried, I felt the world around me begin to tilt, as if the ground beneath my feet was no longer solid. I didn't know if it was the magic playing tricks on me or if it was my own fear twisting my perception, but I couldn't shake the feeling that, one day, I might not be able to stop it from consuming me.

"Kael..." My voice trailed off, too raw to continue. I had no idea how to explain the chaos inside me, the fear that gnawed at my insides, or the uncertainty that lurked in the shadows of my mind. How could I tell him that I didn't feel like a hero anymore? How could I admit that I felt more like a time bomb waiting to go off?

His hand was on my shoulder now, grounding me, pulling me back from the edge I didn't even know I was teetering on. "I know you're scared," he said, his voice steady, unwavering. "But fear's just a reminder that you're still alive. And if you're still alive, then you still have a chance to control what comes next."

His words didn't instantly make everything clear, but they did something else—something unexpected. They gave me permission to feel the fear without letting it define me. Maybe I didn't have all the answers. Maybe I didn't have control over the Ravenmark. But I still had my choices. And I would make them, no matter how terrifying that might be.

As if on cue, a distant siren blared from several blocks over, cutting through the silence like a razor-sharp scream. It was just another reminder of how precarious everything was—the world spinning on its axis, a city alive with its own pulse, yet teetering on the brink of something I couldn't fully grasp. I could feel the tension rising in the pit of my stomach, the faint stirrings of the Ravenmark within me, like the calm before the storm.

"Let's go," I said, the words coming out more determined than I felt. "We can't just stand here."

Kael gave me a sharp, approving nod. "Lead the way."

We began to walk, the city unfolding around us, the bright lights and darkened alleys blending together in a dance that only the night could choreograph. Every step I took felt heavier, each footfall a reminder that there was no going back. The Ravenmark might have been a part of me, but so was the city—the energy, the rawness of it, the constant pulse of life and death that echoed through every street. It was as much a part of me as anything else. And I was beginning to think that maybe, just maybe, that was what would save me in the end.

The streets of the city stretched out before me, veins of asphalt snaking beneath the neon glow of the corner shops and old diner signs that hummed like ghosts from another era. It was late, or early depending on who you asked. The air was thick with the smells of cheap coffee, fast food, and the metallic tang of rain that never seemed to fully fall in this part of town. Somewhere in the distance, a subway screeched to a halt, a shrill, grinding sound that seemed to reverberate deep within my chest, sending a shiver across my skin.

Kael kept pace beside me, the steady rhythm of his footsteps matching mine as if we were walking toward some inevitable conclusion. I could feel the weight of his gaze, but I didn't look at him. Not yet. Not until I could make sense of what had just happened—the crackle of power that had surged within me, the strange pull of something ancient and wild that had almost swallowed me whole.

The Ravenmark, if it could even be called that anymore, had become something so much more complicated. I could still feel its imprint, burning beneath my skin like a living thing. It wanted out. It wanted to stretch, to consume. And I was stuck holding it back, like trying to tame a wildfire with nothing more than a damp rag.

"You're quiet," Kael's voice cut through the fog of my thoughts, steady, unwavering, like the calm in the middle of the storm. I knew that tone. It was the one he used when he was trying to draw me out, to get me to talk about whatever was crawling around in my brain. The thing was, I didn't even know how to put it into words. Not yet.

"I'm just thinking," I muttered, my gaze fixed on the sidewalk ahead, where the pavement cracked like a patchwork quilt, as if the city itself had been pieced together by hands that didn't know what they were doing. I took a deep breath, feeling the cool night air burn my lungs. "I don't know what's happening to me, Kael. Every time I try to fight it, it gets worse."

The words tasted bitter as they left my mouth. I'd spent so long trying to keep this thing contained, convinced that I was strong enough to control it. But every moment felt like I was dancing on the edge of a knife. The Ravenmark was like an addiction, something that whispered at the back of my mind, promising relief if I just gave in. But the price was steep, too steep.

Kael's steps faltered for a moment, just enough for me to notice. But his voice, when it came, was calm, as though he hadn't just been unsettled by what I'd said. "You don't have to face this alone, Corinne. Whatever it is you're feeling, it's not yours to carry on your own."

I knew what he meant. I knew he was offering me a lifeline, a way out of the dark, but it didn't seem that simple. The Ravenmark wasn't something I could just hand off to someone else, no matter how much Kael might want to take it from me. I was the one who had been marked, the one whose blood was tied to its ancient roots. If anyone was going to control it, it had to be me.

But control, as I was quickly learning, was an illusion.

A sharp, jagged pain rippled through me, and I gritted my teeth, stopping dead in my tracks. The world around me seemed to tilt, the city blurring in and out of focus. The pulse of the Ravenmark surged again, this time stronger, more insistent, like it was trying to rip its way through my skin. My head swam, the weight of it pressing down on my temples, and for a moment, I thought I might collapse right there on the sidewalk.

"Corinne." Kael's voice was low, urgent, but there was no panic in it. Not in the way I might have expected. "You need to breathe. Focus."

It wasn't the first time he'd said something like that. But this time, I didn't want to listen. I didn't want to focus. I wanted to let go, to release the pressure, to stop pretending that I could hold it all together.

I pressed my hands against my chest, feeling the rapid, erratic beat of my heart beneath my fingers. It wasn't just the Ravenmark anymore. It was everything—the weight of the choices I had made, the lies I'd told myself, the sacrifices I'd thought I could live with. They were all crashing down on me, one by one, and I didn't know how much longer I could hold my ground.

"You have to fight it, Corinne," Kael said, stepping forward, his voice rough with something I couldn't quite place. "You can't give in."

I looked up at him then, meeting his gaze for the first time since we'd started walking. There was something in his eyes, something fierce and dark, but there was also... something else. A depth that made my stomach twist in a way I didn't quite understand. It was like he was asking me not to give up, not just for me, but for him, too.

"I don't know how," I whispered, my voice barely audible, even to myself. "I don't know if I can."

The Ravenmark pulsed again, as if in answer, and this time, it felt like a roar, not a whisper. It surged through me with a force that I could no longer ignore. I could feel the heat radiating off of me, could almost taste the power building within me, threatening to break free. My breath hitched, and before I could stop it, my hand shot out, grabbing Kael's arm.

The world spun, dizzying and disorienting, as the magic cracked open inside me like an unstable star. Everything felt like it was coming apart, and then—

Everything stopped.

For one heartbeat, there was silence. A stillness that swallowed the chaos whole, leaving only the echo of my breath in my ears.

And then, from somewhere in the distance, a voice.

A voice I had hoped I would never hear again.

"You think you've escaped me, Corinne?" The voice was smooth, predatory, a velvet rasp that made my skin crawl. "You're mistaken."

Chapter 39: The Crimson Rift

The air tasted of sulfur, thick and oppressive, curling into my lungs like a bad memory. It hung over the Crimson Rift, a jagged scar in the earth that pulsed with a violent hum, as though the very fabric of reality trembled beneath its weight. The ground beneath my boots shuddered intermittently, sending small tremors through the mass of bodies that surrounded me. The armies were restless, each one a seething mass of anticipation and dread.

I stood on the precipice, the broken earth stretching out before me, its edges scarred and darkened by centuries of magic and malice. The rift itself was a gaping wound in the world, and every whisper of wind that passed through it carried the taste of something ancient—something far older than time itself. And yet, despite the unnatural air that hung heavy over the battlefield, I could feel the steady pulse of power that had brought us all here, to this moment. To this war.

Kael stood beside me, his hand wrapped firmly around mine, his grip unyielding. His presence was a constant, a quiet strength amidst the chaos. His eyes, dark and steady, never left mine as he whispered those words, a vow that hung in the air between us like a promise sealed in blood. "We finish this together."

The weight of his words settled over me, heavy and comforting, like a warm cloak on a cold night. But the anxiety twisting in my stomach reminded me that promises, no matter how sacred, were fragile. The stakes had never been higher. If we lost this battle, the rift would tear the world apart. And the world was already breaking in ways I couldn't begin to understand.

Seraphina's voice rang out over the gathered forces, cutting through the murmurs and the shifting of armor. "This is our last chance!" Her tone was sharp, clear, unyielding. "Selene is not invincible. Not anymore."

A cheer erupted from the crowd, but it was a hollow sound, the kind that only pretended to be confident. No one truly knew how this would end. The truth was, I didn't even know what Selene could do now that she had the rift at her command. She was more than a tyrant; she was the storm that had swept through this world, and we were just the debris caught in her wake.

I glanced around, my gaze catching on the faces of those who had joined us. Their eyes were filled with the same mixture of fear and hope that I felt. We were united, but only just. The rift had torn so many things apart—families, allegiances, hearts. And still, we fought. Not for honor. Not for glory. But for survival.

A sharp wind cut through the battlefield, sweeping the ash-like remnants of the city's broken buildings into the air. I breathed it in, the scent of decay clinging to everything. The war had taken its toll on this place. What had once been the vibrant heart of the city was now little more than a shadow, a reminder of what had been lost. The towering skyscrapers had crumbled under the weight of Selene's magic, their glass and steel now littered on the ground like the skeletons of some forgotten civilization.

"You look pale," Kael's voice was low, teasing, but I could see the worry in his eyes. "You sure you're ready for this?"

I smiled, though it didn't quite reach my eyes. "Are any of us ever truly ready?" The question hung in the air between us, heavy and unspoken.

He squeezed my hand, his thumb brushing over my knuckles. "Just stay close."

I nodded, my heart thumping in my chest. The battlefield was already a cacophony of tension—shouting orders, clinking armor, the murmur of spells being cast in the distance. But even amidst the madness, it felt as though time had slowed, the world narrowing down to this single moment.

It had been months since I had last seen Selene in person, but I could feel her presence here, like a dark shadow that loomed just beyond the horizon. Her legions were advancing, a sea of darkness on the march, their eyes burning with the promise of destruction. They moved in formation, disciplined and cold, but there was something different about them now. Something twisted.

I drew my sword, the steel humming softly as if recognizing the weight of the task ahead. The blade was cold, unforgiving, but it was mine. It had been with me through every battle, every loss, every moment of uncertainty. It had been my constant in a world that was anything but.

"You ready?" Kael asked again, his gaze steady on the distance, where Selene's forces were starting to appear from the shifting mists of the rift.

I inhaled sharply, my breath steady despite the chaos swelling around us. "I don't think anyone's ready for this."

His lips curved into a wry smile. "Fair enough. But we're still going to do it."

I turned to face him fully, meeting his eyes with a fierce determination. "We have to."

The battle would come soon. I could feel it in the way the earth vibrated beneath my feet, in the way the rift seemed to pulse with a strange, malevolent energy. The forces of Selene were closing in, and the time for hesitation was long gone. This was it. This was the final stand.

But even as I looked at Kael, the unease settled in deeper. Because deep down, I knew this fight would take more than we could possibly give. And when the blood-red sky above us finally broke open, there would be no going back.

The ground beneath me felt alive, trembling with the distant rumble of approaching chaos. The army of Selene was near—her soldiers, twisted by the same dark magic she wielded, moving like a flood of shadows across the scarred earth. I could see them now, their forms like whispers in the fog, and the unspoken question hung heavily in the air: how much longer could we hold this ground?

My hand, still tightly grasped in Kael's, was clammy with sweat, though the air had cooled in the evening's encroaching shadow. He hadn't let go. He wasn't going to. And for that, I was grateful. Still, the uncertainty crawled along the edges of my mind, a creeping thing, gnawing at my confidence. My breath hitched in my chest as the rift pulsed again, sending ripples of energy that made my skin prickle. It was as if the very ground we stood on was at war with itself, torn between the pull of the rift's dark magic and the weight of reality trying to resist it.

"Look at them," Kael muttered, his voice tight, eyes scanning the approaching legions of Selene's soldiers. "They don't fear death. They embrace it."

I knew what he meant. There was something in the way they moved, a sinister rhythm that spoke of discipline, of obedience, and something far colder: an absolute disregard for life, their own and ours. They were coming for us, but not in the way an enemy does. This wasn't just a battle—it was a slaughter.

"Not today," I said, my voice fiercer than I felt. "Not today, Kael."

He met my gaze then, his lips curving into a brief, half-hearted smile. "Not if I have anything to say about it."

A part of me wanted to believe him. But the rift, that infernal wound in the world, seemed to laugh at our defiance. The very air around it felt thick, suffocating—alive with dark magic that tasted like copper on the tongue. The rift was feeding on everything: the city's ruins, the magic we wielded, the hopes we carried into battle. I could feel its insidious pull even from here, as though it were whispering, calling, trying to drag us all into its endless chasm.

I was about to speak again when a voice rang out, sharp and clear, slicing through the murmur of anxious soldiers.

"Listen up!" Seraphina's voice carried across the field, every syllable crackling with authority. "We're not here to die. We're here to make sure Selene doesn't win. If that means standing between the rift and her army, then that's what we do. We fight until we can't anymore, and then we fight some more."

Her words, though fierce, did little to settle the storm within me. Every word from Seraphina was a battle cry, but I knew this fight wasn't going to be easy. She knew it too. The grim set of her jaw and the sharp edge in her eyes betrayed the weight of the truth we all tried to ignore: we didn't know how much longer we could hold the rift closed. We didn't know how much longer we could even stand before it.

The rift trembled again, a deep, unsettling pulse that seemed to echo through the bones of the city itself. From the depths of the rift, I saw movement—distant at first, but unmistakable. Creatures that defied reason, their twisted forms stepping out of the mist, their eyes glinting with malice and hunger.

"Things just got worse," I muttered, my grip tightening on my sword.

Kael's eyes narrowed. "They're not just soldiers. They're spawns."

"Wonderful," I quipped, though my voice wavered slightly. "Spawns. Just what we needed."

The ground cracked beneath the advancing creatures, a sound like thunder splitting the heavens. Seraphina's shout rang out again, calling our forces into position. But it wasn't a smooth transition. It never was. The soldiers, while brave, were visibly shaken, the weight of the unknown pressing heavily on their shoulders. They didn't know what they were up against, but they would soon learn, much to their detriment.

I felt the presence of something dark, a sudden cold that swept through the crowd, a sensation of being watched. I turned instinctively, my eyes meeting Kael's. There, in the distance, just past the battalion of spawns, a figure appeared, outlined by the shifting fog that seemed to emerge from the rift itself.

Selene.

She stood taller than the rest, her silhouette draped in shadow, the red glow of the rift casting long, sinister lines across her figure. Her hair, dark as night, hung like a shroud over her pale face. She was the embodiment of the rift itself—vile, unyielding, and utterly untouchable. She did not move with the urgency of a commander who knew she was leading an army. She moved with the cold certainty of someone who had already won, who had already claimed the world as her own.

Kael's hand found mine again, a silent gesture of reassurance. But it did little to ease the panic that rose in my throat. Selene wasn't just another threat. She was a force of nature. Her power, her presence, seemed to bend the very world around her.

"We end this," I said, my voice trembling with a resolve that barely hid the fear clawing at my chest. "We end this now."

"We will," Kael replied, his tone steady, though his eyes betrayed the storm within. "Together."

And for a fleeting moment, I almost believed it. But the rift pulsed again, darker this time, as if mocking me. And I knew, with a sickening certainty, that this fight was far from over.

The battlefield stretched out before me like a fractured mirror, the remnants of a city I once knew now twisted and ruined by the rift. The soldiers around me shuffled nervously, their hands trembling on their weapons, as if they too could feel the weight of the approaching storm. Above us, the sky had darkened further, the red hue casting long, eerie shadows that seemed to stretch endlessly across the desolate landscape. It was as though the world itself had forgotten what it meant to be light.

I gripped my sword tightly, the familiar weight of the hilt grounding me in the present, even as the chaos around us escalated. Kael's hand never wavered from mine, and as he turned to face me, his eyes locked onto mine with a fierce intensity that both comforted and terrified me.

"Stay focused," he whispered, his voice low, meant only for me. "We've trained for this. We've prepared. We can do this."

I wanted to believe him, I really did, but the cold truth gnawed at the edges of my mind. No amount of preparation could ever truly prepare us for Selene. She wasn't just a ruler; she was a force of nature. She had already brought the rift into this world, twisting it into a weapon more powerful than any of us could fathom. The legions at her command were no longer mere soldiers—they were the twisted remnants of something darker, something far beyond what we had ever faced.

"Easy for you to say," I muttered, my voice sharp despite myself. "You're not the one facing her."

Kael smiled faintly, but it was a smile laced with something else—something I couldn't place. He raised an eyebrow. "True. But I'd be lying if I said I didn't think you could handle her."

I rolled my eyes, half-amused despite the grim situation. "Flattery will not save us, Kael."

"Who said anything about flattery?" he teased. "I'm being honest. You've faced worse and walked out alive, haven't you?"

I glanced at the army around us—some still milling about nervously, others already steeling themselves for the inevitable fight. We weren't the only ones who'd faced darkness, though none had come this close to it. Selene's magic was something I could feel in my bones, a deep, unsettling hum that crawled through my skin like a thousand needles. It was drawing closer. I could almost taste it.

Before I could reply, the ground beneath us quivered. The tremors that had become a constant reminder of the rift's power intensified, sending a ripple of panic through the ranks. I could hear the soft gasp of a soldier, the rustle of armor, the muted sound of weapons being tightened in preparation. There was no turning back.

"Here they come," Kael muttered, his voice low but certain.

I followed his gaze to the horizon, where the mist that always clung to the rift began to part, and from it, they emerged. First came the spawns, their grotesque forms almost hidden by the fog, their eyes gleaming with hunger. They were no longer mere shadows—they had taken form, solid and terrifying, standing between us and whatever hope we had left.

Then came Selene, walking through the mist as though it parted for her, her figure outlined in a black cloak that billowed around her like a living thing. Her eyes, redder than the sky above, locked onto mine across the field. The space between us seemed to stretch, an abyss too wide to cross. Her lips curled into something like a smile, but it was a smile born of malice, of power.

"Seraphina," she called, her voice carrying over the field, a sound that vibrated in my chest. "You've brought your little rebellion to the rift. How quaint."

I felt the collective tension of the soldiers around me. No one dared move, not even to breathe. The world seemed to hold its breath, waiting for the first strike, the first moment of chaos that would spiral everything into madness.

"You're the one who's about to be disappointed, Selene," Seraphina's voice rang out, clear and commanding, cutting through the tension like a blade. She stepped forward, her armor gleaming under the blood-red sky. "We've had enough of your tyranny. This ends today."

Selene's laughter rang out across the battlefield, high and mocking. It was the sound of someone who knew they had already won, who had already claimed victory before the battle had even begun. "Do you think I fear you, Seraphina? Do you really believe you can undo what's already been set in motion?"

Her words were like daggers, sharp and piercing, and I could feel them burrowing deep into my soul, feeding the doubts I'd tried to suppress. But I couldn't let that show. Not now. Not in front of these people. They were looking to us for leadership, for strength. And despite the gnawing fear at my core, I would not falter.

Kael squeezed my hand, as though reminding me I wasn't alone. He was right. No matter how impossible it seemed, we had to keep fighting. For ourselves. For the people we loved. For everything that still mattered.

The battle began with a deafening roar, an eruption of noise and movement as our forces clashed with Selene's legions. Steel met steel, magic crackled in the air, and the ground beneath us shattered with the force of a thousand blows. But as I stood there, caught in the chaos, my eyes were drawn to her—the way she moved with terrifying grace, her fingers weaving in the air like a conductor leading an orchestra of death.

And then, just as quickly as it began, something shifted.

The rift pulsed again, violently this time, sending a shockwave that threw me to the ground. The earth cracked open beneath us, swallowing everything in its path.

For one heart-stopping moment, the battlefield seemed to freeze in time. Then, I heard the faintest sound—a whisper, barely audible, carried on the wind.

It was a name.

My name.

The air grew colder. My breath caught in my throat. And I realized—far too late—that this battle was about to take a turn no one had anticipated.

Chapter 40: The Final Betrayal

The night was suffocating in its silence, a hush that hung in the air as though the city itself had paused to watch. The cool breeze fluttered through the tall, glass towers of downtown Chicago, sending ripples through the shadows cast by streetlights that bathed the sidewalks in a pale, flickering glow. Above, the sky was a deep bruised purple, the occasional flash of distant lightning illuminating the clouds, as though the heavens themselves couldn't decide whether to weep or rage.

I had never thought I'd end up here—standing on the edge of everything I had built, teetering dangerously between hope and devastation. The cold steel of the rooftop beneath my feet felt like the final stage in a story that had been written long before I ever realized it. But now? Now, everything I thought I knew was being rewritten with every second that passed. I had walked into this battle believing in my strength, in the small but stubborn fire inside me that had always refused to be extinguished. I had trusted, I had fought, and I had persevered.

But trust, as it turned out, was an illusion.

The figure in front of me was a ghost from my past, a face I thought I had long buried. The last time I had seen Victor, he had promised to disappear from my life for good. I had believed him, as I always had, because he was the first to show me kindness when the world had been nothing but cruelty. He had whispered the sweetest promises, his voice soft and warm like honey. But that had been years ago, before the betrayal, before the secret he kept from me shattered everything we'd ever shared.

Now, here he was, standing before me, his eyes cold and unreadable. His appearance was as it always had been—dark hair, tousled just so, a sharp jawline that had once made me think of home, but now looked like the edge of a knife. He wore a tailored suit that had never lost its impeccable crispness, even under the pressure of the moment, a stark contrast to the chaos that swirled around us.

"You look surprised," he said, his voice a smooth, almost mocking drawl, as though the revelation of his betrayal was nothing more than a trivial detail in a game he had long since mastered.

"You think you have the right to do this?" I managed to force the words through clenched teeth, my pulse thudding in my throat, each beat a reminder of everything I had been fighting for. I wasn't sure what hurt more—the shock of seeing him or the crushing weight of the truth he was bringing with him.

Victor took a slow step forward, his gaze never leaving mine. His eyes were darker now, colder, the warmth that had once been there snuffed out by years of calculated ambition. "You don't get it, do you?" He laughed, a hollow sound. "This was never about you, or Kael, or any of this. It was about what was always meant to be mine."

There was a moment of clarity, like the clouds parting just enough to reveal a glimmer of the truth beneath them. The game had been rigged from the start. My entire life, the very foundation of everything I had worked for, had been part of some grand design. Victor had played his part, as had Selene, and I—poor, naïve me—had been nothing more than a pawn in their twisted chess match.

His words hung in the air like poison, seeping into my veins, and for a moment, I thought I might collapse under the weight of it all. But I didn't. I couldn't. Not when Kael's voice, sharp and steady, cut through the fog in my mind.

"This doesn't define you," he said, his hand gripping mine, steady and unyielding.

The pressure of his touch, the warmth of his presence, was the lifeline I needed. Despite the betrayal, despite the truth I didn't want to face, Kael was still here. Kael, who had never once faltered, who had stood by me through every storm, every twist, and turn. His support was more than enough to ground me, to remind me of who I truly was.

Victor's gaze flicked toward Kael, and the tension in the air thickened, crackling with unspoken history and old grudges. I could feel the weight of the past pushing down on us, threatening to break everything I had fought for. But I wasn't going to let it. Not now.

"Let's finish this," I said, my voice low but resolute, my hand tightening in Kael's, drawing strength from him. The city around us seemed to hold its breath as the night stretched out into infinity. For a moment, all I could hear was the sound of my own heartbeat, louder than anything else. My pulse, steady now, thudding in perfect rhythm with the steps I was taking. This was my fight. No one else's.

Victor's lips curled into a bitter smile. "You think you can stop me? You're not strong enough."

But I didn't flinch. "We'll see."

The world had tipped on its axis, but I wasn't about to let it swallow me whole.

The silence that followed Victor's words was the kind of stillness that stretched until it felt like it could snap. The city around us—usually so alive, so full of movement—seemed to hold its breath. I could almost hear the thrum of every inch of Chicago, its streets like veins pulsing beneath the surface, each one connected to this moment, to the revelation that had just shattered my world.

Victor stood, so certain, so poised in the face of my turmoil. But then there was Kael, whose presence filled the space with an almost tangible force. He stood beside me, his fingers tightening around mine as if he could tether me to this reality, this fight, with nothing more than his touch. The city lights flickered behind him, casting shadows that seemed to stretch and dance like specters, but I didn't care about the shadows. I only cared about the truth that Victor had dragged from the past, flinging it into my face as if it had never been buried, as if it had always been waiting, ready to strike.

I turned to Kael, my chest tight with the kind of emotion I couldn't put into words, the kind that clawed at my insides, trying to drag me under. "He's right," I said, my voice barely a whisper, the weight of the words threatening to crush me. "Everything I thought I knew, everything I've fought for... It was all a lie."

Kael didn't flinch. His gaze didn't falter, even as the ground beneath us seemed to quake. Instead, he leaned in, his lips brushing my ear as he whispered, "Then we fight for what's real."

And it was then, standing on the rooftop with the wind rushing through the city, that I realized something else: Kael was more than a man beside me. He was my anchor. He was the one who would keep me tethered to the world I knew, even if that world was burning around us. My hand clenched around his, and for a brief moment, I felt stronger than I had in days. Maybe in years.

Victor, of course, didn't notice the shift. He was too busy calculating, his mind always two steps ahead of everyone else. But that was his mistake. He was so used to being the puppet master that he didn't realize how much of a fool he had made of himself. He might have controlled the strings for a while, but the dance was over. The game was changing.

"You think you've won, don't you?" he said, a smirk curling at the edges of his lips, his voice dripping with contempt.

I shook my head, taking a step toward him, feeling the cool night air against my skin, steadying myself against the pull of old feelings, the gravity of memories that tried to remind me of who I used to be with him. But I wasn't that woman anymore. She was gone, buried beneath the weight of the truth.

"No," I said, the word coming out sharper than I expected. "I think you're about to lose."

Victor's eyes narrowed, the smile slipping from his face as he realized something had changed. It was too late for him. I wasn't the same woman he had once manipulated. The lies he had fed me were stale now, and the mask he wore, so carefully constructed, was beginning to crack.

"Don't you see?" he pressed, his tone a little more desperate now, the mask faltering. "Everything I've done, I did for you—"

"For me?" I scoffed, disbelief filling every syllable. "You destroyed everything for me. You dragged me into your mess of lies, thinking you could control me. But I'm not yours to control anymore."

The words hit him like a slap, and for a brief moment, I thought I saw something—something human—in his eyes. But it was quickly replaced by that cold, calculating stare. Victor had never been capable of true vulnerability, not in any way that mattered. He had built his world on manipulation, and I had been foolish enough to let myself be swept into it.

"Enough," Kael's voice rang out, strong and unwavering. He stepped forward, pulling me slightly behind him, his protective stance a quiet declaration that he wasn't about to let anything happen to me. "You've made your move, Victor. It's over."

Victor scoffed, but there was a flicker of doubt in his eyes, like he wasn't entirely sure anymore. I could see the gears turning in his head, his mind working out the next step in his plan, but there was something about the way Kael stood that seemed to make him hesitate. It was as if, for the first time, he didn't know what came next. And that? That was the most dangerous thing of all.

"You think I'll just walk away?" Victor sneered, his gaze flicking from Kael to me. "You're wrong."

"No," I said firmly, my voice steady and unyielding. "You've already lost."

It was the last thing I would say to him before the world, as I knew it, began to unravel once again. But it was enough. The final pieces of the puzzle fell into place, and Victor realized, far too late, that this time, I was no longer his to control. This time, I wasn't alone.

"Let's end this," I said, stepping forward, my heels clicking sharply against the concrete of the rooftop, the sound echoing like a warning.

Victor stood tall, but I could see the cracks beneath the surface—the uncertainty in his stance, the tightening of his jaw. He had been so sure of his victory, but now, he wasn't even sure how to fight. And I would take that uncertainty and use it against him. I wasn't just playing for survival anymore. I was playing for freedom. For something far more precious than I had ever realized.

And this time, the rules were mine.

The tension hung in the air like the heavy weight of a summer storm, thick with the promise of something volatile. The chill of the night should have been a relief after the chaos, but it only seemed to amplify the unease swirling in my gut. Victor's smirk had faded, replaced by a thin line of frustration that tugged at his jaw. His eyes darted between Kael and me, as if searching for some weakness, some crack in the armor that had just been forged between us.

But there was none.

"You're making a mistake," he said, his voice rougher now, a flicker of uncertainty breaking through his polished demeanor. "You think this will end well? That you can just turn the tables on me, after everything I've done? Everything I've sacrificed for you?" He spat the last word like it was poison.

I tilted my head, regarding him with the kind of calm that felt like a dangerous thing to possess. "Sacrifice?" I laughed, the sound bitter and hollow, even to my own ears. "You've never sacrificed anything, Victor. You've taken. And now it's time to pay the price for everything you've stolen."

His face hardened, the lines around his mouth tightening as if he were holding back the urge to lash out. He knew as well as I did that there was no getting out of this unscathed. Not this time.

"You've never understood," he muttered, mostly to himself. "All of this, the games we've played, the lies we've told—it was never personal."

"Don't pretend that this was anything but personal," I shot back, stepping closer, my voice steady but sharp. "You always wanted more. More power, more control. You used everyone. Especially me."

Victor's eyes narrowed, his fingers twitching slightly at his sides. It was a small movement, but I saw it—a flicker of the man who had once been my greatest ally, my greatest weakness. And then, just like that, it was gone. The mask had slipped back into place, cold and unreadable.

"You've made a lot of mistakes, Cora," he said softly, almost too softly. "But the biggest one? Underestimating me."

Before I could react, the sound of footsteps echoed in the distance, sharp and purposeful. I froze, every muscle tensing, my breath catching in my throat. Victor's smirk returned, but there was something else behind it now—something darker, something that made the hairs on the back of my neck stand at attention.

"You're not the only one with allies, Cora," he said, his voice low and dangerous.

I didn't have time to react before the figure stepped out from the shadows, and I felt the world tilt beneath me. It wasn't Selene. No, this was someone else, someone far too familiar.

My blood ran cold.

There, standing in the shadows of the rooftop like a specter, was Evan.

My ex.

The man who had once promised me the world—only to destroy everything I had ever trusted. The same man who had disappeared from my life without a trace, leaving me to pick up the shattered pieces of my heart. The one who had turned his back on me the moment it suited him.

Except, I hadn't thought about Evan in years. Not in the way he was making me think about him now. Not with his dark eyes that still carried that touch of danger, the smile that could once melt my resolve in an instant.

"You've got to be kidding me," I muttered under my breath, a bitter laugh escaping me before I could stop it. "You? Really?"

Evan's gaze flicked over to Victor before landing on me, that same charming, too-slick-for-his-own-good grin playing at the corner of his mouth. "Cora," he said, his voice smooth as honey, every syllable a deliberate caress. "Long time, no see."

I was stunned into silence for a second. Kael's grip tightened on my hand, his warmth grounding me even as the shock of the revelation rocked through me. Evan's reappearance was like a slap to the face—painful, unexpected, and far more personal than anything Victor had done.

"Did you really think I'd let you have all the fun?" Evan continued, his voice a taunting whisper in the cool night air. "You've been playing checkers, and I've been playing chess, sweetheart."

I couldn't move. I couldn't breathe. I was caught somewhere between disbelief and fury, and the two were blending together in a haze of confusion. Why? Why now? Why him?

"Don't listen to him," Kael said, his voice low, but filled with warning. "He's playing you, Cora."

I shook my head, trying to clear the fog from my thoughts. I'd never been good at forgetting the past, especially when it came to Evan. The love we had shared had been intense—too intense—and in the end, that's what had broken us. But I had moved on, or at least I thought I had. Seeing him now, standing there with that smile, pretending like nothing had ever happened, tore open wounds I had spent years trying to heal.

"Why, Evan?" I asked, my voice barely above a whisper, though it felt as though the weight of the question was enough to topple mountains. "Why would you do this?"

He chuckled, stepping forward with slow, measured movements, his eyes never leaving mine. "Because, darling, you're still the best thing that's ever happened to me. And I don't plan on letting go of that—no matter what it takes."

I felt a chill run down my spine, as though his words were a promise wrapped in ice. And as much as I hated to admit it, I knew this wasn't over. Not by a long shot.

Then, from behind Evan, I heard the unmistakable sound of a gun being cocked.

My heart skipped a beat.

"Did you really think you had all the pieces?" Victor's voice was a low murmur, his smirk widening as the gun glinted in the dim light.

My stomach twisted. This wasn't just a fight anymore. This was war. And we were all about to lose.

And then, as the night stretched long and unforgiving, a figure appeared from the corner of my vision—a figure I hadn't expected.

Someone who was about to change everything.

Chapter 41: The Sacrifice

I stood in the middle of the darkened street, the moonlight casting long shadows across the cracked pavement. The sounds of the city had faded, replaced by the steady thrum of my heartbeat in my ears. Selene's silhouette loomed ahead of me, her features outlined in a soft, almost cruel glow. Her eyes gleamed, twin pools of amber light, as if she could see straight through me, straight into the very heart of the decision I was about to make. The air around us seemed to hum, thick with anticipation, the wind holding its breath.

I could hear Kael's voice, distant and pleading, but it was muffled by the weight of what I was about to do. "Don't," he begged. "You don't have to. We can still find another way."

But there was no other way. Not for me, not now. The prophecy had made it clear—this was the cost of wielding the Ravenmark, the price of power. Bound by choice, unbound by sacrifice. I had known this moment would come, had known it was inevitable, but the knowledge didn't make it any easier.

I closed my eyes, taking a slow breath, trying to steady my shaking hands. The Ravenmark had been with me for so long now, an indelible part of who I was. But to unlock its true potential, to unleash the full power it promised, there was something I had to give. Something I was unwilling to lose, yet knew I must. The air shifted, a crackle of electricity sparking around me, and I felt the Ravenmark stir beneath my skin, thrumming with an energy that felt both familiar and alien.

Selene's laughter rang out, sharp and mocking, slicing through the tension like a blade. It was the kind of laugh that made your blood run cold, the kind that told you she knew something you didn't—something that you were about to learn in the hardest way possible.

"You think you're ready for this, little girl?" she sneered, her voice low and venomous. "You think you can control it? Power like that never comes without its consequences. Never without a price."

I didn't respond. What was there to say? She was right, after all. The price was everything. And yet, I stepped forward, my feet moving of their own accord, as if the decision had already been made long before this moment. The Ravenmark flared to life on my wrist, the dark sigil glowing with an intensity that seemed to burn through the air around me.

Kael's voice reached me again, desperate now, but I couldn't stop. I wouldn't stop. "Please, stop! I can't lose you too!" His words cracked something deep inside me, but I swallowed the pain, focusing on the task ahead. This wasn't about Kael. This wasn't about anyone but me.

"This is my choice," I said, my voice steady, even as the weight of what I was about to do threatened to crush me. The words felt foreign on my tongue, but they were mine, and they were the only thing that mattered.

The Ravenmark surged, its energy coursing through me like liquid fire, and I could feel the edges of myself begin to unravel. My body trembled, not from fear, but from the sheer force of the power now at my fingertips. The world around me blurred, reality bending to my will as I reached for the full force of the magic within me.

Selene's smile widened, her eyes flashing with dark amusement as she stepped back, her hands raised in mock surrender. "I warned you," she purred, her voice a silken promise of the pain to come. "You think you can wield it, but the Ravenmark never gives without taking."

And in that moment, I felt it. The shift. The break. Something deep inside me fractured, like glass shattering under the weight of an unbearable pressure. I gasped, falling to my knees, the power writhing inside me, a beast that could not be tamed. The pain was excruciating, a raw, unrelenting force that stole the air from my lungs and the strength from my limbs.

"Kael," I whispered, but the words were drowned in the roar of the magic. The world around me dissolved, the city, the street, the shadows, all falling away like sand slipping through my fingers. There was only the Ravenmark. Only the power. And the price.

I could hear Selene's voice, distant now, fading into the chaos of the magic. "This is the cost," she said, as though it were an afterthought. "This is what you've given up."

The pain was unbearable, a gnawing emptiness that spread from my chest to every fiber of my being. I could feel the Ravenmark's energy seeping into me, filling the hollow space where my heart used to be, where my soul used to live. I had lost something. Something vital. Something irreplaceable.

But in the midst of it, I felt a flicker. A small, stubborn ember of something that refused to die. It was Kael. His voice, his presence, his warmth—something anchored me to this world, to the reality that still existed beyond the haze of power.

I fought to stay conscious, to hold on to what little of myself remained. But the price had been paid, and the Ravenmark had claimed its due. The world, the power, it all seemed to collapse in on itself as I fought to make sense of the chaos. And yet, somewhere deep within, I knew the fight was far from over.

I had made my choice. And now, I would live with it.

The world shifted as the Ravenmark surged through me. The edges of reality flickered, the neon signs from the nearby dive bars and the distant hum of city traffic blending into an eerie symphony. My skin prickled with an electric charge, as if every nerve in my body had been rewired to absorb the power, the sacrifice. I felt the unmistakable pull of the magic—heavy and dark, like an anchor dragging me into an unknown sea.

And for a brief, fleeting moment, I was weightless.

Then, the pain came. It started in my chest, a gnawing, aching pressure, as if something inside me was being squeezed, twisted, and pulled out of place. I collapsed, my knees buckling under the weight of it, but the magic held me steady. The street around me was a blur—sidewalks, cars, and buildings warping into nothing. The only thing that mattered was the pulse of the Ravenmark, beating through me like a second heart.

I could hear Kael, his voice muffled by the crushing darkness that had swallowed us both. "Don't do this, Isla! I can't lose you. You—"

His words splintered and disappeared, as if the magic was devouring them too. He sounded so far away, his presence fading, as though the distance between us had stretched to miles. I wasn't sure if he was still standing there, still watching me in horror, or if he'd already retreated into the shadows, unable to face what I had become.

"Isla, please. You don't know what you're doing," Selene's voice cut through the haze, far too calm, far too knowing.

I tried to lift my head, to meet her gaze, but the weight of the power pressing down on me was unbearable. Through the blur of pain and the pulsing darkness, I could see her standing there, a figure of cruel beauty, her face unreadable as she watched the price of my choice unfold. She had warned me. She had told me it would cost everything, and I had believed her.

But nothing could have prepared me for the emptiness that came with it.

I swallowed against the rising tide of despair, the cold grip of power tightening around my throat, suffocating me. My breath came in short gasps, my body trembling violently as I fought to stay conscious, to cling to the reality I knew.

Then the ground beneath me began to shift, the familiar concrete and grime of the city turning soft, like wet clay. I was falling.

Not physically, but something within me was unraveling, disintegrating, and it was happening so fast I couldn't hold on. Every memory, every whisper of my past, seemed to be slipping away, like smoke caught in the wind. Kael's laugh, the quiet way he touched my arm when we were alone, the sound of my mother's voice when she called me inside for dinner—everything, every piece of myself that had once felt real, felt tangible, was fading, slipping into the abyss that the Ravenmark had opened inside me.

"Isla." The voice was soft now, distant, but undeniably real. It wasn't Selene's. It wasn't Kael's either.

It was mine.

I barely recognized it, the tone thick with grief, thick with the weight of loss. But as soon as the words left my lips, the world came into sharper focus. The Ravenmark's power didn't just take— it also gave. And now I understood the full cost of the magic that had claimed me. It was a quiet, haunting exchange, one that I couldn't escape.

"You think you've won, don't you, Selene?" I whispered, my voice hoarse but defiant, even as my insides twisted with a gnawing emptiness.

Selene didn't answer, but I didn't need her to. I could feel her presence like a shadow, just behind me, always there, watching. But something in her was different now too—less certain, less invincible. The edges of her control were beginning to fray, and I knew it. She had known the price too, but she had never truly understood what it meant to pay it. To give up everything in exchange for something so... so intangible. The Ravenmark wasn't just a weapon. It was a soul-taker, a devourer of the self.

Kael's voice, finally breaking through the darkness, was a lifeline. "Isla!" He sounded frantic now, desperate. I could hear his feet pounding against the pavement, the sound growing louder, closer. "Isla, look at me! Please."

I tried. I really did. But the further I reached for him, the further I seemed to slip away.

There was a moment, one single, fleeting instant, when everything stilled. The power inside me hummed, steady and cold. Selene's laughter was no longer a sound I could hear, only a faint whisper in the back of my mind. And Kael... Kael was there, close enough that I could almost reach him, his voice a steady presence, grounding me, anchoring me to this reality.

"You have to fight it, Isla," he said, his words soft but fierce. "Please, don't lose yourself. Don't let it take you from me."

I didn't know how to answer. I didn't know if I could.

But I could feel it then—the shift, the change. The Ravenmark was no longer my enemy. It was me. It had become a part of me in a way that went beyond choice, beyond sacrifice. It had woven itself into the very fabric of my being, reshaping me, remaking me. And I knew then that this was the point of no return.

But what if... What if it didn't have to be?

I reached for him then, as if by will alone, and for the first time in what felt like forever, I felt the Ravenmark's grip loosen, just a little. And maybe, just maybe, I could still save myself from the abyss.

I felt the ground shift beneath me, the world flickering like a dying lightbulb. Reality itself seemed to warp, folding in on itself with a sickening lurch, the cityscape bending and breaking into impossible shapes. I was spiraling through a whirlpool of chaos, drowning in a current of my own making. And then, just as suddenly, everything stopped.

It was so still, so quiet, that for a moment, I thought I had disappeared entirely. My thoughts felt muffled, as though someone had stuffed cotton in my ears. My body was heavy, as though I were made of stone, unable to move, unable to feel anything but the cold pressure pushing against my chest. The Ravenmark, still flaring in painful bursts beneath my skin, pulsed with an almost hungry intensity. It was no longer a mere tool—it was an entity, living and breathing within me.

And somewhere beneath the suffocating weight of power, I heard Kael's voice again.

"Isla. Isla, please, you're scaring me."

It wasn't enough to break through the haze of magic swirling around me, but his voice was something solid. Something human.

I focused on it, pushing back against the overwhelming force of the Ravenmark. It wasn't easy. It felt like trying to keep my feet on the ground during an earthquake, as if every fiber of my being were being dragged in different directions. But I had to fight it. For him. For myself.

I opened my eyes, the world slowly coming back into focus. Kael was kneeling beside me, his hand hovering over mine but not quite touching. His brow was furrowed, his lips parted in the effort to hold back what was likely a stream of expletives. He looked... scared. And the fact that I could see the fear in his eyes only made the weight of my decision heavier. He was scared for me. He was scared of me.

"Isla, talk to me. Tell me what's happening. Please." His voice cracked on the last word, a vulnerability that hit me like a physical blow. I hated that I couldn't give him the reassurance he needed. I hated that I couldn't tell him that everything would be okay, even though I knew it wouldn't be.

"I... I don't know." My voice sounded strange, as if it wasn't even my own. "I think it's inside me now. The Ravenmark. It's... taking everything. I don't know how much of me is left." The admission felt like a betrayal. I wasn't supposed to admit this to him—not yet. Not while there was still hope. But the truth tasted like ash on my tongue.

Kael's hand finally settled on mine, the contact a balm I hadn't realized I needed until now. His fingers were warm, a stark contrast to the coldness I felt creeping into my bones, and I could feel his pulse—strong, steady, alive.

"You're still you, Isla. You hear me?" His grip tightened, and I had to swallow the lump in my throat. "You're still you. You're just... you're just in a fight right now. We'll figure this out. I swear we will."

His words were kind, but they didn't pierce the fog in my mind. What if he was wrong? What if this was it? What if there was no coming back from this?

I could see Selene now, watching from the shadows, her presence like a dark cloud in the corner of my vision. She was enjoying this, I realized. She had orchestrated it all, set the pieces in motion like some grand, twisted game. The prophecy. The Ravenmark. My sacrifice. She knew the cost, and now she waited, a patient predator, for the inevitable unraveling.

"You should've stayed away, Kael," I whispered, the words thick with regret. "This wasn't meant for someone like you."

He shook his head, the stubborn tilt of his chin the only answer I needed. "It's too late for that. You're not getting rid of me that easily."

I tried to smile, but it came out crooked, laced with the bitter taste of reality. The power of the Ravenmark was still there, in my veins, growing stronger by the second. It wasn't just a magic that could be controlled; it was a force, a tempest that consumed everything in its path. And as I felt the last vestiges of myself slip away, I realized something that made my stomach twist in horror.

I had already lost.

But then, something shifted.

There was a crack. A small one, barely perceptible, but it was enough. The Ravenmark's power began to fray around the edges, its hold on me weakening, just for a moment. And in that moment, a fleeting breath of freedom, I caught a glimpse of something else—something unexpected.

"Kael," I gasped, my voice shaking. "I— I think I can... I think I can control it. I can fight it. I—"

But before I could finish, before I could even think to act on the revelation, a searing pain shot through my chest. My vision blurred again, the world slipping away as if someone had turned off the lights.

"Isla!" Kael's voice was frantic now, his grip on me tightening in desperation. But it didn't matter.

The darkness came for me with a vengeance, the Ravenmark tightening its grip once more.

And through it all, I could still hear her voice, Selene's laugh—soft, victorious, echoing in the hollow space of my mind.

"I told you, little girl," she murmured, her tone rich with malice. "You can't escape what you've become."

And just like that, everything went dark.

Chapter 42: The Aftermath

The air was thick with the metallic scent of rain, an unrelenting drizzle that fell from the bruised sky above. It wasn't the kind of rain that cleansed—it merely washed the earth in sorrow, dampening the remnants of a world that had been rearranged. If anyone had bothered to look, they might have seen the ash-like remnants of the battle swirling in the gutters, uninvited whispers of destruction. But for me, all of that was secondary now. My gaze stayed fixed on the tender place where Kael's fingers brushed against mine.

The city, once a buzzing hive of human ambition, now felt hollow. Puddles rippled beneath the feet of the few souls who dared walk through the shattered streets. I could almost hear the thrum of its pulse fading, the way a heartbeat grows weaker before it ceases entirely. But we weren't dead, not yet, and the weight of the moment was heavy enough to make me dizzy.

"Are you real?" I asked, voice low and brittle, my eyes not leaving his face.

Kael didn't respond right away. Instead, he searched my face as though the question had cut deeper than I had intended. He wasn't one for softness, but the way his brow furrowed, the way his thumb traced a small, absent pattern over my knuckles, told me he understood the fear lingering just beneath my skin.

"Is this the part where you tell me it's going to be alright?" I asked, a half-laugh escaping my lips even though I had no reason to find any of this amusing.

His lips twitched, that half-smile that I had come to recognize as his silent admission of everything he didn't know how to say. "If I could make that promise, I would," he said softly, his voice rougher than usual. "But it doesn't matter. We're here now. Together."

And there it was. The one thing that mattered. The word that had once felt so foreign to me, now a lifeline I clung to with desperation. Together.

I let out a breath, one I hadn't realized I was holding. The Ravenmark burned hotter beneath my skin, a sharp reminder of everything I had sacrificed, everything I had to become to survive. But it didn't matter. It could never be undone. I turned my face to the sky, letting the rain soak my hair, sting my cheeks. I needed the discomfort, needed something to ground me, to remind me that I was still here, still alive, no matter how hard it seemed to breathe in this strange new world.

There was a distant sound of someone shouting, breaking through the heavy quiet, but it was nothing I could focus on right now. Not with the aftertaste of the battle still lingering in my mouth, bitter as ash. My heart, heavy with a kind of sadness I couldn't quite name, pulsed with an odd, unexplainable relief. Selene was gone. Her twisted magic had vanished into nothing, swallowed by the ether that had once been our battleground.

And yet, the silence felt like an accusation. A verdict. Was it over? Had we truly won, or had we merely outlasted something far worse? I couldn't bring myself to ask the question, not yet. I was too tired, too broken, to look for any more answers right now.

"I don't know what comes next," I whispered, pulling my gaze back to Kael. The words hung between us like an unspoken agreement—something we both understood but had no interest in voicing. Not now.

His hand tightened around mine. "We figure it out," he said, his voice steady, even though his own exhaustion was palpable. The dark shadows beneath his eyes were impossible to ignore. We'd been through hell, and it had marked us both.

The city felt strange now, even though it was the same one I'd known my entire life. It was quieter, more subdued, as though it too was mourning. The bars that lined the street, the ones I had passed countless times before, now seemed irrelevant. Who would go there now? Who would seek comfort in a drink when the world had shattered so violently?

"You're quiet," Kael observed after a long pause. I could feel him studying me, his gaze warm and familiar.

"I'm thinking," I said, a little too sharply for my own liking. I regretted it immediately. "Sorry. I don't—this is just so much. I don't know what to do with it. Do you?"

He exhaled through his nose, a sound of frustration, but he didn't let go of my hand. "Not yet. But I will."

I glanced up at him then, meeting his eyes for the first time since we'd stood on the battlefield together. There was a quiet determination in the way he held himself, like he could face the impossible and still come out the other side. I wasn't sure if I believed that for either of us, but I wanted to. God, how I wanted to.

But there was something else, something gnawing at the edges of my mind. A sensation I couldn't shake. The strange feeling that while Selene's darkness had been banished, something else was still lurking, just beyond the reach of my awareness. It wasn't fear, exactly, more like an instinct that had learned to never fully trust the silence.

"I'm scared, Kael," I admitted, the words slipping out before I could stop them. I hadn't realized how badly I needed to say them until they were already hanging in the air.

He squeezed my hand tighter, his voice soft but unyielding. "I know. Me too."

It wasn't the comfort I had wanted, but it was the one I needed. Because, for the first time, I wasn't alone in that fear. And maybe that was enough. For now.

We didn't move for a while. I could feel the weight of the rain, the uncomfortable heaviness of a world that had just recalibrated, trying to make sense of itself again. Kael and I stood there, side by side, as though the ground beneath us had settled into some unspoken rhythm. I could hear the soft thrum of life beginning again—the distant hum of a passing car, the murmur of someone shouting down an alley, the faint rustle of trees still swaying in the breeze. But those sounds felt far away, like the echoes of another life.

"How do we go from here?" I asked, my voice softer than I had intended, a question born more from the uncertainty clinging to my ribs than from any hope of an answer.

Kael's fingers tightened around mine, his hand warm and familiar. His thumb ran over my knuckles, steadying me the way I had once hoped for a gentle breeze to calm a storm. But there was nothing gentle about this moment. There was a hard, tangible uncertainty, a broken thread in a tapestry we had barely begun to piece together. He didn't respond right away. I hadn't expected him to. Some things, no matter how desperately we wanted answers, were not meant to be solved.

"I think," Kael began slowly, his voice low, "we start by breathing. I think that's step one. We breathe, and then we figure out the rest."

I shook my head, a wry smile tugging at the corner of my lips. "Step one sounds like something you'd get on a 'How to Survive a Crisis' pamphlet."

He looked at me then, his lips curving into a crooked smile. "If it worked, would you really complain?"

I paused, my smile flickering out like a candle in the wind. There were moments in life when you didn't know how to react to the truth, when words felt too small for the reality that swallowed you whole. This moment, this fragile peace we had managed to carve from the wreckage, was one of those times. The past week, hell, the past few months, had been a blur of chaos. There was no way to name what had happened, no neat little bow to tie the package up with. Not yet, maybe not ever.

But there was Kael, standing beside me. His presence was a steady constant, the only thing that still made sense in this upside-down world. And in that small, ridiculous smile, I found the first sliver of normalcy I had been craving. Maybe that was enough.

The street was still mostly empty, but I could see the beginnings of life stirring. A couple emerged from a nearby coffee shop, their faces uncertain, like they hadn't yet decided if it was safe to trust the sun. The man had his arm draped around the woman's shoulders, and they both moved with the same cautious grace, as though the world was still unraveling just beyond their sight. It made me wonder how long it would take for anyone to feel truly safe again. How long it would take for the city, for all of us, to believe the worst was really over.

I let out a breath, finally pulling my hand away from Kael's. It wasn't that I didn't want to hold on to him, but there were things that needed to be said, things that had been simmering for far too long. We couldn't keep standing in the middle of the street, pretending like nothing had changed.

"You said we were together," I began, my voice steady but tinged with the smallest thread of doubt. "But what does that really mean?"

Kael stiffened for a moment, his posture straightening, the ease that had settled between us faltering ever so slightly. He was a man of few words, one who preferred action over rhetoric, and that silence between us was more telling than any grand speech could ever be.

"I don't know," he admitted, after a long pause. His gaze held mine with an intensity that was almost too much to bear. "But I do know this: we've been through the worst of it. And I'd like to believe we've earned something real. Maybe not perfect, but real."

A hollow laugh escaped me. "Real is the part that terrifies me."

"I know," he said quietly, almost too quietly, like the weight of that truth had fallen upon him as well. "I'm scared too. But we don't have to have it all figured out right now. We just have to try."

And that, I realized, was the difference. While I had spent most of my life running from things I couldn't control, Kael had learned to face them head-on, even when they were too big, too dangerous, to ignore. It was the kind of bravery I hadn't known I needed, and maybe, just maybe, it was the kind of bravery I was finally learning to believe in.

The rain was easing now, falling in a steady, soft rhythm. I felt it on my skin, cool and comforting, washing away the remnants of a day that had torn through us all.

"I don't think I ever really understood what it meant to be afraid," I confessed, my voice nearly drowned out by the soft patter of water against the pavement. "Not until now."

Kael's smile softened, a quiet understanding passing between us. "I think that's the hardest part. Learning to be afraid and still keep moving forward. Not letting the fear stop you."

I nodded, not trusting myself to speak, and together, we stood in the fading rain, breathing in the strange, fractured peace that had settled around us. The city was still broken, and so were we, but there was a chance. Maybe, just maybe, that was enough.

We didn't move for a long while, standing side by side on that cracked sidewalk, our feet slowly sinking into the wet earth, as though the city was trying to claim us. The steady drip of water from the trees above felt more like an accusation than a cleansing, like it was trying to wash away something that couldn't be scrubbed clean. People passed by, their faces blank slates, each of them lost in their own private grief, just as we were.

The streets, which had once been vibrant, had become something foreign—empty, cold. The quiet was suffocating, almost oppressive, as though the city itself was waiting for something. It reminded me of a moment just before a storm breaks—when the air is too thick, too pregnant with possibility. I looked up, catching the gray clouds as they loomed over us. The storm had passed, but the weight of it lingered.

"I don't know if I'm ready for the world to go back to normal," I said, the words slipping out before I could stop them. Kael's gaze flickered over me, that quiet understanding filling the space between us. He didn't offer false comfort, didn't tell me that everything would be fine. Instead, he just waited, the silence becoming a conversation all its own.

"What if it doesn't?" he asked after a beat, his voice quiet but insistent.

I exhaled, feeling the sting of a breath I hadn't realized I was holding. "I'd be okay with that," I admitted, the weight of those words settling heavily between us. I wasn't ready for normal. Normal hadn't kept us alive, hadn't held us together through the wreckage of everything we had survived. Normal was a lie.

Kael didn't speak again, but his presence spoke volumes. There was something between us now that hadn't existed before—a deeper connection, one forged through fire and blood, through loss and rebirth. And, despite everything, I couldn't help but feel a flicker of hope, no matter how faint it was.

The faint hum of city life began to seep back in, though it felt hollow, like the world had turned down the volume. A man in a well-worn jacket passed by, his eyes averted as though he were a stranger in his own skin. A woman with a child on her hip hurried past, glancing back as though afraid the sky might fall again. Everything seemed muted, but the undercurrent of life, of survival, still pulsed beneath the surface.

"We'll never really get back to normal, will we?" I asked quietly, half to myself.

"No," Kael answered, his hand brushing against my arm. "But maybe that's okay."

His words, though simple, anchored me in that moment. It wasn't the answer I wanted, but it was the truth we both had to face. We weren't the same people we had been before the battle. And maybe, just maybe, the world wasn't the same, either.

I turned to him then, needing something more—something real to tether me to this new reality. "What happens now?" I asked, voice barely above a whisper.

Kael didn't flinch at the question. His eyes, though heavy with exhaustion, met mine. He didn't offer promises or grand declarations. Instead, he took a slow breath, his gaze never leaving mine.

"We figure it out. One day at a time."

I could have laughed, but instead, I nodded. That was all we could do, really. One day at a time. It wasn't comforting, but it was enough for now.

"Alright," I said, more to myself than to him. "One day at a time."

The sound of distant sirens broke the quiet between us, a harsh reminder that even after the battle had ended, the world hadn't stopped spinning. There were still things to be done, people to be found, lives to be rebuilt. But in that moment, standing in the heart of a city that felt as broken as I was, it didn't matter.

"Maybe we should get out of here," I suggested. "Find somewhere quieter. Somewhere we can breathe."

Kael raised an eyebrow, the corner of his mouth twitching. "You think it's quiet anywhere these days?"

I shrugged, a half-smile tugging at my lips. "A girl can dream, can't she?"

His laughter, low and rich, was the first real sound of joy I had heard in what felt like an eternity. It felt good, almost healing, to share that fleeting moment of levity.

"I'll take you anywhere you want to go," he said, his tone serious but with an undercurrent of something lighter, something hopeful.

"Anywhere, huh?" I teased. "Even out of the city?"

He hesitated, but only for a beat. "Maybe not out of the city. But I can promise you a quiet spot with a good view and a drink in hand."

"That sounds like the best offer I've gotten all day," I said, lifting my chin toward the distant skyline, now smudged with the darkening twilight.

He smiled, pulling me along in the direction of the subway, his fingers wrapping around my wrist, firm but not possessive. It felt right, like it was something we could hold on to, just for a little while.

But as we moved through the thinning crowd, something caught my eye—a flash of movement, too quick, too out of place. I froze, Kael's grip tightening instinctively as I turned toward the source of the disturbance. In the distance, a figure darted into an alleyway, their silhouette disappearing into the shadows before I could make sense of it.

"Did you see that?" I asked, my heart racing.

Kael's gaze was already locked on the spot, his eyes narrowing with suspicion. "Yeah," he murmured. "Stay close."

I didn't need to ask who or what we were chasing. I knew, just as I knew that the peace we'd fought for might still be a fleeting illusion.

Chapter 43: A World Reborn

The rain had stopped, though the gray clouds that clung to the sky looked like they had no intention of leaving anytime soon. The city, once so vibrant and full of life, felt like it was waking from a long, unsettled dream. I could hear the distant hum of traffic—people trying to return to normal, as if normal even existed anymore. I stepped out of the small apartment I had come to call home in the heart of Portland, the city that had been both my sanctuary and my battleground. The smell of wet asphalt filled the air, a scent I had grown accustomed to, as did the faint rustle of the leaves in the trees lining the streets.

Everywhere I looked, I saw remnants of the chaos we'd just emerged from—the broken windows in storefronts, the streets littered with debris, the once-pristine murals that had been defaced by desperation. And yet, beneath it all, there was a flicker of something new, something fragile but undeniable. People were starting to talk to each other again, to smile and nod as they passed on the sidewalk. It wasn't perfect, and it wasn't fast, but it was real.

I pulled my jacket tighter against the chill of the autumn air, my boots clicking against the pavement as I made my way down the block toward the café I'd frequented for years. The small, brick building with the faded sign was a haven for people like me—those who needed a quiet place to think, to breathe. Inside, the low hum of conversation and the clink of coffee cups filled the space, a comforting rhythm that I had come to cherish.

Kael was already there, seated at our usual table in the corner, his eyes scanning a newspaper as he absently stirred his coffee. There was something about the way he sat, so composed yet so effortlessly at ease, that made him a fixture in my life. We'd been through a lot together, Kael and I. More than I cared to recount, though I knew the past few weeks would be enough to haunt me for the rest of my life.

But in all of it, he had been my anchor. Not in the way most people might think—steady and unwavering—but in a deeper, more unpredictable way. He had the uncanny ability to make even the hardest moments seem less suffocating, simply by being present.

I slid into the chair across from him, my fingers still cold from the brisk morning. He looked up from his paper, his lips curling into the faintest of smiles, the kind that only I knew meant he was trying to hold back something wry. It was a smile that made me want to laugh, even when there was nothing to laugh about.

"You look like you've seen a ghost," he said, folding the paper and setting it aside.

I rolled my eyes, though the corner of my mouth twitched. "Maybe I have. It's hard to tell these days."

Kael's brow arched, his eyes flickering with that signature curiosity of his. "Something on your mind?"

"Just... thinking," I said, my voice trailing off. I didn't want to talk about it yet. About the city, about the people, about the role they wanted me to play. They had called me a symbol of hope, but to me, I was just a woman trying to pick up the pieces of a broken world. And the weight of those pieces was starting to feel unbearable.

"Thinking, huh?" he mused. "Care to share?"

I took a deep breath, leaning back in my chair and glancing out the window. The city, still waking, seemed to mirror my thoughts—fractured but yearning for something more. "Do you think people really change, Kael? I mean, after everything we've been through. After all the destruction, all the lies... can we actually rebuild, or are we just pretending?"

Kael's gaze softened, his expression unreadable for a moment. He looked at me like he could see through the layers of doubt I had carefully wrapped around myself. "I think people can surprise you. Sometimes, the change is quiet, almost invisible, like the way the rain stops and the sun starts to peek out from behind the clouds. It might not feel like much, but it's there. And it's real."

I nodded slowly, chewing on his words. He was right, in his own way. I had seen it—the subtle shifts in how people interacted, the small acts of kindness that seemed so out of place in the wake of chaos. But it was the big picture that terrified me. Could we rebuild the society we had destroyed? Could I actually be the one to help lead them there?

"You always know what to say," I said, my voice softening, almost in awe.

Kael's smile returned, this time more genuine. "I wouldn't say that, but I do know how to listen. And right now, that's probably what you need."

I let out a shaky breath, my fingers drumming against the edge of my cup. "I'm not sure I'm ready for all of this, Kael. For the responsibility, for being what they want me to be. It's a lot. Too much, maybe."

He reached across the table, his hand brushing mine in a gesture that was equal parts comforting and intimate. "I don't think anyone is ever really ready for something like this. But you're not alone. And I'm not going anywhere."

The simplicity of his words hit me harder than I expected. I wanted to believe him, wanted to trust that we could navigate this new world together, that we could heal it. But fear was a stubborn thing, always lurking beneath the surface, threatening to pull me back into the darkness.

Before I could respond, the door to the café opened, and a gust of wind blew in, carrying with it the smell of fresh bread and something else I couldn't quite place—hope, maybe. The city was moving forward, whether I was ready or not. And maybe, just maybe, that was the first step in finding a way to move with it.

The barista behind the counter set a steaming cup of coffee in front of me, her hands quick and sure, as if the rhythm of the café had become an extension of herself. She didn't look up, though, her focus locked on the steady pouring of milk, creating intricate whorls in the froth. I wondered if she ever got tired of it—the monotony of perfecting lattes day after day. But then again, maybe it was the one thing in her life that was reliably unchanging, and in a world where everything had fractured, stability felt like a luxury.

"I'll take the same," Kael said, his voice warm, though the slight hint of amusement tugged at his lips.

"You really need to cut back on caffeine," I muttered, watching as he pushed his empty mug toward the counter.

"Don't tell me what to do," he replied, his eyes still lingering on me with a sharp intensity that was impossible to ignore. "You should know by now that I do whatever I want."

"Yeah, clearly," I snorted, glancing away to hide the smile that crept onto my face. "It's what makes you so... insufferably charming."

"Someone has to keep you on your toes," he said with a wink.

The conversation lulled, and I found myself lost in the soothing rhythm of the café's ambiance. The conversation was easy, like breathing in a world where it felt like the air was always a little too thick. I was grateful for it, though, for these small moments where nothing was expected of me except to be present. But it didn't last long. The nagging weight of what lay ahead crept back in, inching under my skin, making the back of my neck prickle.

The door chimed as someone else entered, cutting through the comfortable quiet. I glanced up and froze. There was something about the woman who stepped inside—the way she moved through the door like she knew she had the right to be here, like she had nothing to prove. She was tall, her coat immaculate, and her posture was so perfect it could have been rehearsed. A sleek black bob framed her face with military precision, but her eyes—those cold, calculating eyes—were anything but composed.

She was looking straight at me.

For a second, my heart skipped. She wasn't someone I knew, but the way she carried herself, like she was about to make an announcement to the world, made the air in the room tighten. I turned my gaze away quickly, but not before I saw the faintest of smiles curl at the edges of her lips.

Kael, noticing my shift, followed my line of sight. His eyebrows furrowed slightly, his expression unreadable, but I could tell he was weighing the situation.

"Do you know her?" he asked softly, keeping his voice low, casual.

I shook my head, suddenly feeling uneasy. "No idea. But she's definitely... interesting."

Kael didn't look convinced. "Interesting how?"

The woman made her way to the counter, her heels clicking with a rhythmic precision that seemed almost deliberate. She ordered something—something obscure, like it was her trademark—and then, to my surprise, she walked directly toward us, as if she had been summoned by some unseen force.

My pulse quickened, a little too fast, a little too loud. I tried to steady my breath, but it was no use. She was standing in front of us, her eyes never leaving mine, and the smile on her lips had shifted from passive curiosity to something far sharper.

"Excuse me," she said, her voice velvet-smooth, though there was a bite beneath it. "You're the one they've been talking about, aren't you?"

I tilted my head, trying not to let my discomfort show. "I'm sorry, I'm not sure what you mean."

Her smile didn't falter. "The symbol. The hope. The one who saved us all." Her voice dripped with mock sweetness, and I had to fight the urge to shift away from her. "I suppose I should be grateful, but…"

"But?" Kael interjected, his voice low, but there was no mistaking the hint of warning in it.

The woman's gaze flicked to him, and for the briefest of moments, I thought she might say something sharp, something cutting. But instead, she laughed—soft and disarming.

"Oh, don't worry," she said, her eyes narrowing, "I'm not here to make trouble. I just wanted to see what all the fuss was about."

Her words hung between us, thick with the weight of unspoken challenges, and I could feel my heart rate quicken once again. Who was she? What did she want from me?

"Do you always drop by uninvited?" I asked, trying to match her calm, though my words were clipped. I wasn't sure if I was angry or just scared. Probably both.

"I like to make an entrance," she said with a shrug, as if the answer were self-explanatory. "And if I'm being honest, I was curious. People like you don't come around often."

"People like me?" I repeated, my voice dipping into a quiet challenge.

She leaned in slightly, her eyes gleaming with something darker, something more dangerous than I could place. "People who change things. People who make things happen."

I swallowed, her words sinking deep into me like a weight that I couldn't shake. I hadn't thought of myself that way, hadn't allowed myself to think that I was the one who had caused the change, who had been part of something that felt so much bigger than anything I could understand.

But she saw me differently, didn't she? She saw me as someone to be reckoned with.

"Well," I said, forcing my voice to remain steady despite the tension rising in my chest. "If you're just curious, then maybe you should find someone else to bother."

For a moment, she didn't speak. Instead, she simply regarded me with that unnerving smile of hers, as if she were measuring me for something far more serious. Then, with a tilt of her head, she straightened and turned on her heel, walking back toward the door with the same confident stride.

I felt the tension in the air recede as soon as she was gone, but my heart didn't slow. Something about her—the way she had looked at me, the way she spoke—made me feel like a target.

The door closed behind her with a soft click, but the tension she left hanging in the air refused to dissipate. My hands gripped the edge of the table, the faintest tremor still running through my fingertips. I didn't like being under scrutiny, and her gaze—too calculating, too knowing—had unsettled me in ways I couldn't explain.

Kael hadn't spoken for a few moments, his eyes still fixed on the door as if he was waiting for her to reappear. I could feel the shift in the room, the subtle shift from casual to cautious. I cleared my throat, pulling myself back into the present.

"Okay, that was... weird," I said, more to break the silence than to truly expect an answer.

He didn't laugh, though. He didn't even smile. Instead, he leaned back in his chair, folding his arms across his chest, studying me with that unreadable expression of his. "You're right. It was. But I don't think she's just curious. She knows something, and she's playing her cards close to her chest."

I shifted uncomfortably, pushing my cup aside as if the warmth might help soothe the rising discomfort in my chest. "You think she's here because of me? Because of what we did?"

Kael's eyes softened just a touch. "You've made waves. People like her... they can sense that. They want to know if they can control it, harness it, whatever it is you've sparked."

I couldn't meet his gaze. He was right, of course. We'd done something huge. Together, we had torn down walls, forged alliances that no one had expected, and built something new from the ashes of the old world. But in all of that, I had never once considered that others might view us—me—like a pawn in a game I didn't even understand.

I had always thought I was just trying to survive.

"Do you think I can control it?" I asked, barely above a whisper.

Kael's lips twitched, the faintest hint of a smile tugging at the corner of his mouth. "I think you can do whatever you set your mind to. You just have to decide what that is."

It was a simple answer, but the weight of it pressed on my chest. I had to decide. What did I want to be? A symbol? A leader? Or something else entirely?

I wasn't sure. In the months since the battle, I had become something I hadn't asked to be, something bigger than myself, and it was suffocating. The more the people looked to me for guidance, the more I found myself wondering if I was really the one they needed.

Before I could respond, the café door chimed again, and I glanced up reflexively. This time, I wasn't so much startled as I was wary. The new arrival was a man—tall, dark hair, and a gait that made it clear he wasn't here for the usual post-work caffeine fix. He scanned the room, his eyes lingering just long enough on us for me to feel the weight of his scrutiny. And then, just as quickly, he made his way toward the counter, ordering with quiet confidence.

I felt Kael tense across from me, and I knew he had noticed it too—the way the man had looked at us, as though he had recognized something about me, about us. He was here for a reason.

"You think he knows something, too?" I muttered, trying to keep my voice steady.

"I don't know," Kael replied, his tone still calm but edged with something sharper now. "But I don't like it. We should go."

I glanced at him, surprised. "What, you're just going to run away?"

"I'm not running. I'm being smart." Kael pushed his chair back with a soft scrape, but I didn't move.

I wanted to stay. I didn't know why. Something about the café, the smell of freshly ground coffee beans in the air, the murmur of quiet conversations around us, felt like the last semblance of normal I had left. But that nagging feeling in the pit of my stomach told me Kael was right. We didn't belong here anymore.

"I'm not sure where to go," I admitted quietly. "I'm not sure what's left."

Kael stood and offered me his hand. His eyes were steady, unwavering, though there was a flicker of something behind them—something uncertain. I reached for him, my fingers brushing his as I stood, the movement slower than usual, as though I was trying to delay whatever was about to happen next.

We made our way to the door, the quiet buzz of the café fading behind us. The man at the counter didn't look up, but I could feel the prickling awareness of his gaze on my back as we stepped outside.

The air felt different now, like the world had shifted again and we were caught in the middle of something bigger than us.

"Where to?" I asked, my voice barely more than a murmur.

Kael didn't answer immediately, his brow furrowed in thought. Then, with a tilt of his head, he gestured toward the street. "There's a place I know. It's... not far. We can talk there."

I hesitated, but only for a moment. He wasn't wrong—talking was the last thing I had done for myself in a long time. The weight of the city, of everything I'd been carrying, was starting to crush me. It felt like I was suffocating in all the expectations they had of me. If I didn't get some answers soon, I was going to explode.

We walked through the streets of Portland, the cool breeze carrying the scent of the river that snaked along the edge of the city, and my mind raced. Who were these people? Why did they keep appearing in my life, unsettling me at every turn?

I could feel the tension building with every step, as though we were walking toward something I wasn't prepared to face.

And then, as we turned a corner, I saw him.

The man from the café. He was standing there, in the shadows of an alley, his face partially obscured by the dim light.

He was waiting for us.

And for the first time in a long while, I wondered if I had made the right choice in leaving the café.

Chapter 44: The Raven's Legacy

The salt in the air was sharp, like a reprimand from the ocean itself, and the steady crash of waves against the jagged cliffs below was the kind of noise that soothed the jagged edges of my thoughts. I hadn't realized how much the endless horizon calmed me until I stood there, on the edge of the world, with nothing but the sky above and the restless sea below. The Ravenmark on my wrist felt like it was thrumming, almost alive. I had once believed it was a mark of doom, a relentless reminder of a legacy I hadn't asked for. But now, as the wind tugged at my hair and the ocean mist kissed my skin, it felt less like a curse and more like a mantle—something earned, something that was mine by right.

Kael's footsteps were muffled behind me, but I didn't need to turn to know he was there. I could feel the weight of his presence, like the pull of a storm that promised either destruction or rebirth. He'd always been a mystery, a man wrapped in layers of contradictions, but today, his silence spoke volumes. I'd thought I'd known him, had even dared to believe I understood him, but there was always more lurking beneath the surface—more than either of us had been willing to admit.

"Still here, then?" I asked, my voice carrying the edge of amusement that only Kael could elicit. He had this way of slipping under my skin without even trying, like a shadow that followed me everywhere I went. Sometimes, I wondered if that was his only purpose—being my shadow, always there but never quite in reach.

He didn't respond immediately, but I felt the shift in the air as he stepped closer. The breeze picked up, ruffling the edges of his black coat, and I could feel the weight of his eyes on me.

"So what's next?" His voice was low, steady—unchanging, as always.

The question hit me like a brick, and for a moment, I was at a loss. What was next? There had been so many years of running, of surviving, of existing in the shadows of things I hadn't understood. I'd been a weapon for too long—too long for someone who had never asked to wield such power. But now, with the Ravenmark etched into my very skin, I knew that this was my legacy. It was part of me, and I would carry it forward, but how?

The answer didn't come easily, and I couldn't help but wonder if Kael was expecting something grander, something more decisive. But that wasn't how I worked. Not anymore.

"I don't know yet," I admitted, my gaze never leaving the restless sea. "I think I just need to be for a while. To figure out what it means to live with all of this... to make it mine."

I could feel him watching me, could almost hear the skepticism in the way his eyebrows drew together. Kael was a man who had always prided himself on his decisiveness, on knowing exactly what he wanted and taking it. But I wasn't him. I never had been.

"I'm not like you," I said, turning to face him at last. "I don't need the world at my feet. I don't need to conquer or control. I just want to be... free."

His expression softened just the slightest bit, though I could see the doubt still flickering in his eyes. "And what happens if you don't get that freedom? If it's taken from you?" His voice was quiet, but the weight of it struck me like a heavy stone.

I smiled, but it was more for myself than for him. "Then I'll fight. But this time, I'll fight on my own terms. No more blindly following orders. No more living for someone else's vision of what I should be."

His gaze narrowed, and I could tell he was processing my words. Kael didn't speak often, but when he did, it was always like a carefully aimed blade—sharp, direct, and hard to ignore.

"You don't think this world is full of people who'll try to make you fit into their mold?" He gestured out toward the sprawling city below us, the bustling streets and towering buildings. "Everyone is trying to claim their own piece of power, and not all of them will play by your rules. Some of them will drag you down into the muck if they have to."

I could see the world through his eyes—his experiences had taught him that truth the hard way. I'd seen it too, in the bruises and scars that marred his skin, the way he kept his emotions under lock and key. But I wasn't him. I couldn't live like that.

"And if they do?" I asked, tilting my head just enough to catch the glint of his eyes. "What are you going to do, Kael? Fight for me?"

He didn't answer immediately, and I could feel the tension in the air, thick like smoke. The truth was that I didn't need his protection. I'd spent my entire life building walls so high that nothing—nothing—could penetrate them. I wasn't interested in being anyone's pawn, not even his.

"Maybe I will," he finally said, the corners of his mouth curving into that rare, almost imperceptible smile. "I wouldn't mind the fight."

I laughed softly, the sound of it carried away by the wind. "You've always been one for a good fight, haven't you?" I said, and for the first time in a long while, I felt the weight of everything I'd endured slip from my shoulders. Maybe this wasn't a curse after all. Maybe it was something more. Something to build on. Something to create.

The city sprawled out beneath us, its lights winking like stars in the distance, and for the first time, I allowed myself to dream. Not of power or vengeance, but of something real—of a life I could carve out for myself. The Ravenmark was mine, yes, but so was the future. And if Kael was right, maybe that fight wasn't over after all.

The city below was a hum of restless energy, the constant pulse of a million stories unfolding in pockets of quiet chaos. From where I stood on the cliffside, the world felt both infinitely small and immeasurably vast—like a place caught between what was and what could be. The sprawling skyline stretched towards the horizon, an intricate web of steel and glass, while the waters below crashed with reckless abandon, as if they, too, were trying to escape the confines of their boundaries. I let out a long breath, the cold air biting at my skin, and for the first time in as long as I could remember, the weight of expectation didn't feel suffocating.

"What are you thinking about?" Kael's voice broke the moment, low and steady, like the earth itself had spoken. I glanced over at him, and there it was again, that rare softness in his gaze—the kind that didn't quite belong to him, but seemed to slip through the cracks when he thought no one was looking. The man who was always calculating, always three steps ahead, was suddenly waiting for an answer to a question that, even I wasn't sure how to answer.

"I'm thinking about how many times I've been told what I'm supposed to be," I replied, my tone wry, though the truth behind the words clung to me like the remnants of the storm clouds overhead. "And how few of those times anyone bothered to ask me what I wanted to be."

Kael didn't offer a word of reassurance, nor did he mock me. Instead, he simply nodded, his lips pressed together as if he understood something unsaid. I hadn't expected him to understand, but then, I never had expected much from him beyond the sharp edges of his loyalty, the black-and-white certainty of his methods. It was strange how, over time, the space between us had shifted, twisted even, until I wasn't so sure what lay on the other side of that space anymore.

"So," I ventured, stepping away from the edge of the cliff and brushing the sand from my jeans, "what about you? What's next for the ever-present shadow?"

He didn't flinch at my teasing, the nicknames never seeming to faze him. Kael had a way of remaining still, as if he'd been carved from stone and hadn't yet figured out how to move. His smile, when it came, was so fleeting it almost seemed accidental, like he was too busy hiding parts of himself to notice.

"I never expected you to ask me that," he said, his voice more rueful than I was accustomed to. "But I suppose the question is fair."

I raised an eyebrow, and that small shift in my posture must have been enough to make him decide to elaborate. "I suppose I'm figuring out what it means to keep fighting for a cause that's no longer... clear. It's easier when there's a single target, something you can point to and destroy. But when the target disappears, when the fight becomes about what happens next... it gets messy." His gaze flicked to the horizon, and for once, there was no calculation in his eyes—just weariness.

"What if we don't have to keep fighting?" I said, my words hovering between us, like an idea that had never been dared. It sounded almost foolish to say aloud, but there was something liberating about the thought. I wasn't a soldier, and Kael wasn't my commander. Perhaps it was time to step off the battlefield, even if I wasn't sure where that left us.

His eyes turned back to me, narrowing with an intensity that was at once familiar and foreign. "And if the fight isn't over? If the battle we've only just begun is bigger than either of us?" His tone softened, as though he were speaking to the part of me that still didn't want to believe in easy answers.

I glanced down at the Ravenmark on my wrist, the intricate design of the bird's wings etched into my skin like a permanent reminder of a past I could never outrun. The mark had once been the symbol of a legacy I didn't want to claim, of a future that had been thrust upon me. But now, in the silence of the moment, I realized that it no longer felt like a sentence. It was more like an invitation, one I had to accept on my own terms.

"I don't think the fight ever ends, Kael," I said quietly, a faint smile tugging at my lips. "But maybe the fight doesn't always have to be the same. Maybe we fight for something different now. Something we choose."

He regarded me with that inscrutable look of his, and for a second, I wondered if I had said too much. But then, he gave a single nod—almost imperceptible—and I knew that, for all his secrets, Kael was starting to see the same thing I was.

"You're right," he said, the words coming out with an ease that surprised me. "Maybe it's time to fight for something worth fighting for."

I didn't know how long we stood there, the wind whipping around us like an unspoken agreement, both of us standing on the edge of something larger than either of us could fully grasp. Maybe we were both afraid to speak the words aloud, afraid to believe that we could have something that wasn't built on power or control. Something quieter, something real.

It wasn't until the sun dipped below the horizon, casting a final wash of amber and violet over the sea, that I turned back toward the winding path leading down to the city.

"You know," I said, breaking the silence, "maybe I'll buy a small apartment in the city. Somewhere close to the water."

He looked at me, his lips quirking slightly. "And what are you going to do with your newfound freedom?"

"Figure it out, I suppose," I answered, my voice light, but underneath it all was the weight of the truth. "Maybe I'll learn to live with the choice to simply be."

Kael let out a breath that sounded like he was both relieved and, at the same time, hesitant to hope for too much. "And if the world doesn't let you just be?"

I smiled, a slow, unhurried thing, as if I had all the time in the world. "Then we'll deal with it together. But this time, I'm calling the shots."

For once, I believed that it could be true.

The city seemed to buzz with a new rhythm beneath the rising tide of my thoughts, a pulse in the air that I hadn't noticed before. The last rays of sun clung to the skyline, painting everything in shades of copper and rose, while below, the streets stretched out like an intricate web of possibilities. A hundred thousand lives played out in their own corner of the world, each one clinging to their own version of survival. And here I was, standing at the edge of it all, with nothing but the open sea before me, and the weight of choice heavy in my chest. For once, I wasn't drowning in it.

Kael's presence at my side was a steadying force, the kind of weight I'd never admit I needed. But it was there, like a familiar shadow. The kind that always seemed to stay just out of reach, yet never really let you go. I knew I wasn't the only one feeling the pull of the unknown—his silence had grown deeper in the last few minutes, as if he too were searching for something in the shifting sea breeze.

"So, what's the plan now?" I asked, the teasing edge of my voice masking the seriousness that still lingered in the air between us. It was strange, this new sense of freedom that seemed to unfurl inside me, like a tight knot in the chest loosening for the first time. I had no idea what came next, no real path to follow, but I didn't feel the desperate need to find one just yet.

Kael's eyes flicked to me, an unreadable expression flickering behind the stormy gray. He could've stayed silent, as he often did, his typical aloofness intact, but instead he spoke.

"You don't have a plan, do you?" he said, the corners of his mouth turning upward ever so slightly.

I snorted. "What's the fun in a plan? Besides, you're the one who always has a backup for everything. I'm starting to think you'll be just fine if we go completely off-script."

His laugh was low, more a rumble than anything, and it surprised me. Kael wasn't the type to offer amusement without some hidden agenda, but in this moment, his easy laughter felt like a breath of fresh air. I almost forgot how rare it was.

"You know," he said, his gaze returning to the horizon, "you've changed since we first met." The words were said casually, but there was a weight to them—like he was measuring the shift, marking the distance between who I had been and who I was now.

"Can't say I'm sorry about that," I replied with a lightness I didn't quite feel. The truth was, I didn't recognize the person I had been before the Ravenmark. I didn't even recognize the one standing beside Kael now. The Ravenmark had done something to me—it had forged a different version of myself, a version that didn't just survive but demanded to live, to thrive, even if it meant fighting against the forces that tried to shape me into something I didn't want to be.

Kael turned toward me then, his face serious again, all traces of humor gone. "What do you want, really? What does a life of 'just being' look like for someone like you?"

I hesitated, taken aback by the question. It was too simple, too raw. Too close to something I didn't quite know how to answer. But I didn't flinch. Instead, I stepped forward, letting my gaze take in the city below—its lights already flickering on, one by one, like stars in a land-bound constellation.

"I want to find a place where I can choose my own battles," I said slowly, my voice steady. "Where I don't have to answer to anyone but myself. A place where I can just... exist. Maybe I'll do something with this power, maybe not. I'm not interested in becoming the villain of someone else's story."

Kael was quiet for a long while, watching me, the words hanging in the air between us. For a moment, I thought he might say something—some cynical remark about how naive my dreams were, or a sharp observation about the difficulty of finding such a place. But instead, he just nodded, as if accepting something I hadn't fully realized yet.

"You've come a long way, haven't you?" he said finally, his voice softer now. The sharpness was gone, replaced by something I couldn't quite place.

I met his gaze, the weight of all that had passed between us hanging in the space between us. I wasn't sure what had shifted—whether it was his recognition of my growth or something deeper that I wasn't ready to define.

"I've had to," I said simply. "You don't survive without learning how to evolve."

The wind kicked up around us again, colder this time, bringing with it the scent of rain that hinted at the storm that would inevitably break. I felt it before I saw it—a tension gathering in the distance, a ripple in the air that signaled more than just a change in the weather. I looked at Kael, my heart suddenly beating harder in my chest.

"You feel that?" I asked, my voice a little quieter now.

He was already moving, his body tense, every instinct switched on. "I do. And I don't like it."

Before I could ask what he meant, a flash of movement caught my eye. It was fleeting, just a shadow darting between the buildings below, but it was enough to make the hairs on the back of my neck stand up. Kael's hand went to the hilt of his dagger without a second thought, and I felt a sudden shift in the air, as if something was about to break wide open.

"What is it?" I asked, my pulse quickening.

He didn't answer at first, his gaze narrowing as his eyes scanned the skyline, flicking from one building to the next with laser precision. "We're being watched."

The words hit me with an unexpected jolt. My instincts flared, and I followed Kael's gaze, but there was nothing there—nothing obvious. And yet, the feeling lingered, pressing in from every direction.

"By who?" I asked, barely above a whisper.

Kael's eyes flashed with the kind of danger I hadn't seen in him for a while—a kind of danger that said we weren't going to be left to our own devices for much longer. "Doesn't matter," he said, his voice low and deadly. "We're about to find out."

Before I could react, a shot rang out. The sound echoed across the city, ricocheting off the buildings, and for the briefest moment, the world around me held its breath.

Chapter 45: A New Dawn

The streets of New Orleans had a rhythm to them that was all their own. A mix of jazz spilling from hidden corners, the rich scent of crawfish and spices curling through the air, and the soft shuffle of footsteps on cracked pavement. It was a city that pulsed with life in the most unexpected places, a city that welcomed both the worn-out and the wild-eyed with equal fervor. I had lived here long enough to know that it never really let go, not entirely. And yet, standing on the balcony of my tiny apartment on Chartres Street, I realized that for the first time in years, I felt like I could slip free of its grasp, if I chose to.

The early morning mist clung to the cobblestones like a ghost reluctant to leave. The bayou was just far enough from the city's heart to keep its mysteries untold, but close enough to feel like it was always watching. The French Quarter stirred slowly, like the opening notes of a song that you didn't know you knew by heart. In a few hours, the streets would be swarming with tourists, but now, at dawn, it was a place for the locals—those who understood the quiet conversations the city had with itself.

I watched the sun inch over the horizon, a delicate streak of orange against the soft, gray sky. The world was still asleep, but not me. I never slept when the dawn arrived; not anymore. There was too much history in my bones, too many stories left untold. I had learned long ago to listen to the quiet hum of the world, to recognize the moments when change was coming, even if it was only a whisper at first.

Behind me, I could hear the muffled sounds of Kael moving around in the apartment. He'd made coffee—strong, bitter, just the way I liked it—and I could practically taste it on the air, a reminder that some things never changed. He didn't need to ask. He never did. I could always tell when he was near, even without seeing him.

His presence was as much a part of the fabric of my life now as the city itself. It was strange how easily we had woven ourselves into each other's existence, as though we had always been here, in this moment, and would always be.

When he finally appeared in the doorway, a mug in hand and his hair still a tangled mess of dark curls, I couldn't help but smile. There was something comforting about him in the mornings, like the world was a little less complicated when he was near. He didn't speak at first, just leaned against the doorframe, watching me. I knew what he was thinking; he had that look in his eyes—the one that said he was trying to figure out if today was going to be one of those days.

"I thought we agreed you wouldn't drink that much coffee," I said, raising an eyebrow as I gestured to the mug in his hand.

He chuckled softly, setting it down on the railing next to me before joining me at the edge of the balcony. His gaze followed mine, taking in the view of the Quarter as it began to wake.

"We did," he replied, his voice smooth and low, "but I also remember you saying that you'd need it for whatever was coming next."

I turned to him, my heart giving a little jolt. There was something about his expression that made me feel like we were standing on the edge of something, as if the next moment might be the one that changed everything.

"You're not worried, are you?" I asked, keeping my voice light, though I wasn't sure I believed my own words.

He tilted his head, considering me for a long moment. "Worried? Maybe. But not about you. Not anymore."

I didn't know what to say to that. It was the truth, and it wasn't. Not really. Because if there was one thing I had learned over the last few months, it was that the Ravenmark wasn't something that could just be cast aside. It would follow me, in some form or another, wherever I went.

But there was a certain peace in the way Kael looked at me, as though he didn't care what I carried with me. He had his own ghosts, and somehow, they had become my ghosts, too. We had become more than just survivors of a shared past. We had become a promise—of what, I wasn't entirely sure.

I reached for the coffee, taking a sip as I turned my gaze back to the street below. There was something about the way the light was spilling over the rooftops, touching everything with a soft glow, that made the city feel new again. The cobblestones, the buildings, even the trees seemed to come alive with the promise of a fresh start.

"Have you ever wondered," I began, feeling the weight of the question settle on my chest, "if we can ever truly leave the past behind?"

Kael's silence stretched between us like a bridge, and when he finally spoke, his voice was filled with a kind of quiet certainty.

"Maybe we can't," he said softly, "but we don't have to let it define us either."

His words lingered in the air, and for the first time, I found myself wondering if he was right. Could we really move forward, unburdened by what had come before? I wasn't sure, but in that moment, with him beside me and the city slowly stirring around us, I felt like it might just be possible.

Maybe today was the day we would stop being haunted by ghosts. Maybe today, we could finally begin to live.

The coffee shop was packed by the time we arrived, the heavy scent of roasting beans mixing with the faint clatter of mismatched chairs and the soft murmur of conversations floating in the air. New Orleans had a way of embracing contradictions, of taking the quiet and the chaotic and folding them into one perfectly imperfect package. This was my favorite place on Decatur Street—a little corner shop tucked beneath the overhanging balconies, its walls a patchwork of vintage signs and local art, its floors worn smooth by the shuffle of countless feet.

Kael was already scanning the room, his gaze sharp as always, but I could see the softening at the edges of his mouth, the way his shoulders relaxed when he spotted the corner booth. It was a rare thing, to see him look anything but tense. It was a moment of peace, brief as it might be, and I wanted to hold onto it.

"We should've gone to the French Market," I said, my voice teasing as I nudged him toward the table. "You know, to give ourselves the full tourist experience."

He raised an eyebrow, a mischievous glint lighting up his eyes. "I'm not sure 'tourist' is what I'd call it. More like 'undercover agents.' You know, trying to blend in with the crowds so we don't attract attention."

I snorted, sliding into the booth opposite him. "Right, because that's worked so well for us so far."

"I prefer to think of it as an art form," he said with a smirk, glancing over the menu as the barista took our order.

I glanced at Kael, amused by the way his mind always seemed to work in riddles. He was no stranger to danger, to running from it, but there was something magnetic about him—something that made you forget that his past was as complicated as any tangled knot. He had a way of pretending it wasn't there, of wrapping it in layers of charm and confidence, and I couldn't help but admire that about him. It made me feel as though I was living in a moment where anything was possible, even when I knew better.

We both leaned back, the murmur of conversation around us a comfortable backdrop, the heavy mug of coffee in my hands warming me from the inside out. Outside, the world was unfolding in the familiar ways it always did—tourists laughing as they snapped pictures, the clinking of beads on necklaces, the distant sound of a trumpet drifting on the breeze.

It was the kind of day that made you think, maybe, just maybe, everything might be alright.

"Have you ever wondered," Kael said suddenly, his voice soft, a little too quiet for the bustling cafe, "if we're just playing at being normal?"

His words, uncharacteristically somber, made me pause. I set the cup down on the table, my fingers curling around its edges. There was an edge of vulnerability in his tone that I rarely heard.

"Normal?" I repeated, not quite sure how to respond. "What's normal, anyway? Do you mean... like them?" I gestured vaguely to the crowd. "The tourists and the street performers? The ones who think they've cracked the code to life because they've got a cup of café au lait in their hands?"

Kael's lips twitched at the corners. "Something like that. I guess I mean—" He hesitated, his gaze wandering out the window, as if searching for the right words among the people passing by. "There's a kind of mask we wear, isn't there? I think we've gotten so good at pretending we fit into all of this, that we forget we're not really part of it."

The air between us seemed to shift, an unspoken understanding passing through. We were both out of place in the world, no matter how much we tried to blend in, no matter how much we tried to convince ourselves that normalcy was within reach. The truth was, we'd both been shaped by something larger than us—something that left marks that couldn't be erased, no matter how far we ran.

I leaned forward, picking up the conversation where he'd left off. "You don't think that's the point?" I asked quietly. "That we're never supposed to be 'normal' in the way people expect? Maybe it's about finding peace in being... not normal. In being exactly what we are."

He met my gaze then, the shadows in his eyes giving way to something else—something warmer, less guarded.

"I suppose that's one way to look at it." He shrugged, the old tension already creeping back into his posture. "It's just—sometimes I don't know how to do that. How to let go of what's behind me."

I smiled gently. "I'm not sure anyone ever really lets go. We just learn how to carry it, don't we?"

"Maybe," he murmured, his fingers tracing the edge of his mug. There was a long silence between us, filled only by the sounds of clinking plates and the murmur of other voices. It was the kind of silence that didn't need to be filled, but that didn't stop my mind from racing.

The coffee arrived, and for a moment, we both returned to the rhythm of ordinary things. The steam from my cup curled upward, fragrant and familiar, and I felt a strange peace settle into my chest. Despite everything, despite the past that refused to stay buried and the dangers that still lurked at the edges of our lives, I could feel the tug of something new—a thread of hope weaving itself through the chaos.

"Tell me something," I said after a beat, my voice light, as I took another sip of coffee. "What would you do if you didn't have to worry about anything anymore? If everything just... stopped being so complicated?"

Kael's gaze darkened for a second, then softened. "I'd keep drinking coffee with you. I'd keep watching the world go by and pretend it was all as simple as it looks."

I laughed, the sound bright and easy. "You know, that's the most honest thing I've heard in a while."

And for that moment, it felt like we might just have found a way to make it work. Together.

The afternoon crept in like a secret, stealing the warmth from the city's bones and leaving behind a cool breeze that whispered against the brick facades of the French Quarter. I hadn't planned on wandering further, but something about the air—something about the way the streets seemed to hum with possibility—pulled me along, and Kael, as ever, was content to follow. He never seemed to need much convincing when it came to my whims, even the most inexplicable ones. I had never quite figured out what it was that made him so unreasonably patient, but I wasn't about to question it. Not yet.

We passed a street vendor who was setting up shop for the evening crowd, his cart loaded with freshly spun cotton candy, the pink and blue clouds of sugar gleaming under the fading sunlight. The smell of it—sickly sweet, comforting in its simplicity—reminded me of childhood, of fairs and summer nights that seemed to stretch forever.

"Remember when we used to eat this?" I asked, nodding toward the vendor. "Like it was the answer to all of life's problems?"

Kael chuckled softly, his eyes crinkling at the corners. "I do. It's funny how something so sticky and sugary can make everything feel better."

I laughed, but there was a knot tightening in my chest. That kind of innocence, the kind that allowed you to believe that cotton candy could fix anything, had long since evaporated from my life. I didn't know how to get it back, or if I even wanted to. But it wasn't the kind of thing you could just push aside, either. It lingered, like the scent of rain on pavement.

"Maybe that's what we need," I said, trying to lighten the mood. "A good dose of sugar and nostalgia."

"Or maybe," Kael replied, his voice low and thoughtful, "we need something a little stronger than that."

I glanced at him, surprised by the shift in his tone. "What do you mean?"

He didn't answer immediately, his gaze sweeping across the street, where a group of tourists were laughing under the shadow of St. Louis Cathedral. The air was thick with the sound of a trumpet playing somewhere in the distance, the notes drifting lazily on the breeze.

"I mean," he said slowly, his voice dropping lower, "maybe it's time to stop pretending we can outrun what's coming."

I froze. His words felt like a sudden gust of wind, sweeping through the stillness between us and leaving nothing but cold air in their wake.

"We've been running long enough," he continued, his gaze now focused entirely on me, his expression unreadable. "It's time to face it. Whatever it is."

I opened my mouth to respond, but before I could form the words, something shifted in the atmosphere, something just outside my reach. The world felt... wrong. The laughter of the tourists, the music, the hum of the city—all of it felt suddenly far away, muffled, as though a storm was about to descend.

And then, I saw him.

At first, I thought it was a trick of the light. But no—there he was, standing across the street near the entrance to Jackson Square, a figure dressed all in black, his face obscured by a wide-brimmed hat. He wasn't moving, just standing there, watching us. I knew that gaze. It wasn't the kind you forget.

The Ravenmark.

I didn't need to look at Kael to know he had noticed him, too. His entire body tensed, a low growl escaping from his throat before he could stop himself.

"What the hell is he doing here?" Kael muttered, his hand already reaching for the small blade tucked inside his jacket. It was an instinct I knew too well. It was the kind of instinct that came from a life spent in the shadows, a life where every unfamiliar face could be a threat.

"We need to move," I said, my voice tight, but not because I was afraid. No, it wasn't fear—fear was too familiar. It was something else, something I couldn't name. The Ravenmark had never been anything less than dangerous, and I'd always known that it would eventually catch up with me. But standing here, feeling the weight of that gaze on me, it was as though I were a pawn in a game I couldn't remember starting.

Kael nodded sharply, his eyes scanning the streets. "Move where? He's blocking the way."

I turned, scanning the alleys and side streets that branched off from the square. There was a narrow passageway to our right, a way I'd used before to slip through unnoticed.

"This way," I said, grabbing his wrist and pulling him toward the alley. "We can't let him trap us here."

We moved quickly, slipping through the shadows, but the feeling of being hunted never left. My breath came faster, the beat of my heart thudding in my chest. This wasn't just some casual encounter. The Ravenmark didn't show up without a reason, and the fact that he was here—at this moment, in this place—wasn't some coincidence.

"Do you think he knows?" I asked as we rounded the corner, the light dimming as the sun dipped lower behind the rooftops.

Kael's jaw tightened. "If he knows anything, it's that we're not running anymore."

We reached the alley, and just as I thought we'd gained some distance, the unmistakable sound of footsteps echoed behind us. Quick, deliberate. Too close.

"He's following us," Kael said, his voice low, taut with frustration.

I turned, my pulse racing. In the fading light, I caught a glimpse of movement—faint, but unmistakable. The figure in black. The Ravenmark was closing in.

And then, just as I opened my mouth to tell Kael to keep moving, a voice—sharp and commanding—cut through the air.

"Stop right there."

My blood went cold.

I knew that voice.

I turned to face him, the shadows of the alley swallowing us whole, but the figure—his face now visible—stepped into the dying light. And in that moment, I realized I wasn't the only one being hunted.

Milton Keynes UK
Ingram Content Group UK Ltd.
UKHW030902011224
451693UK00001B/162